PARADISE COVE

Also by Davin Goodwin

Roscoe Conklin Series

Diver's Paradise

PARADISE COVE

A ROSCOE CONKLIN MYSTERY

DAVIN GOODWIN

OCEANVIEW PUBLISHING
SARASOTA, FLORIDA

This book is a work of fiction. Names, characters, businesses, organizations, places, and incidents either are the products of the author's imagination or are used fictitiously. Any resemblance to actual events, businesses, locales, or persons living or dead, is entirely coincidental.

ISBN 978-1-60809-485-1

Published in the United States of America by Oceanview Publishing

Sarasota, Florida

www.oceanviewpub.com

10 9 8 7 6 5 4 3 2 1

PRINTED IN THE UNITED STATES OF AMERICA

For Double L

ACKNOWLEDGEMENTS

To my lovely wife, Leslie (Double L). Your countless proofreads, tenacity to detail, and steadfast dedication to story continuity were paramount. None of this would've been possible without your love and support.

To Bob and Pat Gussin and the wonderful people at Oceanview Publishing. Your flawless guidance and feedback have made my writing the best it can be. Thanks for taking a chance on an unknown, debut author.

To my agent, Kimberley Cameron. I'm lucky to have you in my corner!

To our daughter, Elizabeth, for her many suggestions, overwhelming support, and constant encouragement.

To Ruth van Tilburg-Obre, the undisputed Queen of Bonaire. Few can provide the insights and knowledge regarding Bonaire that you can. As always, thanks for the love.

To all my beta readers—John "Smack" Anderson, Rich Atkinson, Kerri Schreiber, Alan and Joan Zale, Tom and Kate Kudzma, Tom

Weber, and John "Divesergeant" Belknap. Your time, feedback, and effort were greatly appreciated.

To Doug Searle of The Bonaire Helpdesk. Thanks for the answers to some interesting questions.

A big thank-you to Martin de Weger for keeping my Dutch correct.

To Sandra Griffis, John "Smack" Anderson, David Brown, and Lucas Walker for the use of your names. Hope you enjoyed your characters.

PARADISE COVE

CHAPTER 1

SOUTHERN CARIBBEAN SEA,
NORTHWEST OF BONAIRE, C.N. (CARIBISCH NEDERLAND)

TOP QUALITY KNIVES easily slice through muscle and fat. But the human body is composed of much more. Bone, cartilage, and the occasional ligament are more difficult. A sharp knife is essential, but not always enough. Regardless of how well the blade held its edge, separating the larger joints required a hatchet. And, in the case of a hatchet, almost any would do, sharp or dull, when delivered with ample force.

Smashing and splitting the joints made a cracking sound, like breaking a large stick, and echoed through the boat. But not to worry. No one would hear.

Only one person on board.

One *live* person, that is.

The skin was still in place, wrapped tightly around the flesh. No need to remove it. All the body parts went over the side and into the ocean; two arms; two legs; three sections of torso; and a head, pounded flat enough to be unrecognizable. After dissection, and before being discarded, the parts were secured with wire to weights. Flat, round, iron weights with a hole through the middle. The kind bodybuilders use to bulk up. Make sure everything went to the bottom. Quickly.

The weights might be unnecessary. But not using them would be a rookie mistake.

Prevailing tides and the easterly trade winds would push the remains—blood, bones, skin—west, away from the island. The aquatic predators and scavengers would feast for days, saltwater eventually shriveling away what remained of the body parts as they dissipated into the vastness of the Caribbean Sea.

No trace.

And an easy cleanup.

Except for the blood.

Which seemed to be everywhere.

Plastic tarps covered most of the deck to catch the blood—and other bodily fluids—dripping off the carving table. And, for the most part, worked as intended. But the boat rocked in the gentle waves, and eventually, some of the blood and gunk made its way off the coverings, seeping into seams between planks of the wood deck. It'd take hours to clean.

The Boss hadn't planned for that.

But improvisation was the name of the game. Like a guitar, piano, or bass player taking their turn on the lead. Or sometimes a vocalist. Making it up as they went along. No printed music; no script.

A quick blast of the hose—again everything over the side—and the deck was, at least, surface clean. Anyone coming aboard would be none the wiser. They'd have to look closely, deep into the deck seams, probably with a light of some sort, to see anything amiss. And who does that? No one, that's who. It's as if the particles of blood and guts were invisible.

Same with the Boss's work clothes. Black fabric covered with blood and flesh. Probably piss, shit, and who knew what else. Packed in a plastic bag with weights, they went over the side and into the sea. No problem. Along with the deck shoes, which happened to be new. That *was* a rookie mistake. The Boss sighed and dropped them into the water.

Job complete. For now, anyway. The detailed cleaning would be done later, by someone on their hands and knees, scrubbing till their arms went numb and felt like falling off. Shit work by any definition.

And The Boss didn't do shit work. At least not on a regular basis.

A sensation of tiredness, one of fulfillment as opposed to exhaustion, swept over The Boss. It had been a sweaty job under the high tropical sun. Not a cloud in the sky, the day ending with a beautiful sunset, streaks of orange reflecting off the now-calm waters. Sails lowered, the boat sat motionless and quiet in the pending nightfall, its mast casting a long shadow away from the sinking sun.

A few gulls dove at the blood-covered sea, snatching bits of flesh and guts floating on the surface. Others hovered above, squawking at their peers, waiting in line for their chance to scavenge. Two of the birds landed on the deck, a dozen feet or so from The Boss, and picked at near-microscopic remnants of viscera drying and sticking to the wood planks of the deck.

Whatever, thought The Boss. *Have at it.*

Leaning against the deck rail with a glass of wine, basking in the day's success, The Boss enjoyed the cooling effect of the evening breeze and reveled at how simple the job had been. Not much different than cutting up a chicken to fry. A slight chuckle. In retrospect, though, more than six steps.

Coaxing that dumbass onboard had proven . . . *challenging.* But once aboard, he was put in his place. A good hatchet-smack to the head, and the guy fell to the floor like the worthless piece of shit that he was. Then, using the halyard, even The Boss had no problem loading the body onto the carving table.

That's when the fun began. Fun The Boss knew and had experienced before.

The carving. The blood; the mangled tissue; the cracking bones. Reliving the event, The Boss's breathing increased, and a tingling spread from the chest outward. Fun like this didn't happen every day. Nor should it. But sometimes it was necessary. A large swig of wine and The Boss calmed, breathing regular again.

Loose ends always needed to be tied up.

And The Boss excelled at tying up loose ends.

CHAPTER 2

West shore of Bonaire, C.N.

Finished with my morning swim, having pushed myself hard the last quarter mile, I sat on the end of the pier with my legs dangling over the edge. No clouds in the typical Caribbean-blue Bonaire sky and a faint hint of salt floated in the air. The wind shoved waves, larger than normal, against the shore.

An iguana lay a few feet away, basking in the sun, overweight from gorging itself on the remnants of the nearby garbage can. It sat motionless, one eye tilted in my direction, the other skewed over the edge of the pier at the water. It was a resident of the area and joined me regularly on the pier after my swims.

I had taken to calling it Charlie.

As I towel-dried my arms and hair, I noticed two teenaged boys using a stick to poke at an object near the water's edge, a stone's throw south of the pier. The object had washed ashore and was covered with random strands of dark seaweed.

I watched the boys take a few steps forward, jab the stick at the object, then retreat, as if expecting something to happen. Nothing did, so they repeated the process several times with the same result.

Some younger children ventured forth, staying well behind the brave teenagers. Wide-eyed, high-pitched streams of Papiamento—the native language of Bonaire—filled the air as they half-talked, half-screamed. They gawked at the object, then raced back up the beach to their mothers, sitting on towels.

One mother stood, nodding her head, and, appeasing the child, walked toward the water. She stopped a few feet shy of the shore. Her eyes widened and she shuffled backward to the other women, grabbed her cell phone, and, with a shaky hand, put it to her ear. She pointed at the object and spoke, her Papiamento not as high-pitched as the child's, but every bit as excited. Unfortunately, I didn't understand a word they said, my Papiamento being only slightly better than my Klingon.

The base of my neck tingled.

I no longer carried a badge, but nearly three decades as a law enforcement officer, specifically with the Violent Crimes Division of the Rockford, Illinois, Police Department, had trained my curiosity to remain on high alert. Of the hundreds of traits, quirks, and ticks conditioned into my psyche during those years, the sense of inquisitiveness, along with a constant need to know and understand, were the most deeply engrained.

I shook my head, stood, and walked down the pier to the beach. This was something I probably needed to see.

My sudden movement startled Charlie and he darted to the other side of the pier, both eyes now pointed in my direction. I gave him a shallow wave. "Sorry, Charlie."

The water surface on the west side—or leeward side—of the island remained consistently flat, almost glasslike, aided by a solid wind from the east. The wind also swept most of the seaweed, litter, and other debris out to sea. Few items floated ashore on the leeward coast of Bonaire.

Except during wind reversals. Over the last few days, the easterly wind had changed direction and blew in from the west, bringing with it all kinds of surface floaties.

I plodded through the sand, closing the distance to the water's edge. Most likely, an unfortunate tuna or tarpon had met its demise. But based on the actions and behaviors of the children, and the concern of the mother, I quickly changed my mind. A fish washing ashore was too common an occurrence and wouldn't generate the reactions I'd just witnessed.

Then I remembered the epidemic affecting the green moray eels. For some reason, a strange parasite was attacking the green morays, causing the deaths of many. The occurrence was so rare that a group of marine biologists had recently arrived on the island, and with the help of local researchers, were studying the phenomenon. The situation was declared serious, possibly affecting the entire green moray population of the local reefs. When a dead eel washed ashore, the researchers wanted to be informed so they could harvest the carcass for study.

The teenagers moved back a few steps as I worked past them and stood over the object. It wasn't a tarpon or tuna. Or a diseased moray eel. I turned back toward the beach and scanned the area, noticing the increased crowd size. I admit, the word *crowd* is relative on a small island like Bonaire, but, even so, a small horde of lookie-loos had gathered. Some vied for a better view, meandering closer to the water's edge.

But not too close.

I sighed and shook my head. Few things draw a crowd to the beach faster than a human body part washing ashore.

And in this case, the human body part was a leg.

Mostly, anyway.

It laid along the water's edge, backside facing up, and looked to be from a few inches below the hip down to and including what remained of the foot. Lots of pockmarks and nips from fish and other scavengers. No toes remained, and the skin reminded me of a crinkled, wet paper bag pulled over the bone. Since the wind swept in from the sea, there was no avoiding the smell, which was, to say the least, invasive and barely tolerable.

Long ago, as a young detective, I learned that death had a particular smell and death mixed with seawater upped the ante to a whole new level. The stink seemed to coat my nasal passages. I bent over and gagged. Luckily, I hadn't eaten breakfast yet.

I straightened and took a couple of deep breaths.

As I studied the dismembered body part, an unexplainable horror clicked in the back of my brain. A passing thought turned unthinkable. I knelt beside the leg and let out a long, slow sigh, dread slashing through me. Sweat ran down my nose and dripped onto the sand, the cooling effect of my swim having already worn off.

Carefully, hands trembling, I used a stick to lift one side of the leg while using another stick to brush away wet sand sticking to the skin, an empty, fluttering feeling in my stomach. Ignoring the smell, heart pounding, I knelt further for a closer look.

Please be wrong.

My stomach went heavy as a cold shiver swam down my spine. The faint outline of Bonaire tattooed on the front side of the thigh caused my throat to go dry. My fears confirmed, I gently lowered the leg back to the sand. Realizing the teenagers and I had already disturbed the scene, I used care to minimize any further contamination.

However, something looked strange near the foot, a clump of seaweed entangled around the ankle. I tried using one of the sticks to clear the snag, but it was caught on something and wouldn't budge. After reverting to brute force and giving the strands of seaweed several good jerks with my hand, a clump pulled free and I saw the hang-up.

A piece of wire wrapped around the ankle.

Not barbed wire or chicken wire or electrical wire or telephone wire. A faded shade of green, it wasn't coated in rubber or plastic and appeared to be the type of wire used to wrap a crate or bind items together.

I slowly stood and scanned the sea, wondering if more body parts might wash ashore. Being a possible crime scene, the beach would soon be closed. Police divers would search the nearby waters for evidence or any additional human remains.

As I stared at the wire, a police siren whined behind me. Two police—or *Polis* in Papiamento—trucks skidded to a stop on the gravel shoulder above the beach. I walked in that direction.

A pair of officers jumped from one of the trucks and scurried down the beach. One struggled with a camera; the other held a roll of crime scene tape. They were young, and although Bonaire is a small island, I didn't recognize them. However, one knew me.

As they passed, she nodded and said, "Hello, R."

My full name is Roscoe Conklin; however, most folks refer to me as R.

I waved and returned her hello.

The driver's-side door of the other truck opened, and Officer Arabella de Groot stepped out. She tilted her head and spoke Dutch into her shoulder mic, then yelled something in Papiamento to the two officers scurrying down the beach. Originally from the Netherlands, she'd been on the island police force for more than ten years and spoke at least three languages.

The two officers turned in her direction, listened intently, then nodded and continued for the shore. Probably new recruits. Had to be. They displayed a lot of enthusiasm. Maybe too much, considering what they were about to encounter.

Officer De Groot walked toward me, her blond ponytail bobbing from side to side in cadence with her strides. She stopped mere inches away. Her near six-foot stature should've allowed me to peer into her ocean-blue eyes, except for her pair of dark, curved sunglasses. The epaulets on her shoulders displayed a crown encircled by a wreath, along with a gold button, denoting her rank as Sergeant, or *Brigadier.*

Usually when we were that close, one of us leaned in for a kiss. But she was in uniform. Any form of fondness ceased while on duty. We had both agreed to that.

Her more so than me.

As always, the edges of her mouth were curved upward, ever so slightly, ready to break out in a smile or spontaneous laughter. She stared into my eyes, as if teasing me to afford her some level of affection. I held my ground and stared back. The breeze lashed at my shirt and pushed her ponytail sideways.

Neither of us leaned in.

"Hey, Conklin," she finally said, holding her vigil, but allowing a relaxed smile to cross her face. "What do we have?"

I took a breath, coming out of my trance, disappointed she was in uniform. "A leg washed ashore."

She stepped back and turned to survey the scene; eyebrows raised. "It is true, then. That was the call that came in, but we did not believe it. Thought it was a mistake. Or even a bad joke."

"It's Rulio's."

Her mouth gaped open for a moment. "Are you sure?"

I nodded.

"How can you be so—" She stopped talking. Her shoulders slumped and she tapped her index finger on her right thigh. "The tattoo."

"Yup. I was able to make out the outline. Faint, but it's there."

"Does Erika know?"

"It's a small island, so she might by now. But there's more."

"What?"

"There's a piece of wire wrapped around the ankle."

She turned her head and eyed the area of beach where Rulio's leg swayed in the mild surf. "*Oh mijn god.*"

CHAPTER 3

ARABELLA AND I walked across the street toward a ten-unit ma-and-pa-type hotel, the YellowRock Resort, which I owned, courtesy of my life savings and a large chunk of my pension. I lived in a small apartment upstairs, and Erika worked in the office on the first floor.

Whether purposeful or accidental, being a few years older than me, Erika often played the role of my big sister. I believe she enjoyed keeping me focused and pointing out the errors of my way every chance she got. Over the past five years, I had gotten used to it and didn't mind. I enjoyed having a big sister.

She was a great office manager, to boot, and kept the business organized and running smoothly.

The mechanical closer on the screen door stuck as we entered, forcing me to pull it shut with some extra force. It had been broken for several weeks, and, regardless of Erika's persistence on moving it to the top of my to-do list, I hadn't found the time—or ambition—to repair it.

She sat behind an old gray desk that could've come out of a 1960's secretarial pool, her yellow polo, embroidered with *YellowRock Resort* on the upper left shoulder, deepening the tint of her dark skin.

Peering over black-rimmed glasses, she said, "Nice of you to come and help me at work today." A Bonaire native, and having lived on the island her entire life, Erika spoke English as a third, maybe fourth, language. As with most of the local population, her speech contained a hint of Dutch accent and reminded me of someone who always wanted to sound formal and correct. She pointed at the door. "You could fix that if you did not spend so much time in the water."

Based on her demeanor, I guessed Erika hadn't yet heard what had been found.

Arabella didn't make eye contact with Erika and went straight to my desk—another old, gray behemoth—and sat. She leaned back and stared at the dirty ceiling tiles, wiping the bottoms of her eyes. I could've told her from experience; those old ceiling tiles never held any answers.

Erika glanced over her shoulder at Arabella, then laid her glasses on the desk. "What is happening at the beach?" she asked me. "I was busy at work and did not right away notice the disturbance." She glanced out the office window. "But now I can see police trucks, yet Miss Arabella is here." My mouth opened, but I couldn't find the words. "Why?" she said, eyebrows scrunched.

Death notices are one of the most difficult tasks a cop must perform, and no one ever gets comfortable with them. Especially when delivered to a friend or relative.

Tough and emotionally draining, they must be done with as much tact and compassion as possible. And caution. I dreaded the next-of-kin's reaction most of all; impossible to know their response. I'll never forget the time I held a grieving mother whose son had died in a car accident. I squeezed her tight with one arm while keeping a firm grip on my weapon so she couldn't grab it.

Retirement should've meant I had delivered my last death notice.

Guess not.

I walked to Erika's desk and sat on the edge, putting us at eye-level with each other. A squeaky fan in the corner oscillated back and forth, pushing warm, moist Caribbean air across the room, providing little cooling effect and no comfort.

With a deep breath, I said, "I have some bad news."

"What?"

"It's Rulio."

Her lower lip quivered. "What about him?" She looked over my shoulder, out the window at the beach, then down to a framed picture of Rulio on her desk. The breeze blew through the office. "Tell me!"

Arabella sat forward, elbows resting on her thighs. We made eye contact and she shook her head.

What could I say? Rulio had been missing for ten days. How could I explain to Erika that a piece of her nephew had washed ashore and was laying across the street in the sand?

The manual didn't cover this. Her relationship with Rulio was more than aunt and nephew. Much more. Erika had raised him since he was a toddler, his parents having died in a car accident. Whereas she played the role of big sister to me, she had always been *mother* to Rulio.

And always would be.

I would much rather have been sitting on my deck playing banjo, listening to the sea waves caress the shore, a cold one within arm's reach. But this had to be done. She needed to hear it from someone who cared.

My chest tightened.

I took her hand. "Part of him . . . Part of Rulio—"

She jerked away, clenching her hands into fists. "What do you mean 'part of him'?"

My eyes watered, knowing what this would do to her. "Rulio's leg washed ashore."

She made a whining sound and her face flushed. "What? No, you are wrong." Tears streamed down her cheeks. "I need to go there." She tried to walk around me and make for the door, but I stepped up and wrapped her in a hug.

"No, you don't," I said. "There's nothing there for you to see or do." She tried to resist and squirm out of my grasp, so I squeezed tighter. "Nothing for you to do."

"Please, please . . ." She buried her face in my chest and sobbed. "No . . ."

I knew she needed to get this out, and nothing I could say would help. I had more experience with premature death than either she or Arabella, so I held Erika tight and let her cry. Her tears soaked my T-shirt, mixing with sweat and some not-yet-dried seawater. The cries turned to moans as her entire body spasmed several times. I held her tighter, concerned her legs might give out and she'd collapse.

I fought the urge to break down myself. Arabella wiped her own tears.

After a few moments, Erika's emotions drained, she relaxed, and I helped her into the chair. She took the picture of Rulio from her desk and held it close to her body.

Living on Bonaire all her life, she had acclimated to the heat. Seldom had I ever seen her sweat. But now, perspiration seeped through her shirt and drenched her hair and face. Arabella brought over a stack of fast-food napkins from my desk and placed them in front of Erika. She took one and wiped her eyes, already red and bloodshot, then her forehead and face. Her breathing ragged, she stared at the floor, still clutching Rulio's picture.

"I must ask what happened?" she said.

I looked at Arabella. She shrugged, which I took as a pass back to me.

"No way to know right now," I told Erika, my voice low and soft. "There'll need to be an investigation."

"You will find out how this happened?" She raised her head, piercing me with her bloodshot eyes. "You will?"

"Erika . . . The police . . ."

Outside, an ambulance arrived, slowing to a stop near the two parked police trucks. Erika, Arabella, and I watched out the office window as the driver exited the vehicle, opened the back, and pulled out a collapsible gurney. Before leaving the truck and heading for the beach, he stuffed a waterproof bag under his arm.

The significance wasn't lost on any of us.

They were going to zip Rulio's leg into a body bag and haul it off.

Erika's eyes widened and she began crying again. "You must find out."

"I . . ."

"Yes," Arabella said with a sniffle. "We will find out how this happened."

Leaning closer, with a cracking voice, Erika said, "Promise."

It wasn't a plea from a friend, or even a big sister. It was a demand from a victim's relative. I'd been here before and knew how I should answer. Investigations held few guarantees, if any. Impossible to make promises.

But, reluctantly, I nodded.

A promise I had no idea how to fulfill.

CHAPTER 4

ARABELLA HAD ASKED if I'd join the underwater search and recovery team being assembled to look for evidence in the area Rulio's leg had washed ashore. She and I had chatted and neither of us were confident anything would be found, but for the sake of thoroughness, a search needed to be conducted.

Now, preparing for the dive, I tightened the regulator to the tank and opened the valve, the hoses stiffening slightly as they filled with air. Putting my lips around the mouthpiece, I breathed in and out several times verifying it worked correctly. Satisfied the gear worked and ready to dive, I hauled my tank, regulator, fins, mask, and buoyancy compensating device—BCD, or BC as most divers refer to them—to the shoreline, then awaited further instructions. I laid my tank on the coral rubble and sand beach, securing my regulator so it wouldn't dislodge and fall into the sand.

A young female broke away from a group of officers huddled around a police truck and walked up to me. She wore a black wetsuit trimmed in purple with a dive mask dangling from her neck. I recognized her as one of the first officers who responded at the beach. The one who knew my name.

"I am Ingrid," she said, extending a hand. "Officer De Groot said I am to dive with you today."

She was Bonairian and appeared much too young to be a police officer. I shook her hand and glanced at Arabella, who nodded.

Turning back to Ingrid, I said, "I'm R, but you already know that. Glad to meet you."

A half smile and a nod. "Yes, all of us know who *you* are." She momentarily looked in Arabella's direction, then back at me. "You are ready for the briefing?"

By *us* I assumed she meant the other officers. Small island, so most of the police force was probably aware of the relationship between Arabella and me.

"Yes, I'm ready," I said as we walked up and joined the rest of the search team assembled around Arabella. "How long have you been on the force?"

"Oh, just now one year."

"How long you been diving?"

She frowned slightly and gave me a sideways glance. "Almost since I can remember. Not to worry, though. I have a dive master certificate and am working on my instructor rating." As we joined the rest of the group, she leaned in closer and whispered, "We will be fine."

Surrounded by myself and the other six divers, Officer Josef Vendel stood in the center of the makeshift circle and spoke for ten minutes reviewing our mission, the search pattern, and the procedures for gathering potential evidence we might encounter. He concluded his comments with a standard overview of basic safety precautions.

Ingrid looked at me after the briefing and said, "Should we get our gear and do a buddy check?" She pointed at the beach. "I will meet you there."

At the water's edge, I donned my gear, secured the straps of my BC, and waited for Ingrid. Accompanied by two of the other officers on the dive team, she trudged across the sand, making her way down the beach in her scuba gear. Being on the petite side, she had to lean forward as she walked to prevent the eighty-cubic-foot tank—which probably weighed nearly a quarter of what she did—from pulling her over backwards.

Out of breath and red-faced, she suggested we perform our buddy check while standing waist deep in the water. Sounded like a good idea, sweat rolling down both sides of my face. Wrapped in a wetsuit was akin to being trapped in a sauna. Especially after standing in the sun waiting for Vendel's briefing to conclude.

I walked into the water, squatted momentarily, submerging myself to cool off, then performed a "buddy check" with Ingrid identifying possible equipment problems *before* we submerged. We verified that each other's hoses and straps were correctly routed around our gear and not tangled. Also, we checked each other's dive weights, making sure they were positioned correctly, and the release mechanism wasn't obstructed. I checked the air pressure gauge connected to her tank and verified it was full and that her breathing regulator functioned correctly. She made the same checks of my equipment.

Four groups of two divers each comprised the search team. One group would search the shallows, depths of less than thirty feet. Ingrid and I had been assigned the medium depths, from thirty-five to seventy feet. Since deeper dives limit the amount of time underwater—known as *bottom time*—two groups, one led by Officer Vendel, had been assigned the seventy-to-ninety-five-feet depths. No need to search any deeper as the sea leveled off along this section of the shoreline at less than one hundred feet, becoming a sandy bottom.

Ingrid carried an underwater camera to photograph anything we found before touching and retrieving it. After the pictures were taken, I'd use a pair of forceps to retrieve the object and stash it in a mesh bag attached to my BC. As a disincentive to touch coral and marine life, marine park rules strictly forbid divers from wearing gloves underwater. If caught with gloves, the diver could be fined, and their equipment confiscated. In addition, they might be banned from future trips to the island. Considering fingerprints can be obtained from recovered items even after being in water, the dive team had received special permission to wear latex gloves.

All eight divers descended at roughly the same time. Ingrid and I slowly dropped down the reef to seventy feet and began slow kicking from north to south, keeping the upslope of the reef—and the direction to shore—on our left. Earlier, she and I had agreed to remain at seventy feet and comb the area in one direction the length of the search region. Then, we'd ascend to sixty feet, reverse course one-hundred and eighty degrees, and continue searching till we reached the other boundary of the region. We'd ascend ten more feet every time we turned around and started back in the opposite direction.

Our first two passes—seventy feet and sixty feet—took us about ten minutes each. Checking my air pressure gauge, I determined that we'd have more than enough tank-air to complete our search in about ninety minutes, leaving extra air for either a safety stop or a leisure swim through the shallows to shore. The additional air would also act as a safety margin in the event we found evidence that needed examining, requiring us to remain underwater longer than planned.

With nearly one hundred feet visibility, zero current, and water temperature in the low eighties, conditions were perfect for a dive. Unfortunately, it was a "work" dive and not for pleasure. Most of my time underwater consisted of observing the marine life, preferring such things as watching a turtle perched on the sea bottom munching on crustaceans or searching the soft corals for an elusive seahorse.

Unregimented, relaxed, and at my discretion.

The opposite of this dive.

Having done only a few search dives in the past, I had forgotten the difficulty in concentrating on the task at hand. These types of dives required structure and procedure. No time for fun and games.

I turned slightly to check on my dive buddy, swimming on my right side, half a body length behind me. Her exhaled bubbles were consistent, rhythmic, and evenly spaced. She shot me an "okay" sign and I reciprocated. I gazed into deeper water and made out the silhouettes and bubbles from one of the deep-depth teams. They moved along at the same pace. I glanced up the reef and located the shallow-depth team. It didn't appear as though anyone had located anything that resembled potential evidence.

Decades ago, before the reef surrounding Bonaire had become a protected marine park, this section of shore was used by the islanders as a municipal metal dumping site. That past was still visible with a plethora of engine blocks, old barrels, cans, and other objects littering the reef floor. Coral had grown over the larger, solid objects, while small creatures had made lairs of the bottles and cans. We didn't disturb anything already claimed by the reef or its inhabitants. I found a few yards of old fishing line and, not wanting any marine life to become entangled in it, bundled it into a ball and stuffed it in the mesh bag.

Completing our pass at fifty feet, we ascended to forty and were turning to reverse course when a brief flash of light caught my eye, and I jerked my head in that direction. Dancing through the water column, a ray of sunlight reflected off something buried in the corals.

Maneuvering as close to the coral as I dared without touching it, I exhaled half the air in my lungs then held my breath, allowing my body to sink a few feet, and peered between two coral heads. I studied the area, looking for the source of the reflection. Several small yellow and purple fish, known as fairy basslets, darted across the coral surface feeding on planktonic crustaceans. A white fish with black vertical stripes, called a sergeant major, swam aggressive circles near the base of the coral. I knew it to be a male because of a patch of blueish-purple eggs splattered like jelly on an old, rusty can lying on the sandy bottom. The males guarded the eggs.

I sensed Ingrid nearby and looked up. She had stopped her swim and was hovering, waiting for me to either continue our search or signal her that I had found something. I gave an exaggerated shrug and continued my examination of the area. I repositioned slightly and again saw the reflection, this time noticing the source.

Before grabbing the object, I made a take-a-picture gesture to Ingrid. She kicked over to my location, and moving around the area, snapped several photos of the object and the surrounding location. When finished, she gave me the okay sign.

The fairy basslets scattered as I reached between the coral heads for the object, half buried in the sand. Considering the forceps and my hand as a threat, the sergeant major darted out and nipped at my wrist. A quick flick of my finger, and he retreated, resuming his sentry duty over the eggs. Using the forceps, I gently retrieved the object from the sea bottom and shook it free of sand. I held it up so Ingrid could take photos, then I examined it closer.

It was a man's scuba watch. Round, stainless steel, spinnable dial, blue background with white arms. I wasn't an expert, but I guessed it to cost several hundred dollars. No telling how long it'd been in the water. I looked for an inscription on the back and on the strap, but no such luck. Ingrid signaled for us to continue, and I acknowledged, stashing the watch in the mesh bag.

Our passes at forty and thirty feet were uneventful, meaning we didn't find any other objects. Just as we completed our last pattern, Ingrid signaled that she had five-hundred PSI of air remaining in her tank, our agreed-upon indicator to swim to shore and exit the water.

"Any luck?" Arabella asked as I trudged out of the water, fins in hand.

"Not sure." I shook my head, clearing water from my ear. "We found a man's dive watch."

She frowned.

"I know," I said. "Big surprise, finding a scuba watch on an island known for scuba diving."

Speaking to Ingrid, Arabella said, "Label it and place it on the table." She pointed at a table set up in the shade near one of the police trucks.

I handed the bag to Ingrid, then dropped my gear on a nearby chair. Still in my wetsuit, water squishing out from my neoprene boots, I walked over to the table. It took Ingrid a few moments to label the watch and place it alongside items found by the other dive teams. Arabella handed me a clipboard and pointed at a piece of paper. Chain of evidence. It had sections for the case number, date, time, photo description, and photographer name. It also required signatures. I signed below Ingrid's.

Arabella photographed the table from different angles and perspectives and allowed only needed personnel to approach. When she barked orders, people scrambled. The entire scene could best be described as organized. Strictly procedure.

"Thanks for the help," Ingrid said. "I enjoyed having you as a dive buddy."

"You're welcome," I said and watched her saunter over to a shade tree where a few other officers huddled around a cooler of water and soda.

The sun shone from directly overhead as I unzipped my wetsuit, sweat beginning to replace the remnants of seawater. Down the beach, beyond the police line, several tourists sat in chairs drinking beers. As bits of their conversations and laughter drifted my way, I suddenly realized how thirsty I'd become.

I surveyed the items on the table. In addition to the watch, there were a few beer cans, an athletic shoe, a wine bottle, a small metal box of some sort, the fishing line I'd gathered, and a knife.

Shaking my head, I said to Arabella, "Don't think you have much here. Looks more like a reef cleanup dive than evidence gathering."

"I agree, but we will analyze it anyway." She motioned with her head at the officers under the tree. "She likes you."

"What? Who?"

"Ingrid. She likes you."

I glanced at the group. "Yeah . . . well . . ." I turned back to Arabella and gave her an exaggerated once-over with my eyes. "I prefer my female officers a little . . . *older.*"

Eyebrows raised, she said, "Lucky for you."

I took a step closer to her. "Speaking of getting lucky . . ."

She rested a hand on her service weapon and looked me up and down. "After a strenuous dive, you think you are capable of a night with *me*?"

I wiped sweat from my brow and snapped my arms out of the wetsuit. "I'll die trying."

A thin smile crept across her face as she drummed her fingers on the handle of her holstered sidearm. "You just might."

CHAPTER 5

A WEEK LATER, I sat on a blue barstool at Vinny's drinking an Amstel Bright waiting for Arabella to arrive. The advertisements described Brights as a "Euro Pale Lager," whatever that meant. Most of the bars and restaurants served them with a slice of lime wedged atop the bottle's neck. When at home, I didn't waste time slicing limes.

In true island fashion, Arabella was late. Being that Bonaire took the term *Island Time* to the extreme, I had purposely arrived a bit late thinking maybe Arabella and I would show at the same time.

Nope. Didn't happen.

No biggie, though. After all, that's what Island Time was all about—not being in a hurry and not letting the little things become an annoyance. I sipped my beer and watched sailboats pass by, sails full, making their way to the harbor before sunset. The wind blew normally, the reversal having corrected itself a few days ago, so the boat owners were trying to make up for lost time.

Steel drum music came from an open-air establishment down the street. I couldn't help tapping the rhythm with my foot on the bar's footrail.

Built on concrete and wood piers, Vinny's was one of the few outdoor bars that stretched over the water, offering a great view of the sea. Horns beeped and car stereos roared as traffic choked and crawled along the single-lane one-way road that weaved through downtown Kralendijk, Bonaire's largest settlement. Vinny's was only six blocks from my apartment, and I found it easier to walk rather than drive and hope for a parking spot.

I'd been avoiding Erika the best I could since making the unwieldly promise to find out what happened to Rulio. A promise I should've never made; one I doubted I'd be able to fulfill. She expected me to dig up some information—or "clues" as she said—about Rulio's disappearance and probable foul play. Each time she asked about my progress, a coldness swept through my body, my chest and limbs becoming heavy and tight. Her head drooped and her shoulders and facial features lowered as I responded. A distant, dull stare would wash over her face and in a monotone voice she'd eventually say, "I understand."

Not much I could do, though. I wasn't a licensed private investigator. Besides, the case was in an open, active status with the island police department. Based on prior experience, they'd be reluctant to provide any info.

Especially not with Inspector Schleper in charge of the investigation. He and I had gone a few rounds in the past and the wounds were still open and bleeding. They might never heal. If I probed him for information, he'd just tell me to go sit on a beach somewhere.

"You are drinking alone tonight?" Jan, the bartender and owner of Vinny's, said, jolting me from my thoughts. His name is pronounced *Yohn* and is the Dutch version of John.

"Waiting for Bella."

He gave a dismissive wave. "Ah . . . She is just like her sister. Always late."

If I had a nemesis on the island, a proverbial burr under my saddle, it was Arabella's redheaded sister, Ruth, who also happened to be Jan's wife. On a regular basis, Ruth made it obvious she preferred I had never come to the island. For Arabella's sake, I always let it pass and never let on the feeling was mutual.

Jan opened another Bright, squished a slice of lime in the bottle neck, and sat it in front of me. "If you must waste time and wait, you should drink."

In agreement, I tipped the bottle and took a swig.

Drinking was never a waste of time.

* * *

As I finished my beer, Arabella strolled through the open-air entrance, beneath the green oval Amstel sign hanging in front of Vinny's. I hadn't seen much of her since Rulio's leg washed ashore, my breathing quickening as she zigzagged through the small crowd of tourists. Being a senior officer on the force, she'd been carrying a heavy workload and putting in extra hours. My face and neck felt warm as she plopped onto a yellow stool beside me.

She wore khaki shorts and my black RPD—Rockford Police Department—baseball hat, hair loose and flowing over her shoulders. Her gray T-shirt had a silhouette of a cowgirl riding a bucking bronco. The caption read: *Well-behaved Women Seldom Make History.*

"I need a beer," she said as she swiveled in my direction.

"My thoughts exactly."

Before I could wave him over, Jan produced two beers and handed them to us.

"Nice shirt," Jan said to Arabella. He turned to me, winked, and said, "You, too."

I wore a dark green Longtail T-shirt from Duluth Trading Company, along with a brown pair of cargo shorts and sandals. No socks. Jan had seen this outfit countless times. Pretty much my standard attire since moving to the island.

When I didn't respond, he gave another dismissive wave and said, "Ah . . . Tell me when you want another." He roamed down the bar, tending to other customers.

"How is Erika?" Arabella asked.

"Not sure. I've been avoiding her."

She scrunched her eyebrows. "You work in that same small office together. How do you avoid her?"

"I've been doing errands to get out of the office." We both took a swig of beer. "It's not easy and I feel bad. She wants me to investigate Rulio's death . . ." I shook my head as my voice tailed off.

"I know she does." Arabella looked out at the distant horizon, where the darkening sky touched the sea. "She called and asked me some questions. I could not talk to her about the case."

"I understand, and I'm sure she does, too. Deep down, anyway." I paused a beat. "She said she'd work for free if I'd investigate. She even offered to pay me."

"She cannot do that." Arabella thrived on procedures and protocol. Her posture straightened, muscles tightening. "*You* cannot do that."

"I know. Besides, I wouldn't take her money. But she expects me to tell her *something*." I hoped that Arabella might give me a little insight into the investigation. Some morsel of information I could take back to Erika. Any tidbit would buy me some time.

Part of me wanted to coax Arabella into giving me the file. The other part knew taking advantage of our relationship wasn't the right thing to do. She'd probably do it if I asked. Or maybe begged. But if Schleper found out, it'd be the end of her career, and I couldn't be responsible for that.

Two sandpipers landed on the deck railing alongside the water. They strutted back and forth, hoping to score a bit of French fry or potato chip. Anything would do, but they seemed to prefer junk food.

I tossed a bar cracker at them, the wind carrying it into the sea, and they both dove after it.

"I told her these things take time," I said. However, from experience, I knew that if a case didn't break within ten days, the odds of it being solved went down drastically. "She said the police are too slow."

"Too slow? *Ach.*" Arabella studied the floor for a moment and rattled her beer bottle on the bar. "Well, to speak the truth, it seems the investigation has halted."

"You mean stalled?"

"*Ja hoor.* We have no clues or leads." She put her elbow on the bar and propped her head up. "I do not know what Schleper now expects. We are not proceeding."

I decided not to press any further. She couldn't tell me anything—wasn't *going* to tell me anything—and it was better to have Erika mad at me than put a strain on Arabella.

At that moment, a voice behind me said, "Hey, R." I turned and saw Chuck Studer, another ex-pat American living on the island. Beer in hand, he strolled up and stood beside Arabella and me.

Chuck had an apartment above one of the storefronts across the street making Vinny's his favorite—and closest—hangout. Being an Air Force veteran, he usually wore a surplus USAF pilot outfit. He served as a mechanic in the military but wore the pilot suit claiming it attracted "the ladies." Beyond my comprehension, the island women—especially the younger ones—found him irresistible. Chuck seldom drank alone.

But tonight, he wasn't in his pilot getup. He wore shorts and a polo shirt, so I assumed he wasn't on the prowl. He stood five feet, nine inches tall with short-cropped graying hair and a clean-shaven face. Without much effort, he maintained the build of a former military person, albeit, these days, a bit thicker around the waist, the result of beer, late nights, and too many late mornings.

"Hey, Chuck," I said.

Arabella acknowledged Chuck with a slight nod, then turned to face the bar. "*Ook dat nog,*" she said. Jan chuckled, visibly holding back a larger outburst. My Dutch was only slightly better than my Papiamento, but I knew what she had said. And it was regarding Chuck's unexpected appearance at Vinny's. Translation: "That's all I need."

Chuck was oblivious to what Arabella had said or its meaning. Even if he had known, I doubted he'd have cared.

"You almost look like a tourist tonight," I said. "What gives?" Telling an ex-pat living on Bonaire they looked like a tourist was akin to an insult.

Arabella paid no attention, her hand tapping a rapid cadence on the bar.

Chuck straightened his posture a bit. "I'm meeting my new girlfriend for a drink."

I swiveled my head in all directions. "Here? Where is she?" Chuck had never referred to any woman as a girlfriend. This was someone I needed to meet.

"No, no, not here. In a few minutes at my place," Chuck said. "Want to stop up and meet her?"

Quickly, almost too quickly, Arabella said, "*Nee!*" She jumped off the stool, put her arms on my shoulders, and looked me in the eyes. "Are we not going somewhere to eat?"

A warm sensation, originating at my shoulders, spread throughout my body. "Yeah, whenever you're ready."

"Hey, Arabella," Chuck said, eyes wide, a smile working across his face. "Know what type of people eat at underwater restaurants?"

Arabella shook her head. "No, and I do not want to know."

"Scuba *diners*," he said with a chuckle.

I moaned and put a hand over my face, covering my half-snicker.

Without even cracking a giggle, Arabella stared at Chuck a moment, then turned to me. "Now." She tipped her beer up and drained the last few drops, then put it on the bar with a bit too much force. "I am ready now."

Chuck shrugged and finished his beer. "I'm headed to my apartment anyway, so I'll walk out with you."

"*Schitterend*," Arabella said, already two steps ahead of us.

As we strolled out of Vinny's headed to the Thirsty Goat, a restaurant a few blocks north where Arabella wanted to have dinner, I noticed Chuck's four-door pickup parked in a spot alongside the sidewalk. As we passed it, I glanced into the open bed.

"Why do you have a speargun in your truck?" I asked.

Spearfishing is illegal on the island. The Marine Park officials have levied serious fines on perpetrators.

Chuck shook his head. "Not mine. It appeared there a few days ago. In the bed of my truck."

"Hope the police don't see it," I said.

Arabella, who had been rubbing the ears of a stray black mutt that had appeared from an alley and had been following us, stood and glared at Chuck.

"I think they just did," Chuck said, looking down the street, away from Arabella's stare.

"Spearguns are not advised on the island," Arabella said. "You should know better." It was as if she'd been waiting for an opportunity to scold him.

Chuck held up his hands in a surrender fashion. "I know, I know. That's why I haven't touched it. I'm parking my truck out front every night hoping the person who put it there will come back and get it.

Or maybe it'll get stolen. I don't want anything to do with it. Hell, I don't even scuba dive."

Arabella crossed her arms in front of her chest and widened her stance. "You should get rid of it. And soon."

CHAPTER 6

Eyes closed, I sat at my office desk, leaned back in the chair. The warm Bonaire breeze drifted through the screen door and the dusty windows couldn't stop the sunlight from streaming into the room.

A stack of invoices lay in front of me. Erika handled paying the bills, but she insisted I approve them before she wrote the checks. Paperwork always gave me a headache.

Erika and I had just finished another *discussion* on my inability to investigate Ruilo's incident. The hairs on the back of my neck lifted thinking about the word "incident." It didn't do Rulio justice. Around Erika, I avoided the word murder, but with his ankle wrapped in wire, the obvious conclusion was foul play. Although she may've realized the truth, and I'm sure she did, I doubted Erika could handle the word "murder." Until she spoke it out loud, I wouldn't use it. At least not around her.

A ping of guilt shot through me as I again stared at the "to-do" list Erika greeted me with when I had first come down from my apartment earlier this morning. Like a seagull with a French fry, she seemed happiest when keeping me busy. Scribbled on white paper with bold black lettering, I checked off the first item—a trip to the hardware store to pick up some odds and ends. But afterwards, instead of returning to the YellowRock and completing the remainder of the list—much of which depended on the stuff from the hardware store—I had stopped at a local watering hole for lunch and a beer.

Or two.

Now, back at my desk, I barely held my eyes open. Time for my daily nap. I envisioned floating off into a Zen-like slumber while listening to Creedence Clearwater Revival, the sea breeze gently rocking my hammock.

But first, another beer.

I reached into the small refrigerator sitting along the wall behind my desk and grabbed a Bright, tossing the top into the waste basket beside Erika's desk. Condensation dripped off the bottle onto my T-shirt as I took the first pull. She gave me a sideways glance as I smiled and let out an exaggerated "Ah." Usually, when I pulled such an antic, she'd mumble something in Papiamento and possibly scold me, just as a big sister should. Instead, today, she just smirked and refocused on her monitor.

Rulio's murder, and the torment she'd been experiencing, had understandably disrupted things. Neither of us were the same right now. Maybe things would never be the same again. Either way, I hated seeing Erika in such pain and turmoil.

Arabella had said the investigation was stalled. I wondered why but knew there could be several reasons. The stall might present an opportunity for me to get involved, find out more about what happened and what the police knew.

As I contemplated ways of getting involved in Rulio's investigation—none of which seemed easy or remotely feasible—the screen door creaked open and a child, maybe eleven years old, entered the office. He walked to Erika's desk and stared at a basket of assorted candies, which lay next to the framed picture of Rulio. Erika nodded. The young boy took two pieces, smiled at her, and left.

A few moments later, the door creaked open again. This time a young girl walked in holding the hand of a small boy. She led the smaller child to Erika's desk, and they both stood in almost the exact place the eleven-year-old had. Erika smiled and nodded. They each took a piece of candy but didn't leave. Instead, the girl said something in Papiamento. Erika responded and each child took another piece of candy and headed out the door. The younger one stopped, turned, and said, "*Masha danki.*" His sister then ushered him out of the office and into the Bonaire sunshine, destined for the small beach across the street.

The beach where Rulio's leg had washed ashore.

Erika sat motionless, staring out the door. After a moment, she placed a hand on Rulio's picture, then blotted her eyes with a tissue. She let out a long breath and went back to work.

I took a swig of beer.

It had started soon after Rulio went missing. Erika set the basket of candy on her desk and, on a regular basis, invited youngsters into the office to indulge. Bonaire is a small island and news spread fast.

Now, since the washing ashore of Rulio's leg, it seemed everyone under the age of twelve knew about Erika's candy basket. Children walking in and out of the office had become a common occurrence. Kind of like a self-serve, year-round, trick-or-treat station. But without the costumes.

In some way, I guessed it to be therapeutic for her, the children reminding her of Rulio. Or did she see the children as some reincarnation of Rulio? In her eyes, maybe every child was, in some way, Rulio.

My hand got slapped once when I had reached for a piece of candy. "Those are for the children," she had said.

In my mind, it was all harmless. If giving candy to children helped her cope with the tragedy, then so be it. I'd support her any way I could. Including getting myself into the investigation.

But how?

I grabbed another beer from the fridge and was about to hit the stairs up to my apartment, leaving the paperwork for later, when the screen door creaked open again. This time is wasn't a kid looking for some candy. It was someone I hadn't seen for a long time and had hoped not to see for even longer.

Inspector Schleper.

He sauntered across the office as if he owned the YellowRock. He nodded at Erika, stopped at her desk, and took a piece of candy from the basket. Erika sat back, folded her arms across her chest, and blew out a breath, rattling her lips, but didn't slap his hand.

He popped the candy in his mouth and laid the wrapper atop an organized stack of papers on Erika's desk. When he turned away, stepping in my direction, she said, "You are welcome."

Half smiling, he said, "Yes, *masha danke*." He paused a moment, the smile disappearing and his expression softening. "I am truly sorry for your loss."

Erika continued to glare at him. After a moment, she pursed her lips and said, "Thank you."

Schleper went to the back wall of the office, grabbed an extra chair, and placed it on the opposite side of my desk. He sat and looked at me. I looked back. Neither of us smiled.

I hadn't encountered Schleper in a long time, not since the final reports and interviews involving Wayne Dow Jr., aka, Mandy W. Driver, a crazed nutjob who'd gone on a vengeful spree across the island, killing people close to me.

Not seeing Schleper was a good thing.

Unfortunately, most good things come to an end.

He wore a button-down shirt, open at the top, and khaki shorts. White gym shoes with ankle-cut socks. More casual that I'd ever seen him. His hair had grown out and needed a good combing. Maybe even a wash. A distinct difference from his normal high-and-tight military cut. He could've passed for any typical Dutch fellow on the island.

Except for his demeanor. In or out of uniform made no difference.

After silently counting to ten, I opened my beer and flicked the cap across the desk. It skidded to a stop inches from the edge on his side.

"What can I do for you, *Inspector*?" I asked.

He stared at the bottle cap for a few moments, then sighed and shook his head. "Are you not surprised to see me?" he said, slowly looking up at me.

I was but would never admit it. "Small island. I run into people all the time." I drank some of my Bright.

"Mr. Conklin . . . R," he said, his voice softening. "I . . . I need a favor."

I half-choked on the beer. "You need what? From me?"

He glanced over his shoulder at Erika. "Is it possible for us to have the room privately?"

"Erika—" I started.

"No! I will not leave," Erika said. "You two *men* can talk in front of me."

I raised my eyebrows at Schleper.

"Miss Erika," he said. "Please—"

"This must have something to do with Rulio," Erika said. "Otherwise, *you*"—she pointed a finger at Schleper—"would not worry about *me*."

I smiled and gave Erika an approving nod.

Schleper cleared his throat and rubbed the back of his neck. He turned in my direction, face painted with confusion, looking for assistance. Undoubtedly, most people didn't speak to him like that, let alone Erika, who had to be the last person he'd expect it from. Schleper only knew edicts—he had little tact, and from what I'd seen and experienced in the past, even fewer people skills.

He now found himself alone in a boat, cast adrift by Erika. And I wasn't about to throw him a lifeline.

"Okay, you can stay," Schleper said through a clenched jaw, his arrogance convincing himself he had the right to tell Erika what she could or couldn't do.

Erika pressed her hands together as if in prayer. "Thank *you*, Inspector," she said.

Schleper may not have had a choice in the matter, but letting Erika hear what he had to say could prove interesting. It often seemed Erika was related to half the people on the island and friends with the other half. She acted as a human conduit for gossip and information. By the time Schleper got back to the station, half the island might already know what he had asked.

But I wasn't about to warn him.

"Unfortunately, my request . . . my favor . . . has nothing to do with your nephew," Schleper said. "Please forgive me."

Erika slumped in disappointment.

I closed my eyes and took a deep breath, trying not to let my jaw muscles tighten. "What do you want, Schleper?" I said in a deeper and much more controlled voice than normal.

After a quick glance at Erika, he leaned over my desk, closing the distance between us, and in a low voice said, "I need you to follow my wife."

I let that sink in before asking, "Why?" An unnecessary question, I realized immediately, the answer being obvious.

"She might be seeing someone." Rather than sitting in his normal, upright posture, he slumped in the chair, hands resting in his lap. He locked eyes with me, his becoming moist and red. "I think she is having an affair."

None of us spoke. I didn't know how many friends Schleper had on the island—if any—but he sure needed one right now. Guess I'd throw him that lifeline after all. I reached into the fridge and took out two beers, opening the first one for myself. The second one I opened and handed to Schleper.

This time, I threw the caps in the garbage.

Erika cleared her throat and stood. "I need to do some errands." Her hand shook as she gathered some envelopes and her purse. She didn't have any errands to take care of. I'd done them all earlier. "I will see you tomorrow," she said to me and headed out the door.

The lowering sun and few scattered clouds promised a nice sunset, which would be impossible to witness from the office. Besides, I'd been sitting at this desk far too long.

"Let's drink these beers on the veranda," I said.

Schleper agreed and I led him up the inside stairs to my apartment and out onto the veranda. Several months ago, my trusty lounger had finally worn out. In its place, I had strung a hammock, which I worked myself into as I offered Schleper a chair. He sat and looked at the sun, which hung several inches above the horizon.

Wind rustled the palm trees and vehicles worked their way past the YellowRock on the one-way street, horns honking, engines revving. None of it, though, overpowered the sound of the waves striking the small beach on the other side of the road.

Nothing could overpower that . . . except maybe Schleper's silence.

"Why me?" I finally asked. "There must be others—friends, officers on the force, who could help you."

Schleper took a small, hurried sip. "I do not have many I can trust."

"You trust me?"

"I have no reason not to." He took another quick sip, looked at the bottle for a moment. "Think how it would be. An inspector asking another officer to follow his wife. Most would love to talk about that."

He had a point. Sounded scandalous when I thought about it. Almost worthy of grocery store tabloid material. I'd hate to be in his shoes.

"How do you say?" he said. "I am in a pickle?"

"Not being a licensed PI could land me in trouble," I said. "I don't know. Might get into a pickle myself."

"I can protect that from happening." He paused a moment, then said, "I am fine that you do not like me. The truth about my wife will hurt me, which you will no doubt find joy with. Yet, you would not lie. You have dignity and that is why I asked you."

I said nothing. Speechless. Not what I'd expected from Schleper.

We both drank our beers for a moment and looked at the sea. Folks on the beach and pedestrians on the street had stopped what they were doing and gazed westward, anticipating the pending sunset. The bottom portion of the sun had touched the horizon, sending radiating streaks of orange across the water. The few clouds had all but disappeared.

Schleper must've considered my silence as confirmation, some sort of agreement to follow his wife. Or maybe he was tired of our back-and-forth. He reached into his shirt pocket, removed a picture, and handed it to me.

"Her name is Tessa," he said. "Not Theresa, just Tessa." He smiled, but I wouldn't have called it a happy smile. I couldn't explain it. Maybe a sad smile, if such a thing existed.

I studied the picture. Tessa was shorter and heavier than Arabella, but the two women could've been sisters. Long blond hair, high cheekbones, and, possibly, a slight overbite.

"Thank you for doing this," Schleper said.

Swinging back and forth in my hammock, I said, "I haven't said yes yet."

Schleper tightened, his body going rigid.

I held up the picture of Tessa. "I'll follow your wife, but you need to do *me* a favor in return."

"What?"

I got out of the hammock and squared off in front of him. "I want to see everything you have on Rulio's case."

"I cannot do that."

"Then I won't follow your wife." I held the picture out for him to take back.

"It is an open case," he said.

"Yes, but I understand it's stalled."

His lips tightened. "Officer De Groot told you such?"

"I just want to see the file. And be allowed to ask a few folks some questions. No harm in that. And I won't get in the way." I waved the picture of Tessa in front of him.

His eyes narrowed. "You think you can do better than us? You are from a big city but that does not mean we are not capable."

"Don't make this into a big-city cop, small-town cop thing, Schleper." I paused a beat. "I'd just be another set of eyes. Couldn't hurt."

After a moment, he took a breath and relaxed. "All right, I will see what I can do." He jabbed a finger at me. "But you promise to stay in the background. And no one can know what you are doing."

"Understood," I said, although on a small island like Bonaire, keeping something like this quiet would prove, at best, difficult.

"And that goes for Officer De Groot, as well. She cannot know."

Reluctantly, a lump forming in my chest, I nodded. It just became even more difficult.

"Okay." He finished his beer and walked across the veranda to the outside stairs that led to the front sidewalk. "I will call you when I want you to start."

"And you'll send the file?"

"*After* you make progress on Tessa. But I will not give you my cell phone. Too risky. Tessa might become nosey and see a number or a message or . . . something. Call me on my desk phone at the department." He started down the stairs.

"Hey, Schleper." He stopped and turned. I held up Tessa's picture. "I'd never take pleasure in any of this hurting you."

The sun had fully set, and he looked across the street at the darkening horizon, a ghostly sliver of orange accentuating the far-off sky. After a moment, he nodded and left.

CHAPTER 7

All stakeouts are boring. Until something happens. General Dwight D. Eisenhower once said, "*No plan survives first contact with the enemy.*"

Schleper didn't waste any time getting me on the hunt. The day after our talk, he called and said Tessa would soon be leaving their house. He gave me the address and approximate time she'd be pulling out in her car. He wasn't sure where she was headed or who—if anyone—she was planning to meet. "That is the reason I want you to follow her," he had said, which I already understood.

Many times during my career, I had tried to get comfortable in an unmarked squad car that smelled of stale coffee, fast food, and vomit, barely able to hold my eyes open and pay attention. Every cop car smells the same and every cop knows the smell.

The countless hours of boredom were usually followed by one of two things. The person under surveillance would make a move and there'd be a level of excitement following them to the next location. Or, more commonly, the next shift arrived, allowing the current surveillance team to go home and get some rest. The best stakeouts end in an arrest, whereas the worst stakeouts end with several wasted days, the result of either bad intelligence or simply bad luck.

When possible, I opted out of surveillance work.

But here I was, about to do it as a retiree. At least this stakeout was on Bonaire. And I'd be using my Wrangler that, as far as I knew, had never contained vomit.

Standing in my bedroom, I thought about what to wear. My wardrobe was very narrow, consisting of various colors of the same type of T-shirt, along with neutral-colored cargo shorts. And two pair of sandals. Other than when wearing my jogging shoes on runs with Arabella, I hadn't worn socks since coming to the island over five years ago.

A simple wardrobe.

And, according to Arabella, a very dull one.

Depending on where Tessa went, blending in could take on several different looks. However, it was never a surprise to see tourists anywhere on the island—they wandered all over.

I dug to the bottom of a seldom opened dresser drawer and pulled out a T-shirt given to me long ago by a YellowRock customer. Overall red and mimicking the design of the international scuba diver flag, a white stripe ran diagonally across the front. White letters above and below the stripe read *Diver's Paradise*, the self-imposed motto of Bonaire.

In the back of my closet, I found a new floppy hat that'd never been worn, price tags still dangling from the brim. I don't remember buying it; probably left behind by a guest. Surprising what some folks forgot to pack when leaving.

I put on the hat and let the draw string dangle in front, hanging below my chin. My sandals and a pair of black socks completed the ensemble. I'd grab my sunglasses on the way out.

Erika turned in my direction as I trotted down the stairs to the office.

She put her hands on her cheeks. "Oh my, do you not look cute," she said. "Would you like to rent a room, Mr. Tourist?"

"Is it that bad?"

"No, you look fine. Just like the average island visitor."

Erika had heard Schleper ask me to follow his wife. However, she didn't know about my deal to get involved with Rulio's case. And now wasn't the time to mention it.

"You are going to follow Mr. Schleper's wife?"

"Yes, I am." I paused a moment. "Technically, it's called *surveillance*."

"Hmmm." She looked at me over the rim of her black glasses. "That is a big word for snooping on someone."

"Maybe so, but you didn't mention my *snooping* to anyone, did you?"

"No, it is too sad. He does not appear to be a nice man, but if what he says is true, no one deserves that."

I nodded. "I agree. And thanks." I headed for the door, keys in hand.

"Besides," she said, "who would I tell?"

"Yeah, right."

As I put a hand on the door, ready to push it open, Erika said, "Wait, I have something you should wear."

I turned back and she walked toward me, an object in her hand.

"This has been lying on the shelf for a long time," she said. "It is the perfect time to use it."

She showed me a waterproof ID case known as a *dive wallet*. It's a plastic case to hold driver's licenses, credit cards, money, etcetera while diving or snorkeling. A black string lanyard allowed it to hang over the owner's neck, the case resting mid-chest level. Most people wore it under their wetsuit while diving. But some tourists used it even while not diving, on a day-to-day basis, over their regular shirt.

Having this around my neck would brand me a tourist in a second.

Erika eased the lanyard over my head. "Perfect," she said, amused with her antics. Not that a frown or scowl painted her face on a regular basis, but a smile from Erika was a rare event, and lately it'd been even rarer. She was a focused, serious individual, and the loss of her nephew had dulled her outlook. This might be the first smile since Rulio's disappearance.

It gave me hope.

"Thanks," I said. "Just don't tell Chuck."

She laughed and patted me on the back of the shoulder as I turned and went out the door. "Snoop well," she said.

Out front, I stopped at my Wrangler and realized it may not be the best stakeout vehicle. Several things made it stand out. Although there were numerous Jeep Wranglers on the island—one of the rental agencies had a fleet of them—few of them were yellow, the color of mine. Also, years ago, I had removed the top and doors from my Wrangler, which the rental agencies don't allow, making my vehicle even more obvious. I considered reattaching the doors and top but wasn't sure where they were stored or how to re-mount them. Especially on such short notice.

Didn't matter. I'd have to make do.

Bonaire is a dry island, receiving on average less than twenty inches of rainfall per year, most of it coming in quick bursts that lasted only thirty minutes or so. Just enough to wet everything down and create dark puddles alongside the streets.

But, as luck would have it, it had rained the previous evening, water still standing in low spots along the roadside. The Wrangler seats were covered in vinyl, so a quick wipe with a towel and they were dry. At least dry enough for me. Living on an island and spending large amounts of time in the water, I had grown accustomed to being partially wet on a regular basis.

The sky was clear with no indication of further rain as I drove north through Kralendijk. I pulled into Santa Barbara Crowns, an upscale neighborhood dotted with modern houses, most built into a hillside providing panoramic views of the Caribbean Sea. After a few turns and cutbacks, I parked across the street from the Schlepers' residence. Not the most expensive-looking digs on the street, but certainly not a dump.

I pulled down the hat brim, partly to shade my eyes from the sun and partly to hide my identity. My well-planned tourist outfit might only go so far. Couldn't remember if I'd ever met Tessa, or if maybe she knew who I was, so I needed to take every precaution in case she caught a glimpse of me.

A half-bottle of water into my stakeout, Tessa's dark blue Toyota backed out of the carport. I slouched in my seat pretending to study my cell phone as she drove past. In the outside mirror, I saw her turn onto a side street a block behind me. I fired up the Wrangler, did a U-turn across the shoulders on both sides of the street, and headed in her direction.

Following another vehicle on Bonaire was easy. And hard.

With few roads, particularly main thoroughfares, driving behind the same car for long periods of time wasn't unusual. Many times, I'd traveled from the south side of the island, through Kralendijk, and toward the north section, noticing the same vehicle in front or behind me the entire time. There just weren't that many reasons to turn off the main streets. However, Tessa might think it odd if she noticed my Wrangler behind her at different times, possibly on multiple days.

She turned into the parking lot of one of the island's major grocery stores and parked in a spot near the building. I slipped into a stall at the rear of the lot, under a nearby watakeli tree, turned off the Wrangler, and put on my *Eagles Greatest Hits* CD, keeping the volume low. Not sure how long I'd be waiting—no way to know if Tessa was shopping or just picking up a few items.

The fragrance of the white flowers on the watakeli drifted through the Wrangler and the tree's abundant dark green foliage provided ample shade. I took a breath and called to check in with Erika, see if she needed anything. She didn't.

The sun was starting to sink, and luckily, had slid below the roof line of the grocery store, casting a long shadow that reached my Wrangler and allowed me to remove the sunglasses. A food-truck vendor across the street cooked chicken on an open grill, the smoke drifting across the parking lot, carrying with it the sweet smell of charcoal, spices, and sauces. My mouth watered. The barbeque hound that I am, I strolled up to the truck, glancing occasionally at Tessa's vehicle, and bought an entire roasted chicken, along with two Brights.

As I crossed the street, headed back to the parking lot, Tessa walked out of the store, a bottle of wine in each hand, and got in her Toyota. She pulled out of the lot as I threw the chicken and Brights onto the passenger-side seat and cranked up the Wrangler. I cut off a small pickup truck full of tourists, tires squealing as I pulled onto the street, and ended up two cars behind Tessa as we went through the nearby roundabout, or traffic circle as they're called on Bonaire.

Being two cars behind wasn't an issue. I saw Tessa's dark blue Toyota ahead of me and easily followed her, traveling down the street called Kaya Industrial. The problem came when, after driving through town and heading north, she turned onto a side road that went into a residential area. I knew the neighborhood all too well. Arabella's sister, Ruth, ran her business nearby.

Tessa skidded to a stop along the gravel shoulder in front of Ruth's place. I wasn't expecting that and jammed my brakes to the floor, stopping the Wrangler several houses away. At first, I thought maybe Tessa had gotten wise to my tailing her and wanted to confront me. Or maybe call her husband for assistance. Neither option boded well for me and my snooping.

The Jeep idled and I sat motionless, as if moving might worsen matters. The smart play would've been to slowly back up, turn around, and drive away in the direction I'd come. Try and tail her again another day. I was tired of following her anyway and calling it quits sounded like a good idea. I still had time to sit in my hammock, eat the chicken, drink the Brights, and listen to the ocean until Arabella came home.

But I didn't get a chance.

To my surprise, Tessa's door opened, and she got out, carrying the bottles of wine. She strolled up to the front door and was greeted by Ruth with open arms. She walked in and Ruth started to close the door but paused and looked in my direction. Even from two houses away, I saw her eyes narrow as she studied my Wrangler. A scowl crept across her face, her stare not wavering until she eventually closed the door.

Was I busted? Ruth had to wonder why I was sitting in my vehicle two houses away from her place. Would she rat me out? Did she suspect why I happened to be on her street? It'd be a huge coincidence that Tessa and I were just "in the neighborhood" at the same time.

No plan survives first contact with the enemy.

I decided to call Schleper. Arabella had told me several times that he worked a lot of hours, so, as instructed, I dialed his office number. He answered, and I suddenly realized I didn't know what to tell him.

"I followed Tessa," I finally said.

"And what did you find out?"

I lied. "Not much. She bought some groceries and did some shopping downtown."

"Where is she now?"

I lied again. "She's back home."

He paused a beat; I didn't say anything. "What do you think?" he asked.

"Not much right now. I'm headed home."

"Okay, you can try again. I know there's more to this than shopping. I need better results."

Schleper must've thought he was my new boss. I wanted to remind him that I was retired and didn't have a boss. Except for Erika, which reminded me why I was doing this.

For her.

And Rulio.

"You'll send the file tomorrow?" I asked, making sure he lived up to his end of the bargain. The whole ploy could be a bust if Ruth told Tessa she saw me.

He paused a moment and sighed. "Yes, tomorrow I will send it."

"Thanks," I said and disconnected.

I sat in the Wrangler and stared at Ruth's. I pulled a leg off the chicken and tossed part of the skin on the ground. A small lizard scurried over to investigate. When another lizard ran over to see what all the fuss was about, the first one grabbed the skin and made for some underbrush. The other one followed close behind.

I finished the chicken leg and almost opened a Bright but didn't. As I turned the Wrangler around and headed for the YellowRock, I considered the lies I'd just told Schleper. I hated doing it but saw little choice.

How could I tell him his wife had just carried two bottles of wine into a brothel?

CHAPTER 8

"There is a package for you," Erika said the following morning as I moseyed down the stairs from my apartment to the office. "It came for you first thing." She pointed at a box sitting on my desk. "It is from the police department."

"Thanks."

She sat sideways in the chair and leaned an elbow on her desk, hand propping up her head. "I must wonder what the police department might send you."

"No idea." Lying was becoming second nature for me.

"Uh-huh." She straightened and faced her desk. Before going back to work, she said, "I might think it has something to do with the deal you made with Mr. Schleper."

No idea how she'd know that. As far as I knew, Schleper and I were the only two privy to our arrangement. I hadn't told anyone, and guaranteed Schleper hadn't. Definitely not Erika.

However, over the years, I'd discovered that, somehow, very few things escaped her. I should probably operate under the assumption that she knew everything I was up to, which was usually the case.

Just like a big sister should.

"What do you mean?" I asked.

She jabbed a finger at the file. "That is about Rulio. Mr. Schleper wants you to watch Tessa. And he agreed to let you look into Rulio's . . ." Her voice trailed off as she lowered her head, eyes pointed at the floor but staring into space.

Time to come clean.

"Yes, this package is the file on Rulio." She hadn't used the word "murder," so I didn't either. "I'm going to take a look at it, but I can't make any promises." Probably should've said *any more promises.* I sat at my desk. "I just don't know if there's anything I can do."

She looked up. "Thank you."

"But no one can know about this, okay? That was part of the deal I made with Schleper. I can't even tell Bella."

Her mouth gaped open for a moment. "Not even Miss Arabella?"

"No, so please don't tell anyone."

With scrunched eyebrows, she said, "Who would I tell?" Then, she began entering numbers into a spreadsheet displayed on her monitor.

"By the way," I said, "who told you about this?"

Not interrupting her typing, she just shrugged. I knew better than to pursue the matter. Suffice it to say, she knew. And the air was clear between us, which made me feel better. A little anyway. My guilt would evaporate when I cleared the fog between Arabella and me.

But that would have to wait.

Before tearing open the package, I leaned back in my chair. The office door was open, a slight breeze filling the room with the faint smell of ocean. Tourists wandered past, their laughs and excited chit-chat telegraphing their anticipation of another splendid day in paradise. It's how vacations were supposed to be—fun. No stress and no worries.

But I wasn't on vacation, and if I were to spill the contents of the package onto my desk, I'd be committed to following it through, no matter what it'd tell me; no matter where it'd lead. And I'd have to do it without Arabella's help or knowledge.

Wasn't sure I wanted to make that commitment. I'd rather get back to my retirement routine. Quit following Tessa, spend more time with Arabella, and nap regularly in my new hammock, listening to the sounds of the island. Or the Eagles. Or Creedence. Or maybe nothing at all.

But I had made a promise.

My heart raced. With shaky, sweaty hands, I sliced through the tape on the package, flipped open the top, and pulled out a stack of papers enclosed by a single manila folder. The file was barely an inch thick, much thinner than I had anticipated. Not sure why I'd set my expectations as such.

The investigation has halted, Arabella had said.

"So . . ." Erika said. "What do you think?"

Not looking away from the file, I said, "Well, I *think* I'll need to read the file first."

Erika shrugged, but didn't say anything further.

Thick or thin, I'd be relying on these few pieces of paper to propel me forward in determining what happened to Rulio. My Golden Ticket to suspects, interviews, evidence, clues, and theories. I had needed this file, and now—surprisingly—I had it. Letting out a long, slow breath, I opened the folder.

At first, I couldn't believe what I saw. The elation I experienced just seconds earlier quickly drained away. I dropped the file on my desk and slumped into my chair, speechless.

Erika glanced at me, but I didn't acknowledge her.

I picked up the folder again and leafed through the first few pages. I leaned my head back and studied the ceiling tile. What I saw in the file shouldn't have surprised me.

It made perfect sense.

After all, Bonaire is part of the Netherlands.

So why *wouldn't* the file be written in Dutch?

I shook my head. For several years Arabella had been trying to teach me Dutch. I wasn't an ideal student and, for the most part, she'd given up on the project. Over time, anything close to the term *learning Dutch* or *Dutch lesson* had morphed into code for jumping in bed and fooling around.

Should've paid better attention. At least occasionally.

I pictured Schleper sitting at his stuffy desk in his stuffy uniform with his stuffy demeanor having a big laugh over this. Probably thought he had the upper hand, maybe teach the big-city cop a lesson.

That image was all I needed. This wouldn't be a deterrent or slow me down. I needed to continue forward and keep the momentum going my way.

The first few pages were easy to decipher, dedicated to specifics; Rulio's full name, address, date and place of birth, parents, what appeared to be their death certificates, his occupation and employer, etcetera. Although in Dutch, the information was identifiable, like countless forms I'd seen and used in the past. A two-inch by three-inch portrait of Rulio was stapled to the upper left corner of the folder. It looked like a picture from the DMV, or OLB—*Openbaar Lichaam Bonaire*—the Bonairian government's equivalent. I flipped through the pages, not finding anything of interest.

Several eight-inch by ten-inch pictures of the leg followed the informational page. The photos were taken from varying angles and distances. Some showed the small pier in the background, while others showed the beach and the sea. Several were taken after the leg had been rolled over, showing the Bonaire tattoo on the thigh. Two pictures were close-ups of the wire wrapped around the ankle.

Arabella's photos of the table containing the items recovered from the search dive followed the pictures of the leg. Again, various shots from different angles and distances, along with close-ups of each item with its corresponding information tag. I saw my signature at the bottom of the chain of evidence document.

The most telling part of the file would be the report from the tending detective, or inspector as they're called in Bonaire's *Polis* Force. And this *inspecteur*, not surprisingly, was Schleper. However, since the report was in Dutch, it'd be a challenge for me to garner any useful information from it.

I plugged *English-Dutch translator* into an internet search and received one hundred and seventy-one million hits. Breezing through the first few pages of the results, there appeared to be three basic options. One option was to translate specific words; another would translate simple sentences; and the third would be to scan an entire page at a time and send it to a place for translation.

The third option was a no-go. I couldn't take the chance of someone seeing this file. It contained confidential police information and I needed to keep it that way. Too risky not knowing who might do the translation and where the information might eventually land.

I decided on a combination of the first two options. I'd translate specific words in the report, then, if need be, the entire sentence.

Sentence by sentence, hours passing, I translated Schleper's notes. Rulio had disappeared and wasn't heard from in over a week. Bonaire is a small island, but folks have been known to go missing, especially if they were so inclined. On Bonaire, the police department was responsible for immigration, making it easy for Schleper to check Rulio's passport status. They had not found any evidence he left the island through immigration.

Since his disappearance, Rulio's credit cards hadn't been used and his bank account hadn't been accessed. His laptop and phone couldn't be located, and several calls to his cell number went unanswered.

From what I could translate, the police had initially determined the only explanation possible from their point of view—Rulio had chosen to go missing. Not the best conclusion, but one made by the process of elimination, excluding all other possibilities until the least provable one still existed.

Seemed reasonable.

Until Rulio's leg washed ashore.

A coroner's report was part of the file, but some of the medical terms didn't translate well, slowing my progress even more and making bits of my translation project appear more like gibberish than something official.

The tattoo of Bonaire on the thigh made it easy to guess who the leg belonged to. However, samples of Rulio's DNA were taken from his apartment in order to make positive identification. The final report was still pending.

Bijl is Dutch for "hatchet," so I zeroed in on a few specific sentences and determined the leg had been removed with some sort of "hacking tool." A diagram was included that had a red arrow at the pelvis, just below the ball-socket of the hip, I guessed, showing the separation point. Other red marks on the bone near the joint must've been used to denote scrapes, indicating a chopping motion.

I noticed Erika get her purse, stand, and stretch.

"I am going to lunch," she said. "Should I bring you back something?"

I glanced at the clock on my monitor. The morning had slipped by, and I wasn't even half finished translating the report. "No thanks, I'm not hungry."

"Still thinking?" she said with a raised eyebrow.

"Yeah, still thinking."

"Looks hard."

"Always is."

She left and I returned my attention to the report.

The line-by-line translation was exhausting. In some cases, what came back didn't make sense. I didn't know if it was because of slang, dialect, or inadequacies of the translation app. A friend of mine, David Brown, worked at the hospital. I'd call him later. Maybe he could provide additional information; more than I could decipher from the report.

I moved on.

No longer did Schleper believe Rulio chose to go missing, and reading between the lines the best I could within the translation, it's possible Schleper never believed it in the first place. Beyond finding a body or some trail of Rulio's mobility, he had no initial explanation for Rulio's disappearance. Now, with the leg washing ashore, he did. Especially with wire wrapped around the ankle. The coroner's report contained information beyond my translation capabilities, and I hoped my friend David Brown could provide greater detail for me.

But the conclusion was obvious.

Moord. Murder.

Speculation was that Rulio had been dismembered and his body parts cast into the sea. Referencing Caribbean water current charts and wind data for the days before the leg washed ashore, the educated guess from island experts was that it occurred somewhere northwest of Bonaire. Normally, the currents and wind would've carried it farther northwest, away from Bonaire and into the open ocean.

The ankle wrapped with wire was enough for Schleper to assume premeditation, and the recent wind reversal that pushed the leg to the shores of Bonaire—a random act of nature the murderer hadn't anticipated—highlighted the intent. No mention of a theory regarding the rest of the body. Most likely lost to the sea forever.

Without a body, though, all conjecture.

Out of the gate, Schleper's team stumbled. Motive and suspects. They weren't close on either.

Rulio had been certified as a dive master and instructor. Schleper alluded to a diving accident that had impacted two divers under Rulio's instruction. I vaguely remembered the incident but didn't know the specifics. And since those specifics didn't have bearing on the murder case—aside from possible suspects—Schleper hadn't gone into details within the report. He did, however, list the names and contact information of the two divers involved: one, an American, deceased as a result of the accident, and the other, an Antillean, who lived on the nearby island of Curacao, injured in the accident. His occupation was listed as carpenter.

The report detailed interviews conducted with Rulio's girlfriend; the staff at Island Diver's, his former employer; the Curacao diver involved in the incident; and the family of the deceased American diver. The report didn't explicitly mention it, but I guessed that some of these individuals had been suspects at some level and at one time or another. There was no mention in the report as to whether these "suspects" had been cleared. But I assumed they had been since the report made no further mention of them.

My stomach grumbled, and I looked at the clock. Midafternoon. I reached into the fridge behind my desk and pulled out a yogurt.

"So, now you are hungry," Erika asked.

I'd been so engulfed in the report and translation, I hadn't noticed her return from lunch.

"The lunch of champions," I said and went back to my work.

Miscellaneous family and friends were spoken to, but no other suspects were identified. And no mention of motive, although I was sure revenge had been discussed. The investigators could check with immigration to determine if any of the suspects had returned to Bonaire, but it'd be almost impossible to check every passenger on every flight and determine any relationship to the suspects.

One notation in the report caught my interest. Whereas I couldn't find anything regarding the other suspects having been cleared, Schleper had taken the time to specifically mention that Joost Obersi, the carpenter and diver residing on Curacao, was at one time a person of interest. Immigration records showed that he had arrived back on Bonaire the day before Rulio went missing and departed three days later. I made a mental note to dig deeper into Obersi.

Finally, I finished the report.

I rubbed my eyes and reached into the small fridge for a Bright. I leaned back in the chair and considered my translation job. All in all, not too bad. It gave me a good read on what the police knew and a few ideas about my next steps.

However, there were countless mistakes I could've made. No guarantee I didn't miss something or that the app hadn't given me a bad translation. I'd just have to go with what I had and hope for the best.

Not my preferred strategy, but, at the present, all I had.

It was late afternoon, nearing Erika's quitting time, and I needed to talk to her before she left for the day.

"Erika," I said, "please tell me about Rulio's dive accident."

"You do not know? I talked to you about it before."

"I remember, but please refresh my memory."

She glanced at the papers on my desk. "Did the police refer to it?"

"Not directly, but I'd like to know more."

She took a deep breath and slowly exhaled, looking at the ceiling. Her eyes teared. After a quick glance at Rulio's picture, she dried them with a tissue. "It was a bad thing," she said softly. Then, in a raised voice, "But it was not Rulio's fault!"

"What wasn't his fault?"

"The man dying, the American."

I remained silent, waiting for her to continue.

"Rulio was instructing them on a dive," she said. "They wanted a new certification. I don't know diving too well, but they were using . . . double-breathers?"

"Rebreathers?"

"Yes, rebreathers."

A rebreather is a breathing apparatus that absorbs the carbon dioxide of a diver's exhaled breath and replenishes it with additional oxygen so it can be breathed again, allowing the diver extended time underwater. This differs from regular scuba where the exhaled gas is discharged directly into the water, creating bubbles. Rebreathers discharge almost no bubbles. They require special training to use and maintain.

"What happened?" I asked.

"I do not know the details. All I know is something went wrong. The students got scared and went to the surface. Rulio always told me that going to the top too fast is bad. One man, the American, something went wrong with his lungs and he died underwater. Rulio brought him to the top. The other man, the one from Curacao, was injured. He recovered, but blamed Rulio."

"I remember Rulio lost his job."

"Yes, Island Divers said he could no longer work for them. Then, no dive shop on the island would hire him. He was terribly upset." More tears flowed. She wiped her eyes again, hands trembling, then continued in a softer tone. "He loved diving. Now he could no longer make a living. What was he to do now?"

"Where was he working before . . . before he went missing?"

"He was a dishwasher."

"Where?"

"A restaurant at the new resort, the one they are building near the south end of the island."

I knew of the place. It was an all-inclusive resort with a proposed grand opening about six months away. However, the restaurant had already opened.

"Do you know the name of the place?"

"No, I do not. I do not pay attention to the new places being built." She waved her hand. "Far too many of them." She seemed caught up in thought for a moment, then said, "But it probably has the word *Paradise* in the name. In some way, most all of them do."

CHAPTER 9

After our conversation, Erika left for the day and I leaned back in the chair, considering my next move. Schleper had told me to keep my mouth shut about the Rulio case, meaning, in my assumption, not to discuss the facts, details, or theories. However, he hadn't said I couldn't *investigate.* And investigating was, in large part, talking to people.

Throughout history, countless murders had been committed to "get even." People rationalize their actions—to themselves and others—trying to justify murder. As well as a powerful emotion, revenge is also a powerful motive. But, other than in cases of self-defense, homicide of any kind is never justifiable.

The two divers involved in the training accident would be difficult to interview—one lived on Curacao; the other was dead. However, Schleper's crew had already spoken with the diver on Curacao, and in the case of the deceased one, they had spoken with his brother. The police had determined neither were seeking retribution.

In any investigation, especially murder, family members are the first suspects. I immediately ruled out Erika. No motive. After Erika, the next closest person to family for Rulio would be his girlfriend, Sandra Griffis. Schleper's team had interviewed her and ruled her out as a suspect. I had never met her, but Rulio had once showed me her picture. She lived on Kaya Powhatan in the Noord Salina neighborhood. No idea if she was home, but I jumped in the Wrangler and headed that way. Ten minutes later, I parked in front of her blue, one-story residence, a rectangular structure of maybe eight hundred square feet.

I let myself through a rusty metal front gate, a blue, chest-high concrete wall surrounding the entire property. Not uncommon on Bonaire. Most of the traditional structures had perimeter walls to keep wild donkeys and wandering goats at bay. The "yard" consisted of gravel and stone, a few thirsty blades of grass pushing up between the rocks, basking in the late afternoon sunlight. A pair of sheets hung on a rope strung between two poles anchored in the yard. A concrete slab ran the width of the front with a warped tin roof hanging haphazardly above, supported by a few wood pillars.

Feeling as if my legs were anchored in place, I plodded toward the front door. A small lizard darted across my path, stopping in the shade of the makeshift porch. He cranked his head and watched as I stepped onto the concrete slab, knocked, and moved back. My hand shook as I wiped sweat from my brow.

Poking through a front window alongside the porch, dripping water onto a cluster of grateful weeds, an air conditioner whined and sputtered rhythmically.

Before I knocked a second time, the door opened halfway, exposing a mid-twenties Bonairian girl dressed in a bright orange T-shirt and dark capris. Large, welcoming dark eyes, smooth skin, and a perky, yet sad, smile. Two chains dangled around her neck, one gold and one silver. A figurine of a dolphin hung from the end of the silver one. Pulled back in a tight bun, strands of hair wafted out around the edges of a black visor.

When I saw *Paradise Cove* printed in pink letters on the front of the visor, a quiet bell rang in the dark recesses of my brain.

She leaned against the doorframe, appraising me. "Can I help you?" she finally said. The younger Bonairian generation spoke English well. Probably something to do with the amount of American television shows the island cable service provided.

"Sandra?" I asked in a quiet voice.

"Yes."

Almost immediately, I came to the same conclusion Schleper's team had. Without asking one pertinent question, I ruled her out as a suspect in Rulio's death. Sandra Griffis stood five feet, two inches tall and weighed, maybe, a hundred pounds soaking wet. Unlikely she could wrestle Rulio—a muscular, one-hundred-and-seventy-five-pound six-footer—into a position to chop off his leg.

But maybe she wouldn't have to wrestle him into position. If he loved her—and trusted her—he might voluntarily make himself vulnerable. A modern-day Samson and Delilah.

Bill Ryberg, my old partner back in Rockford, now deceased, had kept a wooden sign on his desk that read "Follow every lead, no matter how small."

Sandra Griffis was a lead I needed to follow.

"I'd like to talk to you about Rulio," I said.

Her eyes teared. "Why? Is there some news?"

"Just some follow-up." A bead of sweat trickled down my cheek. I had no intention of impersonating law enforcement, but it might work to my advantage if she thought I was a cop. I'd tell the truth if she asked, but so far, she hadn't.

"Okay," she said, fully opening the door and gesturing me into the house.

Although the air conditioner fought a valiant struggle against the Bonaire heat, it was losing the battle miserably, the temperature inside barely lower than the temperature outside. Sandra offered me a seat and a glass of water. I declined the water and dropped myself into a brown, twice-worn-out chair held together in places with gray duct tape. She sat across from me on a red, plastic loveseat that looked as though it could've come out of an inner-city laundromat.

Neither of us spoke. A picture of her and Rulio, standing in sand under a palm tree near the sea, hung on the wall behind her.

Breaking the ice, I said, "Is that Pink Beach?"

Without looking at the photo, she said, "Yes. It was taken last year." She bowed her head, looking at her hands resting in her lap.

We were both quiet for a few moments.

I searched for something reassuring to say but ended up just nodding. For a lack of anything else, I said, "I'm sorry for your loss," with a cracked, shaky voice.

She turned away for a moment, sighed, and looked back, chin trembling. "What can I do for you?"

I swallowed. This would be tough. It'd been a long time since I'd interviewed a victim's loved one and my throat had already gone dry. I hoped I wouldn't choke on my words. Probably should've taken that water. Or a beer.

"How long had you and Rulio been together?"

"About three years or so." She half laughed, a reminiscent smile brightening her face. "We had just bought this house before the . . ." Her voice trailed off, and she wiped a tear with her index finger. "Before the accident." She paused a moment. "Not sure I can afford it on my own."

"By 'accident' you mean the dive accident?"

She nodded. "Rulio felt awful about it. It was just one of those things. Do you dive?"

"Yes, I do."

"Well then, you understand that diving can sometimes be unpredictable. Rulio always said, 'You try to reduce the risks as much as possible, but they're always there.' Most of the time, everything's fine. It's enjoyable. But sometimes, things happen. *That* was one of those times."

I didn't know exactly what happened to cause the problem, especially one so severe that an experienced dive master like Rulio couldn't handle it. I could find out, if need be, but just like Schleper's report, the specifics of the dive accident weren't important right now.

She continued, "Then, after the man from Curacao confronted him—"

"The man from Curacao?"

"Yes, the diver who survived, he lives on Curacao."

"I know, but what about a confrontation?"

"He confronted Rulio at work. He pushed Rulio several times, and finally Rulio pushed him back. The guy fell off the pier and into the water. He panicked, and Rulio had to jump in and pull him to the ladder. *That* made the guy even more mad."

"Did you witness this?"

"No, but Rulio told me about it. The man was upset and blamed Rulio for his injuries."

"When did this happen?"

"Several days after the accident, after the hospital released him. Rulio apologized and tried to explain to Island Divers what had happened, but they fired him anyway. He was so distraught. And none of the other dive shops would hire him." She threw her arms in the air. "How was he to make a living? He was a good dive master, maybe the best on the island. Before the accident, several other shops offered him employment."

"Why didn't he take any of them?"

"He liked Island Divers. They were big enough to offer him a range of opportunities." She wiped another tear. "In a year or so, he thought he might be the dive shop manager. It looked good."

I didn't recall the words *confrontatie, worsteling,* or *gevecht,* the Dutch words for "confrontation," "struggle," and "fight," in the police report. "Just to verify, did you mention this confrontation to the first officers you spoke with?"

She repositioned in the chair, her eyes becoming teary again. One hand fingered the dolphin attached to the silver chain around her neck. "I don't remember."

I stared at her.

"Seriously," she said. "I don't remember what I said." She closed her eyes, shook her head. "It's been very difficult."

We were both quiet a few moments. The air conditioner whined in the background.

"I understand he was working at a restaurant," I said.

Her face brightened somewhat, a faint smile trying to emerge. "Yeah, I got him a job as a dishwasher."

"Where?"

She pointed at her visor. "Paradise Cove. That's where I work. It wasn't a great job, but Rulio knew it helped pay the bills."

But it probably has the word Paradise *in the name.*

"You also work at the restaurant?"

"Not exactly. I'm an accountant for the corporation that runs the restaurant. I know the owners and asked them to hire Rulio. When I explained what he'd been through, they didn't hesitate."

"That was nice of them."

"Yes, it was. And it gets better. They really liked Rulio and asked him to manage the new dive shop. When it opened, that is."

"The dive shop?"

"Yeah, the owners of the restaurant are also building the dive shop." She smiled. "Rulio was very excited." The smile faded, her shoulders sagging. "It would've been a great opportunity for him . . . for us . . ."

The dive shop made sense. A new resort on the island would need a place to sell equipment, give lessons, fill and rent tanks, and schedule dive excursions. It surprised me, though, to learn the restaurant owners would also operate the dive shop.

After a moment of silence, I stood. "I don't want to take up any more of your day."

She stood. "Is there anything new about Rulio?" Her eyes teared again. "The investigation, I mean?"

"Not that I can talk about, but thank you for your time."

"You're welcome. I hope it was helpful."

"Sometimes it's impossible to know what is helpful until more information is gathered." It was the truth, but I regretted saying it the moment the words left my mouth. A mixture of confusion and sorrow spilled across her face. I wanted to leave her with something positive, so I added, "But in this case, you've been very helpful."

She walked me to the door, which was less than ten feet away. Before I left the ninety-degree inside for the ninety-five-degree outside, I said, "Can I ask one more question?"

"Sure."

"Who are the owners of Paradise Cove?"

Her eyes widened and she smiled. "An American couple, the Andersons. His name is John, and her name is Danielle." She went quiet a moment and bit her lower lip. "To be honest, Mr. Anderson scares me sometimes, but—"

"Scares you? How?"

"He's very intense. Acts like he wants to fight everyone. And he hits on all the women. I heard him once tell a member of the wait staff, 'Sweetie, I walk into every room as though I'm James Bond.'" She paused a beat, then said, "Yup, in a nutshell, that pretty much sums up Mr. Anderson."

"I can see how that might be difficult to work around."

"Yeah, but Mrs. Anderson is super nice. She's the kind of person who lights up any room she walks into. And she keeps Mr. Anderson in his place. Most of the time, anyway. She says he's more bark than bite."

Her right hand fidgeted with the dolphin again, a nervous habit or something she didn't know she was doing. After noticing my stare, she bowed her head and held up the dolphin, an invitation for me to examine it closer. "Rulio gave it to me," she said. Her eyes moistened. "I always considered it a pre-engagement gift."

"It's beautiful," I said

"I thought it was a dolphin; Rulio insisted it was a porpoise." She paused, wiped an eye. "When he gave it to me, he said I was the *porpoise* in his life." She looked at me and half-smiled. "It's a play on words. Porpoise for purpose."

I had already figured that out but didn't say so. After a moment, not knowing anything further to ask or how to end this conversation, I simply thanked her again for talking with me and walked out into the sun. The air conditioner whined and fought its never-ending battle against the Bonaire heat, water still dripping onto the small cluster of weeds. The metal gate creaked as I shut it behind me. Stopping at the Wrangler, I looked back at the house. Sandra Griffis had not asked who I was, whether I was a cop, or why I was interested in Rulio's murder.

Standing guard over the yard in the hot sun, the lizard had repositioned itself on a large rock near the road.

It sat motionless and watched me get in the Wrangler and drive away.

CHAPTER 10

On a single breath, I pulled myself through the water the last few strokes, touching the dock pylon ten seconds before Arabella. For me, our swims were never a race, but I couldn't say the same for her. At ten years my junior, she could easily outrun me on the roads. However, at swimming, I had the edge. At least for now.

The swim started with her in the lead, but only slightly. By the time we turned and started back, I had overtaken her and led the remainder of the way. She would consider it a defeat, but she always told me not to let up. She couldn't improve if I let her *win*.

The moment she finished, she raised her swim goggles and studied the GPS-stopwatch-heart-monitor-workout-data-accumulator gizmo strapped to her wrist. A frown or two later, and after pressing a few buttons, she slapped the water.

"That is not a kilometer," she said.

"I said it was two-thirds of a mile."

"Not even that." She checked the gizmo again. "And it was a slow time."

"It's the same pace I always swim."

Eyebrows raised, she nodded at me. "Yup. Slow." Then she smiled and laid back, floating on the surface, catching her breath.

It had been a good swim. For me anyway. I preferred swimming in the morning, but Arabella liked swimming later in the day, after her shift. She said it relieved the day's tension.

Calm water; a sinking sun; a cooler of Brights on the pier. I could float on the surface like this for hours.

Arabella sprang upright. "I need a beer." She swam to the ladder, climbed up, and tossed me a swim noodle. I wrapped it around my upper back, tucking an end under each arm. I could easily float all night, but the noodle made it effortless.

The wind had died. The nearby sailboats, moored fifty yards away on the reef's edge, moved gently back and forth to the almost non-existent waves. Their tall masts and the low sun created long shadows across the water. A few spotted sandpipers scavenged the sand looking for scraps of food left behind by vacated sun worshipers.

Arabella slipped a T-shirt over her one-piece red swimsuit and sat on the edge of the pier, munching an apple, a beer resting alongside her. A can. We never brought glass to the beach.

"What about me?" I asked.

"What about you?" she said, mouth full of apple.

"I could use a beer."

"Are your legs broken? Climb out and get it." The print on the upper portion of her T-shirt read *Gun Safety Rule #1* and along the bottom *Don't Make Me Mad!* The middle of the shirt contained the outline of a revolver with a trail of smoke oozing out the barrel.

I tilted my head. "I'm comfortable."

She stared at me a moment, then mumbled something in Dutch I didn't understand. She reached into the cooler, grabbed a beer, and tossed it to me.

"Thanks," I said, popping it open. "By the way, I know what you just said."

"No, you do not."

With her left hand, she rubbed her right shoulder. Then, she made slow looping motions with her right arm, like she was warming up to throw a baseball. But she wasn't warming up to throw a baseball. Not long ago, while saving my life, she'd been shot in the right shoulder. The injury was nearly healed, but she said it was occasionally stiff, usually after exercise.

"A little stiff?" I asked.

"Yes, but getting better." She stopped the looping-arm motion, and a thin smile swam across her face. "Soon, very soon." She took a swig of beer.

Her competitive juices overflowing, the implication was she'd soon be out-swimming me. Probably so. Only a matter of time. But it didn't matter to me whether I came in first or not. Just being with Arabella was a win in my book.

"Thought any more about the move to inspector?" I asked.

A while back, Arabella had decided to test for an inspector role, but put that desire on hold after being wounded. My concern was that her change of heart was partially based on our relationship. She said she didn't want to leave me, even for a short time. I didn't want to see her go, but she shouldn't make career decisions based on me.

She had recently passed the written portion, and now just needed to return to the Netherlands for some extended training. Physically and professionally, she was ready. All that remained was the mental part—the act of deciding. It'd be a decision that could very well unfold a road map to the rest of her life.

She took a bite of apple and chewed. "Yes, I have thought about it." She swallowed and took a swig of beer. "But I have not made up my mind. I am still thinking."

I held back a smile. "Don't hurt yourself."

She grabbed a piece of ice from the cooler, then leaned forward and tossed it at me. "No, I will not."

The ice fell well short of me. "If you want to talk about it, let me know. I'm all ears."

She nodded.

We watched a passing boat loaded with divers coming in from a late afternoon trip. Some of the passengers standing near the stern waved at us as they passed. We waved back.

Not sure why people on boats felt compelled to wave. Seemed commonplace for passengers to wave at people on a passing boat or on the shore. Maybe it's an unspoken solidarity thing. *Water-loving people unite!* Or maybe it's an excess of alcohol and vacation bliss.

"What do you know about Paradise Cove?" I asked, the words still meaning something to me, but I didn't know what.

She shrugged. "It is a new construction site on the south end of the island. The restaurant is open already. Lots of construction."

"Know anything about a dive shop there?"

"No, I do not."

"Think you could find out who the owners are?"

Her eyebrow scrunched. "Of the dive shop?"

"Of both, the restaurant and the dive shop."

"Why?"

I took a nervous swig of beer. This was going to hurt. "Well, it's a resort, so it's competition to my business."

Arabella stung me with narrowed eyes. "Since when do you worry about competition?"

"The more I know about the entire operation, the better off I'll be." I hated lying to her. Like a thousand jellyfish stings, my entire body throbbed. With an uneasy hand, I drank some beer.

She shrugged. "I will see what I can do."

"Thanks." I finished my beer and tossed the empty can onto the pier. "How about another?"

From the dive shop down the block came the pinging of scuba tanks clanking together. People talking, laughing, and preparing for a night dive. Moments earlier, the sun had slipped below the horizon and slivers of orange, red, and purple now streaked the sky. The Bonaire sunsets tend to display all the colors missed during the day.

My cell phone rang from where it lay beside my T-shirt on the pier.

"Should I get that for you?" Arabella asked.

"Unless it's Erika, let it go to voicemail."

Arabella glanced at the phone's display. "Hey . . . I know this number." She looked at me. "It is Schleper's desk phone."

"Schleper?" I said with a cracking voice. I hadn't put his number in my address book, concerned that such a situation might arise, Arabella looking at an incoming call on my cell and seeing that it was from her boss. Made sense she'd know the number, but I never considered the scenario occurring.

"Why would Schleper call you?" she asked. Again, the narrowed eyes.

"I have no idea." Another lie. "Let it go to voicemail."

"Happy to."

"How about that beer?"

"I have a better idea." She had finished her apple, devouring every part of it—core, seeds, skin, pulp—except the stem. She flicked it at me, the stem landing in the water a few inches away. The ripples attracted the attention of several small, slender, silvery-blue fish with long, narrow beaks called a needlenose that hang out near the surface. They feed on almost anything.

Except apple stems.

The fish darted to the surface and took turns nipping at the stem. By the time the ripples faded away, they had lost interest and swam off in search of other opportunities.

Arabella pushed off the dock and plunged into the water feetfirst. She remained underwater a moment, then surfaced in front of me and put both arms around my neck. We kissed.

She smiled. "Time for a Dutch lesson."

"What about dinner?"

She smirked. "Later. We will figure that out."

CHAPTER 11

ARABELLA HAD RISEN and left for work long before I woke. I rolled out of bed and opened the sliding door that connected the bedroom to the veranda, sunlight and warmth bursting into the room. The bathroom smelled of shampoo and wet towels, with a hint of cucumber-melon body wash. It was her favorite. She had told me several times I should try it.

I declined—cucumber, melon, or any other type of fruit. For me, a plain white bar of soap had always done the trick.

My plans for the day involved Jan. In addition to owning Vinny's, he also owned *The Dutchman's Pleasure*, a thirty-six-foot boat called a Topaz, built around 1988, which he hired out for excursions. Aside from his wife, Ruth, *The Dutchman's Pleasure* was Jan's pride and joy, and he worked tirelessly to keep it in pristine condition. When not tending bar downtown, he was on the *Pleasure* fixing small maintenance items or cleaning its hull of barnacles.

A group of tourists had booked him and the vessel for a snorkel trip to the small, neighboring island of Klein Bonaire—which means *Little Bonaire* in Dutch—located a half mile out to sea. Jan had asked me to tag along and help with logistics and oversee the snorkelers.

He kept the *Pleasure* moored at the marina north of Kralendijk. Running late, I hurried through town, knowing the snorkelers, refreshments, and gear would already be loaded by the time I arrived. Island Time notwithstanding, Jan ran a punctual operation, and he'd want to depart on schedule.

The *Dutchman's* twin engines hummed at idle as I stepped over the side rail and onto the boat's deck. As I lay my gear bag under one of the side benches, eight tourists glared at me. One of them, standing near the stern, cradling her mask and fins, was Sandra Griffis, Rulio's girlfriend.

A coincidence? I wondered.

My old partner, Bill Ryberg, hadn't believed in coincidences. Neither did I.

But what else could it be?

I waved at her. She smiled and waved back.

With his back to me, Jan yelled from the captain's chair, "Nice of you to join us, R. Get the lines."

I leaned over the side of the boat and wrenched the ropes holding us in place off the dock cleats. Jan eased the boat out of the slip and into the harbor, weaving around buoys, careful to produce as little wake as possible. After entering open sea, he pointed the bow in the direction of Klein Bonaire. Fifteen minutes later, we were moored at our snorkel site, a spot called Forest.

Jan had chosen this site partly because of its shallow, lush corals and abundant sea life. But, in addition, its location on the west side of Klein would allow the island to block some of the wind whipping in from the east, making the water surface flat and smooth, ideal for snorkeling.

I watched as the group donned their masks and prepared to get into the water. On the short ride over to Klein, Sandra had told me the divers weren't tourists as I had previously assumed. They all worked at Paradise Cove. Mr. Anderson, the owner, had paid for the trip as a company outing. He and his wife were also on board. Sandra pointed them out to me.

John Anderson, barrel chested, stood about five feet, four inches tall. Light-brown curly hair, grayish-blue eyes, and a pointed nose. He had a machine-gun laugh that could be heard from one end of the vessel to the other, and possibly all the way to Bonaire. His teeth were perfect—white as snow and flawlessly aligned.

Mrs. Anderson had an infectious smile and loved sharing it with everyone. *She's the kind of person who lights up any room she walks into.* True statement. I could tell. Social butterfly by any definition. Blue eyes and dirty blond hair, she gracefully moved from person to person, laughing, talking, and engaging. She seemed to know something about everyone and asked questions about topics *they* wanted to talk about—family, hobbies, recreation. People eagerly responded to her and not because she was the boss's wife, but because they liked her.

Jan gave me an okay sign, so I rolled backwards off the boat rail and into the water. I wore a thin lycra dive suit, mainly for exposure protection against the sun. The suit provided little warmth, but with surface temperatures above eighty degrees, I didn't need any. I floated on the surface and donned my mask, fins, and snorkel, then waited for the others to enter.

Scuba required tanks, regulators, dive computers, buoyance control devices, and, depending on the individual diver, a host of other gadgets. Snorkeling required none of that. Slip on some fins, pull the mask over your face, put the snorkel in your mouth, and it's time to go. Helping a group of snorkelers into the water was much easier than assisting a group of scuba divers.

Within a few moments, Jan had assisted everyone into the water.

Except one.

Legs dangling in the water, John Anderson sat on the platform attached at the boat's stern. The other snorkelers had either stepped off the platform into the water or rolled backward off the rail as I had, but he insisted on entering from a sitting position. Several times, he had removed his mask to blow his nose. He laughed each time he put it back on, his rapid, machine-gun *ha ha ha* containing a tinge of nervousness.

Finally, after drawing several large breaths through his snorkel, he gently eased himself off the platform and into the water. His eyes widened and he refused to descend any deeper than his shoulders. I peeked underwater at his legs. John kicked fast and hard in order to keep his head above the surface. Moving his hands in a circular motion to remain vertical, he bobbed his way to where Danielle Anderson had already begun snorkeling, examining the world below the surface, oblivious to her husband's trials and tribulations.

Jan gave a whistle and pointed at John, my reminder to keep an eye on him. Top priority. I'd also act as a human sheep dog and keep everyone corralled in a defined area—close to the boat.

Other than John, the snorkelers had either caught on to the sport easily or had some level of prior experience. They were doing well. Several adventurous ones did occasional breath-hold dives, plunging to depths of twenty feet or more to examine a coral head or colorful fish.

Forest is known for turtle sightings, but today we didn't see any. I did, however, point out several cleaning stations to some of the snorkelers. A cleaning station is a spot on the reef where larger fish—many of them predators—hover motionless above the coral while small fish or shrimp swarm over them, cleaning parasites off their scales and from their gills. Under different circumstances, they'd be hunter and prey. But not at a cleaning station. Both parties were neutral, and both parties benefited.

Jan's snorkel trips lasted about an hour. Time was money for him, and he didn't like sitting on a boat watching folks splash around in the water. Besides, most people were tiring after sixty minutes and ready to climb back on board.

I had started herding the snorkelers toward the ladder slung over the side of the boat when Jan let out an ear-piercing whistle. I looked in his direction, then to where he pointed.

John Anderson was nearly submerged, his head tilted backwards, his face the only part of his body above water. He had removed his mask and was near motionless in the calm water. Even from this distance—maybe twenty-five yards—I could tell his breathing was rapid and shallow.

I knew what Jan knew.

John was drowning. Or about to.

Contrary to what movies and TV depict, drowning victims rarely yelled for help, splashed, or made a scene. The brain shuts down and concentrates on one thing—getting air to the lungs. In order to conserve oxygen, all muscle movement stops. The person slowly descends, trying to keep their mouth above water. There've been many instances where someone drowned, or was drowning, and the person next to them didn't even realize it.

Interestingly, studies show that drowning victims tend to remove their mask, snorkel, and—in the case of scuba—the air regulator from their mouth. Researchers have no explanation for this phenomenon. Rescuers of missing cave divers are taught to watch the cave floor as they swim along looking for victims. When they see a mask resting on the bottom, they look up and invariably find the drowned diver.

I sprint-swam in John's direction. With fins on, I covered the distance quickly and arrived at John's side within seconds. He pawed at me, wanting to grab hold of something, gaining leverage to keep his head above water. I eased below the surface and he released his grip on me, again going motionless. As I surfaced behind John, an orange lifesaver splashed nearby. I tucked it under John's arms, and Jan pulled him toward the boat as I swam alongside.

John didn't say anything the entire way back to the *Pleasure*. However, several times, he glanced my direction and laughed, his normal machine-gun rhythm ragged and less enthusiastic. White-knuckled, he clung to the ladder as I removed his fins. Before climbing up, he gagged several times, then leaned sideways and vomited. Jan looked over the gunwale and watched. I couldn't help to think better here than on the boat. I'm sure Jan thought the same.

John rinsed his face with seawater and, legs trembling, climbed the ladder. Jan helped him over the rail and found him a place to sit on one of the benches. I removed my mask and lay back in the water a moment, letting the sun beat down on me. I should've paid closer attention to John. He needed it. Not really a close call, at least not in my book. However, he'd probably disagree.

But a close *enough* call to say the least.

"You ready?" Jan said. The engines were already idling.

I sprang upright. "Yeah." I handed him my fins and climbed up the ladder.

I stood next to Jan, sitting in the captain's chair, during the ride back. Most of the passengers were drinking water or devouring some sort of snack. John sat with his elbows on his knees, face in the palms of his hands. Danielle sat next to him, hunched over with a hand on his back. They didn't speak the entire trip back to the dock.

I was the first one off the boat, securing the ropes to the cleats. After taking up the slack and getting the *Pleasure* in its resting place, Jan shut down the engines. Everyone began stepping up onto the dock, me providing help when needed. The Andersons were the last two off the boat.

John still seemed a bit wobbly, leaning partially on Danielle, as the three of us walked down the pier to the parking lot. He smoked a long, brown, slender cigarette, it's smoke causing a near-gag reflex when the wind blew it in my direction.

We approached a black SUV with tinted windows. A chirping sound emitted, and the rear cargo door opened. The Andersons laid their gear bags in the back, then the door slowly closed.

"Thank you for saving my life," John said to me.

"Yes, thank you," Danielle said.

I shrugged. "Not as close a call as you might think."

Two pelicans flew up and perched on pylons positioned ten feet out from the dock, eyeing us intently, probably hoping for some type of handout. Maybe they thought we were fishermen and would throw them some yummy fish guts.

"Well, I'm glad you were there," John said. "I've never been particularly good around boats or water." He held out his hand. "I'm John Anderson." He gestured toward Danielle. "And this is my wife, Danielle."

"John," I said shaking his hand. I turned to Danielle and shook her hand. "Nice to meet both of you."

"Call me Danni," she said, smiling from ear to ear. I understood why people liked her. She was genuine. With a single look, she made a person feel special.

"I'm Roscoe Conklin. You can call me R."

"Yeah," John said, "we know who you are."

"Really?" I said.

Danielle nodded. "Sandra told us."

In my talk with Sandra, I never introduced myself. Apparently, I didn't need to.

"You seem comfortable in the water," I said to Danielle.

"Yeah, I love boats, swimming, snorkeling—anything to do with water." She lightly jabbed John in the ribs with her elbow. "I've never been seasick. And I certainly never came close to drowning." She jabbed him again.

John laughed. *Ha ha ha.*

"I'm just teasing you, babe," she said and kissed him on the cheek.

They stood next to each other, Danielle towering over her husband by about four inches. They reminded me of Sonny and Cher and, with Danielle having just used the term *Babe*, I half-expected them to break out into a rendition of "I Got You, Babe."

John used the tinted SUV windows to check his hair. "I owe you a dinner," he said, turning his head back and forth examining his profiles. Several times, he picked at a few strands of his curls. "Please come to our place any time. Food and drinks on us." He turned away from the windows and handed me a business card. It had *Paradise Cove Seaside Restaurant and Bar* in black lettering. His name—listed as owner—and a phone number were also printed on the card.

"You'll like it," Danielle said. "Lots of Americans come there."

John wiped sweat from his forehead. "I'm burning up. Let's get in, Danni." He opened the driver-side door but turned back to me before climbing in. "See ya at the Paradise?"

"I'll see what I can do."

"And bring a friend," Danielle said.

He and Danielle closed their doors. They pulled out onto the street with all the windows up and, I assumed, the air-conditioning blasting.

I dropped the business card into the glove box after getting in my Wrangler.

No top; no doors.

My kind of AC.

CHAPTER 12

A DAY LATER, alone in the office, I sat hunched over my office desk reading the Rulio file again, hoping to discover something in my translated notes I previously missed. The cleaning company that provided maid service to the YellowRock had called and explained they had resource issues and wouldn't be able to clean all the rooms. In these instances, Erika stepped in and helped with the required housekeeping chores.

Earlier, Schleper had called. He left a to-the-point voicemail demanding to know the identity of Tessa's mystery boyfriend and threatening to pull the Rulio file, forbidding me from doing any further investigation. "*It is time to report into me, Mr. Conklin,*" he had said. "*I need results.*"

The screen door creaked open and a little girl entered the office. She went straight to Erika's desk and stared at the basket of candy. After a moment, she looked at me. I nodded and she took a piece of candy but didn't leave.

Head slightly bowed, she held up two fingers. I nodded again, and she took another piece of candy but still didn't leave.

This time, she raised her chin and stabbed me with her eyes, holding up three fingers. I leaned back in my chair and tried to keep from smiling. This kid would make a good hostage negotiator. I paused a moment, but eventually said, "Yes," curious to see how far she'd push it.

Her posture relaxed. She took all three pieces of candy, smiled at me, and skipped out of the office. Once outside, she gave two other children a piece of candy each.

I had gone back to studying the Rulio file as Erika came through the door, finished with her impromptu housekeeping duties. She paused and turned to face outside, watching the kids, not noticing me hastily covering up the file and putting it in my desk drawer. She didn't need to see the report, and especially not the pictures.

"Are the children not precious?" she said.

"Yeah, they're something, all right."

Erika's brows scrunched and she turned her head. "What is that beeping sound?"

"What beep?" I said. "I don't hear anything."

Since Erika believes she's the only one capable of managing the office alone, I occasionally indulged her and fabricated a crisis that she'd need to clean up. A few moments before she returned, I purposely forced an abnormal reboot of the office server, confusing the workstations linked to it. Ever since then, the server had emitted a periodic beep.

"How can you work with that beep every few seconds?" she asked. "Very annoying."

I leaned back in my chair and smiled. "I don't let the little things stop me."

"Does that mean you got some work done while I was out?"

"I tried, but the computers seem messed up." I tapped randomly on my keyboard, and nothing happened.

After a deep breath, shaking her head, she said, "*Semper mi mes tin ku hasi tur kos aki nan.*" Basically, I believe she was complaining about having to do everything around here.

"Well," she continued, "it is good I am back." Then, in a more condescending tone, she said, "I will fix it so you can get some work done."

I stood. "Actually, I need to go follow Tessa." Erika raised an eyebrow. "You know. Schleper's wife."

"I know who Tessa is." She walked over to the server and power-cycled it. "I thought you had already snooped on her."

"Yes, I did. But a world-class investigator like myself knows that thorough snooping takes time." I headed for the stairs.

"Well, you know police work better than me, so I will have to trust what you are saying. I am not a snooper."

As I got to the top step, about to open the door to my apartment, Erika, satisfaction dripping from her words, said, "Oh, look. I fixed the computers." I could almost *hear* her smile.

* * *

Tessa pulled out of the Santa Barbara Crowns neighborhood in her Toyota and headed for the center of Kralendijk. Dressed in my touristy surveillance threads, in the breezy openness of the Wrangler, I maintained a safe distance behind her. *Journey's Greatest Hits* blasted through the speakers.

Unlike last time, though, Tessa didn't stop for shopping or errands; nor did she go to Ruth's place. Instead, just as Journey was telling me to don't stop believing, she parked in a municipal parking lot a block off the center of downtown Kralendijk. I nudged down Journey's volume and drove past, parking on the adjacent block, then double-timed it back on foot, picking up Tessa as she turned the corner and walked down the sidewalk on the one-way street.

At first, I thought she was headed to Vinny's. Maybe rendezvous with her date at the bar—if Schleper was correct and that's what this was all about—then head off for some afternoon delight.

But Vinny's didn't seem clandestine enough. It was in the center of town and wide open. Anyone could happen in or drive by. On a typical day, Vinny's crowd was as much locals as it was tourists.

She didn't stop at Vinny's.

Tending bar, Jan noticed me as I walked past. He did a double take as he reached for a glass and dropped it. His eyes bulged.

"R, is that you?" he half yelped, half said. "What are you doing?"

I put an index finger to my lips, mocking a *Shhhh* gesture, and kept walking. Jan sees a lot of crazy stuff, and I doubted my outfit shocked him for long. Although, I knew he'd ask me about it later.

Several blocks north of Vinny's, Tessa stopped in front of the Thirsty Goat, the restaurant Arabella and I had eaten dinner at a few nights ago. Only slightly less clandestine than Vinny's.

A man stood near the door speaking to Tessa. He held his gaze on her as she made quick glances through the glass door into the restaurant. He laid a hand on her shoulder but removed it after she said something to him. Public display of affection when you're meeting a secret lover wasn't a good idea. Maybe Tessa was a pro at this stuff. She knew better. He didn't.

The guy was over six feet tall and slender with long, droopy arms. Black hair pulled into a loose ponytail hanging almost to his beltline. He wore a black sleeveless T-shirt and holey black jeans. White deck shoes and a tan cowboy hat, maybe a Stetson.

Not sure why, but I got the feeling he wasn't a tourist.

Using my cell phone, and being as discreet as possible, I snapped several photos. After the last one, Mr. Ponytail looked my way. He narrowed his eyes for a moment. I pretended to analyze my pictures, then turned sideways and took several more of the shoreline. When I turned back, he had opened the door for Tessa and followed her into the restaurant. As the door closed, he held another stare on me. This time, I stared back. After a few moments, he disappeared into the Thirsty Goat.

Now what?

If I followed them in, my cover would be blown. But I couldn't wait on the sidewalk. Tessa would need to walk past Vinny's on the way back to her car, so that's where I headed.

I positioned myself at the bar so I could watch the street for Tessa. Jan tossed a coaster on the bar and sat a Bright on it. He leaned on the bar with both hands and didn't move.

"Well?" he said.

I took a swig of beer. "Well, what?"

"Your clothes."

"Long story."

Jan swiveled his head left and right. Other than me and two locals watching a rugby game on the wide-screen TV, the place was empty. "I have time," he said.

"Not sure I do. Later?"

"Sure," he said and started to wander off.

"Hey," I said, "you see Chuck recently?"

"He drank earlier but left." He rolled his eyes. "Hot date." He smiled. "As always."

That got me thinking. I scrolled to one of the photos on my phone of Tessa and Mr. Ponytail and held it up to Jan. "Ever seen these two?"

Jan studied the picture, then eyed me for a moment. "Not the cowboy. But of course, I know the woman." He laid the picture on the bar and pointed at Tessa.

"You do?"

"Yes," he said. "Tessa. She is a friend of Ruth's. They drink wine almost every day." He shook his head. "Too much, I tell her." He leaned over the bar, his facial features tightening. "Tessa, she is married to a police inspector."

Yeah, I know.

"Why do you have their photograph?" Jan asked.

Studying the photo, I said, "Another long story." I wanted to add *And I'm not sure how this one ends.* But I thought wiser of it and kept my mouth shut.

Maybe a first for me.

CHAPTER 13

I LEANED OVER the edge of my bed, slipping into my sandals. An open beer I'd been nursing for the last twenty minutes sat on the dresser. One last swig and I tossed the empty into the trash. With the sliding door to the veranda open, the early evening breeze drifted through the room. Hanging from a nail on the wall, the lone picture of my late father, taken years ago of him standing tall and proud in his US Postal Service uniform, a role that defined most of his too-short life, gently rapped back and forth, the edge of the frame slowly scuffing away the paint, deepening the existing gouge in the plaster.

Arabella and I prepared for a night out at Paradise Cove. After the *coincidence* of meeting the Andersons on Jan's boat, maybe a closer look at them and their establishment might prove interesting. Not sure why or what or how, but something just didn't feel right. Several decades of investigating people, watching and doubting what they said or did, had heightened my tendency to question everything.

No such thing as a coincidence. At least, not in my experience.

Arabella came out of the bathroom and did a playful 360-degree turn with her arms out, allowing me to examine her outfit.

She wore loose-fitting, capri-length jeans, ankle-strapped sandals, a red T-shirt, and a strand of white pearls. No ponytail, hair loose and flowing over her shoulders. On the T-shirt was a picture of a banjo with dark lettering that read *I'm with the banjo player, but don't tell anyone.*

"Wow, you look great," I said.

"Thank you. As do you," she said. The upturned ends of her lips broke out into a small laugh. "Quite formal tonight?"

I wore my standard cargo shorts and T-shirt but had taken the effort to iron them both. A rarity for me. "Yeah, thought I should make a good impression."

Her eyebrows scrunched. "Why?"

I twisted my nose. It was a good question. "Not sure."

* * *

I drove the Wrangler through Kralendijk then turned south, toward Paradise Cove. With the top off and the doors removed, the evening breeze swept through the inside. I never left old cans, napkins, or discarded cups in the Wrangler for fear they might blow out. Bad enough to litter. Worse yet for the rubbish to find its way into the sea.

Arabella seemed to enjoy the wind blowing her hair, wafting across her face, giving her a moderate rustled look. She rhythmically smiled and brushed it aside. Her right leg dangled out the door opening, her entire body silhouetted by orange remnants of the recent sunset. She gripped the handle attached to the roll bar, the seat belt crossing between her breasts, splitting the picture of the banjo in two. She sipped on a bottle of water.

Luckily, I was sitting. If I had been standing, my knees would've gone weak.

My grandmother once said that Cupid had an arrow for everyone. Mine was etched with Arabella's name and I didn't plan to give it back. I could've ridden with her all night.

But all too soon, we arrived at Paradise Cove.

I pulled into the gravel parking lot, littered with potholes and full of vehicles and, as usual, parked at the edge, as far from the door as possible. The resort section of the complex was under full construction on a parcel of land directly north of the restaurant. Haphazardly parked end-loaders and dump trucks, stacks of concrete blocks, and miscellaneous mounds of wood, dirt, and gravel partially covered with black tarps were all held at bay by an eight-foot-high chain-link fence. Sagging strands of yellow caution tape denoted several "Do Not Enter" areas. Every few feet along the fence hung signs denoting the name and contact information of the construction company.

Based on the partially constructed frame, the rooms would all have a view of the sea. The place looked large. Too large for Bonaire.

The breeze swirled around us and carried a hint of concrete dust and freshly cut wood from the construction area. It mixed with the scent of grease, spices, and prepared food lofting out of the restaurant.

Paradise Cove stood along the sea, the dining area in the back, facing the water, and the main door facing the road and parking lot. Immediately upon entering, I realized why the name Paradise Cove had resonated with me. Hanging in the hallway, life-sized posters of James Garner, the actor who played Jim Rockford in the 70's private investigator series *The Rockford Files*, greeted anyone who entered.

I had never missed an episode.

Arabella pointed at one of the posters, specifically at the word *Rockford*, and looked at me, eyebrows raised.

I shook my head. "Nothing to do with where I worked. This was a TV series and the hero's name was Jim *Rockford*. No connection to Rockford, Illinois."

She studied the poster.

"He lived in a trailer that he kept in a parking lot along the ocean," I said.

She rolled her eyes in my direction, as if saying *Are we through yet?*

I wasn't. "The place was in Malibu, California, and was called *Paradise Cove*."

Patting me on the shoulder, she said, "That is *very* interesting." She shrugged and continued toward the bar.

Paradise Cove had about twenty square dining tables, most of which were outside underneath a large fabric covering. The tables were designed to accommodate four people, although some had been moved together for larger groups. This night, all the seats were occupied. Being low season, it surprised me to see the place full.

The bartender dropped a couple of coasters in front of us and waited for our order. He jerked his head, flipping some stray hair out of his eyes, and stared at me.

I stared back.

Long black hair hung down his back and he wore a black sleeveless T-shirt and black holey jeans. However, no tan Stetson tonight.

Mr. Ponytail.

A voice behind me said, "Lucas, no bill for these folks. It's all on me." John Anderson squeezed between Arabella and me and stuck out his hand. "Hi R. Glad to see you stop by."

I shook his hand and introduced him to Arabella. He gave her the customary three-kiss Dutch greeting. Most Americans aren't comfortable with that. Something to do with violating personal space, but John seemed very adept at it.

We sat at the end of the bar, directly next to the metal swinging doors that led to the kitchen. Each time a server went through, smells of grilled meat, fish, and vegetables rushed in our direction.

"Hold on." John's head swiveled in all directions. "Where's Danni?" He spotted her and waved, yelling, "Danni, over here."

Danielle Anderson, holding a glass of red wine, and wearing a sassy orange top and white silk skirt, scurried over to our position at the bar. John introduced her to Arabella.

"You need drinks," Danielle said, looking at me.

"A couple of Brights, please," I said.

Danielle waved two fingers at the bartender, Lucas, and pointed at Arabella and me. Lucas took two Brights from a waist-high fridge, stuck limes in their tops, and placed them in front of us on coasters. He also produced a glass of red wine for John, who picked it up and laughed, *ha ha ha*, again sounding like machine-gun fire. A three-shot burst.

"You also need a table," Danielle said. She tapped her finger on the bar. "Lucas, see to that." Lucas didn't nod or say anything. He came around the side of the bar and stood next to Arabella, presumably awaiting his next edict.

"We'll stop by later and see how you're doing," John said.

"I'm curious, what's the reason for the name Paradise Cove?" I asked John.

Although facing me, his eyes were cranked to the side, staring at himself in the mirror that covered half the wall behind the bar. "I grew up in LA. As a kid, we used to go to Malibu and swim and boat in Paradise Cove." Still admiring himself in the mirror, he ran his hands through his hair several times and picked at a curl. "I fished off the same pier they used in the *Rockford Files*. Seemed like a fitting name for my restaurant."

I nodded and thought about our first meeting. *I've never been very good around boats or water*, John had said.

As we followed Lucas from the bar area, we passed a large, rusted-steel anchor standing upright in the middle of the restaurant. A plaque was attached to the top of the anchor, but I didn't pause to read it. I also noticed a large black fireplace on the back wall. Probably the only fireplace on the entire island. Glad there wasn't a fire going.

We stopped at a table set off to the side, around a corner not visible from the front, and Lucas pulled a chair out for Arabella. We were next to a white baby grand piano, also not visible from the front.

Wheels on the piano's legs allowed it to be shoved through a large door on the back wall for overnight storage. With the openness of Paradise Cove, everything needed to be brought inside every evening at closing time. All the outdoor establishments on Bonaire did the same thing to protect their equipment.

A waiter came by with another round of Brights. Arabella ordered the tuna; I the Argentinean steak.

Arabella wrapped her arms around her body. "My skin is crawling."

"Is something wrong?"

She swiveled her head across the room. "Just look around."

I did, scanning the entire restaurant. "What?"

"Too many Americans." She smiled and did a fake body shiver.

I raised my beer in a mock toast. "Good place to be."

"Maybe, maybe not." She studied several nearby tables, then asked me, "Why are you Americans always so loud?"

"I don't know." I smiled while sipping some beer. "I've never noticed."

Another fake shiver. "Like a bunch of rowdy cowboys."

We drank a few moments. No TVs broadcasting sporting events at Paradise Cove. A mixture of Latin and Caribbean music played through the overhead speakers. Not too loud to interrupt conversations, but loud enough to enjoy. Laughter flowed from the bar area, but it didn't overpower the sound of the nearby waves. They almost kept beat to the music.

Arabella pointed at a picture on the wall and said, "What do you think of that?"

The picture depicted John Anderson as a boxer, taking an aggressive stance in a boxing ring, wearing black gloves and white silk shorts, ready to strike. The caption below it read *John "Smack" Anderson.*

I shrugged. "Everyone needs a hobby. Seems harmless. Probably good exercise." I shoveled some steak into my mouth.

"I am not sure." Arabella chewed some tuna. "I get a weird feeling about him."

"You just met him."

"I know, but still . . . And did you notice his shoes?"

I leaned sideways and caught a glimpse of John as he maneuvered between a couple of tables. He wore green velvet loafers. "Pretty snazzy. So?" I leaned back in the chair and glanced at the worn sandals on my feet, then back at Arabella. "Probably not something I'd wear."

Her jaw dropped. "'Probably not'? Do you realize they might have cost seven hundred dollars?"

I stole another look at John's shoes. "For a pair of shoes?"

Arabella nodded. "And, anyway, how do you know these people?"

I was looking at my plate, cutting a piece of steak. "They were on Jan's snorkel trip, the one I helped with a few days ago." I raised my eyes to meet hers. "So was Sandra, Rulio's girlfriend. She works for them."

Arabella chewed and stared at me. Her eyes narrowed. "You do not find that odd?"

"Maybe." I took a swig of beer, then leaned in closer to her, lowered my voice, and said, "That's one reason I wanted to come here. Get a better feel for these folks." I resumed my previous posture and took another drink.

"I think I like the way you think." She smiled. "For an American."

We had finished eating as the waiter appeared with another round of Brights and filled our water glasses. He cleared the table and asked if we wanted dessert. We both declined but thanked him for the beers.

Arabella placed her beer on my side of the table. "Someone needs to drive home. Besides, *I* have to work tomorrow."

"Good decision, Officer," I said, tipping my beer in her direction.

Beyond the tarp covering the restaurant tables, people relaxed in loungers lining the beach, each chair coupled with a multi-colored umbrella. Scattered among the loungers, tiki torches glowed atop poles stuck in the sand. A pier jutted out into the darkness, and fifty yards farther out, the faint silhouette of a sailboat, moored at the edge of the reef drop-off, swayed in the gentle waves.

As I took the first pulls of the fresh beer, the crowd started chanting "*Danni and Smack. Danni and Smack. Danni and Smack.*" As the chant grew to a roar, John walked to the piano, placed his cigarette in an ashtray, and played a long arpeggio, starting with the base notes and ending with the higher ones.

"If I could get my lovely wife to join me . . ." he said.

From the other side of the room, Danielle said, "I'm coming."

The crowd cheered as Danielle weaved her way around tables, eventually standing alongside the piano. She kissed her husband on the cheek, then they broke into a raucous version of Dolly Parton's "Jolene." Danielle sang the lead while John played the piano and added harmonies to the chorus.

When they finished, the crowd clapped and yelled for more. Danielle raised her hand in appreciation but shook her head. She moved away from the piano as John started a quiet instrumental of Billy Joel's "Piano Man."

Danielle stopped at our table.

"Nice job," I said.

"Thanks, but I missed a few lyrics in the middle," she said.

"Really? I didn't notice."

She laughed. "Good. My improv skills need work, but I guess I fooled *you*. John has taught me that sometimes, when things don't go as you planned, you just make it up as you go along. 'Improvisation is the name of the game,' he says." She took a sip of wine and glanced at Arabella's T-shirt, then back to me. "I heard you play the banjo. Maybe you could bring it next time and join us for a number." She smiled, making me feel, at that moment, as though I were the most important person in the world.

She's the kind of person who lights up any room she walks into.

"Maybe," I said.

"Well, I think it'll happen," Danielle said with a wink.

I pointed at a picture I had noticed earlier, hanging on the wall near the bar. "Is that you in the cowgirl outfit?"

She looked in the direction of the picture, then back at me, placing a hand on the back of my chair and leaning on it. "That's me, all right. As a little girl, maybe ten years old." She laughed. "I used to think I was Annie Oakley. Skirt, cowgirl hat, and a pair of six-gun cap pistols." She stepped back and put her hands by her side. "Reach for 'em, mister," she said and jerked her hands up to her waist, index fingers pointed at me. "Fastest draw in the west." She made two shooting noises and jerked her fingers, simulating pistol recoils. Then she put her "guns" to her mouth and mimicked blowing smoke off the barrels.

Arabella leaned back in her chair and laced her fingers behind her head, elbows straight out. A see-what-I-mean type of smile crept across her face. She mouthed the word *Cowboys* at me and nodded her head a few times.

"I've been around guns my entire life," Danielle said. "Hell, I learned to shoot when I was twelve."

Before I could ask how, why, or where, Arabella slapped her hands on her thighs and said, "Okay . . . we should go to the bar."

"I'll see you later, Officer," Danielle said, wandering off, addressing the statement to me, not Arabella. Which made me wonder if Danielle knew I'd been a cop. Or if she was just ignoring Arabella. No clue.

As we stood, Arabella said to me, "Did you know *he* would be here?" When our eyes met, she motioned hers toward the bar.

"Who?" I surveyed the area.

Chuck sat on a stool looking in our direction. He held up his beer bottle as we approached.

"R, Arabella, glad I ran into you two," Chuck said.

Arabella leaned into me and whispered in my ear, "Wish I could say the same."

Chuck hadn't heard Arabella's comment. "I'm making a flight to Curacao tomorrow," he said to me, "and thought you might want to tag along."

I've been a pilot for many years and I sometimes flew jobs for Chuck when he was too hungover to fly. Photography flights, sightseeing for tourists, or any other form of flying that he could make a buck at with his Cessna airplane. For whatever reason, he liked the airport lounge in Curacao. I figured he wanted me to go along so I'd fly back after he had indulged in a few at the bar.

For purely selfish reasons, I agreed. Not only did it give me a chance to stay current on my pilot skills, but it also got me to Curacao. Make a trip to Joost Obersi's place, the surviving student of Rulio's dive accident. According to Sandra Griffis, Obersi confronted Rulio, which was part of the reason for his firing. Talking with Obersi might dig up something the Bonaire police hadn't been able to uncover. On occasion, I've been known to leave my better judgment at the door and gamble on a long shot. This was bound to be one of those times.

Follow every lead, no matter how small.

"Meet me at nine o'clock?" Chuck asked.

I nodded and drank some of the beer Lucas had just set in front of me. Arabella had a club soda.

A few moments later, a guy at one of the tables began a ruckus. Not sure of the cause, but he seemed annoyed about something. The folks at his table tried to calm him, but he was having no part of it. He continued yelling, becoming more obnoxious by the second.

John was at the other end of the bar with some customers. I noticed him look at Danielle, sitting near us, also at the bar. Almost imperceptibly, she nodded. More of a slight twitch than an actual nod. Not sure anyone else would've noticed, but I did. Arabella noticed, too, and nudged me in the ribs.

I continued watching John.

He blew out some cigarette smoke and nodded at Lucas behind the bar. Lucas flipped the hair from his eyes and quickly made his way to the obnoxious guy's table. He spoke softly into the guy's ear. John watched intently; Danielle ignored the situation, continuing to sip her wine and chat with a woman at the bar.

When Lucas finished speaking, Mr. Obnoxious jerked his head away. Lucas grabbed him by the arm and *gestured* toward the door. At that moment, two other men, both Bonairian, dressed in white shirts, black pants, and black bow ties, appeared from the kitchen and stood on both sides of Mr. Obnoxious.

Lucas and the two penguins escorted Mr. Obnoxious out of Paradise Cove. No one from the table followed or offered him any help. They were probably as happy to see him leave as everyone else.

John watched the four men exit through the back door, then lit another smoke and turned back to resume his conversation with the folks at the bar. Danielle sipped her wine.

Wide-eyed, Arabella leaned close to me and said, "Was that what I think it was?"

"Yup. They removed a problem."

"I should check on this." She started to get up, but I put a hand on her shoulder.

"Wait."

A few moments later, Lucas came back inside, went behind the bar, and wrapped ice in a towel. He applied it to his right hand, favoring the knuckles. He stood at the far end nursing his hand while his two sidekicks, the Penguin Brothers, tended bar.

I nodded to Arabella, and we walked out the door to the parking lot and strolled between a few of the vehicles. We looked alongside the building and in the shadows near the dumpsters and construction equipment. Nothing, and no one, to be found, but taillights were visible in the distance going up the road. An obnoxious guy getting a few lumps for his indiscretion usually wouldn't bother me, but I didn't like Lucas.

We went back inside.

Lucas tended bar again. The penguins were gone, presumably back in the kitchen. After a moment, he noticed me staring at the red, scuffed knuckles of his right hand. He flipped some hair from his eyes, then leaned over the bar; face flushed. Through a tight jaw and clenched teeth, he said, "That guy is a piece of shit."

We glared at each other.

"Lucas," Danielle said. Lucas didn't back down. "Lucas!" she yelled.

The bar got quiet. Lucas looked at her, then at John. John nodded and Lucas walked into the back. The other two guys reappeared and began tending bar. The crowd murmur returned, at first as a collective whisper, then slowly growing to its normal level.

"He gets a little emotional sometimes," Danielle said.

"I would hate for him to be a trouble person," Arabella said.

Danielle waved Arabella's comment aside. "Not to worry."

Arabella and I had been together long enough that sometimes just exchanging a certain look communicated each other's message. This was one of those times. I finished my beer in one upturn, and we stood to go.

I patted Chuck on the back. "See ya tomorrow, buddy."

"You leaving?" he said. "My girlfriend will be here soon, and I want you to meet her." He held up his cell phone for me to see. "Seriously, she just texted me. She'll be walking in any second."

Arabella and I exchanged another glance. Again, we understood each other, although this time we didn't agree. She was ready to leave, not at all interested in meeting Chuck's new love. I, on the other hand, curious, wanted to meet her, assuming she'd be just another attractive island girl, multiple decades too young for him. Temporary at best.

But if it made Chuck happy for us to meet her . . .

I looked at Arabella. "Maybe we can stay a little longer."

She sighed and plopped back on the barstool. I ordered another beer.

After I had taken one swig, Arabella said, "*Badkamer.*" She stood and walked down the hall that led to the restrooms.

"There she is," Chuck said, his voice high with excitement. He stood and hugged a woman who approached him, then kissed her on the lips and hugged her again. He turned her toward me. "R, this is Tessa."

On shaky knees and with a pit in my stomach, I rose and smiled, then gave her the three-kiss Dutch greeting. "Nice to meet you, Tessa." I sat back on the stool and took a swig of beer. Then another.

Speechless didn't begin to describe my reaction. Schleper's wife. At first, I thought it might be a joke. I scanned the restaurant and bar looking for Schleper, or Jan, or any other familiar face—anyone who might perpetrate such a prank.

I shook my head in disbelief. No one obvious.

I watched Chuck and Tessa for a moment, then realized, it wasn't a joke. Tessa was the girlfriend Chuck had been so enamored with.

The pit in my stomach grew to the size of a basketball. Chuck was flirting with more trouble than he could imagine. Like playing Russian roulette with six cartridges in the cylinder. No way this ends well. *What have you got yourself into, buddy?*

Glancing down the bar, I noticed Lucas standing by the kitchen door, eyeing Chuck and Tessa. Face flush, he drew his hands into tight fists hanging by his side. He'd already proven he wasn't afraid of a fight. And he apparently had friends who'd help him. The Penguin Twins.

My cell phone rang. It was Arabella.

"What's up? You still in the bathroom?"

"No, I am outside, near the Wrangler." She paused a moment. "I saw Chuck's woman and sneaked outside. I cannot come in there, Conklin. I know her."

Not a surprise. Tessa was a friend of Ruth, Arabella's sister, and was married to her boss. Arabella was in the middle of this mess as much as I was.

"I'll be right out." I put my phone away and stood. For lack of anything else, I said, "Nice to meet you, Tessa, but I have to go." I turned to Chuck. "Arabella's outside. She's sick and I need to take her home."

"Okay," Chuck said. He had lost interest in me, spilling all his attention on Tessa.

As I started for the door, I spied Lucas again, giving the eye to Chuck and Tessa. My cadence slowed and I yelled back to Chuck, "Call me when you leave so I know you're okay."

He waved a disinterested hand at me.

I gave one last look at Lucas and walked out the door. Arabella was in the driver's seat of the Wrangler, ready to talk when I climbed into the passenger side.

"She is Schleper's wife!" she said.

I almost said, "*I know,*" but caught myself. That would've been a disaster. Arabella still didn't know about my deal with her boss. Instead, I said, "Really? That can't be good."

"You have to tell him. And soon."

I bit my lower lip. "That won't be good, either."

"You think it any better if Schleper finds out?"

I didn't say anything, and we pulled out of the parking lot and drove up the coast in silence. Tessa was older than the women Chuck usually fell for—by several decades—and she wasn't an island girl.

Hoping to add a little levity to the situation, I said, "What do you think? She doesn't seem like Chuck's type."

Arabella snapped her head in my direction. "She's Schleper's wife!" After a moment, she looked forward and smiled. "Besides, no one seems like Chuck's type."

CHAPTER 14

THE NEXT DAY, rising slightly later—and slower—than planned, the result of overindulging in Brights the previous night at Paradise Cove, and a late evening with Arabella, I rubbed my eyes. They fought any attempt to focus, or even open for that matter, the world being much too bright. My head vibrated from even the slightest movement and my mouth felt as though it had been swabbed with cotton balls. Through experience, I had found that three aspirin and a diet soda seemed to help; however the true remedy was time.

But I needed to meet Chuck at the airport by nine o'clock.

I weighed the prospect of canceling. A few hours nestled in my hammock, The Eagles, quietly playing in the background, interspersed with the random sounds of people and traffic flowing along the one-way street out front, seemed like the perfect augmentation to the aspirin and soda remedy. However, a free trip to Curacao was a good opportunity to speak with Joost Obersi.

After throwing on shorts and a T-shirt, I went downstairs to check in with Erika, let her know I'd be on Curacao for a good portion of the day. I didn't mention my plan to speak with Joost Obersi.

Sitting at the desk, she looked at me over the top of her black-rimmed glasses. "You are wearing sunglasses indoors?"

"Yeah, and the world is still too bright."

She smiled, raising her eyebrows. "Should be an interesting flight." She broke into a laugh as I went out the door. "Have fun," I heard her say as the door closed behind me.

On the short drive to Flamingo International—Bonaire's only airport—I called Schleper. His desk phone.

But I will not give you my cell phone. Too risky, Tessa might see something.

No answer so I left a voicemail. I told him I wouldn't continue following Tessa, to consider me off the case. Schleper was the type who didn't take no for an answer, nor did he handle rejection well. He'd call and threaten to take back the Rulio file and restrict me from further knowledge or privilege. Since I hadn't given a reason for my change of heart, he'd surely go over the edge.

And fast.

Chuck being involved with Tessa changed things. Not to mention the possibility of her being entangled with someone besides Chuck.

Lucas.

I assumed Schleper could be as jealous as anyone. Possibly more. It's a powerful emotion, sometimes causing people to do strange and deadly things. I didn't want to be around—or associated with—him when he blew his stack. Even though I wanted to help Erika and resolve my own curiosity about Rulio's murder, calling Schleper ripped a weight from my shoulders. I wouldn't have to deceive Chuck.

And I wouldn't be lying to Arabella any longer either.

Clear conscience.

Let Schleper take the file back. I wasn't concerned. I had read it twice and had a good grasp of the case status, what the police knew, and what they had accomplished thus far in the investigation. Besides, I could always make a copy before returning it to him.

But, right now, I needed to concentrate on Joost Obersi.

A hundred yards west of Flamingo International's main terminal sat a hangar housing the general aviation businesses—anything unrelated to the commercial airlines. Chuck was too cheap to pay for hangar space, so he kept his Cessna 180 tied on the open tarmac, in front and slightly askew of the large hangar doors.

I met Chuck in the airport parking lot at nine o'clock. We both parked west of the main terminal and walked together to the security gate. My movements were still slow and deliberate, my recovery taking more time than normal. Chuck, however, didn't seem the least bit phased or hungover. I was sure he drank considerably the night before but appeared none the worse for it.

"You feel all right?" I asked as we stepped up to the gate.

"Feel great. Why?"

"I figured you'd be a bit hungover this morning."

He shook his head. "Nope, I don't drink around Tessa."

I didn't say anything, just stared at him, trying to process what I'd heard. If I hadn't known better, I'd have sworn the earth had started spinning backwards.

"She doesn't like me to drink," he said. "She says I'm better when I'm sober."

My whole body seemed to tighten and jerk backwards. "'Better?'"

"That's right. When I don't drink."

"Let me get this straight," I said. "A *woman* has stopped you from drinking?"

"Not stopped. Just taking it easy." He smiled. "And only when I'm around *her*."

"Now I *have* heard everything."

Although I had my own security badge, Chuck buzzed us through and led the way to his plane, serial number N7757U.

Chuck's Cessna spent most of its life on the concrete pad in front of the hangar, the sun beating down on it. Bare aluminum was visible where spots of the vintage '80s red paint had faded, peeled, and blown away. The red vinyl interior had long ago dried and cracked, being held together in places with duct tape, most of it peeling along the edges from the constant heat inside the cabin. The once black plastic instrument panel had seen better days, now faded to a light gray and warped in several places. Ripped and threadbare carpet curled along the floor.

Back in the States, Chuck had parlayed his military training and experience into a civilian career as a top-rated and well-respected FAA-certified airplane mechanic. Mechanically, he kept the Cessna in tip-top shape, it's airworthiness never in doubt.

Chuck propped open the doors, allowing the breeze to ventilate the sweltering cabin. The familiar smell of hot plastic and moldy carpet mixed with traces of aviation fuel—or *avgas* as it's called—wafted out and greeted my nostrils.

As I pulled myself into the coffin-sized cabin and plopped my butt on the hot copilot's seat, I reminded myself Cessna claimed the 180 as one of their mid-sized, single-engine models. If this were mid-sized, I'd hate to see small.

I fidgeted in the cushion, trying to find a comfortable spot, and eventually gave up. I latched the seat belt just as Chuck finished his pre-flight walkaround of the airplane and climbed into the pilot's seat.

Doors shut and locked.

Master switch on.

Flight instruments and radios set.

Engine primed.

Chuck turned the ignition switch, the starter whined, and the prop jerked into motion. The engine fired to life with a slight shudder on the propeller's third revolution. He caressed the throttle and set the RPMs at one thousand. I dialed the tower frequency into the radio.

Not long ago, the plane had experienced a gunshot to the engine block and a propeller strike to a person. Chuck tore the entire engine and propeller assembly apart checking for any internal damage or maintenance issues, replacing worn or damaged parts. This would be my first flight in N7757U since the engine work.

Because of the prevailing winds, we taxied to the easterly-oriented runway—runway one-zero—and the tower gave us a takeoff clearance as Chuck positioned the Cessna on the centerline. He pushed the throttles forward and my body sagged into the seat, the plane lunging forward as the flight instruments sprang to life. We rolled down the runway, the plane's nose becoming light as the airspeed indicator moved past seventy knots. Chuck applied slight back pressure to the yoke, and we were airborne, climbing into the vibrant Bonaire sky.

After takeoff, we made a climbing left turn, bouncing through some early morning, mild turbulence. Curacao lay west of Bonaire, so Chuck picked up a heading of 260 degrees. He stopped our climb and leveled off at two-thousand, five-hundred feet. No reason to go any higher for a short, twenty-minute flight. Climbing burned additional fuel and Chuck liked to save money whenever possible. His business model translated to preserving capital to use for drinking.

However, if Tessa somehow stayed in the picture, that business model might change.

Over the open ocean, the air became smooth with unrestricted visibility. While Chuck fiddled with the engine and fuel controls, I stared out the side window. Many miles away on the distant horizon, the blue Caribbean sky melded with the blue Caribbean Sea.

Satisfied with the plane's configuration, Chuck said to me over the intercom, "feet wet," a term employed by military pilots to indicate the plane had transitioned from flying over land to flying over water.

I turned in his direction, and, in a slightly mocking tone, responded, "Roger that."

He shot me a smile, then shrugged.

Gazing out the window again, I considered my pending surprise-attack meeting with Joost Obersi. Fairly sure the Bonaire police had asked all the pertinent questions, but I didn't care. If I repeated a few, so be it.

I hadn't called ahead—afraid he'd decline talking to me—so there was a possibility he wouldn't be home. If he were, I hoped by surprising him, I'd be able to start a conversation.

"So, R," Chuck said. "What do you think of Tessa?"

Knowing this conversation was inevitable but not wanting it to occur, I didn't say anything, content with listening to the hum of the engine and the wind whisking past the fuselage. My conscience was clear, the voicemail I left Schleper having absolved myself of the situation. Chuck didn't know I'd been following her, and I doubted he knew she was married.

After a moment, Chuck looked at me, eyebrows raised.

"Nice," I finally said. At that moment, the inside of the cabin became extremely hot, the sun beating in through the windshield. I used the sweat-soaked sleeve of my T-shirt to wipe my brow.

"C'mon. She's better than nice."

I shrugged. "Okay, she's *really* nice." More sweat on my brow.

Chuck didn't say anything for a few moments, and the air inside the cabin became heavy with anticipation. He stole quick glances in my direction and struggled to remain still. The flight was nearly half-over, so if he had more to say, time was running out.

After a few heavy breaths, he said, "I have a favor to ask."

I threw my head against the seat's headrest.

"I think she might be seeing someone else," he said.

My face must've shown my bewilderment and shock, but Chuck apparently didn't notice, busy with his piloting chores. The temperature in the cockpit seemed to climb twenty more degrees. I searched for something to say, but came up short, eventually resorting to, "What?"

"Can you follow her? Just for a few days? Check out if I'm right?"

I'd never been a fan of daytime TV dramas—*soap operas* I remembered them being called—and wondered if this could pass for one of their plots. From what I knew, it seemed possible. Deception, cheating, and lies. Not sure they still aired, but at that instant I decided it'd be easier watching soap operas than participating in them.

Something weird was going on. Chuck must've felt it as well and, hence, the reason for his ask. It took a certain skill to juggle multiple, clandestine relationships at the same time. I had tried it once, years ago, and failed miserably. Could be Tessa had experience at this type of thing. Maybe she was a pro at it.

"Let me think about it," I said.

"I'll pay you, no problem."

"I'm retired," I said, my voice cracking as I attempted a meager laugh. "I don't really do that anymore."

Luckily, the Curacao air traffic controller's voice boomed through the intercom, putting an end to Chuck's pleading. "Cessna November Seven Seven Five Seven Uniform, you are cleared to land, runway one-one, taxi to cargo area."

Chuck flew past the airport, made a left turn, and lined up for a final to runway one-one.

"Thanks," he said, as we approached the runway threshold. "We can talk about it later."

Again, like my earlier veranda conversation with Schleper, I hadn't said yes. But unlike my chat with the *inspecteur*, I wasn't about to.

After a smooth landing, and with more than eleven thousand feet of runway, Chuck didn't use the brakes to slow the plane, choosing to let gravity and the loss of inertia do the job for him. Saving the brake pads translated to saving money, which flowed into his business philosophy.

We taxied to the cargo area and parked. Chuck went off to find his freight, and I made my way to the terminal area. I'd have to go through customs and immigration to leave the airport and hail a taxi to Joost Obersi's place.

CHAPTER 15

I NEEDED AN excuse to leave the airport, so I told Chuck some garbage about vetting a new toilet paper supplier. He didn't really listen, more concerned about getting to the bar, happy for some extra drinking time.

"Text me when you get back," he said with a wave. "I'll be at the bar."

There were three cabs in line outside the airport and I jumped in the back of the nearest one and found it driverless. I poked my head out the window and saw a group of men playing a game of dominoes, gathered around an old crate they had laid sideways and employed as an impromptu table. They were nestled in the shade of the outside concrete wall of the terminal. One of them, apparently my driver, glanced at the cab, then waved at the game table, rising from his seat. The low scowl on his face was evident as he walked out of the shade and toward the cab. One of the other men took the driver's spot at the table and bellowed a stream of Papiamentu in his direction. Everyone at the table hooted and laughed. The driver shook his head, smiling. By the time he nestled into the driver's seat, the earlier scowl was gone.

"Sorry to pull you away from your game," I said.

"That would be fine. Anyway, I never win." He continued to smile and looked at me in the rearview mirror. "Where to, sir?"

I gave him the address. He considered it a moment, then gazed at me in the mirror again. "That is a long drive," he said.

Joost Obersi lived in the Lars Thiel area, an upscale, gated community at the southern end of Curacao. I had googled it. The homes were modern, large, and near the sea.

"I'll pay whatever it costs," I said. "I have cash."

His smile broadened. "No problem then, sir."

We used a major two-lane road to exit the airport, then made our way onto a larger road called Schottegatweg Zuid that flowed toward Willemstad, Curacao's major city. We followed that until we exited onto Caracasbaaiweg, which took us south in the direction of the Lars Thiel area.

After passing the MasBango Beach resort, the Mermaid Boat Trips of Curacao, and the Palapa Beach Resort and Marina, the driver, using a handheld GPS mounted on the dash, weaved us through some residential streets before turning onto Kaya Artiko, Joost Obersi's street.

We stopped in front of the house, last one on the left, tightly squeezed onto a small lot, close to the neighboring residence. Even from the front I could tell the place had a substantial sea-view out the back. Made of concrete with a ceramic tile roof, the architecture boasted Dutch and Caribbean influences. Modern construction with square and precise exterior edges, orange pastel paint scheme, and a small, manicured yard of gravel and cactus. Just beyond the lot, Kaya Artiko turned ninety degrees and headed back inland. Joost Obersi lived on the last lot butting up to the sea. Prized property on any budget.

Especially a carpenter's.

I asked the driver to wait for me. Wasn't sure how long this interview would take, but I didn't want the aggravation of trying to find a taxi when finished. He happily agreed, knowing the clock was running even though he wasn't burning any fuel.

Maybe he shared Chuck's business philosophy.

I walked through the gate, along a paved sidewalk, and up three steps to the front porch and pressed the doorbell.

After a few moments, the curtain on the window moved, and a young lady cracked the door open a few inches.

"May I help you?" she asked.

"I'm here to see Joost Obersi. Is he available?"

She glanced away a moment, then back at me. "Why?"

"Tell him it's in regard to his scuba accident."

She paused a moment, then closed the door. I stood there a bit, not sure whether to ring the doorbell again. I turned and walked to the edge of the porch and looked at the houses across the street and up the block. A few palm trees swayed in the wind. They had to be transplants—too perfectly placed in the yards and their trunks too straight to be natural. All the houses had the same look and feel. Fresh; clean; orderly.

And quiet. Maybe even lonely. No people on the streets; no kids out and about playing and laughing; no dogs running and barking. Everyone must've been at work, making enough money to pay the tidal-wave-size mortgages.

Just as I had decided to ring the doorbell again, the door flew open. A man stepped out on the porch and faced me, purposely penetrating my personal space just enough to be bothersome. I took a half-step back.

"What do you want?" he asked.

Dark skinned, he stood eye-to-eye with me at six feet, but weighed at least twenty-five pounds more than me, most of it concentrated in his bulging gut. Completely bald with a long, braided goatee, he had dark eyes and a flat nose. His front top teeth bulged out with defined spaces between them.

"Joost Obersi?" I asked.

"Who wants to know. And why?"

When Schlepper's team questioned Obersi, they would've had a police presence—squad vehicles, uniforms, multiple officers—and were most likely accompanied by members of the Curacao department.

I had no presence at all; just a guy on the porch who arrived by taxi. At least, I should've had the driver park down the street.

Obersi stepped forward, putting himself back into my personal space. I stole a glance at his hands. Calluses, scrapes, and cuts. Hard looking. Workingman's hands. The kind that possibly saw regular fights or scuffles.

"I'm Roscoe Conklin. I live on Bonaire and I'd like to talk to you about the dive accident—"

"Why? What's there to talk about?" He scanned the street and focused a moment on the taxi. "You are not the police, so who are you?"

"A friend of the dive master who was instructing you—"

"I heard he is now dead." He folded his arms across his chest. His ears were curved forward, more so than anyone's I'd ever seen.

"Yes, that's true. That's why—"

"I already talked to the police. Twice."

Silence is a great interrogation technique. I turned my head and looked across the street while I counted to ten. A solitary mangy brown dog scampered down the walk. Still a quiet neighborhood. The mutt looked lonely.

"There is no reason to talk with you." He stepped toward the door.

"Are you sure?" I needed to keep him on the porch, engaged.

He stopped; turned in my direction. "Yes, I am sure."

"You're a carpenter and Rulio's leg was hacked off."

"Yes, I am aware. The police told me as such."

"If you talk to me, maybe I can help you. You and I—"

"I and you what? You think I kill the man?"

"You were on the island when he went missing."

"Yes, I went there. To finish my dive training. I paid for it already and the shop agreed to let me finish. Nothing to do with the lousy dive master from before. He almost killed me."

"That's the problem. He almost killed you—" which I didn't know to be true or not "—and you were on the island when he went missing, and eventually presumed dead."

Neither of us spoke for a moment.

"You had an argument with him." I paused, but he didn't respond. "Don't you see how that looks?"

He was silent a few moments more, then said, "Yes, I do. And that's why there is no reason to talk with you. I told the police everything and they are satisfied. Who are you to question them? An American who thinks he knows better than the police?"

"I'm just trying to find out what happened."

"He is dead. That's what happened. He killed someone else and almost killed me." Joost Obersi poked a finger at me. "Maybe he get what he deserve."

"No one deserves to have a leg hacked off."

He paused and took a deep breath. His eyes averted mine and his eyelids fluttered; he then turned around, facing the door. His upper torso inflated as he drew in a large breath and the muscles in the back of his shoulders tightened. Without turning back, he said, "Go and don't come back. Leave me and my family alone."

"Wait—"

He entered the house and closed the door. I heard the dead bolt latch into place. A slight movement of the curtain, and then nothing.

Neat; clean; orderly.

I walked down the stairs, along the sidewalk, and back to the taxi. The driver was sleeping, and I woke him as I got in the back seat.

"Back to the airport, please," I said.

"No problem, sir," he said, eyelids heavy. After buckling his seat belt, he started the car and pulled onto Kaya Artiko.

I sat in silence as we again passed the Palapa Beach Resort and Marina, the Mermaid Boat Trips of Curacao, and the MasBango Beach Resort.

Somewhere along Caracasbaaiweg I asked the driver, "That was a nice house, wasn't it?"

"Yes, sir, very nice. That is a good part of the island."

"The man I was talking to is a carpenter."

In the rearview mirror, I saw the cabbie raise his eyebrows at me.

"How can a carpenter pay for a house like that?" I asked.

He shook his head. "I do not know, sir. It is not much of my business."

True statement.

But I considered making it part of mine.

CHAPTER 16

I EXITED THE cab in front of the cargo terminal at the Curacao airport. Since I wasn't boarding a commercial airliner, I didn't need to pass through a security checkpoint. However, I still needed to go through immigration, which took longer than I had anticipated. I should've known. Island Time exists for the immigration workers as well.

I texted Chuck with an update and he said he'd finish his beer and meet me at the plane. As expected, he wanted me to fly back.

He had loaded and strapped two crates into the rear section of the Cessna and two more in the back seats, being careful to distribute the load as evenly as possible. Bound shut by crisscrossing wire, each crate was about the size of a large suitcase and made of thick, heavy cardboard. Plain and indiscriminate, the only visible markings were a shipping label taped to each top, along with vigorously applied *Do Not Open* stickers on all sides.

We climbed aboard, buckled in, and fired up the engine. The tower transmitted taxi instructions, then gave us a takeoff clearance. I pushed the throttle forward, lifted us off the runway, and climbed to two-thousand feet. Bonaire popped into view out the front windshield, less than forty miles ahead. A twenty-five-minute flight, straight ahead, into the prevailing winds. As in the trip over to Curacao, the air on our return leg remained smooth.

"Get your toilet paper shit all straightened out?" Chuck asked, obviously proud of his play on words.

"Yeah, all taken care of."

He didn't waste any time getting down to business. "So, will you help me out and follow Tessa?" He reached into a small cooler sitting on the floorboard behind the pilot's seat and pulled out a beer. He popped it open, smiled at me, and said, "Thank you for flying Chuck Studer Airlines."

I double-checked the radio frequency, stalling for time, and made a small, unnecessary adjustment to the throttle. The sun shone through the windshield, baking me to my seat. Hot and thirsty, I longed for one of Chuck's beers.

He downed a long swallow then wiped his upper lip. "Well?"

I had no choice but to answer. "Chuck, I can't follow her."

"Why not?"

"I made a deal with Inspector Schleper."

"Inspector Schleper—" Chuck paused, straightened in the seat, and moved his eyes across the instrument panel. After a moment he shook his head, then said, "What does he have to do with Tessa and me?"

"I agreed to follow his wife, see if she was fooling around."

"So?" As if taunting me, he took a swig of beer.

I wiped sweat from my brow. "If I had known you were involved, I never would've done it."

He waited.

With a long, slow breath, I said, "Tessa is Schleper's wife."

Mouth open, he stared at me. I turned and looked out the side window. Small whitecaps marked the tops of the meager waves two thousand feet below. We passed over a chartered fishing boat, folks on the deck waving at us. I rocked the Cessna's wings.

"I don't believe it. She's not married," he said. "She would've told me."

"It's true." I saw no reason to tell him about Mr. Ponytail, the bartender at Paradise Cove.

Lucas.

He went quiet for a moment. Then, he slapped his thigh with his fist. "I *knew* she was sleeping with someone else."

You mean someone other than her husband? I thought.

The runway at Flamingo International Airport lay straight ahead, less than fifteen miles away. We were the only flight destined for Bonaire at the time, so the tower had already cleared us for landing. Chuck opened another beer.

Then, he froze, the color draining from his face.

"Did you feel that?" Chuck asked.

"Feel what?" I asked.

He pulled one muff of the headset off his ear while scanning the panel, eventually focusing on the engine instruments, specifically the fuel pressure and RPM indicator.

As if on cue, the engine sputtered. A mechanical hiccup, of sorts, that I felt more than heard. A momentary restriction of fuel to the engine caused the prop to jerk, creating a shutter that rippled across the entire airframe, like dropping a stone in a pond. Instantly, the seat frame absorbed the reverberation and transmitted it to my body.

The first one was slight and only Chuck felt it. But the second one was more intense, causing me to sit up, my throat instantly going dry. In unison, Chuck and I both reached for the fuel control knob and shoved it forward, enriching the gas-air mixture, increasing the engine's power.

I estimated the airport to still be ten miles away. Too far for a glide if the engine quit. I stole a glance out the window and looked down at the sea. Those small whitecaps suddenly looked large and ferocious, eagerly waiting to swallow up a single-engine aircraft. Small airplanes and large bodies of water seldom mixed well. Unless the plane was fitted with floats, which this one wasn't.

Then another engine sputter. And another.

Five miles from the airport. Almost within gliding distance. Typically, this is the point where I'd reduce power and set up a long, gentle descent to the runway. But not in this situation. I wanted to maintain as much altitude as possible, not cutting any power until over land. And with nine thousand feet of tarmac, I could wait until over the runway to cut power and still have plenty of landing room.

The words of my first flight instructor, Elif, an old Norwegian guy from Wisconsin, screamed into my thoughts. On a regular basis during my initial flight training, he'd shouted over the noise of the engine, "Altitude is your friend!"

Two miles from the airport, and still over water, I needed that friend.

But, as suddenly as the sputtering had started, the engine began running smooth again. I relaxed—some. Chuck and I nodded to each other and I pulled the throttle back a fraction of an inch, reducing the power, allowing us to begin a shallow descent. We made a high, sloppy approach, landing midway down the runway, and taxied to Chuck's tie-down spot in front of the large hangar doors. Not till I shut down the engine did either of us breathe normally again.

"You got another beer?" I asked Chuck, popping open my door.

"Yeah, one for each of us."

I took a swig and got out of the plane. Chuck went straight to the engine cowling, opened it, and peered into the cavity. "Must be a fuel problem. I'll need to have it analyzed." He closed the cowling hatch. "Might have to drain the tanks."

"How would the fuel go bad?" I wasn't a mechanic—of any kind—but fuel going bad seemed odd.

"Not bad, necessarily, but somehow contaminated. Maybe water or the wrong fuel type."

While I tied the plane to the tarmac, Chuck walked to the hangar and returned with a four-wheeled cart. We loaded the boxes onto the cart and rolled them to Chuck's truck. He planned to deliver them to the client.

After we stacked the freight in the truck bed, I sipped a beer and considered what we'd just done. On previous flights involving packages coming to Bonaire from Curacao, mounds of customs paperwork needed to be completed. In addition, depending on the items, import tax might need to be paid. Things couldn't just be flown to the island and driven away.

I patted one of the boxes with my hand. "No customs or taxes on this stuff?" I asked.

Chuck shook his head. "Never is for this client."

"What?" I asked with an unbelieving half-laugh.

"I shit you not." He shrugged. "The first time I flew for him, he said don't worry about paperwork or customs. Said he had it all taken care of and to just load the boxes and drive away." He took a sip of beer. "I was scared shitless the first time, so I asked the guys in the hangar. They didn't want to talk about it and just waved me away. Told me to drive my load out of here."

"Who's the client?"

Chuck shook his head. "Sorry, R. No way. This is a good deal for me and I'm not going to blow it by breaking confidentiality."

"Be careful, Chuck. This doesn't sound good."

"Nothing ever sounds good to you." He finished his beer, crushed the can, and tossed it in the truck bed. "I'll be fine."

No point in arguing with him. Once Chuck got his mind on a moneymaking scheme, he was determined to see it through. I examined the bed of his truck, the boxes neatly stacked in two rows. "Hey, where's the speargun?"

"Gone. This morning. Don't know who took it and I don't care." He chuckled. "You can tell Arabella not to worry about it anymore."

I studied him a moment. He leaned against the truck, his posture sagging, a vacant stare at the ground. The lines in his face appeared deeper than normal. "Buy you one at Vinny's?" I asked.

"Maybe. I don't know. See how I feel after dropping these boxes off." Not like Chuck to turn down a beer, especially at Vinny's. "I need to think about Tessa and what I'm going to do."

"Well, I'll be there for a bit if you want to stop by."

He drove off and I got in my Wrangler. Before pulling out of the stall, I checked my cell phone. Schleper had called four times but hadn't left any voicemails. But he had texted me.

It read, *"What happened? Where were you?"*

CHAPTER 17

I SAT UNDERNEATH an old Illinois license plate, mounted slightly crooked on an overhead rafter at Vinny's, that read ME N RC. The midafternoon breeze pushed through the bar rattling the branches of the potted palm trees near the front entrance, causing a rubbing sound that was out of synch with the clanking of the ceiling fan. My second Bright sat in front of me, the condensation having run down the side of the bottle, soaking the coaster. A wedge of lime floated in the half-gone beer.

Earlier, when I had arrived, I noticed a commotion across the street, near the building where Chuck lived. Two police trucks and some yellow crime scene tape. A crowd had gathered, mainly locals with a few tourists mixed in. I hadn't stopped or inquired about the issue. Doubted it had anything to do with Chuck or I'd have received a call from him by now. Probably some domestic problem.

I called him anyway. No answer.

Jan cleaned glasses and stocked the beer coolers, preparing for the upcoming happy hour.

"Jan, you know what's going on across the street?" I asked.

He glanced at Chuck's building, then went back to stocking. "No, I do not know."

"How long the cops been there?"

He hesitated, studied a beer bottle for a moment. "A while. Yes, they have been there for a while."

It appeared the crowd was dispersing. Even one of the police trucks left, tires squealing as it took off down the street.

Like the cabbie on Curacao had said, *"It is not much of my business."*

I decided to leave if Chuck hadn't shown by the time I finished my beer. He didn't usually pass up a drinking opportunity, but the news of Tessa might have affected him more than I thought possible. Maybe more than he thought possible. Wasn't sure what I could do for him. Following Tessa wouldn't happen again. That job was finished.

My interview with Joost Obersi came to mind. Not one of my success stories. I hadn't gathered any useful information and doubted I'd get a second chance. Some world-class gumshoe I turned out to be. Should've had that little girl, the one coaxing candy out of me in the office, do the interrogation. She couldn't have done any worse.

Joost Obersi certainly seemed agitated. I imagined the police hadn't cut him any slack in their questioning. Since he was on Bonaire when Rulio went missing, he had opportunity.

As well as a powerful emotion, revenge is also a powerful motive.

Plus, being a carpenter, he'd have the right tools to cut—or chop or hack—off a leg. Or any other body part. In other words, *means.*

Joost Obersi had motive, means, and opportunity. Based on my experience, all of that moved him to the top of the suspect list.

Chuck arrived before I finished my beer. I signaled Jan for two more and he promptly obliged. Chuck sat on a yellow stool and put his head on the bar.

"Not sure I can handle this, R," he said.

I put a hand on the back of his shoulder. "You'll be all right. These things have a way of working themselves out."

He raised his head and swigged some beer. "You're probably right." He shook his head.

I motioned with my head to the crowd across the street. "What's going on at your building?"

"Beats me." He shrugged. "I didn't stop there. Saw the crowd and came straight here." He turned to look at his apartment building. "Probably those shithead, nosey neighbors of mine across the hall." Pointing a finger at the building, he continued, "They gotta know every stinking thing that happens in the place. Plus, they fight with each other all the time." He took another swig of beer. "I hope the cops run their asses in."

I got the impression Chuck was venting. "You'll get through this."

"Maybe. Maybe not," he said.

Jan stopped washing glasses and went to the back, far side of the bar. He made a call on his cell, looking at Chuck and me several times while talking. After the call, he stayed in the back. Several customers across the bar from us needed drinks, but Jan stayed put, not serving them.

I studied those customers and tried to determine what the problem was, why Jan ignored them. Were they troublemakers of some kind? They didn't fit the profile. Looked like run-of-the-mill tourists to me. Dressed almost like I had been when I followed Tessa. Except for the dive wallet. They had more class than that.

"Hey," Chuck said, his head hanging low. "I couldn't get the fuel issue out of my head, so I drained some fuel from the plane."

"Find anything?"

"It'll need to be analyzed, but it looks like the fuel was contaminated."

My throat went dry again. "Really?" The thought of crap fuel caused my heart to skip a couple of beats, my own version of an engine sputter.

"After I let it sit and settle for a while, the contamination separated from the avgas and floated to the bottom. Based on the color, looks to me like jet fuel was mixed in."

I considered that a moment. Aviation fuel differed from gasoline in that avgas types were each a different color. It helped mechanics and pilots verify the correct fuel type was in the plane's tanks. But a single engine Cessna 180 ran on the most basic avgas available.

"How can the engine run on jet fuel?" I asked.

"It can't. Not for long anyway. But a small amount of jet fuel mixed with the regular avgas would make the engine sputter. Kind of like it did. As the jet fuel cleared the carburetors, the engine would run smooth again."

Sweat ran down my brow, but at least my heart hadn't *sputtered* again. I polished off the remainder of my Bright in one upturn and sat the empty bottle on the bar. Jan still hovered in the back. I leaned over the bar and waved my empty at Jan.

"So how did it get into your tanks?" I asked Chuck.

"Not sure, but—"

He stopped mid-sentence as Arabella and three other officers—one of them Ingrid—walked into Vinny's and made a beeline to Chuck and me. As they approached, Chuck looked at me. I shrugged. We both turned back to Arabella as the four of them surrounded Chuck.

Arabella glanced at me, then said to Chuck, "Mr. Chuck Studer, I need to take you to the police station for questioning."

"What?" Chuck said.

"You need to come with me," she said to Chuck.

"Bella, what's going on?" I said.

Eyebrows scrunched and lips pursed, she scolded me, "Stay out of this, Conklin."

Two of the officers stepped closer to Chuck. Arabella waved them back.

She lowered her voice and softened her tone. "Please, Chuck," she said.

"Why? What's going on?" Chuck asked.

"It's Tessa Schleper," Arabella said. "*Inspector* Schleper's wife."

Chuck looked at me for a moment, then back at Arabella. "Yeah, so?"

Arabella took a deep breath. "She has been murdered."

Schleper's text came to mind. *What happened? Where were you?*

Chuck clutched the bar to keep from falling off the stool. Two of the officers grabbed under his arms, helping him back upright. They didn't let go.

I got off the stool and walked toward Arabella. Ingrid stepped in my way and put a hand on my chest. I knew better than to forcibly remove it or cause any type of confrontation with a cop, so I just looked at Arabella. She said something in Papiamentu, then Ingrid, after giving me a short stare-down, backed away.

"You can't be serious," I said.

"We found her"—she glared at Chuck—"in your apartment. Dead."

"But I . . . I didn't do it." Chuck's whole body seemed to be shaking.

"She had been shot with a speargun," Arabella said. "The gun was lying beside her. The same one I saw in the back of your truck."

We were all quiet for a moment, everyone, including me, looking at Chuck.

"Bella," I said, breaking the silence. "You sure about this? He's been with me all day."

Arabella told the two officers holding Chuck to escort him out of Vinny's. She stayed behind with Ingrid.

"His speargun"—she counted on her fingers as she spoke—"his apartment; his girlfriend." She looked at Ingrid and motioned with her head in the direction of the exit. After a short hesitation, and a sympathetic smile to me, Ingrid headed out of Vinny's. Arabella watched her go, then turned to me. "What would you do?"

I slumped back onto the stool. "I'm not sure." I shook my head. "But seriously . . . Chuck?"

"Follow every lead, no matter how small. You always tell me that." She paused a moment. "Would Bill Ryberg not do the same?" She turned and started to leave.

"Low blow, *Officer*," I said under my breath but loud enough that I hoped she'd hear.

She froze, then turned and walked back to me.

"Let me tell you about a low blow. Okay? I stopped at the Yellow-Rock earlier to see if you are back from Curacao, maybe bring you lunch. While I was there, a woman named Sandra Griffis—yes, I believe you know her—came into the office. She remembered something about Rulio and wanted to tell you about it." Arabella shifted her weight to one leg and crossed her arms. "I think to myself: Is Conklin asking around about Rulio's death? Then I think, if he were, he would talk to *me* about it." She shook her head. "But that is not true. No, my *boyfriend* would tell me if that were the case. He would include me and treat me like a partner, not ask me questions and lie about why he is asking them. My *boyfriend* would trust me and not have secrets."

She glared at me for several moments. I stared at the floor, unable to look her in the eyes. Eventually, she left.

Jan placed an open beer on the bar in front of me.

"You called her, didn't you?" I said.

"I had no choice." He closed his eyes and took a breath. "She is my sister-in-law *and* a police officer. She told me to call her if I saw Chuck. What was I to do?"

I didn't touch the beer and walked out of Vinny's.

CHAPTER 18

I SKIDDED THE Wrangler to a stop between two potholes in the Paradise Cove parking lot. This time I parked close to the door. I sat for a moment and counted to ten.

What I was about to do went against my training. A detective seldom confronts a suspect with what the investigators knew. Especially not with as little information as I had and certainly not on the bad guy's turf. Chuck was innocent and I had a good idea who was guilty.

After another ten count, I walked into Paradise Cove.

The place wasn't crowded, too early for most dinner guests. A few servers wandered across the floor preparing tables for the evening rush. A brown dog, white spot over an eye, relaxed at the edge of the dining area, where it met the sand, in the shade of the canopy. Its head raised and turned in my direction, tail banging against the floor, hoping for some attention. When it realized I wasn't headed that way, disappointed, it lowered its head and resumed resting.

In the daylight, I noticed the pier didn't stretch as far into the water as I had imagined. Slightly beyond, the sailboat rested at its mooring, stern pointed at the open sea.

Lucas walked between the beach loungers lighting the tiki torches. At a solid pace, I crossed the floor, weaving between tables, muttering "Excuse me" several times to bewildered workers. I held my gaze on

Lucas and stepped out beyond the fabric canopy onto the beach and trudged through the sand a few more steps to where he stood, stoic, arms at his side.

He wore gray workout shorts and a black T-shirt that read *The Whaler, Venice Beach, CA.* While we stood faced-off to each other, both quiet, he pulled his hair out of his face and tied it into a loose ponytail. Dark, curved sunglasses covered his eyes.

Finally, I said, "I know you were seeing her."

He didn't respond and turned his head, staring away from me. The breeze blew his ponytail over the front of his shoulder. He brushed it back. His hands clenched into fists.

I continued, "And you knew Chuck was seeing her." I pointed at the bar. "He had her here the other night. At the bar. Right in front of you. I know you were angry. I saw it!"

At that point, I wished I hadn't confronted him; wished I had stayed away from Paradise Cove. Letting my anger get the best of me wouldn't help Chuck. And showing my hand to Lucas wouldn't help the investigation. But since I'd come this far, I figured I might as well go all in.

"What I can't figure out," I said, "is how you knew about the speargun."

He snapped his head in my direction, and in a condescending tone said, "What the *hell* are you talking about?"

"The speargun. The one you killed her with."

"Killed *who*?"

I considered his demeanor. After pausing a moment, I said, "Tessa."

His mouth fell open, posture stiffening, muscles becoming rigid. In a low voice, he said, "What?"

Nice performance, I thought. A regular Marlon Brando. Maybe Lucas had taken acting lessons in the past and now thought he could pull one over on me. Good luck. I'd spent far too many hours sitting across the table from dozens of lowlifes who tried desperately to feign surprise.

"Drop the act, Lucas. I know it was you."

He took a step forward. "You don't know what you're talking about. Tessa was a piece of shit. Maybe she got what she deserved."

"Wrong on both accounts."

He turned to leave, but I grabbed him by the arm.

My mistake.

In addition to acting, it seems Lucas was adept at self-defense.

He quickly spun and grasped my hand, twisting and locking it in an unnatural position. Pain shot through my wrist and into my elbow, traveling all the way to my shoulder. Maintaining the wristlock, he twisted my arm more and drove me headfirst into the sand, pinning my wrist behind me, below my shoulder blade.

The pressure on the tendons immobilized me. The best I could do was kick my legs. Just barely. Any movement of my torso intensified the pain in my shoulder, and sent it screaming through my arm to my wrist.

I was at Lucas's mercy.

Lucas bent and, through clenched teeth, said into my ear, "You *don't* know what you're talking about." Accentuating his claim, he tweaked my wrist an additional fraction of an inch, sending an avalanche of additional pain firing through my arm.

The world closed in on me, tunnel vision causing a near loss of peripheral vision. I closed my eyes to fight back nausea and dug into the sand with my free hand, hoping to focus on something other than the pain.

"That's enough, Lucas," a voice said.

The pain let up, but my arm was now numb. I sensed Lucas's release more than I felt it. I opened my eyes and realized the tunnel vision was dissipating. Sweat and sand clung to my forehead, slowly sliding into my eyes.

"Help him up," the voice said, who I now recognized as John.

Lucas grabbed me under the armpit and helped me stand. My legs were slow to cooperate, the world still spinning and my balance a mess, but I tried not to show it. I'd never had acting lessons, so doubtful I convinced anyone.

It took several moments before I could completely straighten. The feeling was returning to my arm. It hurt. It would hurt more later.

I wiped some of the sand off my face and glared at Lucas. John yelled for someone to bring me a beer and a towel. Surprisingly, I didn't feel much like drinking.

"Nothing's changed," I said, wrist still numb. I needed the blood flowing again but didn't want to give Lucas the satisfaction of knowing he hurt me, so I resisted the urge to rub it.

"Mr. Conklin, what's the problem?" John asked, lighting one of his slender brown cigarettes. Luckily, the wind blew away from me.

"You realize what happened?" I asked John. "A woman is dead. Murdered." I turned to Lucas. "And right now, the police are questioning the wrong guy."

"What does that have to do with Lucas? Or us?"

"I think this guy"—I pointed at Lucas—"knows something about it."

John shook his head. "Mr. Conklin, you're always welcome to come and eat or drink, but you won't come here and cause problems." He took a drag from the cigarette and blew out the smoke. "I'm currently in a meeting with an associate and don't have time for this." He pointed toward the exit. "You need to leave."

Lucas put his hands on his hips. "Out," he said.

I gave him one final glare-down, then turned and headed for the exit. As I crawled into the Wrangler, Danielle Anderson stepped out of the door to Paradise Cove.

"You're still welcome here," she said. She wore knee-length black spandex and a pink T-shirt that had *Bulldogs* printed on it. Her hat was also pink and said *Drake*.

"Really? Your *bouncer* has a funny way of showing it. As does your husband."

She twisted her face. "John and Lucas are both harmless."

I rubbed my shoulder and moved it in a small circle.

"Look . . . Lucas is John's old friend. They've known each other since they were kids. John has always stood up for Lucas, and Lucas is like this little puppy dog, with a weird, unyielding devotion to John."

"Sure, a puppy dog." I didn't know what else to say.

"Like I said the other night, Lucas gets a bit emotional. It's just that he admires John *so* much." She placed her hand on my forearm. "Please . . . R . . . don't let this drive you away. Come back. And bring your delightful lady friend with you." She winked. "Don't forget your banjo."

The breeze blew through the Wrangler, bringing with it a touch of salt, seeming to leave a layer of sea on my skin. I needed a good swim, but the job Lucas had done on my arm and elbow would make that impossible for a few days.

Next door to Paradise Cove, construction was finishing for the day; men shouted final instructions to each other, a front-end loader parked and shut down, and a couple of yellow-helmet-clad workers loaded their tools in the backs of pickup trucks.

I removed Danielle's hand from my arm. "Will John stand up for Lucas regarding murder?"

She took in a breath. "Murder? What are you talking about?"

"Ask your husband's puppy dog." I turned the ignition key and pushed in a CD. It happened to be Creedence and "Bad Moon Rising" started playing, so I cranked the volume. After putting the Wrangler in reverse, I held my foot on the brake, and shouted to Danielle, "Can I ask you a question?"

Her face brightened. "Sure."

"Of all the places, why Bonaire?"

She gave me a blank stare.

"Why'd you pick Bonaire to open Paradise Cove?"

"The senior partners." She shrugged. "It was their choice."

"Partners?"

"Yes, R. Even *we* have bosses."

I released the brake and backed out of the parking lot. The sun was near setting on my left, across the sea, as I headed back to the Yellow-Rock. I searched the early evening sky for the moon but didn't see it.

Good or bad.

CHAPTER 19

BLURRY-EYED, I SAT at my office desk the next morning. Sleep hadn't come easy the previous night and I had tossed and turned for hours. It was now nine o'clock and I'd already finished my second Diet Coke. An empty yogurt container lay on a stack of dusty papers.

Erika had the day off. Tomorrow was Rulio's funeral and she needed to tend to some last-minute details. I didn't ask what details but offered my help if needed. She struggled with the concept of a funeral but decided it to be the prudent thing to do. She purchased a child-sized coffin to bury Rulio's leg.

A toolbox sat near the front door, homage to my earlier intention of finally replacing the squeaky door opener. However, I found it difficult to muster the ambition. My thoughts roamed elsewhere.

I decided to call my friend David Brown.

A native Bonairian, Brown had spent twenty years in Amsterdam as a forensics specialist with the National Police Corps, or *Korps Nationale Politie.* He'd recently returned to Bonaire and gained subsequent training that landed him a lab technician role at the island hospital—known as San Francisco Hospital. I had spent a considerable amount of time at the hospital as Arabella recovered from the gunshot wound to her shoulder, the one she sustained while saving my life. Brown and I ran into each other a few times, and hit it off quickly, both of us having spent time in law enforcement.

He told me to call anytime if I ever needed anything.

I fumbled through the hospital phone menu system and eventually got connected to the lab, where David Brown answered the phone.

"Hello, R," he said. "How are you?"

"Good, David. I was hoping you could help me with something."

"Sure, any time. What can I do for you?"

"I need to ask about the leg that washed ashore."

"Ouch. Maybe anything but that." He paused, then said, "Okay, what about it?"

"Well, a few days ago, I saw the coroner's report. But it's in Dutch. I was hoping you could fill in some blanks for me."

Back in the States, it'd be difficult to get this type of information without a warrant, even regarding a deceased individual. Privacy laws, specifically HIPAA—the Health Insurance Portability and Accountability Act of 1996—made it nearly impossible for health care facilities to hand over information about patients without following proper protocol. Especially to private citizens.

But I wasn't sure if Rulio's leg was considered a patient.

I knew about the existence of the EU's Directive on Data Protection but didn't know how it pertained to health information or personal privacy after death.

"How . . ." I could almost hear the wheels turning in his head. "It was considered hush-hush. How could you be looking at a coroner's report?"

"I'm working with a police inspector on the case." Not really a lie, but not really the truth, either. Didn't *feel* quite as bad as an outright lie.

"I could get in serious shit for this. You will owe me some Polar, bud." He referred to a type of beer drunk by many of the island locals.

"Understood."

"Can you snap some pictures of the report and text them to me?" he asked.

I hesitated for a moment, unable to think of any other way. Email was out of the question. Not sure who else might stumble upon a copy stored on a hard drive somewhere. Lacking a better option, I said, "I can do that, but you need to promise to delete them immediately."

He agreed, so I took pictures of the report and texted them to him. After a few moments, he said, "Okay, got them. What do you want to know? I will give you what I can, but I must say, I did not work on this."

"Any idea how the leg was severed?"

A few quiet moments passed

"Well, it was in the water a long time," David said. "But you probably already knew that." He paused. "DNA analysis has not come back yet, but based on the tattoo, they are quite sure whose leg it was. Bloated with lots of flesh missing from fish bites and such. Partially decomposed." Not sure whether David was speaking to me or talking to himself. He continued to mumble as he read more of the report.

He said, "Here it is." Another pause followed by more mumbling. "The femur was severed just below the lesser trochanter."

"The what?"

"A little bit below the ball-socket of the hip, right at the top of the femur, or leg."

"Any indication how?"

"The translation would be something to the effect of 'brute force trauma.'"

"That could mean almost anything," I said.

"Yes, but in this case, it looks to be a hatchet or something like that. Lots of scuff marks on the femur, like a blade coming down with force."

"Not a sawing motion?"

"Does not look that way."

"And not a doctor or trained professional."

"Definitely not."

"Anything classified as *unusual* or *surprising*?"

"You mean, other than a human leg washing ashore?"

"Yeah, other than that."

"It does mention some lacerations on the lower leg, caused by a strand of wire wrapped around the ankle."

"Any specifics about the wire?"

"No, just says wire. In my experience, the coroner wouldn't analyze the wire. That would be the responsibility of the police department."

More silence. I had run out of questions, so I punted.

"Anything else?" I asked.

"Not much. It is a sparse report."

I'd expected as much. Most of what David had told me wasn't a surprise. Nearly impossible to garner any reasonable forensics from a bloated, partially decomposed, waterlogged leg washing ashore. Hence the reason the police had released it to Erika a few days ago. They didn't need it anymore.

Not a complete dead end, though. At least it verified what I already suspected and had been able to translate on my own.

"Hey, R," David said. "There is one strange notation."

"Yeah?"

"It says that small pieces of wood were taken out of the skin."

"What kind of wood?"

"Does not say."

"Any thoughts on that?"

"I would guess they sent the samples out for analysis." He paused a moment. "Wonder how wood got on the leg."

Good question, I thought, considering Joost Obersi's occupation.

"Well, thanks for your help," I said. "I'll get that beer over to you."

"No worries. Help me drink it?"

"Absolutely."

I disconnected and leaned back in my chair, having not heard from Chuck or Arabella. I assumed Arabella—and others—had interrogated Chuck well into the evening, and possibly early morning. Calls to both their cell phones went to voicemail. I figured as soon as Chuck was out, had some rest, and maybe a few beers, he'd call me.

Arabella might be a different story.

A noticeable pain and constant throbbing still emanated from my arm; the one Lucas had tried to coil into a loop. The aching wasn't as bad as last night, but still enough to be annoying, especially if I reached for something. Funny thing, though; the more Brights I had reached for last night, the less my arm had hurt.

I stood and walked over to the open windows. Tourists, dressed in every conceivable fashion and color, all dive or swim oriented, walked along the sidewalk outside the office, their crimson skin telegraphing vacation overindulgence in the Caribbean sun. Conversation and laughs. As multiple groups passed, I caught bits of talk about diving, the reef, lunch plans, meeting up later, and not wanting to go home. On any given day, it'd be the same bits of conversation.

Diving, eating, and drinking. And relaxing.

Vacation in Paradise. If only *life* could be so simple.

Which it isn't when living on the island. Then it's the same as anywhere else. Just sunnier, warmer, and easier access to swimming and diving than most.

But no simpler.

I took a deep breath and kneeled by the door, intent on replacing the door opener. While fumbling with tools, screws, and instructions, I forced myself to concentrate on what I knew about Rulio's case, which wasn't much. Foremost in my mind was Arabella's mention that Sandra Griffis, Rulio's girlfriend, had remembered something additional and wanted to get in touch with me.

After an agonizing thirty minutes, I tested the newly installed door opener. Proud of my handyman success, I stored the tools in the closet and went back to my desk. The Rulio file contained Sandra's contact information. A call to her cell—it was the only number listed—went to voicemail. As an accountant, I guessed she went to work each day at a regular time, probably around eight o'clock. I wasn't sure if her office was at Paradise Cove, or at another location, maybe a rented space in a building somewhere in Kralendijk.

I called her cell again and this time left a voicemail telling her I would stop by her house. If I missed her, to please call me back on my cell number, which I left on the message.

Leaving the office unattended during the day was a common occurrence at the YellowRock. At any given time, Erika and I might both be gone for some reason or another. I checked the day's guest register and noted that no one was scheduled to check in or out, which made leaving easier. My cell number was posted on the outside of the building near the office door. If a guest needed me, they could call.

Ten minutes later, I let myself through Sandra's creaky metal front gate, same as before. The air conditioner still sputtered and whined as I stepped onto the concrete slab under the metal awning and knocked on the door.

No answer, so I knocked again, and again, no answer.

I stepped off the concrete porch and peered through the window above the spot where the AC poked through but couldn't make out anything of interest. Looking through the windows on the other side of the house provided the same result.

Back on the front porch, facing the street, I scanned the gravel landscape and wondered about the small lizard. Last time I was here, it had perched on a rock, acting as a sentry, and watched me drive away. It didn't seem to be around today.

Neither did Sandra Griffis.

Maybe I'd stop later, after "working hours."

I sat in the Wrangler, drank some water, and thought about my next steps. I needed to speak with Chuck, see what had happened at the police station. Hopefully, they hadn't held him over. The concept of bail didn't exist in the Dutch penal code, so if they arrested him, he'd be in jail until tried and acquitted.

Also, now that Arabella knows I'm involved with looking into the Rulio case, she could be a great asset. However, it'd be difficult for her to be around me if she's building a case against Chuck. I couldn't help her with that. If anything, I'd be a detriment, and rightfully so. Chuck was innocent. He had to be.

But that was all a factor of how long she'd stay mad. Usually, when she was upset with me, she got over it rather quickly, within a few hours or, at worst case, overnight. This instance might take a bit longer.

Not surprisingly, she hadn't come to my place the previous night. I had given Arabella a key to my apartment some time ago, and now, sometimes, I wasn't sure whether it was *my* place or *our* place. She never gave up her apartment, an upstairs, one-bedroom studio, in the heart of Kralendijk, and it wasn't unusual for her to stay there one or two nights a week, especially if she had a weird work schedule or stayed late, always concerned about waking me up.

But she had never stayed at her apartment two nights in a row. One night seemed to be the most, then she'd be back at my—*our*—place. Hopefully, this would blow over and she'd make contact today.

I took another sip of water and examined Sandra's house again.

She remembered something about Rulio and wanted to tell you about it.

What had she remembered? And why hadn't she told the police?

I tried her cell another time, and again got voicemail. I left a similar message to the first one, asking her to please call me.

Pausing a moment and studying my phone, I decided to give Arabella another call. As I waited for her to answer, I scanned Sandra's gravel yard for the small lizard. No sign of it and Arabella didn't answer.

I finished the water then cranked up the Wrangler and headed to my next stop.

CHAPTER 20

Tessa had been good friends with Ruth, and they drank wine together, an almost daily afternoon ritual, according to Jan. Maybe there was more to those afternoons than what appeared on the surface, but I'd have to speak with Ruth to find out. Any conversation with her proved interesting—and challenging—and this one might just take the cake.

Halfway to Ruth's, Chuck called.

I answered and asked, "You home?"

"Yeah, got back early this morning." Voice raspy, it didn't sound like Chuck. "They drilled me for hours."

"Get any sleep?"

"A little, but I'm too scared to sleep."

"Tell me about it."

"Well, they think I killed . . . Tessa." His voice cracked on *Tessa*. He didn't continue for a few moments, and I didn't press. To have someone you cared for murdered, then be accused of that murder was almost too much to handle.

Not long ago, I'd walked that mile myself.

"Chuck, listen to me. I know it's difficult, but you have to tell me what they said, what they asked."

He sniffled a few times. "Okay, just give me a minute."

I waited.

I pulled onto Ruth's street and parked on the edge of the road two blocks from her place.

Chuck was ready to continue. "They said they received a call about a disturbance."

"Who from?"

"They wouldn't say. Not exactly very forthcoming. I wasn't allowed to ask much, just wanted me to answer their questions."

"What about the speargun?"

"Oh, man, that's the clincher. They say it has my fingerprints on it."

"Would it?"

"I don't see how. I never touched it. Like I said, when I saw it in my truck, I just left it there."

"Did you tell them that?"

"Yeah, I did, but it didn't matter. They don't believe me."

"Did you explain your alibi?"

"I told them I was on Curacao most of the day, that the flight logs and ATC records would prove it. Then I worked on the plane a little. You know, checking the gas. Then I met you at Vinny's."

I didn't remind him there wouldn't be any record of him being in Curacao. I'm the one who went out and back in at immigration. Unless someone could ID him—either at the cargo hangar or the bar—my word was the only thing that put him on Curacao. And, without asking, I knew he paid cash at the bar. He always did.

As for working on the plane, unless someone saw him, he'd have no one to corroborate his claim. In hindsight, his alibi was shaky. I'd claim he was with me in Curacao, but I was his best friend on Bonaire. What else would they expect?

"Was Bella there?" I asked.

"She did most of the questioning. I swear, R, she's out to get me. She thinks this is her chance."

"She's not like that, Chuck. She's a pro."

"You weren't there! You didn't see how she treated me. You know she's never liked me and now she wants to throw me in jail."

"Not going to happen. The evidence will clear you and this will all blow over." This time, it was *my* voice that cracked. I doubted I reassured him much.

"What am I going to do?" I heard him sob into the phone. "Bad enough losing Tessa, but going to jail for killing her? I can't face that."

"You're a long way from going to jail." I decided against pointing out that he didn't really *have* Tessa. She was married and possibly sleeping with yet someone else. He'd come to that conclusion on his own soon enough. No point rubbing it in now.

It all boiled down to Chuck's prints on the speargun. If that were true, he wouldn't be free right now. The speargun was the proverbial smoking gun in this case, and to have it loaded with prints would be a slam-dunk. Chuck would already be charged and jailed.

Besides, in contrast to what the various entertainment industries would have the general public believe, fingerprint files weren't localized in one spot. They were scattered amongst dozens of agencies and databases, most of which didn't easily interface well. Chuck had been in the Air Force, so his prints would be in a military database somewhere. They'd also be in the FBI's AFIS system, which contained prints of all military personnel and veterans. Arabella would be able to access it through Interpol, but it'd take at least a day or two for the request to go through and receive the information. No way she'd have the match within hours of the crime.

Lying to suspects was typical and commonplace. Done it a few times myself. I was sure that's what Arabella and her crew had done—lied to Chuck hoping he'd confess.

And there was still Lucas to consider. I wondered if Arabella knew about his relationship with Tessa.

"Listen, Chuck, I'll be home in about an hour. Get some grub, then stop by. We can talk some more." I didn't mention beer. Didn't have to. It was a given.

There was a pause, then he said, "Okay. See you then."

I got out of the Wrangler and walked the two blocks to Ruth's. The small amount of exercise helped clear my head, got me thinking about my next conversation.

Ruth conducted business in a one-story house before the road dead-ended. The wrong type of attention is terrible for any business, but more so for hers. She prided herself on being a good neighbor, so the residents turned a blind eye to her trade, as did local law enforcement.

I crossed the yard and stepped up onto the front stoop. Four porch lights were mounted above the door. The first one had a regular colored bulb; the second had a red bulb; the third was regular, again; and the fourth one blue. The two regular bulbs were on, while the red and blue ones were off. Code of some sort, but I had no idea what it meant.

"Hey, R," a woman said. She and another woman sat on lawn chairs under the carport covering. I guessed they were Columbian. They each had a beer and a cigarette. Neither had much modesty. Tool of the trade, I supposed.

I smiled and said hello as I stepped up to the front door and rang the bell.

"You are looking for a *date*?" the other one said as she dropped her smoldering cigarette butt into a can beside her chair.

"Thank you, but not today."

She stood and leaned on one leg, putting a hand on her hip. Then she opened her robe exposing two bare breasts and the tiniest pair of panties I'd ever seen. "You are sure?"

They both giggled.

"You make a compelling argument," I said. "But I'm fine. Just need to speak with Ruth."

"Well, in case you change your mind." She began licking her index finger. The other woman laughed and the first one intensified the licking.

Ruth answered the door. She frowned at the two women, barked something in Papiamentu, and waved them farther back into the carport, out of my sight. I almost told Ruth thank you.

"What do you want?" she asked.

"Can I talk to you about Tessa?"

"She is dead. What about her?"

Good thing Ruth wasn't a doctor. Her bedside manner stunk.

"Do you know what happened?"

"Yes, your loser pilot friend killed her."

I paused and looked at my feet a moment. After a long breath, I asked, "Did she have any boyfriends?"

She stepped out of the house onto the stoop. "What kind of a question is this?" We stared at each other a few moments. "She was truthful to her husband. No, she had no boyfriend."

"Did you know she was sleeping with Chuck?"

"Is that why he killed her?"

Another deep breath on my part. "Did you know?"

She glanced away for a beat, then back at me. "Yes, I did know. But to her, it was not serious. She said she needed more excitement. Occasionally someone different."

I had a hard time picturing Chuck as exciting. All I ever knew him to do was drink. But compared to Schleper, maybe a concrete block seemed exciting.

"Anyone else?" I asked.

"Why do you care? You just want to protect your friend."

"Sure, but I also want to find out who did this."

She narrowed her eyes and the wind pushed her blaze-red hair across her forehead. The wheels were turning as she formed an answer.

"Maybe," she finally said.

"*Maybe?*"

She sat on the stoop. I did the same.

"Maybe a week ago, two men come here looking for Tessa."

"They came here? Who were they?"

She shook her head. "I did not know at first. And I do not know how they would know to look here for her."

"Tell me about them."

"I have never seen them before. Some of the girls say that they see one of the men parked on our street several times. He looks like trouble. The other man was a *mietje*."

"*Mietje?*"

"Oh . . . you might call him a sissy boy."

I nodded.

"The tall one had long black hair in a ponytail." Her breathing became rapid and shallow. "Cold eyes. No emotion." Her face tightened as she stared into space. "I wanted to spit in his face and kick him in the balls." She turned her head and half-smiled at me. "Make him run off and cry to his momma."

I put a hand on her shoulder. "Ruth, how about the other one. The *mietje*."

Her breathing returned to normal and she brushed away my hand. "He was nothing. Short with curly hair. Big chest." She laughed. "He stepped back when I yell at them to leave."

"But the other guy? He didn't step back?"

She looked me in the eyes. "No, he did not."

"Is it possible Tessa was sleeping with him?"

She snapped her head at me. "You are wrong. Tessa was not with that man."

"How can you be so sure? He was looking for her, wasn't he?"

"Not him. Not the man with the ponytail."

"What?"

"The *mietje. He* was looking for Tessa. He said he was her boyfriend."

"Is his name John?"

Her jawline tightened and she squeezed her eyes shut a moment. "I do not know, but I believe Tessa may have slept with him."

"Why?"

She buried her face in her hands. "She would not tell me either way. She told me about your pilot friend, so why not tell me of this man, too?" She straightened. "In my work, I have seen jealous people many times. They think stalking gives them control or power. He followed her many places."

"And the other guy tagged along?"

"Yes, with him always. Right on his heels."

Lucas is like this little puppy dog, with a weird, unyielding devotion to John.

CHAPTER 21

I AWOKE THE next day, alone in my bed. Two nights in a row—two *mornings* in a row. Arabella hadn't texted or called. Before rising, I laid on my back and watched the ceiling fan for a few moments. She must be more upset than I had originally thought. Four empty beer cans accented the dust and usual debris occupying my nightstand. I couldn't remember if they were from the previous night, or the night before.

Didn't matter.

They couldn't be older than two nights. Arabella didn't tolerate empty beer cans lying around.

Rain knocked against the sliding door that led to the veranda. Low, gray clouds moved across the sky and two of the deck chairs had been blown askew. Ripples danced across the surface of small pools of water on the deck.

Perfect day for a funeral, I thought. I wondered if Rulio, kicked back and smiling from somewhere in the Great Beyond, had sent the bad weather.

But blue sky peeked through the overcast in the south, and I knew the storm would be short-lived. After an hour or so, it'd be back to the postcard-perfect sunshine and warm temperatures. The things that kept the island in business.

For the second time in a week, I ironed my clothes. Bonaire funerals tend to be extravagant events and most attendees dressed to the hilt. I chose the same basic outfit I'd worn to Paradise Cove, opting today for a polo shirt instead of a T-shirt. Luckily, the only polo I owned was black. Ironed or not, Arabella would still consider my attire boring, but I wanted to look presentable for Erika. Make her happy that I at least tried. After all, funerals are for the living, not the dead.

The pre-burial memorial service would take place at a small, unimposing building located on Kaya Soeur Bartola, across the street from one of the island's large grocery stores. The Bonaire morgue was in the same structure. I hadn't been near the place since officially identifying the body of my friend Tiffany Wilcox. I'd been avoiding it. I refused to even drive down the street.

But this day was different. I had to be there.

For Rulio, but more so, for Erika.

I parked down the block and walked up to the entrance. A swarm of well-dressed men and women massed at the double-wide entry doors, seeming to resist entering. I assimilated myself into the group, traces of perfume and aftershave melding with the freshness of the post-rain tropical breeze, and shuffled along as we all gradually *Island-Timed* our way inside.

The configuration of the main room lent itself to the service of modest memorials. A podium stood in one corner, adorned with beer-barrel-sized pots overflowing with flowers and greenery. Several semicircular rows of chairs faced the front. Only a few were empty. As would be expected, scattered amidst the seating were several boxes of tissue.

Behind the podium, resting on a riser, sat a child-sized coffin. Erika hunkered in the first row of seats, surrounded by friends and supporters, crying, tissues covering her face. I stood in the back of the room, leaning against the rear wall. I'd give her my condolences later, but right now, she had the support she needed.

Two large floor fans augmented the air-conditioning. A sauna would've been cooler. Sweat dripped from everyone and many of the women carried paper fans, moving them back and forth in front of their faces, pushing warm, humid air across their skin. One kid had a battery-operated, handheld fan positioned a few inches from his cheek. Catching me staring at him, he smiled and moved the fan closer to his face. I wondered how much he'd take for it.

A set of steel doors led to the second room. The building's other purpose.

The morgue.

I glanced at them, but quickly looked away, my mind heavy with memories of a previous excursion into that room. Bright lights reflecting off white floor tile; gurneys lining the walls; beige blankets covering pale corpses; the putrid scent of decaying flesh; and my friend Tiffany lying motionless with a yellow tag hanging from her big toe.

Chuck walked up and stood beside me, poking me in the ribs with his elbow, bringing me out of my trance, away from the darkness of that room. We remained quiet and nodded at each other. I was a bit surprised to see him here. Don't believe he knew Rulio, but he did know Erika.

After all, funerals are for the living, not the dead.

The Andersons sat in a row of seats midway down the aisle, John on the outside. Lucas, the bartender at Paradise Cove, perched in the seat directly behind his boss, leaning forward, as if trying to be as close to him as possible. Danielle gave me a short wave. Lucas turned and stared me down for a few moments while John, smiling, chatted with the woman sitting across the aisle from him.

I scanned the crowd but didn't see Sandra Griffis, Rulio's girlfriend.

Arabella walked through the front door, smiled when she spotted me in the back of the room, and strolled in my direction. She leaned against the wall alongside me, opposite of Chuck. But unlike him, she stood close enough that our shoulders and arms touched. I guessed the room temperature to be at least eighty-five degrees. Even so, the warmth of her body was refreshing. Arms hanging at our sides, she rubbed a couple of my fingers. She wasn't in uniform, so I grabbed her hand and held it. She inched closer, laying her head on my shoulder.

Eventually, a minister went to the podium and the room murmur quieted. He began with a short prayer, then went into the eulogy. His remarks about Rulio being a kind and likeable person were met with a lot of head nodding and smiles, in addition to some tears and tissue usage. He talked about some funny situations Rulio had gotten himself into over his short life and concluded with another prayer.

At that point, everyone moved outside and assembled near the street. Four men carried the small coffin out of the building and set it on a trailer attached to a pickup truck. After the group gathered behind the trailer, the entire procession—the truck barely moving, followed by the crowd—made its way toward a large church in the center of Kralendijk. Rulio's leg was to be buried in the cemetery behind that church.

Along the way, people on the street were encouraged—and welcomed—to join the procession. People prayed; others sang. Most, at one point or another, cried. Arabella and I walked side-by-side halfway from the front. Chuck followed a few strides behind us.

Several times during the fifteen-minute trek to the church, I again scanned the crowd. Still no sign of Sandra Griffis. How could she miss Rulio's funeral? Her bosses were in attendance, so I had to believe they'd have allowed her to skip work for the day.

As the crowd dispersed after the short burial service, Chuck made it a point to let me know he'd be stopping at my apartment for a beer. Arabella said she'd be by later. I figured she hoped Chuck wouldn't stay long.

She should've known better.

Almost as if they were waiting for me, John and Danielle Anderson stood at the edge of the cemetery, directly in my path as I started back toward the YellowRock. Lucas wasn't with them.

"Aren't funerals sad?" Danielle said. She gave me a hug, then pulled back and wiped a tear.

"I didn't see Sandra," I said.

"No, neither did I," John said. "I wonder why." He finished a cigarette and dropped the butt on the ground, crushing it out with his heel.

I stared at the butt a few moments, resisting the urge to ask him to pick it up. "Strange she didn't attend her boyfriend's funeral," I said.

"She hasn't been to work in several days," Danielle said.

I considered the fact that I hadn't heard from her in *several days* either. Seems the last contact anyone may've had with her was when she stopped at the YellowRock office.

She remembered something about Rulio and wanted to tell you about it.

"You try calling her?" I asked John.

"I didn't but Danni did." He looked at Danielle.

"Yes, I called her several times, but no answer."

"I wonder what happened to her," John said.

"What makes you think something happened to her?" I asked.

John looked at Danielle, then back at me. "No reason. Just a figure of speech."

I didn't say anything, just stared at John a moment then shook my head. I resumed my walk and thought, *Yeah, I wonder what* happened *to her, too.*

CHAPTER 22

I SWUNG GENTLY in my hammock holding a beer in my lap. Chuck sat in a chair. Neither of us said much, both looking out at the sea, listening to the vehicle and tourist traffic along the street. Sitting in the veranda's shade, the salty breeze seemed to flush away the sweat and emotion from Rulio's funeral. Along with the memories of the morgue.

Chuck took a swig of beer and said, "Has Arabella said anything? About me? About Tessa?"

"Nope." I paused a moment. "As a matter of fact, she hasn't talked to me since hauling you out of Vinny's."

"Hmmm."

"The funeral was the first time I'd seen her since then."

Chuck picked at the label on his beer bottle. "Sorry about that."

"Not your fault."

"But Tessa's death *is* my fault."

A shot of adrenaline pulsed through my veins. "What do you mean?"

"If I hadn't been seeing a married woman, this might not have happened."

I relaxed. "No, not your fault."

We both drank some beer.

"If anything," I said, "it's my fault."

Chuck snapped his head in my direction, eyebrows scrunched.

"I was following her," I continued. "If I had kept following her, maybe . . ."

Chuck thought for a moment, then stood and pointed a finger at me. "I just realized. That means you were following me, too."

"No, only her. I didn't realize you were seeing her until that night at Paradise Cove."

Chuck leaned against the veranda railing. Sarcastically, he said, "Taking side jobs now?"

I sighed. "Not exactly. Schleper agreed to let me look into Rulio's death if I followed Tessa."

We were both quiet for a few moments.

"As soon as I knew it was you," I said, "I told him I was through, that I wouldn't follow her anymore. Then she gets murdered."

Chuck sat back in the chair. "Well, I still miss her."

"I know you do, buddy."

"They really think I killed her, R." The sorrow of missing Tessa vanished from his voice, replaced with what could best be described as desperation. Face red, hands trembling, he continued, "You have to help me . . . Please."

"I'll do the best I can." Another promise I had no idea how to fulfill.

Arabella walked through the sliding door from my apartment. "Best you can do at what?" she asked. She had come up the inside stairs and stopped at the fridge on her way out to the veranda. She dropped a brown paper bag into my lap and handed me a beer. After glancing at Chuck, she said, "Oh, that."

The bag contained a couple of pastechis. They're a universal Bonaire snack made from a flaky pastry, deep-fried and stuffed with meat and vegetables. Basically, a gourmet Hot-Pocket, but much tastier. As an added benefit, she had also brought an order of fried plantains.

"Sorry," Arabella said to Chuck. "I only brought enough for two." She leaned against the railing and opened her beer.

"Probably not good for us to be around each other right now," Chuck said.

I wasn't sure if he thought Arabella would volunteer to leave. He should've known better.

"Yes," Arabella said. "You are correct. You should leave."

I bit into a pastechi.

"I didn't do it," Chuck said.

"Leave!" Arabella pointed at the stairs.

I sampled one of the fried plantains and chased it with some Bright.

Chuck stood. "You should try to be nicer."

"I will try to be nicer"—Arabella folded her arms across her chest—"if you try to be smarter." Then she smiled.

I ate another plantain.

Chuck said to me, "I'll be at Vinny's." He started down the stairs.

"You know," Arabella said, "Jan turned you in."

Chuck shook his head. "Of course. Keep it in the family, I guess. Right?"

Another bite of pastechi.

"It's a small island," Chuck said. "You'd have found me eventually anyway." He went down the stairs and I watched him walk up the street.

"He didn't do it," I said.

"How can you be sure?"

"He was with me most of the day."

"Maybe, but not all of the day." She hesitated, then said, "Follow every lead. He has motive, means, and opportunity. We have to look at him."

"You're going to ruin his life."

In a raised voice she said, "I'm following the evidence." She paused, then continued in a softer tone. "You should know that."

I didn't respond, just rocked in my hammock and ate the last bite of my pastechi. After wiping my chin, I asked, "What about Schleper? The husband is always a prime suspect."

She looked at me as if I'd just grown a dorsal fin. "Do you not think we checked him out right away? He was in the office the entire day. A whole team of officers to vouch for him."

"Aha! That's what makes it the perfect alibi."

"You are crazy."

"But, seriously, what about Schleper? What's he going to do?"

She shrugged. "I do not know. No one does. He is at home and does not return phone calls." She chewed some pastechi. "He will need to take a leave of absence. He cannot be involved with this."

"No, he shouldn't." I paused a moment. "There's another couple of suspects."

"Who?"

"For one, the bartender at Paradise Cove. Lucas. The guy with long black hair."

"The one who looks like John Wick?"

I had no idea who that was. "I don't know. Maybe. But he'd been stalking her."

"How do you know?"

I let out a deep breath. "I was following her."

"Who?" She thought for a moment. "Tessa?"

"Yes, that was the deal I made with Schleper. I'd follow Tessa if he let me see the Rulio file." I wasn't sure how she'd take this, but I wanted to get it in the open. No more secrets. "I backed off when I discovered Chuck was involved."

"That night at Paradise Cove, you knew who she was?"

"Yeah, but not until then did I know she was seeing Chuck." I thought for a moment and realized I couldn't ignore the fact that I might've been able to prevent Tessa's death. Can't apologize to a corpse, but I could accept responsibility face-to-face with her husband. "Maybe I should go see Schleper. Talk this through with him."

Eyes wide, she shook her head violently. "I do not think that to be a good idea. What if he partially blames you?"

I needed to speak with Schleper but decided to drop the subject for now. I nodded and said, "You should look into that bartender, Lucas. I don't know his last name."

"I can check the employment and tax records. If he has a salary, it would be on file."

"Also, his boss, John Anderson, the owner of Paradise Cove."

"Both of them?"

"Yeah, and you should talk to your sister. According to her, Anderson may've been sleeping with Tessa. At least once anyway."

Arabella's mouth gaped open. "How many boyfriends did she have?"

"At least two. Plus, a husband—"

"Wait! You spoke to Ruth?"

"Tessa was her friend. I had to."

She crossed her arms in front of her and tilted her head. "You have been busy."

"Yeah, well, I'll send you my invoice."

"Right." She took a swig of beer. "Do not spend that money yet."

I didn't want to broach what I was about to say but didn't want any more secrets. "You know I'm going to help Chuck."

She nodded. "I understand. But stay out of the way. With Schleper out, I'll have more work. I do not need you to worry about."

She took it better than I had anticipated. "I love knowing you'd worry about me."

She smiled. "Only a little . . ." Serious again, she continued, "We took Chuck's passport and notified the airport tower about his airplane being grounded. We do not want him leaving the island."

I gave her my intense, gumshoe stare. "Do you really have his prints on the speargun?"

She slumped in the chair. "Of course not. I wish we did. If so, he would not currently be a free man."

"But think about it—why would he leave the speargun? And why do it in his own apartment?"

She shook her head. "I do not know how to answer those questions. Not yet."

We were both quiet for a spell. The sun hung low in the darkening sky, halfway below the horizon, low clouds hiding it from view. The orange glow spread sideways across the water along the sky's edge. A lone sailboat quietly slipped through the water near the horizon.

"I'm glad you went to Rulio's funeral," I said. "And thanks for coming over."

"Yes, I am glad as well. I went to the range this morning and shot two hundred rounds. I feel much better."

Whatever works, I guess. Hate to think how many rounds it'd take if she were *really* upset.

"Did you notice that Rulio's girlfriend, Sandra Griffis, wasn't there?"

"Yes, I did."

I shook my head. "And she hasn't returned my calls, nor was she home when I stopped by her house." I finished my beer. "You said she remembered something about Rulio."

"Yes, that is what she said."

"No clue what it was?"

She shook her head. "I stopped at her house, but she was not home."

"According to the Andersons, she hasn't been to work either." I closed my eyes a moment. "This doesn't sound good."

She typed some stuff into her phone. "I made a note for tomorrow."

I rose to go after another beer. Arabella sprang to her feet and blocked my way. Face-to-face with her, in a low voice, as sultry as I could muster, I said, "You can help me with the Rulio case, Officer, if you're so inclined."

"Maybe, but right now I want to forget about all of that."

I snuggled in closer and embraced her. "You do?"

She flung her arms over my shoulders. "Yes. All I want to do for a while is concentrate on you."

Arabella always made perfect sense.

CHAPTER 23

THERE SHOULD BE a law—written, enacted upon, and regularly enforced—that declares it illegal to roust a retired guy living on a Caribbean island out of bed before nine o'clock AM. If there were such a law, Arabella would've broken it the next morning. But since she was an officer on the Bonaire Police Force, such a law probably wouldn't have mattered.

I relished having her back in my bed. Or was it *our* bed? Didn't matter. Everything was right with the world again and even her reacquisition of the bathroom seemed appropriate.

Except when she nudged me awake a little before seven to join her on a morning run.

"I thought you preferred to run in the evenings, after your shift," I said, eyes still closed.

"Yes, I do. But tonight, I will attend a workout class, so I need to run now." She pulled the pillow out from under my head. "Come, go with me."

I looked at the clock on the nightstand. "It's six forty-five."

"Yes, so we have only enough time for a short run." She pulled my legs sideways, so they plopped onto the floor. I lay half on the bed and half out. She rolled me off the mattress, determined to force me out of bed. She tossed my running shoes at me. "Time to go."

I found it difficult to say no to Arabella, so I relented and joined her for a five-kilometer—three-miles—run. Now, sitting at my office desk, nearly eight thirty in the morning, showered and dressed in a red Longtail T-shirt and my standard cargo shorts, I nursed some yogurt and alternated between a bottle of water and an iced-down glass of diet soda.

"You are up early this morning," Erika said, standing near the filing cabinet, head tilted forward just enough to peer at me over the rim of her glasses.

"Too early."

"My, are we not grumpy this morning." She stared at me a moment, and when I didn't acknowledge, she dropped some papers on her desk and sat in her chair.

I had told Erika to take as much time off work as she needed. Rulio's funeral was the previous day, and I didn't expect her back at the YellowRock so soon. But she said she needed to be at work, that it took her mind off everything.

Sandra Griffis hadn't attended the funeral. I hesitated to ask Erika what she thought about that, fearing it might cause her to start worrying about Sandra. Erika didn't need anything more to concern herself with.

"When I parked my car," Erika said, "I saw Miss Arabella leaving." She turned in my direction. "Is everything back to normal?"

"Is anything ever *normal* around here?"

She puffed out her chest and shot me a big-sister kind of look. "You know what I mean."

I sighed and let a smile creep across my face. But only a small one. Didn't want to give her too much satisfaction. "Yeah, I think so."

"Well then, good. You would miss her if she were gone."

"Yes, I would."

Erika turned back to her monitor but glanced in my direction every few moments. She typed away on the keyboard but fidgeted in her chair.

"What?" I asked.

"What?" she asked.

I sighed. "Something wrong?"

"I do not want to bother you," she said, which I guessed to be far from the truth. She'd never worried about bothering me before. She looked at the yogurt. "You are eating your breakfast."

I ate the last bit of yogurt and tossed the empty container in the trash. "All done, so what's on your mind?"

She swiveled in my direction and wheeled over to my desk. "Have you thought any more about Rulio?"

I sighed and slumped in my chair. "A little, but there isn't much to go on. I talked to the guy on Curacao, one of the divers involved with Rulio's accident, but I didn't get much from him. And I talked to David Brown at the hospital. He said that the leg was definitely removed with a hacking tool, like a hatchet."

I regretted mentioning the hatchet as soon as I said it. Erika's face contorted and tightened, her eyes watering. She still hadn't referred to Rulio as being murdered, and the image of his leg being whacked off took her by surprise.

I softened and lowered my voice, placing a hand on hers. "I'm still looking, but there isn't much to tell. Now that Arabella understands what I'm trying to do, she can help me with this. Soon hopefully, we'll make some progress."

Probably shouldn't have said *we*. Arabella and I hadn't discussed her helping me. Not seriously, anyway. As far as the police were concerned, this case had been placed on the back burner—not old enough to be considered a cold case, but certainly not top priority. Besides, she had said with Schleper out, her workload had increased. I assumed she'd be pressed for time with little available to help me. But if I knew Arabella, she wouldn't be able to resist making progress on a difficult case. It'd eat at her, as it would me, until she couldn't control herself and plunge neck deep into it.

Just as I had.

Barely perceptible, Erika nodded several times. "I understand." She wheeled back to her desk.

"Maybe you should take the day off. Go home."

"And do what?" She buried her face in her hands. "Think more about Rulio?" She patted the edges of her eyes with a tissue. "No, it is best I stay here and work."

"Okay, but if you change your mind, I understand."

She nodded. "And speaking of David Brown." She held out a pink slip of paper. "He called earlier this morning and left a message for you."

"What does it say?"

She shrugged. "I do not know. I did not read it."

I paused a short moment, then said, slowly, "But you *took* the message."

"Yes, but it is *your* message." Stern-faced, she jabbed her hand holding the message in my direction.

I shrugged and took the message and read it. David said he discovered some additional information about Rulio's leg and wanted to meet for lunch to discuss. He suggested a place called The Island Cantina in Rincon.

Erika stared at me. Obviously, she knew what David Brown had said.

I held up the pink slip of paper. "Maybe this is the break we've been waiting for. I'll know more after lunch."

She closed her eyes and let out a breath, then went back to her monitor. I had no idea what David may've discovered but hoped it'd move the case forward. I hated giving Erika any false hope, but she needed something to cling to. Besides, knowing Erika, she had already placed faith in that pink piece of paper long before handing it to me.

I saw it in her eyes.

CHAPTER 24

RINCON IS SITUATED ON the north side of Bonaire in an inland valley. It was established in the 16th century by the Spanish and is the oldest settlement on the island. The Island Cantina is a widely known, small restaurant operated by a local couple. They serve well-prepared traditional meals, including goat stew, and cold beer.

I could take either of two routes to Rincon. Both required the same amount of drive time, and I opted for the one that went past the Karpata dive site. I hadn't driven that road, or been past Karpata, since finding my friend Tiffany Wilcox there, drowned.

The one-lane road winds north along the sea and is a primary thoroughfare for divers and snorkelers seeking access to the northern dive sites. As such, tourists crossing the road, slowing to park, or meandering along the roadside taking in the scenic vista and views might slow my progress. But that'd be okay. Fast or slow, a drive along the sea was what I needed. Besides, being a few minutes late on Bonaire was the same as being on time.

I left the YellowRock and turned north onto Kaya Grandi. At the first side street, a rusty green tow truck almost blew through the Give Way sign—Bonaire's equivalent to a Yield sign—stopping partway into the intersection. I braked a bit and went on past. In the rearview mirror, I saw the tow truck turn onto Kaya Grandi and head north, the same as me.

Continuing north on Bulevar Gob. N. DeBroot and passing the Santa Barbara Crowns neighborhood, I considered stopping at Schleper's house for a chat, but Arabella's admonishment came to mind.

I do not think that to be a good idea.

So, I drove on.

Bulevar Gob. N. DeBroot made a ninety-degree right turn at the dive site Oil Slick Leap and became Queen's Highway, the official name of the coastal road. In front of me, beyond a narrow shoulder, the ground dropped off into the sea—no beach or gentle slope, just a twelve-to-fifteen-foot-cliff—hence the upcoming right-hand curve.

An instant after slowing to make the turn, a flash of green streaked across my rearview mirror. The Wrangler shuddered, lunged forward uncontrollably, and plowed across the small shoulder of cactus and weeds between the road and the drop-off. I stood on the brake pedal, but the Wrangler wouldn't stop.

I was being pushed from behind.

Toward the drop-off.

And the sea.

I'll never forget what happened next. Thoughts of death or the end of my existence didn't come to mind. Nor did the concept of my life flashing before my eyes.

None of that.

For the two seconds it took for the Wrangler to careen over the cliff and plunge headfirst into the sea below, my thoughts turned to a scene from the motion picture *An Officer and a Gentleman*. In the movie, Richard Gere and his fellow Naval Officer Cadets needed to prove they could egress from a submerged aircraft. The cadets were placed in a makeshift cockpit at the top of a large ramp that resembled a small roller coaster. The "cockpit" was then quickly pulled into the swimming pool below by a mechanism attached to the rail. After it settled on the bottom, the occupant had to unbuckle the seat belt, escape from the cockpit, and swim to the surface, all on a single breath of air.

Of course, dramatic music played, and a few of the cadets were unsuccessful, needing to be rescued by pool divers. All in all, I figured the movie producers embellished the scene to make it look more difficult than its real-life counterpart.

I'd seen the movie four or five times, and each time, after watching that scene, said to myself, "Yeah, I could do that. Doesn't look too hard."

It became apparent, as the Wrangler's front bumper punctured the water's surface, I was about to find out.

The airbag deployed, pinning me to the back of the seat with my arms in an upward position, making it impossible to reach the seatbelt buckle. With no doors, water rushed into the cabin, causing the Wrangler to begin sinking almost immediately. No momentary floating and bobbing on the surface while water trickled in through seams around the doors. I was going down fast.

Airbags are designed to deflate soon after deployment. But these didn't, probably having something to do with water pressure forcing the bag against my body. As the Wrangler filled, I felt the weight of the bags slowly easing. Several snorkelers from the nearby dive site, Oil Slick Leap, headed my way, but they weren't going to arrive before the Wrangler pulled me under.

I had practiced holding my breath many times, my personal best being just over two minutes. But that was in perfect conditions. Right now, my heart pounded as if it were going to jump out of my chest. I timed three large clearing breaths and one last deep breath a split second before I rode beneath the surface. I gazed upward, through the empty roof. It'd be an easy escape if I could get free of the airbag and unbuckle the seat belt.

The snorkelers arrived just as I went under. One of them plunged below holding onto the Jeep's roll bar. He fumbled with my seat belt, and after a moment, the tension released, but the airbag still had me pinned.

The Wrangler settled on the bottom at a depth of about twenty feet. Looking at it from the cabin of the Wrangler, the reef appeared different. Seawater stung my eyes, blurring my vision, and I didn't notice any of the corals or sea life. My mind raced for an answer, head swiveling back and forth, searching for something—anything—to help free myself. I was weakening, the urge to breathe becoming more and more overwhelming. As I watched the snorkeler bolt to the surface for his own breath of air, a sense of loneliness—deeper than I'd ever experienced—swept over me.

I was going to die, sitting upright in this Jeep, twenty feet below the surface of the Caribbean Sea.

Just as I had resigned myself to becoming a recovery mission, the airbag deflated. Not much, just a little. But it was all I needed. I squirmed back and forth, freeing myself and feeling a resurgence of strength and hope, and pushed off the floorboard and front seat. Rays of sunlight streaked the water as I rocketed through the top of the Wrangler, swimming upward, and breached the surface, gasping for air.

Three snorkelers rushed to my side.

"You all right, mister?" one said.

I nodded, thanked them, and looked up at the cliff, where, ninety seconds ago, I had been. I put my head in the water, opened my eyes, and made out the blurry yellow outline of the Wrangler, peacefully resting on the bottom.

It was toast. Ruined.

"Need help getting to the ladder?" someone asked.

The Oil Slick Leap dive site is along a rocky cliff. As such, it's one of the few dive sites on the island that has a ladder hanging into the water to allow divers easy access in and out of the sea.

I assessed myself. No broken bones and I didn't see or taste any blood. One massive headache, though.

"Thanks, but I'm okay," I said to the guy and started swimming toward the ladder.

A moment later, someone appeared at the ledge. He yelled down, "Hey, I see who do this. I will follow them and see where they go."

It took me a moment to realize what he meant. "No! Wait!" I yelled back. "Stay there. Don't do anything."

But it was too late. The guy either didn't hear my plea or simply ignored it. He gave a wave, got in his rusted white sedan, and drove up the road. As fast as I could, I swam to the ladder and climbed up. I told someone standing near a truck holding a towel to call the police as I took off up the road in a sprint, drenched and wearing sandals.

I had gone a few hundred yards when three gunshots rang out, stopping me momentarily in my tracks. Most people wouldn't recognize the sound of a handgun when fired outdoors. In the open, they make extraordinarily little noise, especially a small caliber, like a nine-millimeter. But I knew all too well what they sounded like. Indoors or out.

This *pop-pop . . . pop* was from a small-caliber firearm.

And I knew who had just been shot.

Another hundred yards of running and I came to the tow truck, parked in front of a rusty white sedan, the driver's-side door open. The driver of the sedan lay spread-eagle on the pavement, staring at the blue Bonaire sky. His mouth open, a pool of blood had formed under his shoulders.

I wanted to check on him and help, if possible, but knew I needed to clear the scene first. The "+1" Rule assumes there's always one more bad guy lurking about. I'd never cleared a scene without a weapon, but I needed to know the area was secure. Better to find out now than be surprised in a few moments.

I made my way over to the tow truck. With senses on high alert, I peered inside. If things were going to get worse, it'd be at that moment. But the cab was empty. I completed a cursory search of the area but didn't see anyone or anything, so I went back to the body.

As suggested by the *pop-pop . . . pop*, the entry wounds looked to be small caliber. Probably nine-millimeter. Two wounds to the chest and one to the forehead.

The headshot wasn't required. The *double tap* to the midsection would've dropped the victim and led to a quick bleed-out. However, that wasn't good enough for the killer. Cold and heartless, he must've walked up to the terrified driver and stood over him.

Then, while staring into his frightened eyes, put a bullet in his head.

Although I knew there wouldn't be one, I knelt and placed my fingers on the guy's throat, feeling for a pulse. His eyes, open and staring skyward, held an emptiness I'd seen before. The lack of blood circulation caused light to reflect differently off a dead person's eyes, giving them a hollow, far-off, empty stare. Absolutely no movement, either. No twitches, breathing, or blinking. And no sound, which always struck me as odd about homicide scenes. The silence. Normally, I'd hear the things around me—the birds, the ocean, boats passing, and other random noises. But looking at this poor guy lying in the road, I heard nothing. Just the throbbing of my heart through the veins in my ears.

The Bonaire wind blew across the scene, but the salt air couldn't hide the pungent stench of the pooled blood. The coppery scent stung my olfactory lobes. Maybe the smell wasn't there at all. Just my imagination, a mental reminder, involuntarily called up from the recesses of my brain to complete the scene. Make it whole.

Kneeling beside the guy, I flicked away a few lizards vying for position around the blood. He had been someone's son. Maybe a husband; a father; a brother.

"Why would you do that?" I asked the guy, knowing I wouldn't get an answer. "Chase after someone like that. Why?" I wasn't mad at him; I was mad at the tow truck driver, the person I assumed killed this poor guy. Murder is never justified, and in this case, even more so. This guy was trying to perform a random act of kindness, helping locate the person who ran me off the road.

And his kindness cost him his life.

I stood and used my forearm to wipe sweat from my brow.

Sirens screamed from down the road, approaching fast.

I bowed my head over the dead Good Samaritan and let out a long breath.

* * *

Naturally, Arabella took it upon herself to be one of the responding officers, quickly taking control of both scenes—the murder and my Jeep recovery. Although she believed my insistence of sobriety, procedure called for me to have blood drawn for verification. As soon as I had given brief statements regarding the accident and the murder, an officer whisked me away to the hospital. My head still pounded, but their main concern was whether I'd been drinking.

The doctor at the emergency room diagnosed a mild concussion, probably from my head hitting the airbag as it inflated, and gave me a prescription for painkillers, if necessary. Currently, I sat in a chair outside the Priklab—the laboratory area of Hospital San Francisco—waiting my turn to have blood drawn. A young officer sat next to me. He'd been assigned to make sure I did the blood draw and that I didn't do anything to taint the results.

The name tag on the officer's uniform read *Officer Soliana*. He instructed me to call him *Jos*. I couldn't be certain, but he may've been one of the officers who first responded to Rulio's leg washing ashore. I didn't ask, figuring it best not to appear as trying to derive any information from young Officer Soliana.

My cellphone had been in my pocket when I went into the sea. I tried powering it on, but nothing happened.

Time for a new cellphone.

The police said they'd have my Wrangler pulled out of the water and transported to a maintenance facility, but I held little hope of it being repairable. Every piece of circuitry must've been dowsed with saltwater. Too many damaged sensors and computers. Not to mention water in the fuel, lubricant, and transmission systems.

Time for a new Wrangler.

Earlier, my shirt had dried while standing in the sun, explaining to the police what had happened. Now, sitting in the swelter of the hospital corridor, it was again soaked. Only this time from sweat. Jos's uniform clung to his body as well.

The phlebotomist finally called my name and Jos followed me across the hall, into a small room, and behind a curtain. I relented to having a needle stuck in my arm and watched as blood gurgled into a glass tube. Afterwards, Jos and I shook hands, exchanged a few pleasantries, and parted ways.

A beer sounded good right now, and Vinny's was an easy stroll from the hospital, some of it along the ocean.

As I walked down the hallway of the hospital headed for the exit, someone called my name. I turned and saw David Brown. With everything that had happened, I'd completely forgotten about our lunch plans in Rincon.

He strode in my direction.

"I thought that was you," he said. "What brings you to the hospital?"

Not the greeting I had expected. "Had a mild car accident. Just getting checked out."

"Hope everything is all right."

"No worries, I'm fine." I paused a moment, examining his demeanor.

"Whew . . . I've been here since seven this morning. Got called in to cover for someone else." He looked at his wristwatch. "I'm out of here in thirty minutes."

He called earlier this morning and left a message for you.

"You've been here all day?"

"Yeah, and for a part-timer like myself, that's a real bitch." He rubbed the back of his neck. "I haven't even taken a lunch break. My name is on a sandwich waiting for me at home." He slapped me on the arm with the files he carried. "Stop by sometime. And bring that beer with you." He walked back in the direction he had come, giving a short wave over his shoulder.

"Hey, David," I said. "One more thing."

He turned back to me. "Yeah?"

"Did you call me this morning?"

"What?"

"I had a message that you wanted to get together for lunch."

He shook his head. "Nope, wasn't me. But it's a good idea."

I slowly nodded.

"And call me," he said, turning and continuing down the hall.

I watched him walk away, unable to move.

CHAPTER 25

I CHANGED MY mind about the beer.

Although Vinny's was closer, I hailed a cab and, after a quick stop at my apartment for a change of clothes, went to Paradise Cove.

I walked in and sat at the bar. John came over and asked what I needed.

"A beer and a phone," I said.

He signaled Lucas to get me a beer, then handed me his cellphone. "Please, use this to make your call."

I took the phone. "Thanks." I called Arabella.

"How is your head?" she asked.

"Doing better now. Having a beer."

"Vinny's?"

"No. Paradise Cove."

She was quiet for a moment. Lucas tried to engage me in another one of his stare-down contests, but I didn't participate, choosing instead to swivel the barstool and gaze at the sea while chatting with Arabella.

"I'll need a ride home later," I said.

"I will be off soon and come right there."

"Good, but give me some time. I want to hang around here for a while."

"Uh-huh," she said. "Be careful." Then, I could almost hear her smile through the phone. "By the way, Lucas's last name is Walker."

I tried not to laugh. The name *Lucas Walker* couldn't be real. But considering what I knew of him and his buddy John, I wouldn't be surprised to find out Lucas's middle name was *Sky*.

"How'd you find out?" I asked.

"I went to immigration and found his passport. He has not applied for residency, so I assume he's on the island as a six-month visitor."

She referred to the fact that Bonaire visitors can stay on the island for up to six months without a visa, work permit, or applying for residency.

"Also," she continued, "there is no employment records for him, so whatever he is doing at Paradise Cove is—what do you call it?—under the table."

Lucas is like this little puppy dog, with a weird, unyielding devotion to John.

"And, Conklin," she continued, "he arrived on the island *after* Rulio went missing. He couldn't have been involved."

"Well, at least not with Rulio, but possibly other things."

"Yes, possibly."

"Okay, thanks. I'll be watching for you."

John had walked away, so I laid the phone on the bar. Lucas hadn't taken his eyes off me since I'd walked in, but his one-sided stare-down contest broke when he took a cell call of his own.

Above the tables, the canvas canopy whipped and popped in the breeze, forcing the plastic support poles to bend back and forth, absorbing the stress. Drinks in hand, a few tourists strolled along the small pier, sporadically looking over the rail and pointing at the water.

Mounted in a wooden frame I hadn't noticed previously, a painting of a sailboat hung on the opposite wall from the bar area. It looked to be a rendition of the vessel moored beyond the pier, with the name *Dream Crusher* scrolled across the stern.

I pointed at the artwork and asked Lucas, "Is that the same boat as the one moored by the pier?"

Hair loose down his back and over his shoulders, he didn't say anything, preferring instead to readjust his cowboy hat.

"You don't say much, do you?"

"Yes," I heard John say from behind me. "It's the same boat." I didn't turn around and he came into my field of vision as he picked up his cell phone from the bar. "Is there anything else you need?"

"Not that I can think of. Maybe another beer, depending on when my ride gets here."

John pointed at my open beer. "I think you should leave after this one."

Lucas leaned over the bar, again giving me a focused stare, his eyes narrowing.

I turned up the bottle and drank the last of the beer, then sat the empty on the bar. "Okay, have it your way." I stood to leave.

Danielle came through the kitchen doors, smiled broadly when she saw me, and came in my direction.

"Hey, R. I didn't know you were here." She looked me up and down. "You aren't leaving, are you?"

"Yes," John said. "He's leaving."

She gave John a sideways glance. "No, he's *not* leaving. I haven't had a chance to talk with him yet." She turned back to me. "Please have another beer and let's chat."

"No," John said. "He's leaving."

Danielle snapped her head in his direction, lips tight, eyes cutting holes in him. "John!" She paused a moment and when she continued, her tone was softer, almost condescending. "R and I are going to chat. Besides, that's no way to treat someone who recently saved your life."

I wondered whether I had really saved John's life during the snorkel trip or if it might've been some sort of ruse. When Arabella and I had dinner here, John contradicted the incident and mentioned how, as a kid, he had boated and swam at Paradise Cove in Malibu.

Danielle sat on a stool and motioned for me to do the same. She pounded her finger on the bar twice. "Lucas, a Bright for R and some wine for me."

Lucas looked at John.

"Lucas!" Danielle said. "Don't look at *him*. I need some wine and R needs a beer."

Lucas complied, then went through the doors into the kitchen. One of his henchmen—a Penguin brother from the other night—came out to tend the bar. John went around the corner and piano music began playing. Danielle took a healthy sip of her wine.

"I apologize for that," Danielle said. She rolled her eyes. "John always says 'Walk into every room as though you're James Bond.'"

"Yeah, so I've heard."

She frowned a moment, then took a sip of wine. "Anyway, those two tend to get carried away."

Danielle was beginning to remind me of my old friend Tiffany Wilcox. They both treated people well and had a wonderful presence about themselves. They seemed to genuinely like people and everyone responded positively to them.

"No worries." I raised my Bright. "Thanks for the beer."

She gave a dismissive wave. "Like I said before, Luke and John back each other up all the time. Mostly, John treats Lucas like shit, even though Lucas saved John's life one time."

A lot of that going around, I thought.

She continued, "Lucas said that John was like family to him and that's what family does."

"How did he save John's life?"

Another dismissive wave. "Oh, that doesn't matter." She raised her chin, as if looking down her nose at me. "So, R, since you saved John's life as well, that makes *you* part of our family."

"Your family?"

"Yes." Eyes wide, she leaned forward. "How does that sound?"

At that moment, Arabella walked through the door and over to the spot at the bar where Danielle and I sat.

"My ride's here," I said. I finished the beer and stood. "Thanks."

"R, please think about it," Danielle said.

"Sure, I will."

Arabella and I walked out of Paradise Cove and got into her Toyota sedan.

"What was she saying?" Arabella asked. "What are you supposed to think about?"

"Danielle invited me to be part of their family."

"Their family? What is the meaning of that?"

"I'm not sure, but I have my suspicions."

CHAPTER 26

RELAXING IN MY hammock the following afternoon, I watched nearby palm trees sway with the breeze and listened to the waves from across the street. Late afternoon and the road in front of the YellowRock pulsed with traffic. Tourists and locals alike doing whatever it is they needed to do. I held a beer in my hands, cradled in my lap, condensation pooling on the bottom of my T-shirt. The hammock gently rocked back and forth.

Perched high up the trunk of a tree between the YellowRock and the building next door, an iguana basked in the shade beneath the canopy of palm leaves. After all these years on Bonaire, this was the first time I'd seen one in a tree. I knew the locals referred to iguanas as *tree chickens*, but I had never experienced the reason for the moniker. I glanced out at the pier across the street, then back at the iguana resting in the treetop. All iguanas look the same to me, so I couldn't determine whether it was Charlie.

I chastised myself for not putting on some music before climbing into the hammock. Never loud enough to drown out the traffic or the waves, just background stuff, barely discernable. I'd remedy that on my next trip to the fridge.

I had spent the morning acquiring a new cellphone, a much more advanced model than my old one. This one had lots of features and gizmos, most of which I'd probably never use. I chuckled to myself picturing the number of hours it'd take Arabella to train me on this new gadget.

Since the Wrangler was out of commission, I also swung by a local vehicle rental agency. They were rented out, but promised to have one available the next day, which they'd bring by. I told them not to worry about the type; I just needed wheels.

Lastly, I made a stop at the police station. Earlier this morning, an officer called and said there were still a few details to be finalized. Nothing serious—just reaffirming my time statements, the route I had taken north, what I saw before and after the collision, anything I could remember about the tow truck driver, and a description of the scene when I came upon the Good Samaritan. Pretty standard stuff. I'd been on the other side of that table many times. They wanted to make sure today's story matched the one from yesterday.

While at the station, I watched for Arabella as I walked the halls but didn't see her. No Schleper, either, which wasn't a huge surprise.

He is at home and does not return phone calls.

My head and body still ached, the adrenaline from yesterday's exploits having worn off during the night. I rolled my shoulder, the way Arabella had done after our swim a few days ago. Can't fall fifteen feet into the sea strapped to a Jeep without getting a little banged up.

My mind drifted back to the vision of the Good Samaritan lying on his back, lifeless eyes staring at the Bonaire sky. The worst thing about being around a lot of brutal crime is the tendency to become used to it. Sad to say, in the heyday of my career, I'd become accustomed to the staleness of death, the smell of blood, the devastation of murder. Seeing the bullet holes in that man's chest and head reminded me how numb to violence I'd been all those years as a cop. Yesterday proved most of that numbness had eroded away.

Loaded with tanks and divers, a boat from one of the island's larger operations motored past, halfway between Klein Bonaire and Bonaire, headed toward one of the southern sites. Maybe Tori's Reef, the last place I had spent any time with my old friend Tiffany. Because of everything that had happened yesterday, I never made it to Karpata, the site of her death. That was the reason I had chosen to drive up the coastal road in the first place.

As I rose to get another beer and put on some music, Arabella came up the stairs dressed in her full *Polis* uniform. She laid a brown paper bag on the table, along with an additional six-pack of beer.

"I need to change," she said, headed for the bedroom. She pointed at the bag. "Piska kriyoyo and baka stoba."

Dinner.

Piska kriyoyo is a creole-style fish, pan seared and served with a spicy tomato sauce. Baka stoba is a goat stew. The bag also contained several slices of funchi, the island's version of cornbread.

I had the food plated by the time Arabella came out of the bedroom. She wore a black T-shirt. Any color looks great on Arabella, but black is especially enticing. White letters on the shirt said *So Many Guns, So Little Time*. She carried an issue of *Guns and Ammo* magazine.

We took our food to the veranda and sat at a small table against the wall. Arabella dug into the piska kriyoyo, while I let the lava-hot baka stoba cool. A couple of chibi-chibi birds landed on the railing, hoping for a handout. I tossed some crumbs of funchi over the edge and they dove out of sight to retrieve them. A few short moments later, they flew back and resumed their perch on the railing.

Arabella handed the magazine to me, opened to a page in the middle. "You ever shoot one of these?"

I perused the one-page article. "A Makarov? No, I never have." I handed the magazine back to her. "But I've heard of them. Small, Soviet-made, semi-auto pistol."

"Yes. Might make a good backup piece. The cartridge seems strange, though. Says here it is basically a nine-millimeter with a shorter brass." She paused, then dropped a hint. "Might be fun to own one."

I would have loved to have surprised her with a Makarov, maybe as an upcoming birthday gift, but firearms were highly regulated on Bonaire, and it'd be nearly impossible for a foreigner to have one shipped here. Especially a handgun manufactured by the former Soviet Union.

I ignored the suggestion and blew on a spoonful of baka stoba. "Don't you already own three or four handguns?"

"Hey." She pointed at her T-shirt.

I nodded and ate the spoonful of stew.

"Any thoughts about yesterday?" I asked.

She let out a long breath. "Not many. It definitely was no accident."

"If it were an accident, most people would stop and try to help out. Not drive away."

"Yes, and then also kill someone."

My stomach turned at the thought of an innocent bystander being killed. Especially when he was trying to do something nice—*for me.* I laid my spoon down, suddenly unable to eat. I took a swig of beer. "Who was the Good Samaritan?"

"A local man who lived in Rincon, on his way home from work."

On his way home from work. All choices come with consequences, some of them unintended. Sometimes, those consequences can put a person in harm's way. The Good Samaritan made a choice between two routes to take that day, and maybe, like me, he chose Queens Highway—the coastal road—because he wanted to gaze at the sea for a while. If either of us had chosen the other route, he would still be alive.

If...

"Speaking of Rincon," Arabella said, "you were headed there?"

"Yeah, to have lunch with David Brown." I balked at telling her about the supposed message from Brown that got me headed toward Rincon, but decided she needed to know.

No more secrets.

After my explanation, her cheeks and neck flushed, and her breathing stopped for a split second. "So, the message was a possible setup? To get you going to Rincon?"

"Seems that way."

"But who? And how would they know you might take the Queens Highway?"

"Good questions."

We were both quiet for a moment. Arabella's plate was clean, only a few stray fish bones and a lemon peel amongst a thin film of tomato sauce. A small commuter plane flew overhead, clawing for altitude, destined for Curacao, the drone of its engine audible a few moments before the plane came into view.

"He have any family?" I asked.

"Yes. A wife and five children." She wiped a tear from the corner of her eye.

I shook my head. The stew was cooling, but I'd lost my appetite. The chibi-chibi birds still patrolled the railing.

"Any leads?" I asked.

"The truck was stolen. Hopefully, some forensics will be gotten from it. We are also investigating local video cameras."

Video cameras outside of businesses were becoming more common on Bonaire, however, the island still contained many dark spots.

"I want to catch that person," she said. "Badly! *Verdomde klootzak.*"

I stared at her.

"*Fucking asshole,*" she said.

I smiled. "Only you can make those words sound so sweet."

She ignored my attempted levity, hitting me with a stare. "I had to tell his wife." She closed her eyes and pinched the bridge of her nose.

My thoughts drifted back to a few weeks ago when I had to tell Erika about Rulio. Arabella had only delivered that type of news once in her career, and it had affected her then the same as it did now.

Those conversations can't be done over the phone, by email, or social media. They must be delivered person to person. Face-to-face verifies the correct person gets the message and it's not some kind of cruel joke.

In some instances, the death notification can be used as an opportunity to further an investigation, asking questions and gathering information. But in this situation, there'd be no point. This guy wasn't involved with anything. Just a regular person coming home from work, seeing what he thought was an accident, and trying to do the right thing.

"When does telling someone about death get easier?" she asked, eyes reddening.

The face of every person I'd ever given a death notice to flashed through my mind, Erika being the most recent. I breathed in some air, let it out slowly, then took a swig of beer.

"It never does," I said.

CHAPTER 27

THE NEXT DAY, I met Chuck for lunch at a food truck near the police station, eating burgers and fries on a rickety picnic table. We watched as a few police trucks came and went.

Chuck squirmed and continuously rubbed the back of his neck. When he knocked over his beer, I asked, "What's your problem?"

He glanced sideways at several policemen walking out the door of the building. "Not sure I like being this close. They could come right out and grab me."

"It's a small island. They can grab you anywhere, here or farther away."

He bounced his knee rapidly. "Have you found anything yet? Anything that can help me?"

I chewed on some burger and stared at my fries. Not sure it'd be wise to disclose anything Arabella had told me. Not that she had told me much, anyway.

His head swiveled in all directions. "How come you chose this place?"

"Chuck, it'll be fine. Your best defense is that you didn't do it."

He leaned closer to me, over the table. "But what about the prints?"

I needed to consider my answer carefully. "Probably don't have to worry about that."

"Why?"

"Well . . . you said you never touched the speargun, so how could they have your prints?"

His eyebrows scrunched and he got a far-off look on his face. After a moment, he said, "Yeah, you're right. No way my prints are on that gun."

"See? There you go."

"Hey . . . Do you know something you're not telling me? What did Arabella tell you?"

I shook my head. "Chuck—"

Before I could finish, my new cellphone rang. It was David Brown.

"Hey, R," David said. "I had a strange visitor a few minutes ago. Thought you might want to hear about it."

"Okay, sure." I rose and walked away from the picnic table.

"A guy came to my house, asking questions about the leg that washed ashore."

"What kind of questions?"

"Things like, what did we know? Have we discovered anything? What could I tell him? Stuff like that."

"What *did* you tell him?"

"That since I did not work the case, I knew very little. All I told him was public knowledge items." He paused a moment, and I didn't press him. "It was confusing why he wanted to talk to me."

"What'd he look like?"

"About your height, black hair, long and in a ponytail. Wore a black T-shoirt with no sleeves. And, as strange as it sounds, a cowboy hat."

Skywalker.

"He say anything else?" I asked.

"Yeah, and get this: he said he was an undercover FBI agent investigating a case."

"An FBI agent?"

"Well . . . he showed me a badge. I had never seen an FBI badge before."

"He mention what he's investigating?"

"All he said was that it had to do with two murders, the leg being involved in one of them. He came across real cool. Seemed to know what the hell he was talking about."

"Why'd he come to *you* with these questions?" I asked.

"Something about needing my help to tie up a few loose ends." His voice cracked. "R, I hope you haven't gotten me into some bad shit."

"Nothing to worry about." He was quiet a beat. "Anything else for me?"

Sounded like a lot of info for a fed to disclose. Especially one undercover.

After a brief pause, he said, "Hey, R, I was thinking about that wire. You ever get it analyzed?"

"What?"

"The wire wrapped around the ankle. When we talked before, I suggested you get it analyzed."

"Oh . . . Yeah." I remembered him saying the coroner wouldn't analyze it, but I didn't remember him suggesting having it done. He said it'd be the responsibility of the police department.

"R, metal alloy can be broken down to identify a signature," he said. "It's almost like DNA. Every batch can be identified by its unique compound makeup."

I'd need to check with Arabella. She hadn't mentioned anything about it, but it was a lead that needed closing. "I'll check on it. Thanks."

We disconnected. I worried that even if we could somehow identify the wire, it'd be nearly impossible to track down its origin. Must be tons of that wire type manufactured and distributed around the world. But the wire was a loose end and needed to be tied up.

Chuck still sat at the picnic table, head swiveling, fidgeting like a twelve-year-old at the doctor's office.

"Chuck, there's a phone call I need to make."

"I'm out of here, anyway. I'll catch you later." He cleaned his trash on the table, headed for his truck, and waved as he drove off.

I walked toward the YellowRock and dialed the Rockford, Illinois, Police Department on my new phone. When I purchased the service, I'd opted for an international package.

I asked the operator for Larry Penn, an old buddy from my time on the job.

"Penn!" he answered on the second ring with a hint of irritation in his voice.

"Having a bad day?"

"Who is this?" He paused. I didn't say anything. "Is this Conklin?"

"How are you, Larry David?" He liked to be called by his first and middle names. Some sort of ancient, southern tradition. At least that's what he told people, mainly attractive women.

"How the hell are you, R?"

"Doing well, living the dream. Can I hit you up for a favor?"

"Why is it you always want something? Maybe once, you'd call and just say hi."

"You're right. I'm sorry, but I still need a favor."

I heard a hard breath through the phone. "Okay, what do you need?"

"You still have that contact at the DOJ?"

"Yeah, I know a guy."

"Can you check on an FBI agent?"

"What kind of mess you into now?"

"That's the thing. Not sure. I need to find out if one Lucas Walker is actually an FBI agent."

He said the name to himself, as if he were writing it down. "Hold on a second." I heard some keyboard clicks. "Well, that doesn't help." Another pause. "Just googled him. Came back with three hundred and twenty-eight million hits. Then I googled *Lucas Walker FBI* and got over four million hits." Another sigh. "I guess I'll need to call."

"There's a possible problem. He claims to be working undercover."

"If that's true, I may not be able to get anything."

"Understood. I appreciate anything you can do."

We talked a few more minutes. He wanted to fill me in on the status and gossip regarding folks I used to work with who were still with the department. As Larry David droned on, I walked along the sea, coming up to the YellowRock from the south. Watching the boats moored along the reef roll with the waves, listening to the laughs of the tourists, and the wind blowing through the palm trees, I realized my life and Penn's life were completely different. We had chosen different paths, and, of the two of us, I was the luckier.

"Well, I have to go," he said as I came to the office door of the YellowRock. "Got a murder investigation to push forward."

After we disconnected, I thought about what he had said.

Got a murder investigation to push forward.

Maybe we weren't on such different paths, after all. I had two murder investigations to *push forward.*

Three, counting the Good Samaritan.

CHAPTER 28

I WALKED THROUGH the now smooth-operating door into the YellowRock office.

"You have a visitor," Erika said, pumping a thumb at my desk.

Lucas Walker slouched in a chair, one of his legs hanging over the edge of my desk. Face stern, he locked his dark eyes on me as I walked in that direction. His tan Stetson laid on its crown, upside down, on a stack of dusty papers.

I stopped at the edge of my desk and shoved his leg to the floor.

"Manners," I said.

He remained stoic for a moment, then smiled and repositioned a little, eventually sitting up straight. I sat at my chair, leaned forward, and rested my elbows on the desk. Erika texted on her phone.

His smile gone, Lucas and I stared at each other for a few moments, giving me time for a ten count. I didn't want to be the first to speak, but I also didn't want this to drag out indefinitely. Erika pretended to study her monitor, but I knew she paid close attention.

This was the first time I'd truly studied his face, taking interest in his eyes. He didn't look away, so I concentrated on them.

During my years as a violent crimes detective, I had sat across the table from a lot of bad people and tried to decide if they were killers. I can say with certainty: they never looked any different from anyone else. They might've had a rough face with a thousand-yard stare, or they might've come across as unthreatening with kind eyes and a gentle touch. Some were street-hardened by the violence of inner cities, but many who grew up in suburban neighborhoods had the same look, neither type necessarily being killers.

They were regular people with regular faces.

The hard truth was, given the right circumstances, everyone was capable of anything when pushed to the brink. Some people were willing to step up and defend themselves, their families, and those who are not so capable, and that sometimes meant killing. Most people would be surprised, when pushed to the brink, how disturbingly easy it was to take a human life.

Everyone has their line.

Did Lucas Walker have the eyes of a killer? No way to tell. He looked like a regular person.

Curiosity finally got the best of me and I gave in. "Why are you here?"

His smile returned. "I need something from you." When I didn't say or do anything, he continued. "I know you think I killed that woman, but I didn't." He leaned forward. "I need you to believe that."

I eased back in my chair but didn't say anything, even though I did believe him. Mostly.

He sighed and continued. "But I think I know who did kill her. I just need more time to prove it."

I reached into the small fridge behind my desk and took out a Bright. I opened the bottle and flipped the cap into the trash. I didn't offer him one.

"There's more here than you understand," he said. "And, believe me, you don't want to get involved."

I took a swig of beer and sat the bottle on the desk. Erika walked over and stood next to the filing cabinet, alternating her attention between watching out the window and glancing at her cellphone. Lucas kept his attention on me.

"I know you wore a badge," he said. "I'm telling you this out of brotherhood."

I barked a short laugh, tipping my head sideways. "Brotherhood?"

He looked at Erika, then back at me. "I'm an FBI agent."

Immediately, I knew Lucas wasn't with the FBI. I'd worked a few cases alongside FBI guys and had grown to know their lingo: their communication style. They never said anything akin to "I'm an FBI agent." Usually, it's something more like, "I'm with the Bureau."

I'd been waiting for him to mention it and had a response prepared.

"What?" I said.

"I've been undercover for several years working on a case. I can't have it blown now. Especially by you."

I'd heard a lot of stories in my life, but this one may've taken the cake. I studied Lucas's face. He was either telling the truth or was an incredibly good liar. And I'd seen a lot of good liars in my past. I considered again whether he might've taken some acting classes.

"Prove it," I said.

"Prove it?"

"Yeah, let me see your badge or credentials. Something to validate your claim."

He repositioned in his seat. "Well . . . I don't have them *on* me." He repositioned again and I waited. "But I can get them later."

"Sure, you do that. What field office do you work out of?"

"Well . . . I'm not at liberty to say."

"Why not?"

He leaned over the desk. "Have you ever worked undercover?" I hadn't so I didn't reply. "That's what I thought. If you had, you'd understand."

I paused a moment, feeling my face flush. "What's the case?" He didn't answer and we stared at each other. Eventually, I shrugged, and with as much sarcasm as I could muster, said, "Maybe, out of *brotherhood*, I can help."

He shook his head. "No, you can't be involved. And you have to keep this quiet."

Tessa came to mind. Regardless of whether I believed him or not, the last time I kept something quiet, a woman died.

Before I responded, Erika walked out the office door. Through the window, I saw her speak with Arabella. A moment later, Arabella came into the office, followed by the officer who escorted me to the hospital several days ago, Officer Soliana.

Jos.

She and I exchanged nods.

Arabella approached Lucas while Jos remained by the door. Erika stayed outside.

I forgot what I was about to say to Lucas, but it had become unimportant. Instead, I leaned back in the chair, fingers laced behind my head with my elbows pointed out, thumping my feet onto the desk. Too bad I didn't have some popcorn. There was about to be a show.

Arabella looked down at Lucas. "Is there a problem here?"

"No problem, Officer," I said. "Agent Walker was just leaving."

Lucas snapped his head in my direction, eyes narrowed, jaw tight.

Arabella hadn't known about Lucas calling himself an FBI agent, but, like a true pro, didn't hint to any surprise on her part. "Then my job will be easy." She pointed at the door. "Agent Walker."

Lucas rose, but took his time doing so. Gripping his hat by the brim, he put it on his head, wiggling it a little, adjusting the fit. He pointed a finger at me. "You're getting in way over your head, asshole."

"I scuba dive," I said. "I'm in over my head all the time."

"Sir," Arabella said, exaggerating her hand pointing at the door.

Lucas put his hand on Arabella's shoulder. "Officer, please under—"

Arabella slapped his hand away. Jos took two steps forward and rested a hand on his sidearm.

Wide-eyed, Lucas stepped back. Arabella moved up to him and put her fist in his chest. "For your own safety, you should never put a hand on me." She pointed at the door again. "Leave . . . Now!"

Lucas looked at me, then at Jos, then at Arabella. He smirked, then moved around Arabella and headed for the door.

"Officer Soliana will see you out," Arabella said.

Jos held the door open and Lucas walked out of the office as Erika came back in. Jos remained outside, standing guard near the window as Lucas crossed the street and strolled down the sidewalk, glancing once over his shoulder at the YellowRock.

I said to Erika, "Now I know who you were texting."

"I do not like that man," she said.

"Don't worry about him. He's too pathetic to worry about," I said.

"Erika texted me before you arrived," Arabella said. "Then she texted that you are here, but Jos and I decided to come anyway."

"You did the right thing," I said to Erika.

"Yes," Arabella said. "That is why I say to call me anytime." Then she said to me, "Why did you call him Agent Walker?"

"He said he's an FBI agent, working undercover, presumably on some big case."

"You are joking."

"Nope. Said he'd been working on it for years and I was about to ruin it."

"What case?"

"He wouldn't say."

As far as I knew, Lucas spent most of his time at Paradise Cove with the Andersons. Didn't seem as though he had a lot of time to work on a case. Unless the Andersons were working on the case with him. Maybe the whole Paradise Cove business was a front and part of the investigation. Sounded far-fetched.

"Does the FBI work outside of the States?" Arabella asked.

"That's another interesting point. I've only worked with them a few times, and never with an undercover agent or an agent working on foreign soil. I think they're allowed to work overseas, but only after notifying the local law enforcement agencies."

"I do not know of any such notification, but I will find out."

"That'd be helpful."

"I do not believe him," Erika chimed in. "That man does not have the dignity."

Not sure *dignity* was the word she intended to use, but I understood what she meant. I took a sip of beer. I didn't offer one to Arabella. She was in uniform.

"For one," I said, "people working undercover never openly admit it. Especially to a civilian like me. Or David Brown."

"David Brown?" Arabella asked. "From the hospital?"

"That's him."

"Why would he tell David Brown?"

Lucas must've suspected David had given me information about Rulio's leg. But what led him to that conclusion? I hadn't told anyone about our conversation, and I was sure David hadn't either.

Arabella's question was the zinger. As Schleper might say, it had put me in a *pickle*. David had no reason to be involved until I called him, asking specifics about the leg.

No more secrets.

I needed to come clean with Arabella and tell her about my chat with David.

"I called the hospital and talked with David," I said. I looked at Erika for a moment, then down at my desk. "I asked him some questions about Rulio's leg."

Erika put a hand over her mouth and sat, shoulders slumped.

Arabella's jaw went tight, her eyes narrowing at me. "Why did you do that?"

She knew I'd continue investigating. We had discussed it. I slowly raised my head, wanting to remind her of that conversation, but quickly closed my mouth before saying anything.

She tapped her foot several times and folded her arms across her chest. "And what did he tell you?"

"Nothing we didn't already know." I looked at Erika. "I'm sorry." She stared at me for a moment, then returned to her monitor.

Arabella's posture relaxed. "Okay, I will find out more about *Agent* Walker."

I didn't mention to her I had already asked Larry Penn, my buddy on the Rockford Police force, to do the same.

"I will see you in a few hours, when I am off duty," Arabella said as she went through the door. She and Jos walked toward their police ride, parked on the other side of the street.

Erika placed a hand on Rulio's picture and wiped her eyes with a tissue. "I do not think I will ever know what happened to Rulio."

I didn't say it, but I shared her concern.

CHAPTER 29

Arabella and I sat on opposite sides of an outdoor table at the Coral Reef Café. She had the day off and, after a morning swim, we had walked the four blocks up Kaya C.E.B. Hellmund, the road that passed in front of the YellowRock, for a late-morning breakfast.

Across the street, men worked on the city pier, the large commercial pier that serviced supply vessels, military ships, and cruise boats. Two tugs maneuvered toward open sea, headed for a cruise ship positioned on the other side of Klein Bonaire. It'd soon dock and flood the business district with tourists.

Arabella didn't care for cruise ship tourists. Barely tolerated them. Whenever she referred to them, her nose crinkled, and she used the term "cruiser."

"*Ach*," she said. "After I eat, I will stay away from downtown."

I munched on some mango. "Any plans today?"

"I will relax, maybe go to Ruth's and see her."

That would leave me out, at least during the Ruth trip. Arabella had said after the swim that she looked forward to getting away from the madness for a day. Rulio; Tessa; the Good Samaritan. She didn't want to even *think* about them.

Her cell phone rang. She looked at the display, shut her eyes, and breathed out, her entire body seeming to condense into the chair.

After letting it ring for a few moments, she answered and conversed in Dutch with the person on the other end, including several long pauses and a few intense questions. I sat and watched the tugs escort the cruise liner toward the downtown pier. Without saying goodbye, Arabella disconnected the call and dropped her cell on the table. Wide-eyed, she stared off into space.

"Should I say *what*?" I asked.

"Since Schleper has not been heard from, the other department inspector and the inspector chief went to check on him this morning," she said.

She didn't continue.

"*And . . .*" I said.

She looked in my direction and shrugged. "He was not at home. Nor was his car. They don't know where he is."

"That's odd."

"Yes, he is sometimes a strange man."

"Should we be worried?"

"I do not know about *we*, but I am not. He has made it clear many times that he can care for himself."

I didn't press it, although I found it strange he hadn't been heard from.

We both ate some food. Arabella drank coffee; me, iced tea. Workers busied themselves securing the cruise ship to large cleats anchored along the pier as taxis and tour buses began lining the street.

"Speaking of the inspector, have you thought more about doing the training?"

She stopped eating and let out a long breath. "Yes, but I have no decision." She looked at me, her lips unnaturally curled down, her eyes watery. "It is difficult."

Before I had a chance to answer or encourage her, my cellphone rang.

"It's Chuck," I said studying the display. "I should probably answer it. He's in a bad way these days."

Arabella's mouth opened, she hesitated, then shrugged. I answered the call.

"Hey, R," Chuck said. "Can you fly to Curacao for me this afternoon? I can't leave the island. Your police buddies have me grounded."

"Curacao?"

Arabella shook her head.

"Yeah," he said, "that same customer has more packages for me to pick up."

"Doesn't the tower know your plane is grounded? They won't allow it to depart."

"I was hoping you'd talk to Arabella and see if she could fix it so my plane can leave. I promise not to go along."

"Hey, she's sitting right here." I looked at Arabella and smiled. "I'll put you on speaker."

Arabella flipped her middle finger at me. I touched a button on the display and set the phone on the table between us.

"Okay, Chuck, go ahead."

"*Hallo*, Arabella," Chuck said, trying to win her over by using one of the four Dutch words he knew. He's possibly the only person on the island who spoke less Dutch than I did.

"What do you want?" she asked. She showed me her middle finger again, this time jabbing it two inches from my nose.

"Can you okay it with the tower so R can make a flight to Curacao for me this afternoon?"

She didn't say anything. She leaned back in her seat, drinking coffee, looking at me. Considering Chuck's request, flying to Curacao would give me a chance to talk with Joost Obersi again. Another conversation was warranted. His reaction when I questioned him about the wood in Rulio's leg might prove interesting.

"Chuck," I said. "It ran a little rough last time."

"Remember I told you I found jet fuel in the tank?"

"Yeah."

"Well, I drained both tanks and flushed the fuel lines. I ground-ran the engine and everything is fine. You won't have any problems."

"Ever figure out how it got in the tanks?"

"No clue. At first, I thought the guy in the fuel truck must've fucked up. But . . ." He was quiet a moment. "I don't know."

"That doesn't give me the warm and fuzzies."

"Nah, you'll be fine."

Arabella, still leaned back in the chair, ate the last of her toast. "I must think about it."

A few moments of silence and Chuck's voice came over the cell-phone speaker again. "Arabella, this is the way I make a living and I need the money. I'm going to need to pay for lawyers and court costs. I can't do it with my plane grounded."

She laughed. "Not to worry, there are debtor's prisons in the Netherlands. We will find a place for you."

"What?" Chuck said.

"No, they don't," I said, smiling at Arabella. "She's just messing with you, Chuck."

"Meet me at the hangar?" Chuck said.

"The rental agency never dropped off a vehicle for me," I said. "You'll need to pick me up."

"No problem. As far as I know, I'm still allowed to drive, right Arabella?"

"*Ja*, you can drive," she said.

"Besides," Chuck said, "the customer will be at the airport when the packages arrive. He'll be expecting to see me there, too."

All of us were quiet. Arabella made a point of stretching her arms.

"Arabella? . . . Please?" Chuck said.

I pointed at the cruise ship docking at the pier and said to Arabella, "You better make up your mind. The street will be crawling with cruisers soon."

"If I'm broke," Chuck said, "when I'm old and home bound, R will need to change my diapers and wipe my ass."

"Don't worry, Chuck," I said. "Before it gets to that point, I'll smother you with a pillow."

"You will have to beat me to it," Arabella said.

"Please . . ." Chuck said.

She groaned. "All right, I will notify the tower that your plane will depart to Curacao and return a short time afterwards. But you cannot be on it." She looked at me. "Promise?"

I nodded.

"Yes," Chuck said. "And thank you."

I disconnected the call as the cruise ship began regurgitating tourists onto the pier. Sunglasses; droopy hats; multicolored T-shirts; bags draped over their shoulders; cellphone cameras at the ready. Regardless the country of origin, people spilling out of a cruise ship were always the same.

"*Gadverdamme*," Arabella said. "I can smell the suntan lotion from here."

"Let's roll."

Arabella didn't move, just stared at me.

"What?" I said.

"You are going to fly an airplane with a bad engine?"

"You heard Chuck. It wasn't the engine; it was the wrong fuel. He cleaned the tanks and lines. All taken care of."

"You are going to rely on Chuck? Put your life in his hands?"

"Regardless of what you think of Chuck, he's a good mechanic. If he says it'll be fine, I trust him."

"*Ach*," she said, shaking her head. "I sure hope you are correct."

As we rose and laid money on the table, Arabella said, "You owe me."

"I love it when I owe you."

"I do, too," she said, kissing me on the lips. "But I like it better when you pay up."

CHAPTER 30

CHUCK AND I leaned against the outside wall of the large hangar on the north end of the airport. A few yards from us, out on the tarmac, the faded paint job of his plane seemed to absorb more sunlight than it reflected. Chuck drank a beer. Sipping from a water bottle, I enjoyed the shade. We waited for Arabella to call and give us the go-ahead. I didn't dare crank the plane's engine until the tower and airport authorities had been notified. Knowing Arabella wouldn't hurry, I relaxed and savored the coolness of the concrete blocks through my T-shirt. She'd take her time and cause Chuck some anxiety.

"I wish she'd call," Chuck said. He paced back and forth, and I got the feeling more was on his mind than getting permission for this cargo run.

"How you doing?" I asked.

Chuck drank the last of his beer, pulled another from his shorts pocket, and opened it. "Okay, I guess." He turned sideways from me, maybe trying to conceal the watering of his eyes, and took a swig. "I miss Tessa. More than I thought I would."

"I know you do."

"It sucks."

"Yeah, it does. But the answer isn't in those Brights."

Chuck smirked. "You're one to talk."

I agreed. Coming from me, there couldn't have been a more hypocritical statement. But over the last few days, I'd worried about him. Not just the drinking, but the fact that he hadn't shown—other than his initial shock and devastation—much emotion regarding Tessa's death. I was relieved seeing him teary-eyed and hearing him say he missed her.

We'd been waiting almost an hour when Arabella called.

"You are all set to go," she said. "You must be back before dark, though."

"Thanks." I laughed lightly into the phone, hoping to lighten her mood a little. "Haven't had a curfew in about forty years."

"Remember," she said. "You owe me."

"Can't wait to pay up."

We disconnected, and I said to Chuck, "I'm all set. I'll text you before I start back."

"Okay. I'll get the customer and meet you here."

"And you're sure about the fuel issue?"

"R . . . you won't have a problem. It'll purr like a kitten."

Turned out, Chuck was correct, and the engine ran smooth on the flight over to Curacao. No issue with the departure clearance from Bonaire or the arrival on Curacao. It was as if Chuck's plane had never been grounded.

I parked at the same spot on the Curacao tarmac as Chuck had used on our previous flight. After waiting at the customer window inside the shipping hangar for almost ten minutes, a clerk finally came by and asked what I needed. I gave him the paperwork—the bill of lading—Chuck had given me, then informed him I needed to run an errand and would be back for the packages later. He flipped through the documents, then shrugged and said they'd be open 'til six o'clock.

I rented a white four-door pickup, the most inconspicuous vehicle on the island. Both Bonaire and Curacao were flooded with these trucks. They happened to be the vehicle of choice by divers, so the rental agencies kept plenty on hand.

Except maybe on Bonaire, where I couldn't seem to get one.

I left the airport, driving past the guys playing dominoes on the old wooden crate, and navigated across the island toward the Lars Thiel neighborhood. After once again passing the Palapa Beach Resort and Marina, I threaded the same residential streets the taxi driver had taken on my previous trip and turned onto Kaya Artiko. I parked two houses from Joost Obersi's, got out, and walked up to the front door.

After ten minutes of knocking, ringing the doorbell, and trying to peer through the curtain-covered window, I decided either no one was home, or I was being ignored. I went back to the rental truck, settled into the driver's seat with all the windows down, and decided to do some surveillance—or *snooping*—on Obersi. Arabella had said the police verified his alibi, so I wasn't sure what I hoped to accomplish or learn by sitting in the truck watching his house. His reaction to wood being discovered in Rulio's leg would've told me a lot.

The neighborhood appeared as lonely as it did on the previous trip. At one point, a teenager walked down the street bouncing a basketball. He eyed me as he passed the rental truck. I raised my bottle of water to him and munched on a sandwich I'd grabbed from a vending machine on my way out of the airport.

Other than a quick glance, he paid me no attention. Periodically, he'd slow in front of certain houses, almost as if performing some ritual, a signal, a shout-out for his buddies to come out and strike up a game. But no one answered his call and he continued his solitary dribble down the road, the thump of the ball against the pavement—his invitation to others—fading.

Eventually, the street became quiet again, nothing more than the whisk of the wind through the palms. To my left, the sea gleamed in the sunlight, too far away for me to hear the waves against the shore, but close enough for me to almost feel the water.

Obersi's house was stoic. No one stepped out the front door; no movement of blinds; no windows opened or shut; no vehicles in or out of the driveway. Nothing. After two hours, I gave up and headed back to the airport.

I didn't want to exceed my curfew.

* * *

Back at the cargo hangar, I met up with the same worker I had spoken with earlier. He looked at his watch and frowned, even though it wasn't close to six o'clock yet. *What happened to Island Time?* I thought.

The five boxes sat on a wheelable pallet ready for transport to the plane. I signed all the paperwork and we exchanged copies. He rolled the pallet across the tarmac and helped me load them.

All aircraft are sensitive to weight and balance, especially small ones. I wasn't as concerned about the weight of the boxes exceeding the gross limitations of the plane, as much as I was concerned about the equal loading of them. The plane had a center of gravity point, and cargo—be it people or items—needed to be loaded correctly in order to keep the plane balanced. Like a playground teeter-totter, too much weight either side of the center of gravity could cause a tipping motion during flight. A heavy kid on one end of the teeter-totter prevents the small kid on the other end from being able to move.

Either end of a small airplane being forced up or down during flight is a recipe for trouble, and off-center loading can cause such an issue.

I stacked one box in the front copilot's seat, then put three in the back row of seats. My helper put the last box in the small rear cargo area, which helped distribute the weight evenly across the airplane. Everything got strapped into place to prevent movement in case of turbulence.

Satisfied with the loading, I pulled myself into the cockpit and began the preflight checklist. Before engine start, I glanced at the box sitting next to me in the front seat. Somehow, while twisting and turning the box to squeeze it through the door and onto the seat, I had ripped one of the corners. I tried forcing it back into position, but accidently made the rip worse, opening a portion of the box and exposing some of its contents.

My body froze. After a moment, I realized I had quit breathing, and forced open my mouth, gasping, like being underwater and finally breaching the surface. I leaned closer to the box for a second look, using the flashlight feature on my new phone, and peered inside.

I hadn't noticed it on the previous trip, but now studied the wire binding the carboard boxes shut. A faded shade of green, it was bare, not coated in rubber or plastic.

Not barbed wire or chicken wire or electrical wire or telephone wire.

I jumped out and jogged back into the cargo hangar. I borrowed a knife, some duct tape, and a pair of wire cutters, then went back to the plane.

Making a small hole in the exact same location on each box, I verified their contents to be the same as the one in the front seat. I wrapped duct tape in a consistent pattern around each box, covering the holes, hoping to give the impression it was part of the packing process. Then, I used the wire cutters to cut a piece of extraneous wire from one of the boxes. I put the wire in my pocket and returned the tools to the guy in the cargo hangar.

With the engine running smoothly, I departed Curacao, climbing into the clear Caribbean sky. As Bonaire came into view through the front windshield, I glanced at the box in the front seat.

I wondered if Chuck knew what he'd been hauling in those boxes. He knew who the customer was but hadn't shared that information with me.

What had he gotten himself into?

Worse yet, what had he gotten *me* into?

CHAPTER 31

WITH A KNOT in my gut, and too focused on the contents of my cargo, I bounced the landing at Flamingo Airport, then sped down the taxiway to the parking area. As I shut down the engine and watched the propeller slow to a stop, Chuck walked across the tarmac, followed by three other men.

One of them worked at the airport assigned to the cargo hangar. He pulled a wheeled pallet, like the one used by his counterpart at the Curacao airport.

I recognized the other two men as well.

John Anderson and Lucas Walker.

My hands shook and my face flushed as I opened the door and half-stepped, half-fell out of the plane. Affirmation, fear, and concern all at the same time.

"Any problems?" Chuck asked.

Nausea built in my stomach. I turned away from him for a moment and tried to focus. Turning back in his direction, I managed a meager shrug.

John approached me and stuck out his hand. "I appreciate you flying these over."

I shook his hand, my sweaty palms preventing me from maintaining a firm grip. As John tried to decide what to do about his now damp hand, not wanting to wipe it on his expensive jeans, Lucas and the airport worker began removing the crates from the Cessna and loading them onto the pallet.

"How was the flight?" John asked.

"Just fine," I said without looking in his direction while helping Chuck secure the ropes holding the plane in place on the tarmac, one on each wing and another under the tail.

I paid no attention to the small talk John and Chuck engaged in as all five of us walked to the parking lot. Lucas strode alongside and occasionally glanced in my direction from the corner of his eye. Sweat ran down my neck, my wet T-shirt clinging to my back.

I quickened my pace. Chuck always had beer in his truck, and I needed one.

After the crates were transferred into John's SUV, Lucas pressed a wad of money into the airport worker's pocket. He nodded at Lucas and John, then went into the hangar, closing the door behind him.

All taken care of . . . just load the boxes and drive away.

As they left the parking lot, John and Lucas drove past Chuck and me, John offering a slight wave and Lucas making a shooting motion at me with his finger and thumb. Being a quick, imaginative thinker, I finger-shot back.

Chuck and I leaned against the tailgate of his truck, the wind at our face and the sound of a turbo prop coming to life, waiting to taxi. He handed me an open beer, along with two one-hundred-dollar bills.

I looked at the cash. "What's this for?"

"Your cut." His face brightened. "I get paid well for these trips."

I handed the cash back to him. "No thanks."

Chuck had never grasped the concept of someone refusing money. His mouth gaped open and his voice raised in pitch as he said, "You don't want it?"

I shook my head. "How many of these trips have you done for him?"

He tucked the cash into his pants pocket and thought for a moment. "Probably half a dozen or so. He was having some guy from Curacao do the flying, but something happened to him."

I nearly gagged on a swallow of beer, spilling some of it on my shirt. "Something *happened* to him?"

"Yeah, I don't know what. All I know is John came to me and asked if I'd take over. When he told me the pay, I jumped on it."

"Do you know what's in those crates?"

Chuck shrugged. "Restaurant stuff, I guess. Napkins, plates, cups. Hell, I don't know. Could be baby puppies for all I care. Money's good. That's what counts."

"It's not restaurant stuff."

"How would you know?"

"I saw inside of them."

Chuck paused, looked at his airplane tied to the tarmac. "Well, I don't want to know."

I took a swig of beer. "They're filled with US currency."

His head jerked in my direction.

I nodded. "Yup . . . Cash."

He let out a short whistle. "How much?"

"No idea. Tens of thousands? Maybe hundreds of thousands. I've never seen that much currency before."

"Damn," he said, slapping his open palm on the side of the truck. "I knew I should've been charging more."

"Are you crazy? You shouldn't be charging him *anything*. You shouldn't be involved with this."

"Involved with what? It's not against the law to haul cash."

"In this case, it probably is. Especially that kind of loot into and out of sovereign countries. Not going through customs; not declaring it; not paying taxes. All sorts of problems."

"What do you think it means?"

I had a theory, but no need to concern Chuck with it. *If* that were possible. "Not sure, but I'd suggest not doing any more trips for him."

"That could be a problem." Chuck rubbed the sole of his foot back and forth on the pavement. "The other guy I told you about, the flyer from Curacao?"

"What about him?"

Chuck's hand trembled. "Well, the something that happened to him occurred *after* he told John he wanted to quit doing the flights."

My head fell back, and I closed my eyes.

"I don't know if John had anything to do with it," Chuck said, his speech rapid and high-pitched. "Could be a coincidence."

I took a swig of beer.

Great, I thought. *Another coincidence.*

CHAPTER 32

CHUCK DROPPED ME at the YellowRock. I went up the outside front stairs to my apartment and found Arabella standing at the kitchen counter drinking an Amstel. She was out of uniform and wore a T-shirt with writing on the front that read *Homicide Cop: My Day Begins When Yours Ends*. Her belt, weapon, and badge laid next to her on the kitchen counter.

I took the wire I'd cut from one of the boxes and laid it in front of her.

"Any way to compare this to the wire wrapped around Rulio's leg?" I asked. She examined the wire but didn't handle it. "I cut it from one of the boxes I flew back from Curacao."

"I suppose there is no documentation on this," she said.

I shook my head. "No way to preserve anything." She picked it up and looked it over. "David Brown told me there are ways to compare metal alloys. He said it's almost like a DNA signature."

"Who do the boxes belong to?"

I paused a moment, mostly for dramatic effect. After an exaggerated sign from Arabella, I said, "John Anderson."

"John Anderson? From Paradise Cove?"

I took a beer from the fridge. "The one and only. I watched him and Lucas load the boxes into John's SUV."

"But there must be tons of this wire. Is it just a coincidence?"

No such thing as a coincidence. At least, not in my experience.

"Hard to believe. Especially considering the cargo."

She waited. I drank some beer.

"Well," she said, "are you going to tell me or keep me suspended?"

I smiled. I liked keeping her *suspended*. But when she pinched her lips together and began drumming her fingers on the counter, I came clean.

"Cash," I said.

"What?" she said, the pitch of her voice rising a notch. "Money?"

"Yup. US currency." I nodded. "*Geld*."

Her eyebrows squished together. "Are you sure?"

"I think I know dollars when I see them."

"*Je bent gek*," she said. The best translation was something like *that's crazy*. Then she said, "Why would Chuck fly those packages?"

"He didn't know what he was hauling."

She rolled her eyes. "Yeah, right. We are talking of Chuck."

"Seriously, he's not an idiot."

"I am not so sure." She took a drink of beer and drummed her hands on the counter, not making eye contact with me. "Speaking of Chuck, I need to discuss something with you."

I glanced at the veranda, then back at Arabella. "Let's sit outside."

A couple of chibi-chibi birds flew off the railing when I opened the slider out to the veranda. From one of the restaurants north of the YellowRock, tunes from a steel drum band rode on the salt air, the breeze carrying the music in our direction. I slid into the hammock and Arabella sat in a nearby chair. A few children played in the shallow waves across the street.

"I have to formally charge him," Arabella finally said. "I am under a lot of pressure."

"It's a mistake."

Arabella frowned. "A police inspector's wife is dead. Chuck was sleeping with her and she was shot by his speargun."

"It wasn't his."

She tilted her head. "You know what I mean."

I let out a breath. "Yeah, I do. Sorry."

"I cannot put it off any longer. I have tried to be lenient, but we have no other leads."

"Just because you have a lead doesn't mean you're right."

"But it does not mean I am wrong, either."

"Can you wait another day? Maybe two?"

"That is not how it works." She paused a moment, then in a softer tone said, "You know that."

The case Bill Ryberg—my old partner—and I had worked years ago dealing with an alderman's brother back in Rockford came to mind. We were pressured to move forward even though everything we had was circumstantial. It affected both of us. And not for the positive. Bill was never the same and retired shortly afterwards.

Wearing a badge every day meant dealing with stress and pressure, but there's a difference between the everyday stress and pressure brought on by the job and the stress and pressure of being forced to move a case forward when the evidence didn't support it. The latter can change a person, and I hated the thought of it affecting Arabella the way it had Bill and me.

"I will do my best," she said. "But it may become out of my control."

"Yeah, I understand. And thanks."

"It is a two-bladed knife," she said, meaning a double-edged sword, but I didn't have the guts to correct her. "If I charge him, we will not have enough evidence to convict him. But if I refuse to do it, I may be in trouble." She wiped moisture off the neck of her beer bottle. "Besides, if I do not do it, someone else will." She shrugged. "Either way, it will happen."

Far out on the horizon, the distant humidity was forming into low clouds that would eventually hide the sunset. The children playing in the waves across the street had departed and the echo of the lonely waves slapped against the vacant shore punctuating the silence between Arabella and me. Two snorkelers sat on the end of the pier donning their masks and fins, intent on a late afternoon swim.

I sat up and hung my legs off the edge of the hammock, squaring off with Arabella. "Time to make a list. I'll start."

She leaned forward.

"First," I said, "we have Rulio's leg washing ashore—"

"With a piece of wire on it," she said.

"Right, and now we have a piece of wire to compare it to."

"I will work on that. Hopefully, David is right, and we can identify the wire."

I took a swig of beer. "We had two initial suspects, the students from Rulio's accident."

She shook her head. "But we have ruled both out. One is dead, even."

"I talked to Joost Obersi, the carpenter in Curacao."

"When? I did not know this."

"A few days ago. Pretty hostile individual. You know he's a carpenter?"

"Of course, I know that."

"Could that explain the wood splinters found in Rulio's leg?"

She tilted her head. "How do you know about that?"

I shrugged. "It's in the coroner's report."

She smiled. "Yes, but that report is in Dutch. I know your level of Dutch, and you could not read it. So how do you know?"

"David told me."

She nodded. "Well, regardless, the wood is not from Bonaire. A biology teacher at the school said it is a hardwood, most likely oak."

"I don't recall seeing any oak trees on Bonaire."

"No, of course not," she said. "But get this . . . it is sometimes used to build sailboat decks."

I fell back in the hammock. "So, Officer, you've been holding out on me. There's a sailboat moored right off the reef by Paradise Cove."

"Yes, I am aware."

"But how did Obersi get on the boat?"

She pushed the hammock with her knee. "Stop thinking about the man from Curacao. It is not him. We have confirmed his alibi. He is no longer considered a suspect."

"Are you sure?"

"Yes." She tipped her bottle up, but before drinking, said with a smile, "It's in the report. Just read it and see."

"The report said he was a person of interest."

"Yes, initially, but we cleared him."

Apparently, my translation needed some fine tuning. I looked her in the eyes. "You should see his house. Very impressive. How can a person afford digs like that bending nails?"

"Well, if your Dutch was good and you had read the report, you would know that his wife is from Holland and has plenty of money."

I bit the inside of my cheek. "So, he's legit?"

"Yes, as far as we can determine. Besides, how he pays for his home is not my concern. We are not interested in him as a suspect."

It is not much of my business.

If he'd been cleared, then so be it. But something seemed out of whack. I just couldn't determine what.

"Now, let us move on. Back to our list," Arabella said. "Then Tessa is killed with Chuck's speargun."

"With *a* speargun. But Lucas and John seemed to be interested in her as well."

"I spoke with Ruth and yes, she said Lucas and John were stalking Tessa. Also, she thinks John had slept with Tessa, at least once, but Tessa never admitted it to her."

"There you have it," I said. "They should be considered suspects." As should Schleper, but I kept that opinion to myself.

"But we have nothing connecting them to Tessa. Just Ruth's word. Tessa never filed a complaint." She tapped her foot on the floor. "However, Lucas beat that guy up at Paradise Cove."

"Yeah, so we know he has anger problems." If anyone could spot those tendencies, it'd be me. I hadn't told her about Lucas driving me into the sand with a karate move, but now was not the time. "Then, when Rulio's girlfriend, Sandra, remembered something, she miraculously disappeared."

"True, and we have not found her. We entered her house. Her keys and purse were there, and her car was parked on the street in front. Her cellphone showed calls from you, Paradise Cove, and some of her friends. No trace of her."

The thought of Sandra meeting the same fate as Rulio disturbed me. If she had, with no wind reversal, her remains would've been pushed *away* from the island, not *toward* it. In Rulio's case, the murderer hadn't anticipated the wind reversal and the leg washed ashore. I doubted they'd make the same mistake twice.

"She and Rulio both worked at Paradise Cove," I said. "And they both knew Lucas and John. And today we find out Anderson is flying money over from Curacao."

"Everything seems to focus around John Anderson. I need to check him out better. Not to mention file a report about the boxes of cash he is bringing to the island."

"And don't forget," I said. "Lucas claims to be an FBI agent. He told that to David Brown and me."

"Undercover, no less. But why would he admit it?"

"I don't know," I said, "One of the FBI's focus *is* money laundering. It's a stretch but, if he's really a fed, that could be the investigation."

"We do not know if it is money laundering. It could be drug money. Or maybe stolen. We do not even know it is real. Could be counterfeit."

Sitting quietly a moment, we pondered everything we knew.

"That is a big list," Arabella said. "We need to look harder at John Anderson. He may be the key."

"The problem is, he's smart. Maybe too smart. He's not leaving anything for us to connect him to." I drank some beer and watched the glow of the sun behind the low clouds.

"Hey!" Arabella said after a moment. "What about the airplane fuel? Could John Anderson have caused that?"

"I've been thinking about that. If we crashed in the sea, his boxes of money would be gone, and he wouldn't want that. I'm thinking he had nothing to do with Chuck's fuel problem."

"So . . ."

"Don't know. Chuck had done some work on the engine. Maybe he messed something up. As much as I hate to admit, maybe, in this case, it *was* a coincidence."

She raised her eyebrows at me, and I shrugged.

Although Anderson seemed to be at the center of all this, we weren't any closer to an answer than we were days ago. While investigating crimes, frustration can sometimes overwhelm the good guys, leading them to believe it's all hopeless. Many times, I've thrown up my hands and thought, *Now what?*

"Maybe I should make something happen," I said.

"Like what?"

"I don't know . . . tell Anderson I know about the cash he's hauling over here? Ask him about Sandra Griffis? Something, anything, to make him move. Poke at him. Get him to sweat a bit. If he's under some pressure, maybe he'll do something stupid and make a mistake."

"Why would you do that? Tell him things that we know?"

"Might be the only—"

"A good investigator," she said, pumping her beer bottle at me, "does not tell the suspects what she knows."

"I wouldn't tell him everything, just enough to make him nervous." The wind pushed the sounds of paradise across the veranda. "Look, Bella, the stuff circling Paradise Cove has my neck hairs tingling. I need to tweak Anderson a little."

She slouched in her chair. "Well, far be it for me to argue with your neck hairs. But do not plan anything without talking to me first."

I smiled. "Never."

Arabella stood and stretched. "I need a break. Too much work talk."

I raised an eyebrow.

"Yes, too much," she said. "Even for me."

"Hungry? Want to get some grub?"

"I think I want you to pay your debt to me."

I huffed and raised my chin. "What debt?"

She walked over and looked down at me, sitting on the hammock. "You owe me."

I wrapped my arms around her waist and pulled her close. "I suppose you want your payment." I buried my head in her belly, playfully gnawing at her T-shirt.

Her cellphone rang. "It is work. I must answer." She stroked my hair twice, then answered the phone. "*Wat?*" She listened a few moments. "*Ik kom eraan!*" She ended the call and went inside, grabbing her belt, weapon, and badge.

"What happened?" I asked.

"Looks like we have another entry to our list." She headed toward the stairs. "David Brown is at hospital."

"He works at the hospital."

"Yes, but right now he is a patient." At the top of the stairs, she turned back in my direction. "He has been shot."

CHAPTER 33

I FOLLOWED ARABELLA down the stairs and ran to where my Wrangler would've been parked if it weren't wrecked. I forgot the rental hadn't arrived. Standing on the street, I happened to glance at the small coffee shop a few buildings from the YellowRock. A man stood on the sidewalk next to one of the outside tables and stared at me.

He wore a sleeveless T-shirt, baggy cargo shorts, and sandals with no socks. Tall and broad shouldered, he held a gaze on me for an uncomfortable length of time. A low-riding floppy hat and a pair of dark shades hid the upper portion of his face. However, I recognized his stance; his self-imposed, self-important demeanor radiated outward like that of a barracuda patrolling the reef.

Inspector Schleper.

"Are you coming?" Arabella yelled as she dropped into the seat of her Toyota and closed the door, window down. She hadn't noticed Schleper.

I got the sense Schleper wanted me to join him. He laid a newspaper on the table, pulled out a chair, then took a seat on the opposite side of the table.

An invitation? Or a summons?

Knowing Schleper, it was most likely a demand.

"Hey," Arabella said. "I need to go."

She didn't need me at the hospital. I could arrive later, and she'd update me. Being an active investigation, I wouldn't be allowed to speak with Brown nor be in his room.

"I'll meet you there," I yelled back.

She nodded and sped away, her Toyota disappearing around a corner.

I made my way to the coffee shop.

"Inspector," I said, standing at the table. He didn't say anything and motioned for me to sit, again making it feel more like a command than a request.

I sat anyway.

"Mr. Conklin, I hoped we might meet. I think we should talk." He sipped from a cup. A half-eaten pastry of some sort lay on a nearby saucer, a fork and some crumbs lying next to it on the table.

"Please accept my condolences on the death of your wife," I said. "I'm very sorry."

He gave a dismissive wave. "Thank you, but that is not necessary." He leaned back. "I understand you have doubts about the guilt of your friend Mr. Studer."

So much for grieving. Right to business. That's the Schleper we all know and love.

"He didn't do it," I said.

"And you have proof of this?"

"Innocent till *proven* guilty, right?"

"You are not in the States, Mr. Conklin. Do not assume things." He sat up and flipped his paper to the next page, acting as if he were reading during our conversation. "What are your suspicions, then?"

I didn't say anything. I had too many suspicions to count, but that's all they were—suspicions. At least right now.

"You think maybe the bartender person did it?" he asked.

How would he know about Lucas Walker? I doubted Arabella had said anything. As far as I knew, this might be the first time Schleper had been seen in public since Tessa's death.

My face, no doubt filled with confusion and surprise, must've given away my curiosity.

"Rest assured, Mr. Conklin, I have my ways of knowing things."

"Then, yes. I believe he should be considered a person of interest."

He nodded. "I agree."

We both sat quietly for a few moments. The wind whipped at the canvas umbrella mounted above the patio. The couple at the next table jabbered away in Dutch. My whole body tensed, and I wanted to get to the hospital. But my curiosity around Schleper's intent held me glued to the seat.

After a few moments, I said, "Schleper, what—"

"I am going to write down a name for you." He produced a pen and paper from his pocket, scribbled a name, and handed it to me. "You and Officer De Groot should talk to this person."

I read the name, then looked back at Schleper. "Who is this?"

"A local thug who has had dealings with Lucas Walker."

So, he knew the name of the bartender. Earlier, he hadn't let on. Wonder what else Inspector *Barracuda* knows.

"Are you saying he's somehow involved?" I asked.

"I would think you and Officer De Groot can make that determination."

My understanding was that Schleper wasn't involved, off on leave somewhere. I wondered how he knew so much about this situation.

Rest assured, Mister Conklin, I have my ways of knowing things.

"Why are you telling me this?" I asked.

"Because I want the right person caught."

"You think I don't?"

"I am sure you want your friend cleared, regardless of me and my feelings." He tilted his head back for a moment. "I have privately been looking at this individual myself, but I need you and Arabella to look deeper."

Arabella? I had never heard him refer to her in any manner other than Officer De Groot.

"How well do you know the people at Paradise Cove, specifically the owner, John Anderson?" I asked.

"Not enough to help you."

"I still don't understand why you're telling me this. There must be people on your force who could do this for you."

"Yes, there are. But I know you would not let up anyway. If Officer De Groot is involved alongside you, then I am okay with giving this to you." He took a sip of coffee. "Besides, let us just say there are some in the department who enjoy my pain and misery. I would not take satisfaction in letting them in on what I know."

"Not me. I don't take *any* satisfaction in murder." I paused a few moments. "And again, for the record, I'm sorry. If I had been following Tessa . . ." I paused, letting out a long, slow breath. "Maybe things would've turned out differently."

He shrugged. "Yes, well, we will never know. Will we?"

Schleper was right. We'd never know. And that's what I'd been struggling with. He downed the last of his coffee, looked at the remaining crumbs of pastry, then folded the newspaper and put it under his arm.

"What will you do now?" I asked.

"I am not sure."

"Where will you go?"

"Mr. Conklin, I am not going anywhere. I mourn for my wife, but I am realistic. She betrayed me. But none of this is your concern." He pointed at the piece of scrap paper with the name scribbled on it, still clutched in my hand. "That is your concern right now."

I stood to leave. "Thank you, Inspector."

"One last thing. I will ask you to use your influence with Officer De Groot to have her apply for inspector training. She has good instincts." He looked away and half-smiled. "There might be an opening soon."

"Me? Influence her? You know Bella as well as I do. She makes her own decisions. I don't control her any more than she controls me."

He threw some of the pastry crumbs on the ground for some nearby sandpipers. "Mr. Conklin, you have more influence over her than you realize."

I considered that for a moment. Part of me didn't believe it and the other part hoped it wasn't true.

"Take care," I said, for lack of anything better, and headed down the sidewalk.

I might still catch Arabella at the hospital.

Thanks to Schleper, my back pocket held the name of another entry for our list.

CHAPTER 34

THE TREK TO the hospital seemed to take forever. I jogged most of the way, cutting through parking areas and a couple of vacant lots. The glass sliding doors to the emergency room swooshed open allowing a portion of the air-conditioned inside environment to slip out as I walked through. Arms crossed, Arabella stood midway down a hallway, the focal point in a circle of three other officers. One was Ingrid and another was Jos. They all wore serious faces. Heads nodding, they spoke Papiamentu amongst themselves. Based on the noises emanating from behind the gray, floor-to-ceiling curtain behind them, and the coming and going of two nurses, I guessed that's where hospital staff tended to David Brown.

The other officers were in uniform. Arabella wasn't, however, her holster and weapon were strapped around her waist. Her badge rode sideways, clipped to the collar of her T-shirt. As I approached, she broke away from her colleagues.

"Hey, Bella, how's David?" I asked.

She briefly glanced over her shoulder at the other officers, then led me to the far end of the hall. "Gunshot. Two bullets to the chest."

"None to the head?"

She breathed out. "No, that is why I said 'two bullets to the chest.'"

I looked down the hall at the group of police officers. They wouldn't still be here if David were dead. "He still alive?" I asked Arabella.

She bit her lower lip and nodded. "Yes, but only barely. They have him sedated."

"Where'd it happen?"

"Outside his home. According to a group of neighbors, they came up to the house as the shooting occurred and saw someone running away, down the street. We believe they interrupted the shooter and he fled. The neighbors found David near the front door, unconscious and bleeding."

"We have witnesses?" I felt the excitement build. "They get a look at the shooter?"

"No, not a good one. His back was to them. All they could attest to was that he was short." She breathed out. "I have officers asking other neighbors for information." She bellowed a stream of Papiamentu at Ingrid and Jos. They each gave a wave and left the emergency room. "Now I have two more helping."

"Casings?"

"Not yet. And the shots were pass-throughs."

She meant the bullet went through the body, making it virtually impossible to locate. Could be anywhere within several hundred yards of the scene. They'd examine all nearby objects, buildings, and structures in the estimated path of the shot, hoping the slug lodged somewhere, but odds were slim.

"Motive?"

She shrugged.

It was a bit early to have a possible motive, but Arabella knew David and I had recently spoken. No doubt that gave her pause. It did me. Could I be the reason he was shot and nearly killed? I called from my office phone, so how would anyone know our conversation? Only Erika and I were in the office.

A tall Dutch woman walked out from behind the curtain. In contrast to the nurses coming and going in a hurried fashion, she moved slower and with more purpose, examining an iPad-type of device. She wore a long white lab coat and had a stethoscope draped around her neck. Several pens peeked out from a pocket on her coat.

She walked up and stood in front of Arabella, still studying the device's screen. "I am Doctor Amanda Ingerbretzen." I recognized her as the physician who treated Arabella's gunshot wound. "I have attended to Mr. Brown." She looked up from the clipboard. Her eyes moved from Arabella's sidearm to her badge and then to her T-shirt.

Homicide Cop: My Day Begins When Yours Ends.

"Let us hope that is not the case tonight," the doctor said, with a slight smirk. "I can assume you are not family?"

"No," Arabella said. "I am the officer in charge." She then whipped off something in Dutch.

The doctor looked at me, then responded.

In Dutch.

I rested my hands on my hips and let out a slow breath. Talk about feeling like a third wheel.

The Dutch flowed back and forth for a few moments, then, in English, Arabella said, "Thank you. Please keep me informed."

That, I understood.

Dr. Ingerbretzen laid a hand on Arabella's shoulder and squeezed several times. "How is the shoulder doing?"

Arabella jerked away in order to move her shoulder out from under the doctor's hand. "It is fine."

Doctor Ingerbretzen drummed her fingers on the iPad-device several times, then turned away and walked down the hall. She used her body to push through a set of extra-wide double doors. The doors slowly closed behind her, clanking shut and echoing down the hall.

"So?" I asked Arabella.

"He is stable, but serious. They have called a surgeon to repair the internal damage and will move him to the operating room shortly." She stepped over to the curtain and peeked behind it, then returned to me. "They hope he will be conscious after the operation."

"That couldn't have been said in English?"

"Yes, it could. But the doctor was concerned about privacy laws. You are not a relative."

The remaining officer still stood at the other end of the hall. He took a few steps forward and spoke Papiamentu to Arabella. She nodded and said "*Ayo*."

That, too, I understood. Papiamentu for "good bye."

The officer left. Arabella and I followed him out the door into the warm Caribbean night, a cloudless sky with a million stars twinkling at us.

"I spoke with your boss," I said.

Arabella jumped in front of me and stopped so fast I almost bumped into her. Which, in hindsight, was a pleasant thought.

"You spoke to Schleper?"

"Yeah, at the coffee shop." She knew the place. We often went there for a light breakfast or afternoon snack. Arabella liked the fruity iced tea concoction they offered. I usually just had soda or regular tea.

We walked toward her Toyota.

"He said he had hoped to run into me," I said.

"What? . . . He? . . ." She shook her head, eyebrows scrunched. "What?"

I removed the paper from my back pocket. "He said we should check this guy out."

She took the paper and read it. "I do not recognize this name. Why does Schleper think it is important?"

"He said he wants the 'right person caught.' Said he's been looking into this person privately and wants you and I to take a deeper look."

She leaned against her Toyota, staring at the paper. Her shoulders slumped. "But why you? Why not bring this to me?"

"I don't know." She looked up from the paper, eyes reddening. After a moment, I said, "I'm guessing I was just convenient at the time. I'm sure he would've given it to you if he hadn't run into me."

"But you said he hoped to run into you."

I copied her lean against the Toyota, nudging up beside her as close as possible, and put my arm behind her shoulders. She wasn't in uniform, so I kissed her on the cheek. She rested her head on my shoulder.

"The important thing is we have a name to look into," I said.

She straightened. "Yes, I will check that out. Maybe tonight, but probably tomorrow." She slid into the driver's side of the car, me into the passenger seat. "I will drop you off, but then I need to see what my team has discovered. I will be done late tonight, so I will stay at my apartment."

There had been an attempted killing, and work on a homicide investigation continues until there isn't anything to do—either the case is cleared, or the investigation gets stonewalled. Right now, Arabella had a lot to do.

She put a hand on my knee. "You will be okay?"

"Sure. Right as rain."

Leaning over, with a crooked smile across her face, she whispered in my ear, "You still owe me." Then she squeezed my thigh.

CHAPTER 35

I ASKED ARABELLA to drop me at Vinny's so I could grab a couple of beers before heading back to the apartment. A little white lie. What I really intended to do was find Chuck and get him to give me a ride.

To Paradise Cove.

Chuck sat at the bar, alone, with a half-empty beer in front of him. Two stools away, several young tourist gals enjoyed fruity, colorful foo-foo drinks through tall straws. They eyed Chuck every few minutes, but he didn't seem interested, and as far as I could tell, had made no attempt to engage them in conversation. Unusual for him. Elbows on the bar, he watched traffic roll past on the street in front of Vinny's.

I dropped onto a stool between him and the ladies. "Hey, Chuck. You all right?"

"Yeah, I'm fine." He took a five from a pile of money on the bar. "You want a beer?"

I didn't accept and asked about a ride to Paradise Cove.

"Sure," he said and slid off the stool.

"Wait," I said, tapping the bar. "Finish your beer first. I'm in no hurry."

He stared at the bottle a moment, then shrugged. "That's okay. Let's go."

Neither of us said anything during the trip to Paradise Cove. Unusual for Chuck to remain silent for any period, let alone an extended one. Typically, his mouth's going a mile a minute about the women he's seeing or the money schemes he's hatching. And it's especially not like him to leave an unfinished beer behind.

Still a cloudless night, and as we traveled south, farther and farther from Kralendijk, our eyes adjusting to the loss of light, countless stars jumped out of the black sky. I made a mental note that when the Tessa and Rulio messes were cleaned up, Arabella and I would make a trip to the southernmost end of the island one night and lie near the water, drink a six-pack, and gaze skyward. If our eyes adjusted enough, we'd see the Milky Way Galaxy, appearing as a long narrow band of densely packed stars.

Or maybe we'd just fall asleep to the rhythmic slap of the waves against the shore.

Chuck pulled into the parking lot at Paradise Cove. It happened to be a crowded evening, but he found an open spot near one of the dumpsters. We walked through the door into the bar area and Chuck bumped his way through the throng of tourists. He ordered two Brights while I scanned the restaurant for Lucas Walker.

Not an empty table in the joint, as loud, boisterous customers, all decked out in recently purchased T-shirts, enjoyed a night in paradise, wishing life could be so simple. Even the outside chairs were full, the flames from the tiki torches illuminating people's faces and casting flickering shadows across the sand. Hard to tell in the darkness, but the sailboat I'd seen earlier, *Dream Crusher*, didn't appear moored in its usual spot, near the end of the short pier.

No sign of Lucas, but Danielle Anderson appeared from the kitchen.

"Hi, R," she said.

Chuck handed me a beer and I took a swig. "I'm looking for Walker."

"He's not here." She looked at Chuck, then back at me. "Is there something I can help you with?"

I hated to drag her into this mess. Lucas—and John Anderson—were the ones I needed to find and speak with. Her life didn't need to be ruined. Although, once she learned the truth, it would be.

Changing the subject seemed prudent. "I see *Dream Crusher* isn't moored. Someone take her out?"

"Yeah, Lucas went sailing this afternoon. I expect him back any minute. We're pretty busy and I need his help."

"Lucas sails?"

"Yes, he's quite an accomplished sailor. Several years ago, he taught me, although I'm not as good as he is."

Lucas didn't strike me as the sailing type. A surfer, yes, but not a sailor. But since he's from LA, it made sense.

"John sail, too?"

"No," she said, shaking her head. "He'll ride along, but he doesn't want anything to do with controlling the boat." She glanced out at the sea for a moment. "He doesn't know port from starboard. No concept of windward or leeward, and good luck teaching him to jibe or tack." She sighed then refocused on me. "Nope, John's not a sailor. He's a great businessman but knows nothing of the sea."

Chuck talked with the bartender, who happened to be a young island girl. She smiled at him, but I couldn't determine if she was interested or just playing him for tips. I hoped Lucas would arrive soon and kept glancing at the sea, watching for *Dream Crusher*.

Bright-eyed, Danielle asked, "You bring your banjo? John and I are about to sing a few numbers. You're welcome to join us."

"Yeah, you should've brought it, R," Chuck said. "I can drive back and get it if you want."

"No banjo tonight," I said. Taking a breath, I continued. "Look, Danielle, Lucas paid me a visit the other day and told me some pretty interesting things."

"I'm sure he did," she said.

"I just need to clear them up, if I can."

"Did he tell you he was an astronaut?"

"What?"

"Or maybe an FBI agent. Undercover, of course." She half-laughed. "That's what he tells everyone. He's either an astronaut or an FBI agent."

My body slumped. This wasn't what I expected. I never thought Lucas was an actual FBI agent, but I hadn't pegged him as a nutcase. A pathetic slug, yes; but not demented.

"He's obviously not an astronaut," Danielle said. "I mean, look at him. Not exactly a NASA poster boy. And to be an FBI agent, you'd think he'd need to know a little something about guns. Well, let me tell you, he doesn't. I doubt he knows which end the bullet comes out. He can't even load a water pistol." She signaled the bartender for a glass of red wine. I stood there listening, my mouth probably hanging open. "And when it comes to guns, John isn't much better." She took a sip of the wine. "Nope, between the two of them, I doubt they could even spell the word *gun*."

Chuck laughed. "Wow," he said softly.

I couldn't tell whether his reaction was to what Danielle had said or to the fact that she had said it in the first place.

"How well do you know Lucas?" I asked.

"Like I said before," Danielle said. "He and John have been friends a long time. I know him as well as I know anyone."

I bit my lower lip. Chuck stood next to me, but I needed to see how Danielle reacted to this next question.

"Did you know he was seeing a married woman?"

Chuck took a swig of beer and swiveled the barstool he sat on, turning his back to us.

"Not specifically," Danielle said. "But I can't keep up with all of his girlfriends. That'd be impossible."

"Well, this *girlfriend* happened to be the wife of a police inspector."

"Oh my God." Her hand shot up and covered her mouth. "The one who got killed?"

Chuck repositioned on the barstool.

"That's right," I said. I glanced at Chuck, then back at Danielle. "With a speargun."

Danielle accepted her glass of wine from the bartender. "What are you saying, R? Are you implying that Lucas killed that woman?" Her eyes left mine and moved to look behind me. When she spoke again, her voice was louder. "I wouldn't let John hear you talking like that."

"Talking like what?" John said. He appeared from behind me, walked over to Danielle, and put his arm around her.

She leaned down and kissed him on the cheek, saying, "Hey, sweetie." She swayed a little and took a small step sideways to steady herself.

"What did I miss?" John asked.

"Mr. Conklin," Danielle said, pointing at me with her wine-glass hand, her words beginning to slur, "thinks Lucas killed the wife of that police captain." Her face reddened and I doubted this was the day's first glass of wine for her.

Inspector. But I didn't correct her.

John shook his head. "No, not possible."

"That's what I told him," Danielle said.

I didn't say anything. Chuck had swiveled the barstool around, facing us again.

Hands forming into fists, John took a step forward, closing the distance between him and me. He looked up. "You need to leave."

"Probably," I said. "I eventually leave every place I go."

"Wait, wait, wait," Danielle said, interrupting my ten count. Her words were slurred more now than earlier. "Let's all just have a drink, and talk about banjos, music, scuba diving, something." Pointing at

Chuck, she said, "Airplanes! Let's talk about airplanes." Her wine glass was empty again. "Aren't we all friends?"

Too bad she was going to be pulled into whatever it was John and Lucas had going. Money laundering or drugs or whatever it turned out to be. And multiple murders. I hated what was coming her way but wasn't sure I could keep her out of it.

"Yeah, we're friends," I said. "Aren't we, John?"

He hesitated a moment, then laughed. Machine-gun style.

Ha ha ha.

"A beer sounds good to me," Chuck said, smiling at the female bartender as she handed him an open Bright.

"Not to me," I said.

"Anything else you want to say, R?" John asked.

I said nothing.

"What?" he said, cupping a hand around one of his ears and leaning slightly forward. "No witty comeback?"

Still quiet on my end. I said nothing.

"Good," he said, lighting a cigarette. "Since you don't have anything else to say, then get the hell out of here." Then he snarled at Chuck. "If you're going to do business with me, you need to learn to keep better company."

Chuck moaned a little but grabbed his beer and followed me out the door.

CHAPTER 36

WE PARKED AT the YellowRock and went up the outside stairs to the veranda. When I went to unlock the sliding glass door, I noticed it was open about an inch. I didn't usually leave it unlocked, let alone slightly ajar. I must've left it that way when Arabella and I went to the hospital.

"What's wrong, R?" Chuck asked, pulling me from my trance, staring at the lock.

I shook my head. "Nothing. Let's have a few beers."

Clear the scene, I thought as we walked through the door. I wasn't sure if someone had been in my apartment, so I did a covert scan of the living room and kitchen. Then made an excuse to go into my bedroom and bathroom. Admittedly, I'd done, at best, a cursory check but nothing seemed amiss. However, finding my door ajar didn't sit right with me.

Chuck hung with me on the veranda for a two-beer gab session. Mostly he talked gibberish about the young bartender at Paradise Cove and how he should ask her out. From his viewpoint, that's what she wanted. His sorrow and sense of loss over Tessa had only lasted a day or so. But that was Chuck.

"I hope you didn't cost me a client," he said.

"You need to lose that client, anyway."

"The guy pays too well to lose. Cash is king, baby."

"You get caught flying currency onto the island, and no amount of cash will keep you out of the Big House."

He went quiet for a few moments, then, staring at the floor, said, "Yeah, John's aggressiveness surprised me. First time I'd seen that side of him."

"Now you have."

"Maybe you're right. It may not be worth the risk."

Anderson's demeanor hadn't surprised *me*. He strove to be thought of as the gregarious restaurateur, suave and charming. But in essence, he wanted control—*needed* control—over everything and everyone around him. He was correct in seeing me as a threat. The more I poked, the more my curiosity grew and the more he lost control of things. No telling how far he'd go if he found out I knew about the boxes of money. It was pure happenstance the one box broke open enough for me to see inside.

It was after midnight by the time Chuck ventured home. Considering the number of beers he'd drunk, I convinced him to leave his truck and walk. Reluctantly, in true Chuck fashion, he agreed, tossing me the keys for safekeeping.

I swung back and forth in the hammock, sipping a beer, listening to the quiet of the island. An occasional vehicle drove along Kaya C.E.B. Hellmund, and, across the street, the waves never ceased rushing against the shore. A random wind gust floated through the trees, rattling the palm leaves and momentarily rocking the boats moored along the reef. Other than that, complete silence.

Island Silence.

A lone sailboat glided across the water between Bonaire and Klein Bonaire. It seemed to hide in the darkness, the red light atop the mast marking its quiet progress from north to south. I wondered if it was the *Dream Crusher* with Lucas at the helm, headed back to its mooring at Paradise Cove. Too dark and too far away to make out details and be certain.

I considered the possibility that John wanted Rulio dead. Could Rulio have stumbled onto the crates of money as I had? Maybe asked some questions or made some assumptions? Perhaps, Rulio decided to back out of the dive shop venture. And if Sandra, being an accountant for the company, saw irregularities in the numbers, she might've asked questions or had similar misgivings about her employers. If the answers didn't satisfy her, maybe she dug deeper. Deep enough to make John consider her disappearance a necessity.

They removed a problem. Twice.

But why David Brown? He didn't appear involved.

Nor did Tessa. Although, if she had been involved with Lucas or John, maybe she knew more than we thought.

But how to prove any of this?

Even though it was late, I called Arabella, knowing she'd still be working David Brown's shooting. I was right; she answered on the second ring.

"How's it going?" I asked.

"Not good." Her voice sounded scratchy, raw, as if she'd been talking loud for an extended amount of time. "We do not have much."

"Still no motive?"

"No, we will start that investigation tomorrow. Ask around the hospital and his friends about who might want to hurt him, how he was acting . . ." She released a hard breath into the phone. "*Ach*. You know the drill."

David's chat with me was the obvious motive. Somehow, the shooter knew David had spoken to me. But he hadn't told me anything of value, nothing we didn't already know.

"Still no slugs?" I asked.

"No, but we will try again in the daylight. Entry wounds look like small caliber, maybe nine-millimeter."

Same as the Good Samaritan.

"How much longer tonight?" I asked.

"I do not know. Everybody is tired. We can only do so much."

Either the case is cleared, or the investigation gets stonewalled.

I doubted they were stonewalled, but whatever could be completed tonight had probably been done. Her team needed a fresh start in the morning.

"Any update on David?" I asked.

"I checked with the hospital and nothing has changed. Condition is the same. They said again he is lucky to be alive."

"What about protection."

"Conklin, have faith. We put a guard at his door." She exhaled into the phone. "We have some knowledge on procedure."

She was correct. They knew their jobs.

Unable to think of anything else to ask, I said, "Okay, I'll let you go." I was prying and needed to let her get back to it. "Just wanted to check in before I hit the sack."

"Wait," she said. "I have some other news for you." Muffled, as if a hand were over her phone, she barked some instructions to someone. Then she returned her attention to me. "I received a message from a biologist. He had dissected a diseased eel that washed ashore."

The marine biologists studying the eels being killed by the mysterious virus. When a dead eel washed ashore, the researchers wanted to be informed so they could harvest it for study. But why the message to Arabella?

"Okay," I said.

"They found a human toe."

"Where'd the eel wash ashore?"

"Same area as Rulio's leg."

I was quiet a moment, processing what she had said. Morays are territorial, so unless someone on the island had reported being bitten—severely—the toe must belong to Rulio.

Sandra Griffis crossed my mind, but that'd be a long shot. The wind now blew out to sea, not toward the island in a reversal, as it had with Rulio's leg.

"I do not know any more than that," Arabella said. "I plan to contact the biologist tomorrow."

"Any reports of eel attacks or bites?"

"I will find out tomorrow."

Always good to have as much information as possible. If the toe turned out to be Sandra's, it'd spark the possibility that she was truly dead and not just missing.

"Anything else?" I asked.

"No."

"Are you staying at your place tonight?"

"Yes, I am."

"Well, then I guess I'll have to pay my debt tomorrow."

"Yes, you will."

She disconnected.

I hadn't asked about progress on the Good Samaritan shooting. And Arabella hadn't given me an update on the name Schleper scrolled on the piece of paper during our meeting at the coffee shop. I had memorized the name and address before I gave her the paper, so, maybe tomorrow, I'd do some surveillance.

Or as Erika referred to it, *snooping*.

CHAPTER 37

SOMETHING OUT OF the ordinary woke me. A noise; a movement; a smell. I didn't know. Somewhere in the recesses of my brain, a defense mechanism detected an abnormality nearby and startled me awake. A self-preservation wake-up call of sorts.

Lying in bed, eyes wide open, I remained motionless. Judging by the darkness outside, and knowing I went to bed after midnight, I guessed it to be early morning. Ambient light sneaked around the edges of the curtains, casting thin beams of illumination across the walls and ceiling.

I listened. No sound. Made of concrete block and cement, the building didn't creak like a wood-framed structure. No popping timbers or bending floorboards when someone walked over them. A person's weight had much less impact on cement and tile.

As I considered getting out of bed and going into the living area, movement from the small hallway off the bedroom caught my eye. Barely a shadow, little more than a flicker of darkness on darkness, it told me what I needed to know.

Someone was in my apartment.

And it wasn't Arabella.

I jumped out of bed in my boxers. Through the darkness, I made out a few key characteristics of an intruder advancing rapidly in my direction. Long hair; slender build; sleeveless T-shirt.

He entered the bedroom, and before I could take a swing at him, shoved the large end of a baseball bat into my gut. I fell back, landing on the bed, gasping for breath. He dropped the bat, jumped on top of me, and grabbed under my chin, pushing my head back. An instant later, I felt the cool thinness of a blade against my throat.

"Settle down, you piece of shit, and you don't get hurt," he said. "Otherwise, I'll cut you up and feed you to the sharks."

We both remained motionless, eyes locked on each other. His hair hung forward and sweat dripped from his nose and forehead onto my face. The ceiling fan twirled overhead, looking like some sort of satanic halo hovering above his dark features. I closed my eyes and counted to ten.

"What do you want?" I asked through gritted teeth.

"We just want to talk, R." I moved my eyes and, in the darkness, barely made out John Anderson, leaning sideways against the wall near my dresser. He must've followed Lucas into my bedroom. "But first, we thought we'd get your attention." He paused a moment. Lucas maintained eye contact with me. "Do we have your attention?"

John needed control and, in this instance, considering the blade on my jugular, I decided he had it.

"Yes," I said, "you have my attention."

"Lucas," John said.

Lucas, continuing to hold the knife in place, slowly got off me and stood alongside the bed. He removed the blade from my throat and picked up the bat. He held one in each hand. The message was clear. Try anything and I get whacked or cut. Maybe both. I raised myself and sat on the edge of the mattress, resisting the urge to rub my throat or chest.

"Nice work," I said to Lucas. "They teach you that at Quantico?"

"R . . . I'm the one you need to talk with," John said.

I stared at John. "So . . . *talk*," I said.

"In a nutshell, R, you need to stop pressing things. The people I work for want you to back off and let it go."

"The people you work for? . . . Let *what* go?"

"All of it. We like you, R." He pointed at Lucas. "Lucas, Danielle, me. All of us. We're all friends."

"*Friends?*" I glanced at Lucas for an instant, then back at John. "Were Rulio and Tessa friends?"

Lucas's hands tightened around the handle end of the bat and his face boiled into a scowl. He looked at John. John shook his head.

"They can't convict your friend for Tessa's death," John said. "They don't have enough evidence. But if you continue your current path, additional *evidence* might appear. As for Rulio, I don't know what you're talking about. Other than it was a sad situation."

My lips tightened and I glared at him.

"You piece of shit," Lucas growled.

I smiled at him. "You already called me that, *Agent* Walker." I looked back at John. Time to spill the beans. "What about all those boxes, the ones filled with cash?"

John didn't act surprised that I knew about the boxes. He paused a moment, then pushed off the wall and stepped up to me, face flush, neck muscles tight. "Just drop it!" He took a breath. "You can't change anything anyway." He sat on the bed next to me. "And, who knows? If you do as I ask, maybe one of those boxes finds its way into your closet."

"Does Danielle know about all of this?" I asked.

He popped a cigarette in his mouth, but before he got it lit, I said, "No smoking in here." He paused and stared at me a moment, then lit up. I tried to relax the best I could, but my entire body tensed.

"Danielle is not your concern, friend—"

"I'm not your *friend*."

Lucas took a step forward and put the end of the bat in my chest. I knocked it away and stood, squaring off with him. John put a hand on Lucas's arm.

"Lucas," John said, "wait in the other room."

Lucas didn't move.

"C'mon," John said.

Lucas jabbed me one more time with the bat then turned and headed toward the hallway.

After Lucas had left the room, John said to me, "He should be your biggest worry. I can't always control him, and he does whatever he wants. Especially if he thinks he's protecting me or Danielle."

"Yeah, you're a *real* lucky guy."

He sighed. "As I was saying, Danielle isn't your concern. I can handle my wife. You just need to decide if all of this is worth you or your friends getting hurt."

"How many times you going to threaten me?"

He blew smoke in my face. "As many times as it takes. But eventually, the threats become action. My Boss's patience is wearing thin."

"Your Boss. Funny, I thought you were the Boss."

"Hell, R, we all have a boss. You should understand that."

He smiled again and patted me on the shoulder. "I have something for you. Actually, it's for your lady friend." He dropped the cigarette butt on the floor and crushed it out with the toe of his shoe.

In a surprising show of confidence, he turned his back on me and walked over to the dresser. Total self-assurance in his control of the situation. Upon reaching the dresser, he picked up a bag I hadn't noticed earlier. He reached inside and pulled out a box.

"This is a gift," he said, opening the box and tilting it in my direction so I could see into it. "It's a Makarov automatic pistol. I know Arabella had mentioned wanting one, so I thought I'd pick it up for her." He reached into the box again and pulled out three additional, smaller boxes. "And here's some ammunition . . . In case she needs to shoot someone."

Getting a handgun onto Bonaire was no easy task. Not to mention 150 rounds of ammo. Anything firearms related is highly regulated with gun control laws more restrictive than any in the States. John was proving to me his ability to beat the system, shoving his ties to the black market in my face. He had links to the criminal underworld and wanted me to know it.

"That's okay," I said. "She can't accept a gift like that."

"It's brand new, in the box. Never been fired."

I shook my head.

"I'll just leave it here. You can give it to her later." He closed the box and laid it on the dresser, shaking his head. "It'd be a shame—a waste, actually—if somehow her fingers got broken and she's unable to pull the trigger."

"After a while, Anderson, your threats don't mean anything."

"Just remember this, *Conklin*, you mentioned Rulio earlier. Any of your friends could end up like him."

"You mean like Sandra did?"

He raised his hands, surrender fashion. "Danielle handles all the administrative stuff. You'd have to talk to her about Sandra." He cocked his head. "I wonder if anyone has heard from her." A thin smile worked its way across his face. "Remember, R, let's stay friends, okay? So, back off!"

When he turned to leave, I said, "I don't need any more *friends*."

He stopped, slowly turned, and walked back to me. "Tell you what," he said. "If you don't want to be friends, then I suggest you buy a tall bottle of whiskey and find a couple of hookers. Then, after you get shit-faced drunk and fuck the hell out of the whores, you should kill yourself." He patted me on the chest. "That'd be a better alternative than *not* being friends." He stared at me a moment, then left the room.

By the time I followed him into the living room, the sliding door to the veranda was open and he and Lucas were gone. I walked out, looked over the railing, and saw the taillights of a vehicle disappear down Kaya C.E.B. Hellmund.

The door had a key entry from the outside. I examined the lock, which I should've done earlier when I came home and found it open. No scrapes or indications of forced entry. They must've picked the lock. Time to get a new one that's pick resistant.

I checked the time. Four a.m. I needed a beer but didn't want to drink at this hour of the night. Or morning. I knew attempting any additional sleep would be hopeless, so I slipped into the hammock and thought about what had just happened.

Earlier this evening—or was it yesterday evening?—I considered making something happen, getting John to lose control, maybe get him to make a mistake. Not sure what I did to make this happen, but he seemed to have notched things up a level.

Danielle was right about one thing: John certainly wasn't a gun person. He referred to the Makarov as an automatic when it's a *semi*-automatic. Any gun person worth his weight in range passes wouldn't make that mistake.

Both gunshot victims—David Brown and the Good Samaritan—had double taps to the chest. With his limited firearms awareness, doubtful John could perform at that level of precision.

And Danielle had claimed Lucas was just as inept. She was right about John, so I had no reason to doubt her claims regarding Lucas.

So, if the shooter wasn't John, and probably not Lucas, then who?

CHAPTER 38

MY CELLPHONE BUZZED me awake. I lay facedown in my hammock, sweat dripping off my nose onto the veranda floor. Movement proved difficult as I tried to roll over, my coordination slow to catch up with my intentions. I missed the call and it went to voicemail.

The display showed two missed calls from Arabella. I must've slept through the first one. It also showed the time as 8:36 a.m.

Patches of dark clouds filled the southwest sky and they appeared to be moving in this direction. The temperature had already dropped, and the palm trees bent and swayed with the increased wind gusts. By the look of the darkening sky, it'd be raining in less than an hour.

Plopping back in the hammock and sleeping through a rainstorm sounded like a great option. But instead, I stretched, then rested my elbows on the railing, looking out at the sea. A dive boat cruised past. The diving never stopped. A little rain? No big deal on Bonaire.

A Creedence song came to mind. "Have You Ever Seen The Rain?" The events of last night made me consider some of the tune's early lyrics, something about there being a calm before the storm. Just as the clouds approaching from the southwest signaled bad weather approaching, last night's events indicated that John Anderson was panicked and a different type of storm was about to make landfall, somewhere near Paradise Cove.

I turned and leaned my butt against the railing, scanning the wall, the veranda ceiling, the seams where walls and ceiling met, the floorboards, and the corners. It was just a cursory examination, but nothing seemed out of place. Nothing obvious.

John knew Arabella had mentioned a Makarov. But she had only mentioned it to me, here on the veranda. I'd have to check with her, but doubtful she talked about it to anyone else. Especially not anyone from Paradise Cove.

In addition, the person who shot David Brown must've known that I'd talked to him. That conversation took place in the office and the only person nearby was Erika. No secret she often listened to my conversations, but she'd never do anything to jeopardize David. Especially since it involved Rulio's case.

I was convinced the apartment and my office contained multiple listening devices. John and Lucas broke in last night, so I had to assume they could've done it earlier as well.

By leaving the Makarov, John had tipped his hand. He'd have to assume I'd catch on and go looking for the devices. I didn't understand what he'd gain from that and why he'd want me to know.

I needed to call Arabella back, see how things went last night, but it was possible she'd be sleeping. Her 8:36 call may've been when she got back to her apartment and I didn't want to possibly wake her. She'd call when she could.

I wasn't sure how to tell her about last night's visit from John and Lucas. When she found out, she'd want to file a report and go after them. Problem was my word against theirs. No proof they broke into my apartment. And I had in my possession what I believed to be an illegal firearm. That might not go over well in her report, especially if other officers were involved. No proof John handled it or gave it to me and I'm sure he's smart enough to cover his tracks. He'd been doing a good job so far.

Out of curiosity, I opened the Makarov box and examined the gun. At first glance, it appeared new. The box also contained the owner's manual, two magazines, and a small, cheap trigger lock, courtesy of the manufacturer. *Can never be too safe* said the paper tag attached to the lock.

Many firearms manufacturers ship their products coated with a brown wax-like petroleum-based corrosion inhibitor, the most common being trademarked as Cosmoline. This Makarov had been wiped clean of Cosmoline, and the barrel smelled of linseed oil, indicating that the weapon had been recently cleaned, making me question whether it'd been previously fired. The Makarov chambered a nine-millimeter cartridge, albeit a shorter than standard slug with smaller brass. David Brown and the Good Samaritan had both been shot with what appeared to be a nine-millimeter.

If this was the murder weapon, then it'd be important to have. But, again, I wasn't sure how I'd explain it being in my possession.

My word against theirs.

I used a clean cloth to wipe down the weapon, the magazines, and the owner's manual, then put all of it back into the manufacturer's box and slipped the box into a large freezer bag. Then, I did the same with the ammo boxes, putting them in an additional freezer bag. I zipped both bags shut, ready to transport.

I'd eventually tell Arabella about last night and give her the Makarov. But first, I needed to drive to Paradise Cove.

Last night, Chuck had left his truck and keys with me. He never stirs before late morning, unless he had a flight, and since he and his plane were grounded, that wasn't an issue. Good excuse for him to sleep even later.

I went down the interior stairs to the office and checked in with Erika. She seemed surprised to see me.

"You are up early this morning," she said. "And not to exercise, I see."

I put my hands on my hips. "For all you know, I swam to Curacao and back this morning."

She peered at me over the rim of her glasses. "If that were true, you would shower. And I can tell you did not."

I didn't respond.

"Someone from Abby's Seaside Truck Rental called," she said. "They will drop off a truck for you sometime this morning."

"Did they say what time?"

"They say 'sometime this morning,'" she said. "Even *I* know what that means."

"Okay, but I need to run an errand," I said. "I'll be back in an hour."

"You are walking?" she asked.

"No, I have Chuck's truck. He left it here last night."

"Aha!" she said, pointing a pen at me. "You and Chuck drinking late. Today, no exercise and no shower." She smiled.

Facing her, I started out the door, my backside pushing it open. "You should've been a detective."

Her mouth fell open. "Maybe so." Her smile disappeared and her eyelids drooped. "Would it be possible for me to do any worse?"

A tingling swept up the back of my neck and across my face. She meant: *Could she do any worse on Rulio's case than me?* I let out a deep breath. "Probably not," I said.

She looked up at me for a moment, then turned back to her monitor. She wiped her eyes with her fingers.

A lump formed in my throat. My investigation was marginally further along than she realized, but I hesitated to dive into it with her. As much as I wanted to fill her in on my progress—what little of it there was—it wasn't yet the right time. For the next little while, as much as it hurt, I'd have to let her believe what she believed.

I pushed through the door and left.

CHAPTER 39

I SPED TOWARD Paradise Cove, driving Chuck's truck as if I'd stolen it. Not sure how early in the day the workers arrived to prep for business, but I gambled the Andersons spent most of their free time there.

Ten minutes after leaving the YellowRock, I pulled into the empty lot at Paradise Cove. The storm had passed quickly, as it usually did on Bonaire, leaving a few dark puddles in the gravel parking lot.

A brick-sized rock held the restaurant door open.

I walked in. A man polished the wood bar using a white cloth and liquid from a plastic spray bottle as two women scurried between tables positioning chairs, adjusting vases containing fake flowers, and filling salt and pepper shakers. In high-pitched voices, they jabbered to each other in Papiamentu. The man said something and they all three laughed. It might've been in reference to me. I had no way of knowing.

A solitary person walked along the beach behind Paradise Cove and *Dream Crusher* rocked gently at her mooring, a few yards from the short pier. A pelican sat perched on one of the unlit tiki torches, its wings partially unfolded. The canvas providing shade over the dining area moved rhythmically with the wind, which had died down considerably since the storm's passing.

The guy behind the bar stopped wiping and looked up at me as I walked over and sat on one of the barstools. I laid the freezer bags containing the Makarov box and the ammunition on the bar.

"Is Danielle or John Anderson here?" I asked.

He nodded and disappeared through the door into the kitchen.

I swiveled the barstool to face the sea. The breeze worked its way through the restaurant, blowing some napkins off the stack at the end of the bar. I considered how refreshing it'd be to lie on the beach with the sun hitting me in the face and forget about all of this. But that wasn't going to happen today.

Or any time soon.

The bartender returned from the kitchen. "Missus Anderson will soon be out. Would you like something to drink?"

"Just ice water, please."

He dropped a cork coaster on the bar and set a glass of ice water in front of me. After last night, it tasted good. I drained the glass in one upturn, and, when I set it back on the coaster, the bartender filled it again.

My cell rang. Erika.

"Your rental truck has arrived," she said.

"Can you sign for it?" Not uncommon for her to forge my signature for business purposes. This might not have been strictly business, but I wanted them to leave the truck. Chuck would be wanting his back soon.

"Yes, I already did," she said. "And I have the keys. I will lay them on your desk."

"Thanks." I clicked off.

The bartender continued his polishing routine, stopping occasionally to yell something at the women, then chuckling when they laughed. After a few moments, Danielle sauntered out from the kitchen. Her hair was pulled behind her head into a tight bun, covered with a fine black net. She wore a white, full apron, stained with numerous blotches of crimson, and blood-soaked rubber gloves covered her hands.

A frown came over her face. She did a fake quick draw routine with her hands then smiled. "Hello, R."

I looked her up and down and she apparently noticed my unintended, prolonged glance at her apron.

"I sometimes help in the kitchen doing prep work," she said, snapping off her gloves and dropping them on the bar. Without being asked or told, the bartender scooped them up and threw them in the trash. He then wiped the area down with soap and water. Danielle didn't acknowledge him but smiled at me. "Yeah, I know. *Shit* work." She made a chopping motion with her hand on the bar. "I have to admit, though, sometimes it's kind of fun. Nothing like chopping things up to take out your frustration." Then, in rapid succession, she tapped her finger twice on the bar. "Andre."

The bartender stopped polishing and poured her a glass of red wine, leaving the half-empty bottle on the bar within Danielle's reach. He looked at me. I shook my head. Danielle motioned with her eyes and the bartender walked to the opposite end of the bar and continued his polishing.

"I know what you're thinking," she said, sipping from the wine glass. "But I've been up since four this morning. Besides, whoever came up with that stupid rule about not drinking in the morning wasn't married to John *Smack* Anderson." She took a large hit of wine. "Or trapped on this miserable rock of an island."

She shook her head and poured more wine into her not-yet-empty glass. Flushed cheeks, heavy eyelids, I guessed it wasn't her first glass of the morning. I stared at her a moment, then pointed at the freezer bags lying on the bar.

"What are those?" she said, looking at the bags.

"Gifts . . . From your husband."

She laid a hand on the bag containing the Makarov box. "What are you talking about?"

"He and Lucas broke into my apartment."

She sighed, then, under her breath, barely audible, she said, "Those fucking idiots."

I waved my hand across the bags. "John said these were gifts for Arabella."

She took a sip of wine. "Arabella. Your squeeze?"

We stared at each other for a long moment. I took a drink of water.

"I came here, thinking I might return them to you," I said. "But, on second thought, maybe it'd be best if I turned them over to Bella."

She shrugged. "Whatever. We have no use for them."

Maybe. Maybe not.

She caressed the stem of her wine glass. "Well, maybe your squeeze—"

I shook my head. "I'm sure *Arabella* would be happy to look them over. Check to see if they've been used in a crime."

After a moment, she said, "Okay." She finished her glass of wine and laid the empty glass on the bar, then grabbed the bottle and walked toward the kitchen. Before going through the door, she turned back to me. "Did John talk to you about being friends?"

I didn't say anything.

"He did, right? And I hope you listened . . . and understood. I'd hate to think you weren't our friend."

"I don't need more friends."

She took a step back in my direction, put her elbow on the bar, and cradled her head in her hand. Her eyes stung mine and we were both quiet for a moment.

Andre, the bartender, picked up my glass, half full of melting ice and condensation running down its side. He held it up and looked at me.

I raised a hand, palm out. "No thanks. I'm done." I headed for the door but stopped and turned around when Danielle spoke.

"When I was in fifth or sixth grade—I can't remember exactly—there was a bully in my school," Danielle began. She stared through the dining area at the sea. "The bitch was bigger than me and hated my guts. Don't know why, but she did. She'd make fun of my clothes, my hair . . . everything. When I finally taught myself to ignore her, she began hitting and kicking me. It got to where she'd beat on me several times a week. I tried fighting back, but it was pointless. She was just too big. None of the other kids were any help. They just laughed at me. All the other kids were afraid of her, too.

"She was a cruel person, devoid of any feelings." Danielle tapped her fingers on the bar again and Andre brought her a clean glass. She filled it with wine from the bottle she held. "One day, the bitch brought her pet white rat to school, probably for show-and-tell or something—I can't remember. However, I do remember that she loved that animal." She laughed. "How fitting she'd have a *rat* for a pet. Anyway, she baby-talked to it and cuddled it close to her face, being gentler than I thought her capable of." She made a dismissive wave with her hand. "She let all the other kids pet it. But not me, of course. I didn't get to."

She paused a moment and took a gulp of wine. Not sure why, but I waited for her to continue.

"Then, at lunch recess that day, I snuck back into the school building. I took her precious, soft, pink-tailed rat out of the small cage and cradled it against my body as I walked into the bathroom." She turned and faced me, her eyes narrow as she stared into some far-off abyss visible only to her. "I filled the sink and held its head under water till it drowned." Her lips tightened. "Then I broke every bone I could in its wretched, limp body." Drinking the last of her wine, and holding her gaze on me, a thin smile crept across her face. In a matter-of-fact tone, she said, "Then I put it back in the cage."

"That's disturbed. Even for a bullied child."

She let out a small laugh. "Maybe, but watching that bitch fall down sobbing when she found her *Precious* dead in the cage was . . . precious itself." She rolled her head, cracking her neck. "And as a bonus, I learned something that day."

"What? That you're a lunatic?"

She stepped up to me, stopping within a few inches. Swaying, she held up her index finger, wanting to make a point. "What I realized, even at such a young, impressionable age, was that everyone, even bad people, have something—or *someone*—that's important to them." After letting that sink in a bit and glaring at me a quick moment, she bowed her head and picked at a spot of dried blood on her apron. "So, tell me, R"—her eyes rolled up at me—"who's important to you?"

Hands at my side, I instinctively squeezed the bag containing the Makarov. I calmed myself and counted to ten. A heaviness overtook my body, and I may've momentarily forgotten to breathe, returning in a slight hitch. Disappointment, not anger or fear.

Returning her stare, in a low, graveled voice, I said, "Certainly not you."

For a split second, her face tightened, then it relaxed as she broke into a wild laugh. She tilted her head back and said, "I'm so glad you stopped by, R." Still laughing, she waltzed through the door to the kitchen. A moment later, as I stood frozen in place by confusion, she poked her head back out and said, "Next time you stop by, please bring your banjo." Then her face brightened, she smiled, and disappeared into the kitchen.

The Bonaire sun beat down on me as I left the restaurant, forcing me to shield my eyes with a hand, even though I wore sunglasses. The steering wheel was hot to the touch and the vinyl seats singed my legs as I twisted into the driver's seat of Chuck's truck. Tires spinning, throwing loose gravel against the underside of the bed, I stomped on the gas, and pulled out of the parking lot, onto the blacktop road.

I hoped to never visit Paradise Cove again.

Friend or no friend.

CHAPTER 40

CLENCHING THE STEERING wheel tighter than necessary, I sped north, away from Paradise Cove. My neck muscles cramped, and my jaw ached. I fought the urge to pound my fist on the dash.

The interaction with Danielle Anderson wasn't what I had anticipated. Not sure what my expectations were, but I never thought it'd be the same I'd-hate-to-think-you-weren't-our-friend warning that John used.

And the thing about the rat came out of left field. Was it just a pretense to an implied threat? Was Danielle really that disturbed? Or did her laughter at the end telegraph the story as nonsense, something she had made up? If so, why?

Before I processed any of it further, my cell phone rang.

Chuck.

"What?" I should've counted to ten before answering.

A momentary silence, then he said, "Well, good morning to you, too."

I took a breath. "I'm sorry. What's up?"

"I'm at The Rock." Chuck referred to the YellowRock Resort as *The Rock*. "Where are you? I need my truck."

"On my way back. Be there in ten."

Chuck started babbling something about needing to go to the airport. Not interested, I disconnected. More important things for me to worry about.

The conversation with Schleper came to mind and I wondered if Arabella had researched the name he had provided us.

I parked alongside another truck, which I assumed was my rental, in front of the YellowRock. A freshly painted mural of a turtle decorated its tailgate. Not long ago, my good friend Tiffany—the person who played the role of my kid sister—had asked for a rental with a turtle.

But she got a seahorse instead.

Not the time to think about her. Or those days.

Chuck came out the door of *The Rock* and I tossed him his truck keys.

"Any chance Arabella could clear my plane so you can make another flight to Curacao tomorrow afternoon?" he asked. He tugged at his shirt collar then looked at his feet. "Mr. Anderson has more packages he needs delivered."

"You can't be serious."

"This is my chance to keep him as a client. Besides, he's upped the pay to a point I can't refuse."

"You better."

"I'm going to have court and lawyer costs. I need the cash."

"Bringing US currency to the island won't help your defense. If anything, it'll cost you more in legal fees. You're just digging a deeper hole for yourself."

A thin smile worked across his face. "Only if I get caught."

"You'll get caught. Arabella already knows about the packages. She's not going to okay another flight."

His face tightened and flushed. "You told her?"

"Consider it *protecting* you."

He shook his head. "Well, I'll try to find someone else. Let me know if you change your mind. There'll be a big paycheck in it for you."

"Chuck, the police would still need to clear your airplane to fly."

He shrugged and got in his truck. "I'll figure something out."

Hand on the roof, I lowered my head to the door window and looked in the truck at him. "Don't be an idiot. It's not worth it."

He paused a moment and let out a long breath. "Maybe you're right," he said. "But regardless, I still have to meet Lucas at the airport tomorrow afternoon."

I watched him pull away, then went inside to get the keys to the rental.

The one with a turtle on the tailgate.

CHAPTER 41

I DROVE THROUGH Kralendijk, turned off Kaya Gob N. Debroot, and pulled up to a small orange house with a tile roof midway down Kaya Den Haag. Other than a front gate hanging open from a broken hinge and a few weeds sprouting through the gravel landscape, the residence looked reasonable. Could've passed for any working-class home on the island.

It was in a better-than-I-expected neighborhood, given the fact a police inspector had given me the resident's name and address. I assumed the house would be run down and in need of repair, typical of miscreants known by police officers worldwide.

I slipped through the gate and walked across the gravel yard toward the house. A brown mutt lay sprawled in the shade tied by a rope to a small, untrimmed wayaka tree. Its head raised as I approached; tail banging rapidly on the ground. Giving the dog a quick once-over and noting the white patch over one of its eyes, I was certain it was the same animal that had been at Paradise Cove. The day I confronted Lucas on the beach.

The dog lowered its head back to the gravel when it realized I wasn't coming any closer. Its tail continued wagging, albeit at a slower pace, until, after a moment, it stretched, yawned, and fell motionless.

The sun was a bit past straight overhead. The dog must've known it was siesta time.

With the adventures of last night—actually, early morning—and the lack of sleep, my energy level had begun to erode. I envied the dog and wished for siesta time as well.

Two metal bowls lay against the wall near the front stoop. One held remnants of dry dog food and the other a small amount of water, maybe two swallows. The dog food looked old and crusty, a few flies hovering about. A thin layer of dust floated on the surface of the water.

I knocked.

No answer.

I knocked again.

Still no answer.

I peered through the front windows. Dirty curtains and dust-filled screens prevented me from seeing inside. I walked along the side of the house. More windows and dirty curtains and screens. Same at the back of the house.

It'd be illegal to enter the dwelling, so I didn't consider it. Not seriously, anyway. However, if a window were open or unlocked, perhaps I'd manage to hear something or garner a peek inside. But no such luck. Every window I checked was closed and locked.

I stood in the backyard, sweat soaking through my shirt. The gravel acted like hot embers, radiating heat through the soles of my sandals.

A knock on the locked back door produced the same, no-answer result, and I wasn't sure of my next step. I really wanted to chat with this guy. Schleper had said he was *a local thug who has had dealings with Lucas Walker.* That was reason enough to speak with him.

A run-down, twelve-foot by twelve-foot shed stood at the back of the property. Made of metal with a tin roof, it looked to be the type purchased pre-built at a home improvement store, delivered, and dropped into place. The structure leaned sideways about ten degrees. No windows, but a sliding door on the front swayed in the wind, half open.

I stepped sideways through the door and into the dark shed. As my eyes tried to adjust, I ran my hand along the inside wall. I flipped a switch and a single overhead bulb illuminated the space.

Crumpled paper bags and cardboard boxes of all dimensions littered the floor. Shelves lined the two sidewalls containing laptop computers, cameras with underwater housings, and scuba air regulators. I guessed all the items were stolen and this was a storage area for fenced merchandise. Not very secure, but it didn't have to be. Perhaps this guy didn't hold the property long enough to worry about it being found and re-stolen. Or he was well enough known by other crooks that they didn't dare steal his goods. Odds were, he operated as the means of acquiring the property. Higher-ranked hoodlums probably took all of it, paying him a pittance, then fenced it to the real customers.

As I stepped to the center of the dark room, amidst the bags and cardboard boxes, the back of the shed caught my attention. Pegboard covered the wall and tools hung from hooks inserted into the holes of the pegboard. Hammers, screwdrivers, pliers, wrenches, saws, etcetera—all divided into sections. Even a couple of large, rusty monkey wrenches. A black outline surrounded each tool, marking its exact hanging location, walling off each object from the others, forcing them into their own quiet solitude. *A place for everything and everything in its place.* Ben Franklin would've been proud.

There was even a scuba section. Several masks, snorkels, and two sets of fins hung on the wall inside their respective black perimeter. On the edge of the pegboard, near the back corner, draped three spearguns of various sizes, each hanging silently, content with their isolation.

A fourth outline set my heart racing and my mind spinning.

A black perimeter—a reserved spot on the pegboard—but no speargun.

A place for everything BUT NOT *everything in its place.*

At that moment I sensed someone behind me. Then, an instant later, as I turned, I heard a voice yell, "Conklin!"

Arabella stood at the door flanked by Ingrid. Arabella lowered her weapon and placed a hand on Ingrid's arm forcing her weapon toward the ground as well. They both holstered their guns as I turned fully around to face them.

"What are you doing here?" she asked before I could ask her the same thing.

"I wanted to talk to this guy," I said. "But when he didn't answer the door, I thought I'd look around a bit." I pointed at the back wall, hoping to deflect the fact that I shouldn't be in the shed. "Look, a speargun is missing."

She stepped into the shed and studied the back wall. "Yes, and based on the outline, it looks to be about the size of the one from Chuck's truck." She placed her hands on her hips. "But you should not be here."

"Why are *you* here?"

"We received a call from a neighbor about someone looking in the windows and walking around the house."

"But why not just send a patrol? Why you?"

"When I heard the address, I recognized it from the paper you gave me." She wiped sweat off her neck and brushed back some hair. "I thought maybe I should come along. I brought an extra squad just in case."

Someone from outside the shed yelled for Arabella. She walked to the door and looked toward the house for a moment as the person continued speaking in Papiamentu. I stepped to the door and peered out as Arabella spoke to an officer on the back stoop of the house. After a few moments, eyes wide and a concerned look on her face, she pointed a finger at me.

"You stay here," she said, then nodded to Ingrid.

Arabella trotted off and entered the house through the back door. I started to walk out of the shed, but Ingrid put up a hand and shook her head, hard, twice.

"No, Mr. R," she said. "Please stay here."

"Look," I said. "I'm going into that house."

I tried to walk past her, but this time she put her hand on my chest and pushed me back. I knew better than to assault a police officer, but I needed to get into the house.

"I'm going in there," I said, pointing at the house.

She rested her hand on the baton hanging from her belt. "Officer De Groot said for you to stay here."

Bonaire police didn't carry tasers, but they were well trained in the use of batons and pepper spray. Although being tased was five seconds of agony no one wanted to experience, I had confidence Ingrid, using her training and skills with a baton and pepper spray, could make a taser seem mild in comparison.

She likes you.

I sure hoped Arabella was right.

Disrespecting a police office didn't sit well with me, especially when that officer was Ingrid. Being charged with an R&O—resisting and obstruction of a police officer—would be the ultimate humiliation for a retired cop like myself.

But I needed to get inside the house.

"I'm going in that house, Ingrid," I said. "You can stay here or come with me."

She moved slightly aside as I nudged past her and walked across the yard. Right on my heels, she followed me into the house, coming through the back entrance directly behind me. I breathed a sigh of relief and leaned against the kitchen counter for a moment. She stood by the door. I doubted she would've shot me, and I was glad she didn't use her baton or spray. She probably figured it easier to let Arabella deal with me.

"Thanks," I said to her.

She threw her hands in the air and dropped them. "What choice did you give me?" Folding her arms across her chest, she sighed and said, "That was not nice of you."

Loud, anxious voices came from deeper inside the house. I followed their sound and entered a small den or bedroom area. In the middle of the room, a body lay on the floor, a pool of dried blood, glossy and reddish-brown in color, defining its perimeter.

Arabella turned in my direction as I moved closer, careful not to step in the blood or touch anything. I expected a scolding, but instead, she said, "It is him."

By *him*, I assumed she meant the guy who lived here. Owner of three spearguns. Former owner of a fourth.

The body lay faceup, two bullet holes in the chest: one in the forehead.

Rack up another one for our shooter, I thought.

"We got luckier on this one," Arabella said and handed me a clear plastic bag containing a shell casing. "We found it behind the door."

I examined the casing. Looked to be a nine-millimeter, but with a shorter brass, matching the ones John Anderson had given me.

"Also," Arabella said, moving toward one of the walls. "A bullet went through the victim and lodged in this wall. We can dig it out and perhaps do ballistics with it."

I saw the impact hole from where I stood. The bullet had gone into the wall sideways, which meant it probably didn't go very deep. Be easy to dig out. Also, the sideways impact might've preserved the ballistics marks—at least on one side—the bullet not crunching and deforming as it would by a head-on strike against the block and cinder wall.

"Now we will have comparisons when we find the gun," Arabella said. She knelt and looked over the body. "I am guessing he has been dead for a few hours."

I agreed with her, but skin color, smell, and insect activity would later confirm her assumption. If the murder was only a few hours old, then the Makarov John gave me couldn't be the murder weapon. It hadn't left my sight, so I had to assume there were two Makarovs currently on the island. Arabella needed to know about the weapon in my possession, but right now, in front of the others, wasn't the time to tell her.

"I'm leaving," I said. "Buzz me later?"

Arabella stood, moved her head back and forth, looking at the other two officers, then nodded at me. She was about to have her hands full.

Again.

I walked out the front door and across the gravel yard to my rental truck. The brown, mangy mutt still panted under the shade of the wayaka tree, although it had risen to a sitting position. It looked at me, wagged its tail a couple of beats, then yawned.

Upon reaching the truck, I paused and turned around. With its tongue hanging out, tail still wagging, the dog yelped, straining at the limit of the rope. It sat on its back haunches a moment, then yapped again.

I got in the truck and drove off.

After three blocks, I turned around and went back.

CHAPTER 42

I WENT INTO the office, escorted by my new friend. Erika appeared from the large closet in the back.

Her face brightened. "Who do we have here?" She bent over and rubbed behind the dog's ears.

"His owner is dead—"

She looked up at me, brows scrunched. "I heard about a person being shot."

Not a surprise. Again, no island-secrets when it comes to Erika.

"Yeah, that was him." I watched her rub the dog's head. Its tail wagged. "I couldn't leave her there, tied to a tree." I shrugged. "So, I took her."

Erika stood. The dog moved a step closer to her and pointed its nose in the air.

"What will we do with her?" Erika asked.

I shrugged. "Keep her, I guess. We could use an office dog."

"'We?'"

"I'll help take care of her."

"I am *sure* you will." She went to her desk. The dog followed and sat at Erika's feet.

"I also took a bag of dog food and some bowls from the front porch." I went to the truck, got the items, and brought them back into the office, dropping them near Erika's desk. "She probably needs some food and water."

Erika glared up at me.

Before she could say anything, I took the stairs two at a time up to my apartment. I went to the veranda, scanned the area, my head slowly making a circle, stopping on each scant piece of furniture. Not many places to hide a snooping device.

Where would I hide it? I thought.

I flipped over the small plastic table, the one Arabella and I had eaten at when she talked about the Makarov. Two-sided tape secured a small black device not much larger than a pack of gum to the center of the table's underside. Virtually unnoticeable. If either of us had brushed against it with a knee while sitting, we wouldn't have thought anything of it.

I ripped the device off the plastic and held it in my hand. One end had a spot for a USB connector, while the other end had a small, round charging port. I went to the kitchen and put the device in a plastic bag, then laid it on the counter.

I searched the remainder of the apartment. Under furniture, inside closets and cabinets, behind pictures, under end tables. My place wasn't overly furnished, so it didn't take long.

Nothing.

Sweat beaded across my brow as I searched the bedroom. Finding a recording device in that room would be distressing, especially when I told Arabella. And I'd have to tell her. My fists clenched just thinking about someone listing to our most intimate moments.

Luckily, no device in the bedroom.

I went back to the kitchen, dropped the plastic bag containing the device on the floor, and smashed it with the heel of my sandal. I held no preconceived notion forensics could be gained from the device. No doubt the only fingerprints were mine and it looked like something mass-produced, making the buyer virtually impossible to trace. Jaw clenched and hands shaking, I threw the bag in the nearby trash and headed for the stairs to my office.

Downstairs, I dropped to my knees and peered under Erika's desk.

"What are you doing?" she said, rolling her chair back, away from the desk. "When did you go insane?"

"I'm looking for something."

Her face crinkled. "What would possibly be under my desk for you to find?"

I didn't say anything and, not finding what I was looking for, crawled over to my desk. The dog followed.

"*What* are you looking for?" Erika said.

Unable to find anything under my desk, other than dust and a few stray paper clips, I moved to the third office desk, the one in the corner that served mostly as a place to stack miscellaneous papers and small cardboard boxes.

Centered between the ends of the desk and about six inches from the front edge, I found another device. Same as the one upstairs. Black and not much larger than a pack of gum. Held in place with two-sided tape.

I ripped it off and held it so Erika could see.

She took two steps in my direction, cocking her head sideways. "What is that?"

I stood. "It's a listening device. I found another one upstairs."

Her eyes widened and she took a deep breath.

"Yeah," I said. "Someone has been eavesdropping on us."

She stared at the small black device. "Snooping?"

"Yup."

I went to my desk and fired up the workstation, searching for "listening device." The first result was a place called *We-Spy-4-U*. Their homepage featured a picture of a small, black, voice-activated recorder that had a blazing resemblance to the ones I'd just found. According to the website, the device could pick up audio from fifty feet away, had five months of standby power, and could record continuously for two weeks.

With all my might, I heaved the device on the tile floor of the office. It shattered into countless pieces, many of them scattering to all corners of the room. The dog, ears back, tail between its legs, scurried under Erika's desk. I leaned back in the chair and closed my eyes, not bothering to seek advice from the dirty ceiling tiles. If they *could* offer advice, I knew what they'd say.

Don't let the anger control you. It solves nothing.

Erika sighed. "Now you've scared Snickers." She reached under the desk and petted the dog a few moments, then retrieved a broom and dustpan from the closet.

I counted to ten.

Laughter and the random sounds of tourists enjoying their vacation drifted into the office from outside. Bonaire's weather was picture perfect 365 days a year. Sunshine, beaches, and turquoise water. I calmed, sat straight, and opened my eyes. Erika dumped the remnants of the listening device into the garbage, banging the dustpan lightly on the edge of the trash can, then glanced my direction.

"We are all better now, yes?" she asked.

I nodded. "We are." I motioned at the trash. "Thank you."

"You are welcome." She replaced the broom and dustpan in the closet and sat at her desk.

"What was that you said?" I asked.

"When?"

"Something about *snickers*?"

"Oh, yes. While you were *out*"—she rolled her eyes, pausing momentarily on the ceiling "—a child came in for some candy. The little guy dropped a Snickers bar on the floor and the dog began eating it. We thought a good name would be Snickers."

I shook my head. "I was going to call her Dog."

Wide-eyed, she looked at me as if I'd suddenly grown gills. "Just . . . Dog?"

"Yeah. It was good enough for John Wayne."

"John Wayne?"

"A movie actor . . . From the States—"

"Yes, I know who John Wayne is. But—"

"He played in a show called *Big Jake* and had a dog named Dog." I was quiet for a moment. Erika stared at me, her head slowly shaking.

Before she could respond, the landline phone rang, and she answered it.

"It is for you—your friend Mr. Penn," she said.

Larry David from the Rockford Police Department. I picked up the phone on my desk and pressed the Line 1 button. "What do you have for me, Penn?"

"Good to hear from you, too, R," he said.

"Sorry, I'm a little on edge."

"Same old, same old, huh?"

"Yeah, I reckon so."

We were both quiet for a few moments.

"Well, enough chitchat, I guess," Penn finally said. He sighed. "I don't have much for you."

"Oh?"

"Nope . . . My DOJ contact says the FBI won't admit or deny anything about any Lucas Walker person. And they said that's especially the case if he's actually undercover."

"Figures."

"Sorry, R."

"What do you think?"

"I have no idea. But let me ask you this: Have you ever known or heard of an undercover officer—for any agency or force—admit to being undercover?"

I leaned back in my chair and thought for a short moment. "Of course not."

"Maybe that's your answer. Don't overthink this."

I had already considered that scenario. "You might have something there."

"Damn right I do."

"Thanks, Larry."

"R, call me sometime when you want to talk. Not just when you're in the middle of some shitstorm."

"You got it."

I hung up, put my feet on the desk, and within a few moments, drifted into deep thought. The opening of the office door startled me, and I sprang forward, wide-eyed.

A child stood motionless a few steps inside the office, looking at me with eyes almost as wide as mine. Erika touched the edge of the candy basket and waved the little girl forward. She glanced over her shoulder at me and said something in Papiamentu.

The girl smiled and approached Erika's desk. She looked at Dog and Erika said something to her. As if knowing what the conversation was about, and obviously understanding Papiamentu better than I did, Dog's tail began whacking the floor as the little girl went over and rubbed her ears. Erika and the child exchanged a few more lines of Papiamentu, then both looked at me.

"She wonders why you no longer smile," Erika said.

Good question. *From the mouth of babes*, I thought.

I shrugged, not saying anything.

The girl picked out two pieces of candy. She stared at me and took a step toward my desk. She paused, then took another step. After a moment, she walked the rest of the way. She stood stoic for a moment, then gently placed a piece of candy on the desk.

Warmth radiated throughout my body as I unwrapped the candy. Chewing and smiling at the same time, I said, "*Masha danki.*"

A broad smile worked its way across the little girl's face. She stood at the edge of my desk a few moments watching me chew. Then she twirled 180 degrees and waved at Erika as she went through the door, outside, amidst the sunshine, beaches, and turquoise water.

"Imagine that," Erika said, slapping her hands on her thighs. "The young child tamed the grumpy ogre."

Before I could respond, my cell phone rang.

Arabella.

"Conklin," she said. "David Brown is awake."

* * *

I wasn't allowed into David's hospital room, so I paced the hallway. Family members filled the small waiting area near the nurse's station, packed together on a couch and two padded chairs. Their faces seemed to carry a distant look of hope as they sat spellbound, hypnotized by a muted Dutch news station flashing scenes of Amsterdam across the screen of a wall-mounted TV.

I glanced at them every time I passed. Doubted they'd appreciate me joining the group and disrupting their silent vigil. It was their time, not mine. I didn't know David well enough to have met any of his family. They didn't know me from Adam.

After about fifteen minutes, Arabella, another officer, and a doctor walked out of Brown's room. The doctor went to the family as the other officer made for the exit. Arabella motioned for me to follow her down the hallway.

She checked all directions, making sure we were alone, then said, "He's awake and coherent, but very much in pain. He refuses too much medication—"

"Did he say anything?"

She folded her arms across her chest and tilted her head sideways. "Yes, that is what I want to tell you. If you will give me a chance."

I held up my hands, palms out. "Sorry. What did he say?"

"He said he got out of his car and walked to his house door. Someone came up behind him. He thinks he turned around but cannot remember."

"He was shot in the chest, correct?"

"Yes, we know he turned around, whether he remembers or not—"

"Anything else? Clothing? Tall, short?"

Arabella's lips tightened and her eyes narrowed, her posture becoming rigid. She opened her mouth but quickly closed it, then gazed at the ceiling for a moment. "I am trying to tell you," she finally said, eyes glued upward.

I shut up and bit my upper lip, working to keep my excitement contained.

After a long, slow exhale, she said, "All he thinks he remembers is that the person was shorter than him."

John Anderson.

CHAPTER 43

JAN PLACED A full bottle of Bright—lime wedge poking out the top—on the bar in front of me. Last night's intrusion by Anderson and Lucas, a trip to Paradise Cove, a missing speargun, a dead guy, finding the listening devices, and a visit to the hospital all added up to a long day. The first beer had gone down quickly, and I figured the second would disappear just as easily. I drummed my fingers on the bar.

Vinny's was half full, mostly locals. A soccer game played on the large-screen TV and six people sitting at a table nearest it hooted and hollered every so often. It looked like a matchup between two South American teams, but I couldn't determine which team they were rooting for. The only thing I could tell was the score, which was tied with just a few minutes left to play. Crunch time.

I didn't know the exact score in my game, but knew the bad guys were ahead. And I couldn't explain why, but it felt like time was running out. That the *game* was nearing its end.

Crunch time.

Arabella arrived and plopped on the barstool next to me. She'd stopped at the apartment, showered, and changed. She wore my black RPD baseball cap, her hair in a ponytail pulled through the back. Just a plain T-shirt tonight—no cute saying.

She took a sip of my beer as Jan brought one for her and an additional one for me.

"David Brown is resting," she said. "Not much more he could tell us anyway." She held her beer up in a mock toast. "At least we have the bullet."

"The bullet?"

"Did I not tell you?"

"Tell me what?"

"*Ach*! Too much has been happening." She took a swig of beer. "We found a slug at Brown's house. In the outside wall by his front door." She smiled. "Now we can compare to the other one we found today."

"Mr. Speargun's?"

"Yes, see if the two match. They look to be the same size." She gripped her beer with both hands and shook her head. "If only we can find the weapon."

We were both quiet a moment.

"Anything more at the Speargun house?" I asked.

"No, not much. We have talked to some neighbors and will do more tomorrow. I have officers there for the evening, but I will relieve them in the morning."

Darkness had swallowed the island, and downtown Kralendijk glowed with multi-colored lights, the bars and restaurants doing everything possible to draw tourists through their doors. A partial overcast blocked the moon and the ocean melded to blackness a few dozen yards beyond shore. Klein Bonaire, a half-mile out to sea, lay quiet, it's silhouette undiscernible. A few moments earlier, the distant edge of sea burned orange from the remnants of the sunset. Tiffany once said it looked like someone had taken a spoon and spread orange sherbet across the water. It now fused with the black sky forming an invisible horizon.

Jan joined the six soccer fans for a brief instant, cheering with them as something important happened, the announcers' voices raising in pitch. Arabella didn't pay any attention and seemed lost in thought, staring at her Bright label.

Too much has been happening, she had said. But she knew it wasn't the stuff that needed to happen. Many of the pieces were there. She just needed to put them together in the right sequence. I hadn't put the puzzle together yet either, so I shared her pain. And I had two pieces—two *major* pieces—she didn't have.

Lucas and John's visit to my apartment and the discovery of the listening devices.

I swallowed hard; my throat dry despite my second beer. "Bella, there's a couple of things you need to know."

She came out of her trance and swiveled on her stool in my direction. "What?"

Before I could explain, my cell rang.

Chuck.

I sent the call to voicemail.

"Last night, in my apartment—" My cell rang again. I looked at the caller ID. "It's Chuck. I'll get rid of him."

Arabella gritted her teeth and rolled her head, swiveling back to face the bar.

"Not a good time, Chuck," I said into the phone and hung up.

I flagged Jan for two more beers and Arabella swiveled back in my direction.

"What were you saying?" she asked.

Before I could answer, her phone chirped with a text message. Her face grew dim as she read it.

"What?" I asked.

She stood, took a last swig of beer, and put the cell phone in her pocket.

"That was Chuck," she said. I couldn't decide what surprised me more: Chuck having Arabella's number; or her reading one of his text messages. "He is at Paradise Cove. Erika is there and causing trouble. We need to go."

I stood and texted Chuck as Arabella and I went to my truck.

Get her out of there!

CHAPTER 44

THE PULSATING POLICE-TRUCK lights pierced the darkness as we pulled into the lot at Paradise Cove. Erika stood near the back door of the restaurant, as did John Anderson and Lucas Walker. Chuck, holding a beer, stood between them. Two police officers completed the ensemble.

Arabella sprang from my truck, pointed at one of the two officers, and growled something in Papiamentu. Wide-eyed, he stumbled across the gravel and hurriedly switched off the red and blues. He apparently thought it best to stay at the police truck, stand guard, making sure no unseemly soul approached.

His partner wasn't quite so lucky.

Arabella began pelting him with questions in Papiamentu. His answers were jagged and incomplete, partly because Arabella wasn't allowing him to finish a sentence. He pointed at Erika a few times and at the door to Paradise Cove.

John glanced between Arabella and the officers, and a few times at me. Lucas leaned against the concrete wall of the building, occasionally flicking the hair from his eyes, which seemed to be a losing battle considering the direction of the wind. Erika had taken a few steps closer to Arabella, nodding and listening intently to her conversation with the officer.

I stood behind Arabella and waited. Eventually, Chuck walked over to me.

In a low voice, he said, "She burst in yelling about Rulio."

"What was she saying?"

"She wanted to know what happened to him."

Arabella turned her head sideways, just enough for me to catch a glimpse of her scowl. She put a hand up in my direction. I motioned for Chuck to follow me, away from her and the others.

When we were several steps away, I said to Chuck, "Go on."

"She said she had proof."

"Proof? Of what?"

"Not sure." He took a swig of beer. "I got the feeling she meant about this place. That someone here had something to do with Rulio and his . . ." He didn't finish the sentence and lowered his head, staring at his feet.

The two officers got in the police truck and drove away. Arabella waved for me to rejoin the group. As far as I knew, neither John nor Lucas had said anything since our arrival.

"Erika came into the bar and made accusations," Arabella said. Erika stood with her arms folded across her front, toe tapping rapidly on the gravel. Arabella looked at her. "She yelled and caused a disturbance."

Erika pointed at John and Lucas. "They know something!" She breathed heavily; her cheeks red. Sweat ran down both sides of her face. In a lower voice, but every bit as forceful, she repeated herself. "They know something."

A few customers walked out the door and headed for their vehicles, glancing back at us, shaking their heads.

The door flung open and Danielle marched out. She extended her arm and pointed at Erika. "She's costing me customers. And money," she said to Arabella. "Get her out of here."

"Will you press charges?" Arabella asked.

John looked at Danielle, but she didn't acknowledge him. Another group of customers left the building, quietly, voices low, staring straight ahead until they got in their vehicles and drove away.

Danielle said, "I just want her gone. All of you. Gone. And never come back." She turned toward the door. "John, let's go. Inside." She looked at Lucas. "You, too."

Without hesitation, John stormed into the building. Lucas continued to lean against the wall. After a moment, he scuffed his deck shoes on the gravel, stood straight, and smiled at me. He flicked his hair back and walked inside.

I put a hand on Erika's shoulder. "Let's go home."

She swiped my hand away. "They know about Rulio." No one said anything as she moved her head from Arabella, to Chuck, then back to me. Her eyes watered. "I am sure of it."

Arabella let out a long breath. "How are you sure?"

"Because I find this." She reached into her pocket, pulled out a cellphone, and held it out for me to take. "It's a hot phone."

She meant *burner* phone, but I saw no reason to correct her. Her English became more broken as her excitement rose. I took the cell from her. "What's this?" I asked.

"It's a cellphone, R," Chuck said, in a matter-of-fact way, as if bewildered that I didn't recognize a cellphone when I saw one.

I didn't give him the satisfaction of acknowledging. "Why is this important?" I asked Erika.

"I find it in the dog food," she said.

"The dog food?" Chuck said.

Arabella pointed a finger at Chuck. "You should stay quiet." Then she looked at Erika. "The dog food?"

"Yes, the bag of dog food for Snickers."

Arabella cocked her head in my direction. "Snickers?"

"Not important right now."

"As I pour food for Snickers," Erika continued, "this phone fell out of the bag."

We were all quiet for a moment. Throughout my career, I'd seen things hidden by bad guys in all kinds of weird places. The dog food didn't surprise me, but I couldn't make the connection to Paradise Cove. I gathered by her silence that Arabella had the same dilemma.

Running low on beer, which meant he needed this conversation to be over as soon as possible so he could refill, and ignoring Arabella's previous warning, Chuck asked, "But what has that got to do with Paradise Cove?"

"You see, Mr. Chuck," Erika said, "even Mr. R thinks I should be a detective."

Arabella raised her eyebrows at me.

I shrugged. "That's not important right now, either."

Erika continued. "I look at the call history, and there is only one number, so I dial it." She had our attention. Both Arabella and I leaned forward, listening. Chuck nursed the last few drops of his beer. "A woman answers. But not nicely. She say 'What!' like she is mad or something. I say nothing and hang up."

"I still do not see any connection," Arabella said.

Erika held up a finger. "I look up the number." She went quiet for a moment, enjoying the limelight. "It is one of the numbers for here, Paradise Cove."

"But—" Chuck said.

"The man who had the speargun," Erika said. "The one that killed Tessa. It is his phone!"

Chuck looked at me, wide-eyed.

"We do not know that absolutely, not yet," Arabella said.

"The man hides a phone in his dog food," Erika said. "I call the number, and a woman here answers."

"Could be any number of reasons for that," I said.

"You think so?" Erika said. "Well then, Mr. Fancy Detective, let us hear one of them."

I hadn't expected her to challenge me and didn't have a better explanation. Maybe she *would* make a good detective.

Then I remembered the business card John Anderson had given me after the snorkel trip. I retrieved it from the Wrangler's glove compartment, showed Arabella, then compared the phone number on the card to the one in the call history of the burner phone.

"The numbers don't match," I said.

"Might not be the only one for this place," she said.

"I called here!" Erika said. "That woman, the bossy one, she answered when I called."

"Can I see the phone a minute, R?" Chuck asked. Trying to get my mind around things, and without thinking about what I was doing, I handed him the phone.

"And," Erika said, "my friend tells me the wire from Rulio's ankle was traced to here."

She must've meant the wire samples from Rulio's ankle and the one from Anderson's money box. I hadn't heard that. I looked at Arabella, *my* eyebrows raised.

A thin smile crept across her face. "Not important right now," she said.

"The hell with it," Chuck said. "Let's call the number and see who answers."

"NO!" Arabella yelled.

But it was too late. Chuck had already dialed the number and the first ringtone sounded through the speaker. We gathered around Chuck, all quiet, holding our breath, waiting for someone to answer. A collective sigh released when the phone disconnected after five rings.

Arabella yanked the phone from Chuck's hand. "That was stupid."

A moment later, the back door opened a crack, and Danielle peeked out, her eyes locking onto Arabella. When Arabella held up the phone, Danielle quickly pulled her head back inside and closed the door.

Erika pointed at the closed door. "Her! She answered."

"We should go," Arabella said.

We agreed I'd drive Erika home in her car and Arabella would follow us in my rental truck. Chuck decided to stay for another beer.

"What are you doing?" I asked him.

"I need to talk with John. He still needs that flight made."

"But you're still grounded. And so is your plane."

"Yeah, but I think I got something worked out. I won't be here long, one beer at the most. I just need to verify the day and time with John."

I shook my head. "Your life, I guess. Be careful."

Chuck went into the restaurant as we pulled out of the parking lot.

For the second time that day, I left Paradise Cove.

Also, for the second time that day, I hoped to never return.

CHAPTER 45

AFTER GETTING ERIKA settled in her house, Arabella and I stopped back at Vinny's for a nightcap. Considering my second trip to Paradise Cove in a day, it had become an even longer day. Fatigue oozed out of me, but I had a few things to talk through with Arabella.

"Tell me about the wire," I said, wiping condensation off my freshly opened bottle of Bright. Arabella had opted to stand at the bar, whereas I sat on a blue stool, turned in her direction.

"Erika is right. How she would know is beyond me, but the composition of the wire from Rulio's leg matches the one you gave me." She took a swig of beer. "Legally, not much can be done, though."

Chain of evidence. No way to prove the wire I gave Arabella came from one of John's money boxes. I knew that'd be a problem when I snipped the wire, but I needed to know. And now we did. Too much of a coincidence that strands of wire from the same batch just happened to be strapped to Rulio's ankle and around that cardboard box.

John—or Lucas—had to be involved. Somehow. Some way.

"I do not understand the technology," she said. "But it is like a fingerprint, kind of. Both wires came from the same alloy, which is unique with every manufacturer and every batch produced." She raised and dropped a shoulder. "Or something like that."

"That's what David Brown told me."

We were both quiet a moment, watching the crowd at Vinny's. Numerous curvy glasses holding brightly colored drinks lined the bar. Lobster red-skinned tourists, dressed in new, still-creased T-shirts, had replaced most of the locals from earlier.

Sweat dripped from Jan's brow as he set two beers in front of us. His shirt was soaked through. The thick crowd was keeping him on his toes.

People at the table along the rail, a few feet from us, spoke in a low murmur as if not wanting to be overheard. I pondered the conversation to determine if their covertness was necessary. I drank some beer and forced myself to stay focused on current problems, deciding I had enough to worry about.

"What do you think?" Arabella asked me.

"Well, the wire is a red flag, that's for sure," I said. "And the wood in Rulio's leg indicates a ship . . . or more specifically, a sailboat. Like the one moored at Paradise Cove. Did you ever—"

"None of that indicates any special person."

"No, they don't. Same with the speargun. That guy could've sold it to anyone." I studied her for a moment. She studied me back. "But the cell phone Erika found certainly points to a connection between the speargun and Paradise Cove." I swigged some beer. "It boils down to John or Lucas. Or both."

"Might not be Lucas. David Brown said the shooter was short."

"Yeah, my bet is John Anderson."

"Maybe, but how to prove it?"

"We still have to assume Rulio was killed and dumped at sea," I said. I kept coming back to the sailboat at Paradise Cove. "Did you trace the registration of *Dream Crusher*?"

"It is registered to Danielle Anderson, so John could easily have used it."

"Danielle said John wasn't much of a sailor. Lucas is, though. He sailed on *Dream Crusher* just the other day."

"But, like I said earlier, immigration records show Lucas was not on the island when Rulio disappeared."

"And none of this explains or links to Sandra Griffis. Has anyone heard from her?"

"No, she is still considered missing."

I shook my head. "She disappears after remembering something she wanted to tell me. And she worked for Paradise Cove . . . as an accountant. Maybe she found out about the boxes of cash."

"And that's when she went missing."

"Yup," I said. "Maybe she was a loose end."

"How does Tessa figure into this? Was she also a loose end?"

"Maybe. John could've said something to her during a moment of passion. You know, pillow talk."

"Maybe . . ." she said, not sounding convinced. "If what Ruth says is true and John was sleeping with Tessa, maybe Danielle didn't like it. Killed Tessa from jealousy."

A few stools down, a tourist leaned over the bar, words slurring, arms moving in animation, as he told Jan a story. After so many years tending bar, Jan had heard almost every conceivable story known to the island but listened anyway, face stoic, head bouncing in a rhythmic shallow nod. Most tourists who visited Vinny's left with the impression Jan was their buddy.

"What about the stuff from the dive?" I asked, thinking about the watch and other items organized and labeled on the table.

"I do not have hopes for the items collected," Arabella said. "Like you said, more of a reef cleanup." She shook her head while taking a drink of beer. "We should have results in a day or two. Same with the trace evidence from the tow truck that ran you off the road."

"I'm not getting up any hopes. That truck had to be full of sand, dirt, hair, prints . . . you name it. I imagine it's been driven by a ton of people and seldom cleaned."

"Agreed, and with no video camera, it will be hard to track down who stole it."

Investigations are always a series of highs and lows, the peaks and valleys changing direction quickly. One moment everything is looking great, the momentum flowing, whereas the next minute, it's unclear how to proceed, the momentum having withered.

I finished my beer, unsure of the current direction, and waved at Jan, who had escaped the chat with the drunken tourist. Like one of Pavlov's dogs, he instinctively brought us two more beers. Arabella and I would be walking back to my apartment tonight, leaving my rental truck parked downtown.

Sweet smells from the restaurant across the street lofted through Vinny's. Arabella watched a server walk past with a plate of food destined for a nearby table.

"You hungry?" she asked, turning back to me.

I should've been famished but was too exhausted to eat. We were getting nowhere, and it bothered me. My chest muscles tightened, and I felt my jaw clench. Too many coincidences emanating from Paradise Cove.

"I am ordering some food," Arabella said. "Want something?"

"Yeah . . . I guess. Something light."

Vinny's didn't offer food service of any kind, other than peanuts and stale crackers at the bar. Arabella stopped a passing waitress from the restaurant across the street and placed an order. They provided table service and bar food to customers at Vinny's.

"Could we make a case for getting on *Dream Crusher*?" I asked. "Maybe find some trace evidence."

"Yes, I will make that work," she said, smiling. "Almost like finding a smoking gun."

Speaking of a smoking gun . . . No time like the present, I thought.

"I need to tell you something," I said.

Arabella sat quietly as I told her about the listening devices, John and Lucas breaking into my apartment with the Makarov, and finally about my chat with Danielle Anderson. As I droned on, her face grew a dark shade of crimson. Her eyes narrowed, her breathing shallow and quick.

When I finished, I took a long swig of beer and looked out at the dark sea. She straightened her back and tapped her beer bottle on the bar.

"You are just now telling me this?" she said. "People broke into your apartment and gave you an *illegal* weapon? People who are maybe under suspicion for murder, and who are maybe involved with money laundering crimes?"

I didn't say anything. Hard to argue with her implications.

"You are an experienced detective," she said. "And you just now tell me about it? How does that make sense to you?"

My shoulders slumped. "Looking back now, it doesn't."

"*Ach.*" She put her head on the bar, cradled it in her arms, and mumbled some Dutch. "*Ach,*" she said again, lifting her head.

"The good part is," I said, "at least we know who the shooter is."

"Maybe."

"Maybe?"

She looked me in the eyes. "You are convinced it is John?"

"I want to be. Based on what Brown said, Lucas is too tall."

"Could be the wife, Danielle. Especially after the last conversation you had with her."

I nodded. "Wouldn't have thought it possible . . . until *that* conversation, anyway. She is a disturbed lady."

Arabella tipped her bottle in my direction. "Follow every lead."

"Absolutely, but even if she is our shooter, you really think she could've killed Rulio, too?"

"Maybe, if it suited her plans. Kill one; kill many. What is the difference to a psychopath?"

"But you know his size. He was a strapping young guy. How could she force him onto a boat?"

"Maybe he was already dead, and she just dragged him on. Maybe she had help. Maybe she tried to use the lure of sex. Who knows? Maybe he went on willingly. She was his boss."

I scratched an ear, mulling over her logic.

"Besides," she continued, "Danielle said John was not a sailor."

"Supposedly he wasn't a swimmer either, but I've come to think that was a lie."

"People always lie." She pointed a finger at me. "You have told me that many times."

Yup. I used to tell people it's what I did for a living—get lied to.

"I don't lie," I said, tilting my head sideways and leaning closer to her. "At least not to you."

"Ha! Sometimes you do." She playfully pushed me back. "And you do not tell me what you know when I need to know it. You always hold back on me."

"No, I don't," I said, feigning innocence. "I just told you."

"*Ach . . .*"

We were both quiet a moment, the wind pressing the front of Arabella's shirt against her body. Small waves crashed against the nearby beach, the water turning to foam as it failed once again in its never-ending attempt to go ashore, drifting in defeat back to the sea.

I sat down on the stool, reflecting on the conversation. What Arabella said made good sense. Overall, I felt the momentum, ever so slightly, ebbing in our direction. Schleper was right. She has good instincts.

Maybe Arabella and Erika should start their own detective agency. I could walk their office dog.

I took her hand and pulled her close, cradling her between my legs. "You must have some kind of superpower."

She kissed me on the lips. "I do not need superpowers. I am a female cop." She kissed me again, this time deeper, harder. "Take me to bed, old man."

"What about your food?"

"I will change the order to takeaway."

CHAPTER 46

ERIKA LOOKED UP from her desk, raising an eyebrow at me as I took a broom from the closet. "I am surprised you know where that is kept," she said.

Late morning and I had decided to do some office cleaning while I waited for Arabella. She called earlier and said she wanted to do a swim during her lunch hour and invited me to join. I figured something was amiss. The only time she did noon hour workouts was when she needed to relieve some sort of stress.

"Wonderful," Erika said with a roll of her eyes after I finished with the floor and returned the broom to the closet.

Next, I cleared the spare desk of papers and other clutter, sprayed it with cleaner, and wiped it down with a cloth. Late-morning sunlight flooded through the front window and dust particles swam on the beams.

Erika's moderate enthusiasm dwindled. "But you should dust *before* sweeping," she said.

I paused a moment, shrugged, then continued.

For the most part, the cleaning—which, admittedly, I performed haphazardly—should've helped clear my mind, empty my consciousness of deep thoughts. But I was drowning in the magnitude of yesterday's events.

Too many questions. Hopefully, Arabella would have some answers.

"Must you stir up so much dust?" Erika asked, perched in front of her monitor, eyeglasses low on her nose. A pile of manila folders sat on her lap. She'd flip open a file, frown, then shake her head and go on to the next one. Putting her hand over her mouth, she faked a very loud cough. "You should be collecting the dust, not putting it in the air."

"I know that." I gave her a sideways glance and continued dusting, having moved on to the file cabinet. "But I've never been any good at this."

She raised her eyebrows. "When are you swimming with Miss Arabella?" She lifted the stack of folders off her lap and sat them on the desk. "It is near lunchtime and your workday is almost over anyway."

My cellphone rang. Erika recognized Arabella's ringtone.

"Ah," she said, "saved by Miss Arabella."

I answered and Arabella said she'd be at the pier in ten minutes. Just enough time for me to change, grab a towel, and meet her across the street.

* * *

From the start, Arabella swam like she was on a mission. She sprinted out early, led the entire way, and *beat me* by nearly two minutes. By the time I coasted in and touched the pylon, she had finished studying the e-device strapped to her wrist.

"You better not have let me win," she said. "Today is not a good day for that."

I splashed some water on my face. "Nope, I did my best. You ousted me today." I moved toward her, and we slapped a high five. "Nice job."

She half-smiled, not saying anything, and flung her goggles onto the pier. She submerged, popping up a few moments later, and ran her hands over her head smoothing down her hair.

I watched six flamingos fly past, a few yards beyond the boats moored along the reef. Silently, they glided through the air single file just a few feet above the water, their pink feathers in stark contrast to the dark blue of the sea. Bonaire is one of only four places in the world where flamingos breed. Every day, thousands fly over from Venezuela, feed, then make the flight back in the evening. They winged south, out of sight in a few short seconds.

Arabella floated quietly. Her distant stare told me what I needed to know.

"Okay, Bella, what's up?" I was worried about her. The responsibility and stress from multiple cases and the subsequent heavy workload would eventually take a toll on her. She's tough, but everyone, even Superwoman, has her limit. "Anything new?"

She continued to stare into nothingness. "Not much." Her tone was matter-of-fact. "I am working on authorization to board the *Dream Crusher*. Hopefully, in a few days we can search her."

"Good. Anything on the cell Erika found?"

"It is like she said." She shrugged. "A burner and the only number dialed is to Paradise Cove. But Paradise Cover has three phone numbers, and a lot of women work there."

"If only we could talk to Sandra," I said. "She'd be able to tell us where the lines ring. I'm betting one goes to an office and the person who answered was Danielle Anderson."

"That would be my assumption as well. I will see if the phone company has records regarding the installation and where the lines terminate."

Knowing who answered the phone still wouldn't tell us much, but at least it'd be something. My gut told me we were close. I didn't yet know what additional information we needed, but when it appeared, the needle would spin and point at the answer.

We floated on the water, quietly. Arabella stole quick glances at the ladder and a few at her wrist, checking the time. She seemed hesitant to climb the rungs, as if not wanting her lunch hour to be finished.

Finally, she looked at me and said, "Conklin, there is something else . . . Schleper came back to work today."

"What?"

"Yes, he just waltzed into the office like nothing ever happened."

"What did he say? How did he act?"

She grunted. "He was his typical self. Took control of everything. Barked orders like a junk dog."

She meant *junkyard dog*, although I wasn't sure the simile worked. I hadn't expected him back so soon. And based on the inflection in her voice, neither had Arabella.

"He said . . ." She paused a moment, then continued. "He said he needed to be there and get up to speed on everything, if I . . . if I were going to Amsterdam." She looked me in the eyes. Hers moistened, and I wasn't convinced it was from the saltwater. "For inspector training."

A lump formed in my throat and my voice cracked as I said, "Are you?"

There was a long silence. Vehicles crawled along the road that fronted the YellowRock, many of them filled with tourists, inching toward more memories in paradise. Small waves slapped the nearby pylons. I waited, longing for a beer.

"Yes," she said. "I think I will."

Another lump in my throat and another voice crack. "Good, I'm happy for you."

"Are you sure?"

I gathered myself. “Yes,” I said. “I’m sure.”

“But first,” she said, her voice emanating the familiar authoritative tone I had grown accustomed to, “we must finish this mess with Paradise Cove.”

CHAPTER 47

CHUCK LEANED AGAINST the fender of my rental truck drinking a beer as I finished prepping and assembling my dive gear. We were a few hundred yards south of Paradise Cove, parked behind several mangrove trees I hoped would conceal us from the occasional passing vehicle. A light breeze rustled my shirt as moonlight reflected off the water. A billion stars poked through the black night sky and every few seconds a small wave slapped the dead coral along the shore.

"You sure you want to do this?" Chuck asked as he dropped his empty beer can in the truck bed. The quiet and calm of the evening seemed to shatter as it hit the metal, it's echo reverberating across the area.

"Chuck!" I said in a loud whisper.

He looked at the empty as he opened a fresh beer. "Oh. Sorry."

"I'd prefer everyone at Paradise Cove *not* know we're here."

He held a hand up in surrender fashion. "I got it. I got it."

"The only way this works is if they don't see me . . . Or *hear* me." Unlikely that would happen. Based on the laughter, shouts, and music coming from that direction, it'd take a moderate explosion to catch anyone's attention. Just the same, though, I preferred as much stealth as possible.

Chuck took a swig. "You sure about this?"

I zipped up my wetsuit; looked out over the dark water. "Yeah, I need to check that boat, and this might be the only way I get aboard." I continued to slip into my gear as Chuck continued to drink.

By "that boat" I was referring to the *Dream Crusher.* It'd been several days, and Arabella hadn't been successful in getting permission to board and, right or wrong, I was tired of waiting. Time to take matters into my own hands.

While Paradise Cove buzzed with patrons, hopefully keeping the Andersons busy, I planned to scuba out to the *Dream Crusher,* work my way onboard, and snoop around a bit. The key would be to stay underwater just deep enough so no one onshore saw me. Since night divers are common on Bonaire, it'd be unlikely I'd draw any attention.

I latched a dive light to my BC but didn't plan to use it in the water. The Bonaire waters were so clear, a diver using a light underwater could be seen by someone onshore a hundred yards away. If I stayed just ten feet or so below the surface, there should be enough moonlight and ambient light from shore to provide what I needed. But, in case of an emergency, I'd have the light.

Also, the light would come in handy while onboard *Dream Crusher.*

I didn't want to leave fingerprints on the boat, so I pulled on a pair of dive gloves. The Marine Park Rangers didn't patrol the shores at night, so little chance I'd get caught with them. Next, I strapped a knife and sheath to the inner side of my left shin.

"Seriously?" Chuck said. "Aren't you the one who always said a knife isn't necessary for Bonaire scuba?"

"Yeah, I say that. But the knife isn't for the dive. It's in case I need it while on the boat."

Chuck didn't scuba so I wouldn't have a buddy on this dive; I'd be solo. At night. Not the best of situations, but something I'd done before. However, those times had been for pleasure, not for a covert, illegal *mission.* Before wading into the water, I performed a modified, self-buddy check on myself and inhaled a few test breaths from the regulator.

I stood ankle deep in the water, faced the *Dream Crusher*, and took a compass heading to the boat. I planned to swim straight out from shore, then turn right, hopefully making a sweeping circle to approach her from the seaward side, out of view from the Paradise Cove crowd.

I briefly considered using the kick-counting method to determine distance traveled. It's a method of knowing how many kicks it takes to cover a hundred yards. Problem was, it'd been so long since I'd counted my kicks over a specified distance, I had no idea what my rate might be. Also, water current would add or subtract from the number, and at night, it'd be more difficult to judge the current's effect.

Counting kicks wasn't the best choice. A time-in-water technique seemed to be my best option. I'd swim away from shore for a predetermined amount of time, then make my right turn, hopefully far enough from shore allowing me to approach the boat from the seaward side.

I surface-floated to deeper water, turned back to shore, and gave Chuck the okay sign. Since he was my pseudo shore support, I figured he should know I was ready to submerge.

"Be careful!" he yelled, quickly putting his hand over his mouth. A moment later, he held up his beer, tipped in my direction, and took a swig.

I hope he saves me a couple, I thought as I let some air out of my BC and slipped below the surface.

Initially, in the shallows, I saw the floor of the sea. But as it sloped away into deeper water and I maintained a depth of ten feet, the bottom faded into darkness.

Kicking through water that appeared near pitch black, with no clues or references for up, down, or sideways, spatial disorientation, albeit unlikely, became a real possibility. Although not too serious, I didn't want it to complicate or impede my progress. I imagined a worst-case scenario of swimming upside down, possibly even in the wrong direction. Every few minutes, while pushing through the dark sea, I looked up. The moonlight hitting the surface of the water, accenting the barely discernible small waves rolling toward the shore, gave me a sense of position and orientation.

At regular intervals, I checked my compass and air supply gauge. My motion through the water—hands, arms, feet—disturbed nearby microscopic marine animals that thrive in the water column, causing them to create bioluminescence, a heatless light generated by a chemical reaction within their bodies. Whenever I read my compass or looked to the surface, a trail of small, blue-green dots of light trailed my movements, as if a squadron of lightning bugs were mimicking my actions.

After thirty minutes in the water, needing a bearing on my position, I slowly surfaced, lifting only my head out of the water. To my surprise—and delight—the *Dream Crusher* rolled gently in the waves a mere thirty yards away. My right turn in open water hadn't been as precise as I had hoped and left me closer to shore than desired, but my ad-hoc navigation had done the trick. Mostly, anyway. I readjusted course, descended, and swam the remaining distance, resurfacing on the seaward side of the boat, near the stern.

I grabbed the ladder trailing from the aft deck and floated on the water's surface, letting my heart and breathing settle. After listening a few moments for sounds on the boat and watching for movements or lights, I determined no one was onboard.

I removed my BC and tank assembly, then used the straps of the BC to latch all my gear together and secure it to the lowest ladder rung, which happened to be below the water line. Squeezing some air out of the BC lessened its buoyancy and allowed the gear to slip a few feet below the surface. Nicely hidden from sight, yet easily available when I needed to skedaddle. I looped the lanyard attached to the dive light around my wrist.

Checking that no one was on the nearby pier, I took a few breaths, then climbed the ladder.

I stayed as low as possible, trying to remain out of sight, and moved across the deck, headed for the companionway area. I forced myself to move slow, fearing fast, jerky movements might draw the attention of someone at Paradise Cove.

The door and hatch were unlocked, making it easy to enter and walk down the three steps to the stateroom. Although dark, I didn't want to chance flipping on a switch. No ambient light penetrated the structure, so I used my dive light, figuring if light couldn't come in, then it also wouldn't go out. In addition, I could control the flashlight better than a lamp, ceiling-, or wall-mounted light. I kept it pointed down, at the floor, and held my hand over the lens, fingers spread, to further reduce the beam. The light softly illuminated small portions of the room as I moved it back and forth.

Not knowing what I was looking for, I searched bookshelves, drawers, small cubbyholes designed for storage, and under the cushions of a circular couch built into the wall. I checked under the bedroom mattress, careful not to disturb the sheets and pillows. I also checked the bathroom, or *head*.

Lots of junk—old maps, travel brochures, paper, pens, a few dirty swimsuits and towels, cans of nonperishable food stored in the kitchen cabinets, and resting in a dusty rack on the counter, three bottles of wine.

I pulled on the padlock securing the door of the stateroom closet, but it didn't budge. Jiggling the door showed play in the hasp where it attached to the frame, allowing the door to open several inches.

With my hand cupped over the bezel of the flashlight to prevent light from escaping, I placed it to the crack between the door and the jam and peered inside the closet. Impossible to see much—too dark—and the few inches the door opened didn't allow adequate visibility into the closet.

The next action I considered went against years of training. I considered it carefully, but decided that, since I was already onboard, I needed to do whatever was necessary.

I shut the door, put my foot on the wall, and yanked as hard as I could, shifting all my weight backwards in the process. I stumbled back as the hasp splintered off the frame, the door swinging open. Regaining my balance, I shone my light into the closet and peered inside.

Some miscellaneous tools sprawled atop a toolbox on the floor and a broom rested in the corner. A few random items one might expect to find on a sailboat—rope, a box of old maps, life jackets—lay scattered on the floor. The closet didn't seem to hold anything of importance. I was about to give up, wondering why it would be locked in the first place, when I noticed a bundle of wire in the back. Wire I'd seen before and wasn't surprised to find onboard.

Not barbed wire or chicken wire or electrical wire or telephone wire.

Behind the wire, a hatchet hung low on the wall. David Brown had read from the coroner's report on Rulio about scuff marks on the femur, like a blade coming down with force.

I examined the destroyed frame and the hasp hanging on the door, padlock locked in place. It'd be obvious someone had been onboard, and the Andersons would have their suspicions who it was. I doubted they'd be able to prove it and they'd be foolish to even try.

However, my heart raced as a tinge of panic tried to set in. I realized I'd just made it possible for the Andersons to claim that any evidence found implicating them had been planted. It's possible I may've blown the whole case.

I needed to calm myself and find something I could use; definitive evidence I could take to Arabella.

Slowly moving the light around the closet one last time, a flash of silver reflected from the far back corner, catching my eye. It hung from a small nail.

A necklace.

Lifting my left leg, I pulled the dive knife from the sheath. So as not to destroy any trace evidence that might be on the necklace, I reached into the back of the closet and, using the notch near the end of the blade, a feature designed to snag and break fishing line, eased the chain off the nail and carefully pulled it out of the closet.

I cradled the necklace in my gloved hand and flooded it with light. My breathing hitched when I saw a dolphin. Or, more correctly, a porpoise.

He said I was the porpoise *in his life.*

CHAPTER 48

EARLY THE NEXT morning, earlier than I thought Chuck ever rose from bed, he called me.

"Chuck, I can't talk now. I'm waiting for a call from Arabella."

"I'm meeting John and Lucas at the airport around one o'clock." He yawned. "You change your mind and want to make some easy cash?"

"No, I haven't. And you should follow my lead."

"Today's not the flight. They just want to talk things over and prepare a delivery."

"You know this doesn't end well. The money isn't worth it."

"You worry too much."

"Not in this situation. Listen to me—"

"But—"

"Just listen . . ." I took a deep breath. "The Paradise Cove bunch, John, Lucas, and maybe even Danielle, aren't what they seem."

There was a long silence. Through the phone, I heard his breaths. Quietly, he said, "But I need the money."

"Not that bad, you don't. Don't go."

Another long pause.

"Maybe you're right. Thanks."

He disconnected, probably upset at my hounding him. Chuck's determination to make a quick buck will someday be his undoing.

Maybe I got through to him this time, but right now, I had more important things to worry about.

Arabella wouldn't be happy when she heard about my excursion on the *Dream Crusher*, and I doubted she'd be able to use what I found as grounds for boarding. The necklace proved the Andersons and the *Dream Crusher* were tied to all of this. The truth was about to come, I felt it. It was as if everything had slowed down and the world had gone quiet. We'd been waiting for this moment, and now we just needed one last catalyst to push us to the finale.

Problem was, I didn't know exactly what that catalyst was. However, I was confident that, between Arabella and me, we'd figure something out.

I paced the veranda waiting for her to call. She hadn't returned my voicemails from last night or this morning. Driving around the island looking for her would be futile. No telling where she'd be. I called the police department and asked for Schleper. He was *unavailable*, so I asked them to page Arabella. They said they wouldn't, but I could leave a message for her.

So, I left yet another message for her.

She sometimes delayed in returning my calls, but today felt longer than normal. I didn't want the momentum of our investigation to erode. It was only a matter of time before the Andersons discovered the broken closet door, assuming they hadn't already. No telling what might happen then.

With the clock bumping off noon, my phone buzzed.

"Bella," I said. "I've been trying to reach you."

It took me five minutes to tell her about the previous night, how I got on the *Dream Crusher*, and what I'd found. Afterwards, she went quiet. I waited.

And waited.

Finally, she said, "I am on my way over."

* * *

I sat on the edge of the hammock playing my banjo, waiting for Arabella to show. Based on her reaction over the phone, I assumed she'd waste no time getting here. However, it'd been longer than I had expected.

A makeshift lunch of microwaved remnants from leftover takeaways sat on the table next to a half-drank Bright. The banjo playing, a futile attempt at calming myself, was doing nothing to help organize the thoughts banging against my skull.

I picked off some tunes that I'd known for years, playing them the exact way I had played them countless times before. Rote; non-thinking; automatic. Nothing creative. Just killing time till Arabella arrived.

Movement in my peripheral vision startled me, pulling me from my trance. My breath caught and my pulse quickened, a shot of adrenaline speeding through my veins as I stopped playing and looked over my shoulder. I quickly calmed when I saw it was Erika. She had come up the inside stairs to my apartment and stood at the sliding door to the veranda. I breathed out and laid my banjo on its stand, realizing that Lucas and John's visit a few nights ago had put me more on edge than I thought.

My curiosity piqued when I considered her coming upstairs. I could count on one hand the number of times she'd been in my apartment.

"My friend called," she said. "There has been a shooting. I thought you should know."

Her voice was soft, and she didn't look me in the eyes. Her hands, hanging by her side, trembled. I couldn't remember ever seeing Erika scared or shaken like this. I stood, the breeze suddenly feeling chilled.

She wiped the side of her face. "At the airport." Her breathing quickened. "My friend said it was an American."

My entire body seemed to go weak, a heaviness forming in the pit of my stomach.

I checked the time.

Quarter after one.

Chuck!

I'm meeting John and Lucas at the airport around one o'clock.

CHAPTER 49

HANDS SWEATY, BARELY able to hold the steering wheel of the truck, I pulled into the general aviation area of the Flamingo Airport. Two police trucks were parked at an angle to each other near the fence gate. I had clearance for this section of the airport, but my ID badge was in my flight bag, which I neglected to grab before leaving the apartment.

Crime scene tape flapped in the breeze around a large section of the parking lot. I slipped under it and made my way toward the gate, tied open with additional crime scene tape. An officer approached me with his hand out, head shaking.

"Sir, you will need to go back," he said, pointing at my truck.

Beyond the fence line, alongside the large commercial hangar, several other officers stood over a black tarp lying on the dry dirt, gravel, and scattered weeds. Additional tape kept several airport workers at bay on the other side of the scene, where the hangar door emptied onto the tarmac. Tied to the concrete in its usual location, Chuck's airplane sat under the high sun, gently rocking in the breeze.

I had called Chuck twice on my drive to the airport. Both times, the call went to voicemail. Frustrated, pacing along the tape barrier, I tried again to duck under the tape, but, again, the officer stopped me.

I bit my lower lip and swiveled my head looking for Arabella.

"Where is Arabella?" I yelled to the officer who had blocked my way.

He rubbed his forehead and pointed at the parking lot entrance. "Officer De Groot has just arrived."

I spun around and watched Arabella park a police truck next to my rental. She hurried in my direction and, not appearing surprised to see me, motioned her head toward the gate. "Come on," she said.

As we jogged through the gate, a gust of wind blew open a portion of the tarp, exposing what lay beneath it.

A human leg.

Shorts and white deck shoes.

Chuck never wore deck shoes.

I slowed, my breathing returning to normal as I approached the tarp. Arabella knelt alongside it and looked up at me. I nodded and she pulled back the upper half of the tarp.

On his back, lifeless eyes open to the deep blue Caribbean sky, wind whipping his black ponytail across his pale face, lay supposed FBI agent Lucas Walker.

Or, depending on his mood, an astronaut.

Luke Skywalker.

I breathed a sigh of relief.

"Two," Arabella said. "Center mass."

I knelt beside her. Two crimson patches stained Lucas's black T-shirt. As with the other corpses, the shots were well grouped. Precise. Expert by any standard.

"Must not have needed the head shot."

"Witnesses?" Arabella asked one of the officers.

He shook his head.

"*Verdomme.*" Arabella stood and placed her hands on her hips. She examined the outside wall of the hangar, and after a short moment, pointed at an upper corner, near the roof line. "Camera."

She waved a hand and, in Papiamentu, told one of the officers to investigate the status of the camera. I didn't understand all of what she said, but picked out the word *vidio*, Papiamento for *video.*

The officer scurried toward the airport workers lined along the tape. After a brief discussion with one of them, he disappeared into the hangar.

A twin-engine commuter plane, made by Britten-Norman and known as an Islander, taxied to the end of the runway and prepared to depart. Taxis and small buses from the dive resorts lined the main terminal area awaiting the arrival of the afternoon commercial flight from the States. I envied those folks, oblivious to the mess at this end of the airport.

My cell phone rang.

"Chuck," I said to Arabella. Then into the phone, I yelled, "Where are you?"

"Jeez, I'm at home." He sounded hungover, maybe still drunk. "I decided not to meet John at the airport. Thought you'd be happy. I'm—"

"Good. Stay there." I disconnected and returned my attention to the scene.

Arabella gestured at Lucas's body. "What do you think?"

I looked at the corpse, again relieved it wasn't Chuck, then back at Arabella. "I think he was shot," I said. "Twice."

Her eyes narrowed. She pointed at the parking lot and said, "If you prefer, I can have an officer escort you back to the other side of the tape."

Holding back a smile, I held up my hands in surrender. "Okay, okay."

"So . . . *what* do you think?" she said again.

I let out a breath. "I think we pushed and poked enough to spook someone."

"You mean John Anderson."

"Maybe. Whoever it was, they're cleaning up loose ends." I looked at Lucas's corpse again. "But this seems out of place. I didn't think Walker was a loose end. He seemed loyal to Anderson."

"Might not have been him." Arabella raised an eyebrow.

I didn't say anything. The Islander sped down the runway and took to the air, its twin engines howling as the props bit into the air, tugging the small plane higher and higher into the blue sky. Arabella stared at me. The noise of the Islander faded, the area becoming eerily quiet, especially for an airport. She waited for me to admit Danielle could be our killer. Based on my most recent conversation with Mrs. Anderson, I didn't have any reason to argue against the idea.

I nodded. "Possibly."

She looked to the south, in the direction of Paradise Cove. "I am not so sure we need a bigger hotel on the island." Then glanced down at Lucas's body. "But perhaps a larger morgue would be handy."

Before I could respond, the officer who had gone into the hangar to check on the *vidio* yelled to Arabella. When she turned in his direction, he pointed to the inside of the hangar.

"We will finish this later," she said to me. She turned and I followed her. After two steps, she glanced at me over her shoulder. "Sure, you may come."

The officer guided us through the hangar, around several twin-engine planes in various states of disassembly. One had an engine missing and another had the skin of a wing removed. Boxes, wrapped in plastic, stacked shoulder high on wooden pallets, lined one wall and large, wheeled toolboxes lined another. The spotless concrete floor, covered in a rough gray epoxy, reflected light from the overhead fluorescent lamps. Two massive fans hung from the thirty-foot-high ceiling, gently stirring the warm air.

We entered a small office. Between crates of spare parts and shelves of aviation motor oil, an older computer workstation sat on a folding metal table. The system's hard drive chugged and groaned and made a small whining noise. I hoped it'd last a few more minutes.

One of the airport workers sat at the table, his fingers gliding across the keyboard. When Arabella nodded, the officer spoke to the guy at the keyboard. He punched a few keys and a video sprang to life on the monitor. Another mouse click and the picture enlarged, focusing on the area where Lucas's body rested.

The video began with Lucas standing near the building, presumably waiting for Chuck. Black T-shirt, shorts, and white deck shoes. While waiting, he pulled his hair into a ponytail. Based on his disposition, and his increased pacing, it appeared he was growing agitated.

"Move it forward," Arabella said.

A couple of mouse clicks by Keyboard Guy and the video moved along at five times the normal speed. Two minutes later—ten minutes on the video time stamp—it became obvious Lucas was talking to someone. The camera angle limited the field of view, making it impossible to determine how many people were involved. Might've been just one; might've been several.

Without being asked, Keyboard Guy slowed the video to normal speed. We watched a few moments as Lucas carried on the conversation. The other person—or persons—never came into view.

"Is there anything we can do?" Arabella asked. "I need to see who he was talking to."

Keyboard Guy shook his head. "I am sorry, ma'am."

At that instant on the tape, Lucas became animated, as if arguing with the unseen person. He turned around and took two steps, appearing as though he were headed to the tarmac, but then reversed himself, yelling, leaning toward the other person, waving his hands. After a moment, he shook his head violently and held his hands out in front of his body. Then he jerked twice and fell backwards onto his back.

We watched in silence as the video continued to move forward in time.

After a few moments, Arabella said, "I guess that is it. Does not tell us much of anything."

I wasn't so quick to give up, still studying the video, Lucas's dead body lying on the ground. Something earlier in the video had caught my attention.

I said to Keyboard Guy, "Can you please back up to the point before Lucas turns around?" He moved the video backwards. "And slow it down." I watched as Lucas made a motion with his hands and fingers. Based on what I could determine from his facial expression and body language, his gesture appeared to be one of sarcasm, a condescending act meant to irritate the other person.

I nodded. My *Aha!* moment.

A lump grew in my throat, my stomach turning sideways. The killer could only be one person.

And I knew who.

"Conklin, what is it?" Arabella asked. "What do you see?"

We rewound the video and watched it again. I held up a finger in front of Arabella, never a good thing to do, but luckily, she didn't break it. "Watch closely." The section played one more time, and I had Keyboard Guy stop at the point when Lucas brought his hands up from his side. I pointed at the screen, Lucas frozen with his arms bent at the elbows, waist high, and his fingers and thumbs positioned to simulate pistols pointed at a target.

Fastest draw in the west.

"Who else have you seen make that move?" I asked.

Arabella's face grew hard. "Danielle Anderson."

"That's right. *Danni.*"

I headed out of the office, weaving around wing tips and airplane propellers, headed for the large, open hangar door.

"Where are you going?" Arabella yelled.

"Paradise Cove."

"No, you are not!"

Behind me, coming in my direction in rapid succession, footsteps struck the concrete floor.

CHAPTER 50

ARABELLA POINTED AT me and said to one of the officers, "He stays here!" She took a step closer, jabbing a finger at my chest. "Understand?" She focused on me a moment and when I didn't respond, raised her voice several levels. "Understand?"

I averted my eyes, gazing at the runway, and nodded.

Arabella pointed at the other two officers and said, "Come with me."

The three of them hurried out the gate into the parking lot. Arabella jumped in her truck and sped away. The two officers got in a different truck and, tires squealing, followed her out of the parking lot, headed south.

Paradise Cove.

Without realizing it, I took two steps toward the security gate. The officer stepped in front of me, putting a hand on my chest.

"No," he said. "Officer De Groot said for you to stay here."

He stood three inches shorter than me and weighed probably fifty pounds less. He also had a sidearm, a baton, and pepper spray. I shoved his arm away and kept walking. He grabbed me by the shoulder and pulled me sideways, placing a hand on his baton.

"I need to back up Arabella," I said.

"She has backup. Please stay here."

I removed his hand from my shoulder and took a step closer to him. "But I need to be there for her!"

He stood his ground and grabbed his baton, holding it at his right side. "No!"

Wasn't sure how far I could push this guy. I had pushed Ingrid to the edge of police-to-police respect, and I'd gone beyond that realm with this guy. But the urge to back up Arabella, be there if she needed my support, overpowered my common sense.

I pointed at the gate. "I'm going through that gate." I took two heavy breaths. "If you don't like it, then shoot me."

After staring at each other for an additional testosterone-filled moment, I trotted through the gate to my truck. Luckily, he didn't follow. No gunshots rang out; no whack to my head with a baton; nothing sprayed in my eyes.

As I sped down the coast, I pieced together, the best I could, the whole bloody mess.

I had been wrong about Danielle. She was certainly the shooter. She'd killed the Good Samaritan, the Speargun Guy, and Lucas. She had also attempted to kill David Brown. Lucky David had a nosey bunch of neighbors, else he'd be a fatality, as well.

Tessa's murder must've been planned for a while. Someone put the speargun in Chuck's truck as an early setup. If John had an affair with Tessa and spilled something about his and Danielle's operation, then Tessa became a loose end. Too much focus would come to bear if they shot a police inspector's wife. Plus, a gun would've been harder to plant and make obvious. Chuck's affair with Tessa cast him as the perfect patsy. Kept the focus off the Andersons, who made it look like a crime of passion between Chuck and Tessa.

Or it could've been out of jealousy. Maybe Danielle killed Tessa because she had an affair with John. Possible her death had nothing to do with the shit going down at Paradise Cove. Wouldn't be the first time in history a woman scorned took matters into her own hands.

Rulio must've stumbled onto something, possibly the boxes of money, and decided he wanted out. I'll probably never know for certain, but whatever it was or for whatever reason, he became the first loose end. The information Sandra Griffis had most certainly got her killed as well. Probably dumped in the sea like her boyfriend.

I pulled into the Paradise Cove parking lot and stopped behind one of the police trucks. The restaurant door was open, but before going through, I turned my head sideways listening for any noise.

Nothing. Deathly quiet.

I took a step inside. Then another. And another. A corner of the tarp covering the outside tables had come loose and rustled in the wind. Otherwise, no other sounds.

And no people.

I slowly made my way deeper inside. Midway down the bar sat a half-full glass of red wine, an open bottle next to it. In the dining area, several sandpipers jumped between tables, picking at crumbs.

No sign of Arabella or the other officers.

I moved beyond the bar and spied around the interior corner of the dining area. The grand piano sat in quiet splendor, it's top propped open, the white finish polished smooth. On the floor, near one of the legs, lay the remnants of a shattered wine glass. Across the floor were splatters of red wine. I barely made out the features of a person sitting on the piano stool.

I moved closer and saw blood dripping off the stool, pooling near the broken glass. A lit cigarette burned in an ashtray sitting atop the piano.

John Anderson, dressed in a red velvet jacket, blue jeans, and green loafers, sat slumped over, head sideways on the keyboard, arms by his side. Two exit wounds, center mass in his back. Blood had splattered the wall behind him, punctuated by two bullet holes.

I stared in disbelief. Danielle may've been the executioner, but I had figured they were in it together, John being the one in charge. The order *giver.*

The Boss.

But apparently not. He must've become a loose end after his affair with Tessa. He just didn't realize it until a few moments ago.

I scanned the beach, the pier, and the sea. Then the bar and the back-door area. Still no sign of Arabella or the officers. Or Danielle.

No sounds.

I turned to head toward the kitchen and storage areas. I'd never been in either and didn't know what to expect. Would I stumble upon Danielle? Arabella? More dead bodies? After one step, John Anderson moaned. I stopped and jerked my head in his direction. Eyes half-open, blood dripped from his mouth. He didn't try to move.

"Danni," he said, a blood-and-saliva mixture oozing from his mouth.

I remained silent, just staring at him.

"Danni," he said again, lifting his head a few inches off the keyboard.

I knelt in front of him. "Pick up a snake; you're liable to get bit." I paused a moment, then added, "Or shot."

He stared at me through near-lifeless eyes. "I wish . . . I'd have never . . . met you."

I smirked. "You're not the first."

He coughed, dashing the piano with blood, then appeared to try and smile. *No machine-gun laugh now?* I thought. The wind rustled the sheet music as John's body went limp and his head crashed back onto the keyboard. The faint sign of life his eyes had held slowly faded.

Another loose end tied up.

As I raised and thought about Arabella and her team, a gunshot blared from the kitchen area. The door flung open and Danielle ran out, her eyes widening when she spotted me. She swung the gun in my direction, and I didn't have time to duck or take cover—not that there were many options.

However, she couldn't run and aim at the same time. Danielle's marksmanship was near perfect while standing still and aiming at a stationary target. But this time, rushed and breathing hard, her shot went wide right and she kept running, headed toward the pier.

The door flew open again and Arabella, followed by the other two officers, ran through the dining area and into the sunshine, chasing Danielle. I gave chase as well, running across the beach parallel to their path.

Danielle ran to the end of the pier and, without stopping, dove into the water. She surfaced and began swimming in the direction of the *Dream Crusher*. Even with the pistol in her hand, her stroke was powerful and smooth—she pulled herself through the water with long, graceful strokes. She'd be at the *Dream Crusher* in a matter of a few moments.

As Arabella approached the end of the pier, she dropped her gun belt and slipped out of her shoes. She dove into the water and swam after Danielle. I flipped off my sandals, half falling, half plunging, sloshing forward through waste-deep water.

A quick glance at Arabella and I saw she had closed the distance between her and Danielle. Arabella's stroke was quicker than Danielle's, but I wasn't sure she'd catch Danielle before she reached the boat. If not, I hoped Arabella wouldn't follow Danielle aboard. That would be problematic. No telling what other weapons were stored there. Plus, knowing the layout, Danielle would have a definite advantage.

I quickly checked the other officers, our backup. One was on his radio, hopefully calling for a police boat to help. Maybe even a chopper.

The other officer was positioned several rungs down the ladder at the water's edge.

I plunged headfirst into the water and began swimming on an intercept course to them. Because *Dream Crusher* was moored south of the pier, straight out from the beach, I had a good angle—and chance—of cutting off Danielle.

This wasn't a fitness swim; I swam hard. My breathing quickened and my shoulders already ached with every stroke. For the sake of speed, I kept my head down and breathed every fourth stroke.

I paused a beat, treading water, lungs heaving, to check my position in relation to Danielle. Just a few more yards. I changed direction slightly and swam harder to catch her before Arabella did. The salt water stung my eyes and blurred my vision. After a few more strokes, I made out the foam, bubbles, and splashing of Danielle's stroke a few feet in front of me.

Then a gunshot rang out.

I raised my head and saw Danielle pointing the Makarov at Arabella. The wet gun worked perfectly as she took a second shot, which went wide and skipped off the water somewhere under the pier.

Arabella took a breath and dove below the surface. I did the same.

After a few powerful strokes underwater, closing the distance to Danielle, bullet trails passed through the water directly in front of me. The shots missed, but *any* bullet coming your way is too close for comfort.

Danielle wasn't giving up easily.

I swam up to her and grabbed her legs, pulling her below the surface. She jerked and squirmed, flailing her arms trying to push herself back to the surface. Arabella came up behind Danielle, wrapped her arms around Danielle's neck, and put her in a chokehold. I held her underwater until the urge to breathe overwhelmed me, then let go, all three of us breaching the surface and gasping for air.

I didn't see the gun.

Arabella still maintained the hold around Danielle's neck.

"Settle down," Arabella said. "Or I will squeeze the life out of you."

Danielle continued to fight back, so Arabella tightened her grip. Danielle's face reddened and she coughed, water squirting in front of her. Arabella's face grimaced as her biceps contracted. More red flooded Danielle's face, but she quickly went limp. Not unconscious but accepting of her situation.

I swam alongside as Arabella towed Danielle to the ladder attached to the end of the pier. One of the officers helped pull Danielle up, followed closely by Arabella. I came up the ladder last.

The two officers had Danielle's hands cuffed behind her back by the time I stepped onto the pier. Arabella retrieved her gun belt and buckled it around her waist. Then, she took a deep breath and used her fingers to stroke back her wet hair.

She looked back out at the sea. "She dropped the weapon. We will need to get it."

One of the officers spoke into his mic. I assumed he was calling the police dive team to the scene.

"She 'dropped' it?" I said, half smiling.

Arabella gave me an ironic look, then turned to Danielle. She smiled and said, "Take her away."

The officers started to escort Danielle away, but she stopped, stood solid, and looked at me.

"You think this piece of shit rock is going to hold me?" she said. Her head swiveled back and forth several times between Arabella and me. "My people will come for me. Count on it."

Laughing, I said to Danielle, "This isn't the old west." Mocking her, I made the quick-draw gesture. "And you're not Annie Oakley."

She smiled at me and let out a breath. "I sure hope the next time we meet, R, you'll play your banjo for me."

Arabella nodded at the officers, but Danielle jerked out of their grasp. They grabbed her again, this time with more force, and led her down the pier. Over her shoulder, she yelled, "I knew better than to trust a man. They'll let you down every time."

Arabella and I watched in silence as the officers took her through the door and placed her into the waiting police truck. The plank decking of the pier had suddenly become hot on my bare feet and I wished for my sandals, which were somewhere down the beach.

"Is it true?" Arabella said. "Will a man always let me down?"

Time to break a rule, one she and I had agreed upon and honored for quite some time. Even though she was in uniform—a wet uniform—I put my arms around her neck, pulled her close, and kissed her on the lips. "Nope," I said, staring into her blue eyes, sparkling like rays of sun glistening off the sea. "I only let you down half the time."

She pushed away. "Hey, why are you here? I told you to stay at the airport."

I sighed. "Guess this is one of those times."

She playfully punched me in the arm as we turned and strolled down the pier, toward Paradise Cove.

"By the way," I said, looking her up and down. "I like the way your wet shirt clings to your body."

She smiled and punched me again. "You better!"

CHAPTER 51

PARKED IN THE last row at Flamingo Airport, I leaned against the fender of my new Jeep Wrangler. The sky was typical Caribbean blue and the midafternoon sun beat down, my T-shirt sticking to my back like flypaper. The Jeep's doors were still attached, and Dog popped her head out the front passenger-side window as I opened a fresh Bright. People struggled with luggage and carts, tourists in too much of a hurry to end their stint in paradise, fighting their way to the open-air terminal.

Halfway through my beer, a KLM 777 roared down the runway, nosed up, and climbed into the cloudless sky. A few seconds after take-off, it rolled into a shallow left turn and headed north, the engine sound diminishing with distance and altitude. I raised my beer in a mock toast and pictured Arabella, seated somewhere in the bowels of the jet, already fast asleep, settled in for the long journey to Amsterdam.

I rubbed Dog's ears and finished the beer. After Arabella had checked her luggage and received her boarding pass, I stood in the security line with her, which is mostly outside. It offered us the opportunity to drink one last beer together. Neither of us were in a hurry. Arabella nursed her Bright as she offered several groups of people to cut the line and move forward.

She sported a fresh haircut, dark jeans, and a new, crisp white T-shirt, which read *If You Obey All The Rules, You'll Miss All The Fun.* I chuckled every time I read it. Amsterdam may never be the same.

Eventually, the time came. We finished our beers, and she went through the sliding glass doors, into the departure lounge, ready to make the trudge through security and immigration. She turned for one final wave.

I waved back. "*Tot ziens*," I said.

"Not 'goodbye,'" she said. "Just 'see you later.'"

You would miss her if she were gone.

Now, in retrospect, I smiled at the image. Earlier, in jest, I'd reassured her that going to Amsterdam was a chance for her to practice her Dutch. "But I do not need the practice," she had said. "Besides, my practice involves you."

She'd be back in a month or so.

We both hoped.

* * *

Leaving the airport, I decided to drive north, to the Karpata dive site. It was a huge detour from my route back to the YellowRock, but I felt compelled to make a visit.

Time may heal all wounds, but it does so quite slowly.

I parked alongside the rock marking the site, *Karpata* printed in bold black letters against a yellow background. Dog was eager to roam the area as I drank a Bright in the shade, looking down at the sea. Divers, outfitted in wetsuits, fins, and masks of every possible color, sauntered down the concrete steps toward the shore.

Most of my assumptions about the Andersons and their Paradise Cove business had been correct. Initially, Danielle's cooperation with the authorities could best be described as *passive collaboration*. Any bit of information she divulged came with a price. My understanding was she negotiated to the finest detail, drawing out every conversation. Most of the time, she played dumb, feigning ignorance about the criminal operation being run from Paradise Cove. Over and over, she blamed John for everything and claimed he had been the ringleader.

The Boss.

My people will come for me. Count on it, Danielle had said.

Maybe. Maybe not. And if they do, it might *not* be for the reason she had hoped.

As the interrogations crawled along, she had become fearful for her life in lockup and desperate for some type of protective custody. Eventually, Danielle determined that the immediate danger in prison overrode loyalty to her criminal superiors. Her stonewalling faded, and she began to provide pertinent information about the operations. However, she still refused to disclose the names of her partners and claimed not to know the source of the cash. She realized full well those names were her trump card, the proverbial ace in the hole, so to speak. Once that cat was out of the bag, her bargaining position would be gone.

It was slow going and it'd take the authorities months—maybe years—to get the full picture.

The investigation and arrests boded well for Arabella. She was going to Amsterdam for inspector training, having solved a case involving six murders. Sandra Griffis would count as seven, but her body had never been found. She was still listed as missing.

In addition, Arabella had provided valuable information to the Curacao and Dutch authorities pertaining to the boxes of cash the Andersons were flying into Bonaire. The case was ongoing and had been transferred to Dutch and Curacao investigators, but from what Danielle had said and what Arabella had been able to ascertain, the Andersons' partners were shipping money to Bonaire. After arrival,

John commingled it with revenue from Paradise Cove's restaurant and soon-to-be dive operation, then doctored the books so it'd look clean. Being an accountant for the company, Sandra must have noticed irregularities in the numbers and, after inquiring about them, probably necessitated her own demise.

As suspected, Lucas Walker had never been an FBI agent, and no one wasted time exploring the possibility of him being an astronaut. He'd been just a typical thug.

Chuck had been cleared of all charges and it took him two days to recover from the celebratory hangover.

Although she hasn't yet given an explanation or gone into details, Danielle admitted to dismembering Rulio and dumping his body parts in the sea. If it hadn't been for the wind reversal, she might've gotten away with it. The leg would never have washed ashore. Rulio would've just remained missing, and none of this would ever have come to light.

Danielle has yet to confess to the murders of the Good Samaritan, the Speargun Guy, Lucas, or John Anderson. Nor has she admitted to the attempt on David Brown's life.

The tight shot groupings to the chest of those victims demonstrated Danielle's expert trigger discipline, steady hand, and controlled breathing. But the shot aimed at me while I stood near the piano and the ones in the water as Arabella and I swam her down were careless and sloppy, approaching the level of an amateur. Even without formal training, like the kind military and law enforcement agencies use to prepare recruits to fire under pressure, Danielle's shots should've been closer. She had proven herself capable of hitting her target—even if not precisely where she had aimed—but missed widely on all those attempts.

In the end, her confession may not be needed. The Bonaire police had the murder weapon, slugs, and trace evidence.

However, whenever I thought about it, my neck hairs tingled.

Not surprising, Danielle revealed John Anderson to be a philanderer and she wanted to make sure Tessa was his final conquest. When Lucas told her about Chuck and Tessa's fling, Danielle bought the speargun and had Lucas put it in Chuck's truck. She claimed that one day, after a bottle of wine, she decided to kill Tessa.

As for the *Dream Crusher*, after it's no longer needed for evidence, the authorities are donating it to the Marine Park. Several dive shops have volunteered to strip the boat of ecological contaminants and have her sunk. She'll soon become an artificial reef and a new dive site on the island, albeit one with an interesting backstory.

With Dog loaded back in the passenger seat, I left Karpata and headed for the YellowRock. I didn't rush, allowing tourists to pass me along the way. They'd wave; I'd wave. Dog hung her head out the window. Occasionally, I reached over and rubbed her back.

* * *

As I parked in front of the YellowRock, I noticed Erika standing at the end of the pier across the street. The sun hung well above the horizon, so she hadn't ventured out there to view the sunset.

With the late afternoon wind pressing my T-shirt against my back, Dog and I ambled toward the end of the pier. Charlie sat along the edge and watched, one eye keeping close tabs on Dog. I strolled up and stopped beside Erika. We both gazed in silence at the horizon. She cradled the framed picture of Rulio close to her body and took several deep breaths. Dog stood between us, watching a few colorful parrot fish dart back and forth below the water's surface.

Erika reached down and rubbed Dog's ears. "Good girl, Snickers," she said.

Dog looked at me. *Get used to it*, I thought. *The dog with two names.*

Erika and I were quiet for a few long moments, the mild surge splashing against the wooden pylons. A cruise ship's horn blasted as two tugboats assisted it out of the downtown harbor, pointing it at the open sea.

Finally, still staring at the horizon, Erika said, "He was a good boy, was he not?"

I put a hand on her shoulder. "Yes, he was."

PUBLISHER'S NOTE

Paradise Cove is the second novel in the Roscoe Conklin Mystery Series.

The first in the series, *Diver's Paradise*, introduces Roscoe Conklin after he's transitioned from the Rockford, Illinois Police Department to owner of a ten-unit hotel on the small Caribbean island of Bonaire. What he finds is that Bonaire may be a nice place to vacation—but if you're Roscoe Conklin, people close to you keep turning up in trouble—or even dead.

We hope that you enjoyed *Paradise Cove*, the second Roscoe Conklin Mystery, and will also read the first, *Diver's Paradise*, and look forward to more to come.